Shackled to the World

A PHANTOM TOUCHED NOVEL

STACEY BRUTGER

Copyright © 2020 Stacey Brutger

Cover artist: Giusy Ame / Magicalcover.de

Editor: Faith Freewoman (www.demonfordetails.com)
Proofreader: Missy Stewart of Ms. Correct All's Editing and Proofreading Services

All rights reserved.

ISBN-13: 979-8607934118

Other books by this author:
BloodSworn
Coveted

A Druid Quest Novel
Druid Surrender (Book 1)
Druid Temptation (Book 2)

An Academy of Assassins Novel
Academy of Assassins (Book 1)
Heart of the Assassins (Book 2)
Claimed by the Assassins (Book 3)
Queen of the Assassins (Book 4)

A Raven Investigations Novel
Electric Storm (Book 1)
Electric Moon (Book 2)
Electric Heat (Book 3)
Electric Legend (Book 4)
Electric Night (Book 5)
Electric Curse (Book 6)

A PeaceKeeper Novel
The Demon Within (Book 1)

A Phantom Touched Novel
Tethered to the World (Book 1)
Shackled to the World (Book 2)

Coming Soon:
Daemon Grudge (Clash of the Demigods - Book 1)
Ransomed to the World (Book 3)

Visit Stacey online to find out more at www.StaceyBrutger.com
And www.facebook.com/StaceyBrutgerAuthor/

This is for everyone who struggles
day to day with anxiety…don't give up the fight.

It might take you a while to find your pack—the people or pets
or things that make you happy—but once you do, they will
shine like the sun in the darkness and chase away the shadows
where all our doubts and fears linger.
———Annora

Chapter One

One week later...

"**Y**ou can die just as easily as everyone else," Eddie warned, seconds before he vanished.

Annora resisted the urge to growl in frustration. They were at the stadium, teaching her how to fight and use her phantom abilities at the same time.

And she was failing.

In the last week, Eddie had taken it upon himself to train her—or more like punish her whenever she called him by that name, which she did frequently, since she knew it pissed him off. She refused to call him Edgar anymore, not when he lied to her about everything.

Annora concentrated on locating him, able to feel the dark particles move through the air. She whirled and ducked when he appeared behind her, barely missing the fist aimed at her face, his knuckles grazing her cheek slightly when she didn't move fast enough. Living as a ferret, watching her for years, had given him insight into how she moved and fought. He could anticipate what she would do even before she thought it. That insight, added to his lightning speed and reflexes, meant she barely landed any blows.

Sweat coated her skin, matting her hair, and her head pounded from sustaining the hypervigilant focus she needed to survive the training session without ending up a bloody mess. But she refused to call it quits—not until she was strong enough to track down Logan and take him back.

"If you want to survive long enough to rescue your friend, you're going to have to learn to be faster." Eddie scowled and crossed his arms, not even a strand of his black hair out of place. The afterworld glowed in his eyes, adding to his aura of displeasure.

Annora scowled back. There was a ruthlessness to Edgar the others didn't have when training her. He pushed her harder, knew how much damage her body could take, then demanded more.

She glanced at the sideline where she kept her bag. Snug inside were the knives Logan left her. She'd been practicing with them every spare second, still able to feel the tiny nicks and cuts on her fingers from the long hours of working with the blades. She itched to use those knives on Eddie. She knew just the right way to cut a person to cause maximum pain, ways to make him bleed, ways to slow him down and take him out.

Her uncle taught her many things while she was in his care—most of them how to torture, maim and kill.

At night, when she let down her guard and couldn't hold off sleep any longer, she relived the torture, struggling against her need to feel pain in order to feel alive. She relished the lick of pain as cold blades bit into her flesh, the way the lash of a whip landed against her back, the metal tips digging into her spine and shredding her muscles so badly standing was impossible.

As if he knew she was close to breaking and taking all her pent-up rage out on him, Eddie held up his hands, palms out, and backed away.

His nose was long and straight, his eyebrows full, his lips generous if a bit hard, and while he wasn't as muscular as the other guys on the team, he was even more ruthless. The way he moved was different from humans, even different from shifters. There was an elegance to him, an effortless self-awareness that she envied.

Her body ached, every inch of her covered with bruises and scrapes. The pain usually invigorated her, kept her going past her limits, the extra boost of adrenaline like a craving, but she was just too tired. She'd been warned to stay out of the afterworld for fear her presence would be noticed, but the darkness was like an addiction.

As if noticing she was reaching the end of her endurance, Xander spoke from the sidelines, striding toward them, his long, muscular legs eating up the distance. "That's enough for the day."

The man was big and rugged and intimidating as fuck. His black hair was buzzed short on the back and sides, leaving the silvery, frosted tips on top to sweep over his forehead. Stubble covered his jaw, giving him a dissolute look that made him sexy as hell.

As he came to a stop between them, she wasn't sure whether he was protecting her or Eddie. Annora leaned over, bracing her hands on her knees, finding the ground suddenly fascinating as she panted to catch her breath. While she marveled at the way the men were trying to take care of her, she also found it annoying.

She could train more.

She needed to do more.

"Not yet. I need—"

"You need to get ready for school." Xander turned slowly to face her, his sharp teal eyes narrowed dangerously, pinning her in place. "We agreed to help you train, but only if you promised to listen to our advice. If you fall behind in your studies, they will expel you. What use would you be to Logan if you're gone?"

Annora wanted to protest that getting Logan out alive was more important than some stupid classes, but the guys refused to budge on the issue. Since arguing would be a waste of breath, she stomped over to the sidelines, struggling to control her fury. Ever since Logan was taken, the fury had been getting worse.

Escalating.

Close to raging out of control.

Collecting her bag, she headed for the shower, trying to shove all her hurt and anger into a box to keep the uncontrolled fury from spreading.

Tried, but nothing seemed to work.

The rage just continued to grow.

She was tempted to reach for the afterworld and skip home, but Eddie's warning that she could be tracked made her hesitate. She didn't really give a shit if her father or the others located her, but she couldn't risk getting killed, not until after she rescued Logan.

She wouldn't allow anything to get in the way of her mission.

She was in and out of the shower within minutes, her hair still dripping as she headed toward the tunnels, then cursed when she found both Xander and Eddie waiting for her.

Crap.

She glared, then spun and marched away from them down the darkened tunnels.

She suppressed a sigh, hating that she never had more than a few minutes alone to sort out her thoughts. She got that the guys were afraid something would happen to her, but they didn't seem to understand that she'd spent her whole life alone and being around people was draining.

Although, truth be told, being near the guys usually calmed the anxiety that raged inside her.

Now, ever since Logan was taken, there was an awkwardness between her and the guys, a distance that made her ache every time she saw them.

They hovered, fretted, but kept their distance.

She missed their touches, missed their joking. Now they treated her like one of the walking wounded, and she felt isolated, and more alone than ever.

It was as if they could finally see just how damaged she was and were waiting for her to snap.

But she was stronger than that.

She didn't have the luxury of falling apart, not when her psychotic uncle still had Logan in his not-so-loving care.

As she walked down the tunnel, both guys pushed away from the wall, so focused on her it was like the other didn't exist. Water dripped from their hair like they'd shoved their heads under the faucet instead of showering, no doubt worried she'd escape their watchful eyes.

She almost snorted at the absurdity.

Even though the guys restrained themselves from killing Eddie, they made it obvious that they didn't consider him one of the team.

Actually, she was shocked they even allowed him to stay, but maybe it was better to keep the devil where they could watch him.

They were afraid Eddie would disappear with her.

She wouldn't put it past the asshat either.

He wasn't known for his truthfulness.

"I want you to pull on the afterworld to heal yourself." Eddie glared at the bruises on her arms.

"I thought you wanted her to *avoid* going into the afterworld." Xander studied the other man suspiciously, taking her safety seriously.

"Draw on it, not enter." Eddie snapped, clearly annoyed at the other guys for hovering around them all the time. "Only the strongest phantoms can even enter the afterworld. While her bloodlines help, Annora's strong enough to enter in her own right, a survival instinct that has saved her life over the years."

A muscle ticked in Eddie's jaw, and she could tell he was remembering the times he'd come to her rescue, as well as the many times when he couldn't.

"While I was trapped in the afterworld," Eddie continued, "I was able to cloak her and keep the others from discovering her presence." The sharp angles of his face softened when he looked at her, pure joy and possessiveness shining from his fathomless blue eyes. "The more often she enters the afterworld without me there to shield her, the easier it will be for the others to find her."

As they exited the stadium and entered the quad, Eddie scanned the area. He pursed his lips, his expression hardening, probably still pissed that she refused to leave with him. She would not abandon her men.

But right now Eddie's jaw had that strong, stubborn look she was beginning to recognize. "Eddie—"

"Edgar," he growled, and turned his glare on her, as if he knew she used the other form of his name to put distance between them.

Annora dropped her gaze first, but she refused to feel guilty about feeling betrayed.

He was the one in the wrong.

He lied to her for years, pretending to be a ferret. She'd poured out her secrets to him, her hopes and fears, without once suspecting he was anything more than an animal.

She refused to feel bad for treating him as a stranger. Every time he looked at her with intimate knowledge in his eyes, she couldn't forget.

"What would happen if they found her?" Xander interrupted her musings, completely ignoring Eddie's grumpy behavior.

"They will either take her to her father to pass judgment on her or they will kill her outright." The massive frown on his face sent the few students up and about at the butt crack of dawn scurrying in all directions. "With her power, it's unlikely they would want her dead right away. At least not until they can figure out whether she can be…useful."

Annora snorted. "You mean controlled. A virtual slave to do their bidding."

Eddie merely shrugged, ignoring her comment. "Unless her father finds her first."

He glanced back at her, his blue eyes apologetic. "Daxion is a powerful man. He'll only see her as a half-breed, a mistake, and an embarrassment. He'll use any and all means possible to make sure she's never found."

Xander and Eddie continued the conversation, their voices a low rumble, but she couldn't get over his comment.

Oh, not about her father wanting her dead.

What shocked her was her mother must have known.

It explained so much—why they kept moving around when Annora was younger. Her mother had been trying to keep her safe the only way she knew how.

"Daxion?" She murmured, not caring that she was interrupting them.

Eddie lingered close to her, automatically matching his stride to hers. "It's the name of the ruling house, a family name that invokes both respect and fear."

She marveled at finally knowing her last name but quickly rejected it. Her mother was right. It was better not to accept anything from her father. She would stick with Greenwood.

"You're not surprised your father wants to kill you." Xander captured her hand, engulfing it in the warmth of his grip.

Her thoughts scattered at the contact, loving the warmth of him against her cold fingers. Xander was big and gruff, the perfect soldier, but he was always so gentle with her. The scent of fresh sea breeze wrapped around him, tantalizing her senses, as if his gryphon had flexed his wings and wrapped them around her in a protective cocoon. His beard was cropped close to his face, hiding most of his expression, but his eyes gave him away.

He was worried.

About her.

Xander's father was much like her own. While hers craved power, his was a jealous tyrant. She leaned against Xander, soaking up the silent comfort he offered. "Mother warned me not to search for him. Ever. I think she was afraid."

Memories of the many times they left in the middle of the night, often abandoning their belongings, came to her mind.

Maybe afraid was too tame a word.

"You won't be able to hide forever," Eddie interrupted. He didn't appear jealous of their closeness, more like he was craving that same intimacy.

"You need more training in how to stay out of the afterworld, how to use your powers to keep yourself hidden." He edged closer to her, glaring at anyone who looked at her too long. "Tonight we'll practice drawing on your powers without relying on slipping into the afterworld. Only when you're strong enough will we train you how to keep yourself hidden."

"You were stuck in the afterworld." Xander tucked her closer and narrowed his eyes at the other man. "How do you expect to protect her when you couldn't even protect yourself?"

Eddie stopped and glared at Xander, as if ready to flash both of them to the afterworld to duke it out. "With phantoms, family means everything. I refused to bow to their demands. The only way to escape was the afterworld."

But Annora was already shaking her head. "But you got stuck."

His eyes dropped to meet hers, and his face softened. When he took a step forward to touch her, she retreated, her back smacking into Xander, who pulled her close. Eddie stopped dead, hurt flashing across his face seconds before his expression went blank, his hand falling to his side.

"Not stuck, more like finding the doors locked behind me." The corners of his mouth kicked up. "That's when I discovered you. You called to me in a way that I couldn't refuse. I stopped seeking a way out and stayed to help you."

Annora didn't understand, shifting uncomfortably and crossing her arms in front of her. "You think I'm your mate."

"No." Eddie shook his head, his smile softening. "I *know* you're my mate."

"Why return now?" Xander wrapped his arm around her middle, pulling her closer, his voice laden with suspicion.

Eddie noted the gesture, but instead of being perturbed, he shrugged. "She needed me."

As if that explained everything.

She must have snorted, and Eddie's face lost all humor.

"I would protect you with my life." He leaned closer, until he was in her face, daring her to deny it. "I'm the only one standing in the way of you having all your choices taken from you. Phantoms aren't like shifters or vampires or witches. You never leave the family. You do as you're told or you suffer dearly for your disobedience. I didn't agree with that way of life. I was a complication they needed to eradicate, so I banished myself to the nothingness of the afterworld before they could break me to their will."

"You're royalty." She knew it deep in her bones. That they would do such a terrible thing to him...what would they do to her if they ever found her?

"So are you." He straightened, his lips tightening. "And they won't stand for either one of us disobeying the elders. When they find us—and they will find us—we'll have no choice but to fight. They'll either demand we return or try to eliminate us. Only together might we be strong enough to escape our fate."

Chapter Two

Xander reluctantly loosened his hold on Annora, already missing her as she pulled away, and the three of them began to walk back toward the house. He watched Annora carefully, furious that he couldn't do anything to help her. She was so focused on getting Logan back, she was physically and mentally pulling away from him and the rest of the guys in the process.

Every day she became more distant. The harder he tried to hold on to her, the faster she slipped from his grasp, and it was crushing him.

His gryphon ruffled his feathers at the thought of losing her, and he wished he knew how to fix everything. The only thing he could do was train her and wait and hope it wasn't too late to save Logan. Xander very much feared if they failed to rescue the kitsune, Annora would never forgive herself.

He glanced at Eddie over her head. While he wasn't sure he could trust the guy, Xander didn't doubt the man would do anything for Annora, his devotion to her clear to anyone who looked. For now, it was good enough for Xander.

As long as Annora was willing to put up with the man, he could stay.

As they approached the house, Xander nudged her arm. "He's right about one thing...you need to heal before you go inside. If Mason catches sight of your bruises, he's going to lose his shit again."

They made the mistake—although only once—of allowing Mason to accompany them to the stadium to help train Annora. When Eddie went after her hard, pushed her for more, repeatedly putting her on the ground, Mason completely lost it. He transformed into his troll, stomping around for nearly an hour, determined to rip Eddie's head off.

Only Annora was able to calm him, and the man attached himself to her side for the rest of the day, roaring at anyone who got too close. Xander wished he could allow himself to lose control like that, give in to the near-fanatical need to tuck her away someplace safe as his beast urged, but it wouldn't help either of them.

Instead, he watched her get the crap beaten out of her day after day, his gut churning with acid. He couldn't sleep at night, could barely function when she was out of his sight. In no time at all she'd become everything to him.

And he was afraid if anything else happened to any of the guys, she would shatter.

Annora sighed, and he gave her a smile of encouragement and held out his hand. "Heal. You're tethered to me. My touch will keep you from slipping into the afterworld."

"She's never going to learn to do it herself if she keeps using you as a crutch," Eddie grumbled, more in protest than jealousy. "You're not always going to be around to protect her."

Over my dead body.

"Maybe, maybe not, but I'm here now." When Annora accepted his hand and smiled up at him, he silently vowed to do everything in his power to keep her safe.

He hadn't been there for her last time—and it cost them Logan and broke her heart.

He would not fail her again.

Annora squeezed Xander's hand, grateful for his silent support. It had been a week since she visited the afterworld, and she missed it, her body actually aching, her skin tingling as she fought the pull. Being near the guys was the only thing that made it better, gave her even a fraction of peace and made her forget for a few minutes.

But she didn't deserve it.

She was afraid if she allowed herself to feel anything but anger, she would drown in her loss and pain and never surface again.

She couldn't abandon Logan that way.

She wouldn't.

He was counting on her, and she was determined not to let him down again.

"Pulling on the afterworld is a muscle memory, and the more you do it, the easier it will become." Eddie came to a stop in front of her, his blue eyes intense as he gazed down at her. "Most phantoms learn the skills when they're young. In truth, most can't do more than just touch the other side. Very few can actually visit the afterworld. They just aren't strong enough. Some don't even try for fear they'll never be able to return."

Late at night, when she couldn't sleep, she played with the afterworld, watching the particles fill her room, and once even called some of the black butterflies over to watch them dance and chase each other, ignoring the fact that they were carnivorous bugs that fed on the flesh of the dead and dying. She didn't say anything to the others because she knew the guys would bust a nut over her practicing on her own.

They wanted to shackle her powers, afraid she would be pulled into the afterworld and end up trapped beyond their reach. Yet for some reason she felt comfortable in the afterworld. Maybe it was because she'd visited so many times as a child, but the other world no longer held any fear for her.

The real world had more than enough monsters to fill her nightmares.

She studied Eddie, not sure why he didn't spill her secret.

Maybe now that he was no longer living in the afterworld, he couldn't sense her intrusion anymore, but she quickly dismissed that idea as ludicrous.

Right?

She narrowed her eyes on Eddie and saw him stiffen slightly. "You were stronger in the afterworld," she accused.

"Everyone is stronger in the afterworld," he answered smoothly, not missing a beat.

Annora stubbornly shook her head, knowing she was on the right track, and poked him in the chest. "It took something out of you to assume physical form again, didn't it? You're weaker."

The lines around his eyes tightened slightly, as if she just questioned his masculinity. She saw the debate in his eyes over whether to tell her the truth or not, and she placed her hands on her hips. "Spill it."

"The transition weakened me." He kept his face expressionless. "I need more time in the human world to gain my strength back."

"Because of me." Everything inside her went cold, the air freezing in her lungs. "You didn't take the shape of a ferret to trick me," she murmured, the truth taking shape in her mind. "You were scattered in the afterworld. You could only take the shape of small forms because you were trying to pull yourself together. You came early to save me."

He gave a negligible shrug, like it wasn't a big fucking deal that he risked his very soul to save her. "You needed me."

Xander immediately jumped on the only question that mattered to him. "If they come for her, are you strong enough to fight?"

Eddie lifted his chin, his jaw tightening, dark smoke rising from his skin. "I won't let anything happen to her."

"But you'd get stronger if you went into the afterworld, wouldn't you?" It was a hunch, and she assumed she was right when his eyes went blank.

"No, only time will cure me."

Even Xander snorted at the lie, but when she went to shove Eddie in the chest and force him into the afterworld, Xander tightened his hold on her hand. "If you enter the afterworld with him in his weakened state, he won't be able to conceal your location. If your father senses you, he'll hunt you down. Eddie made the right choice. If he can heal on his own, let him."

Annora yanked her hand away from him, her fury surging wildly. "Stop making decisions for me."

Xander's teal eyes widened slightly, his white hair bristling, as if the gryphon's feathers in the other world stood on end, and his face darkened. "If your father is as powerful as Eddie claims, he will easily plow through us to get to you. None of us will let you go without a fight. If you don't care about that, think of Logan before you do anything you can't take back. If they find you and take you from us, he's as good as dead."

She flinched, agony like a gaping wound opened up in her chest, as if he'd physically sliced into her with his talons, leaving her feeling gutted. That he would think she was capable of abandoning them stole the very breath from her lungs. "I would never risk him, or any of you."

"That's not what I meant." He reached for her, his teal eyes sad.

She held up a hand, unable to bear being touched right now. She paced away from them, stopping at the bottom step leading up to the house. While she might not be able to help Logan, she could do something for Eddie.

Before she had a chance to doubt herself, she reached for the afterworld. Magic from the human realm flared around her, exposing secrets and spells, until she could even see the souls of the people around her, and their animal counterparts.

Dark particles began to rise from her skin as she funneled more of the afterworld through her. As she absorbed the particles, the bruises and aches in her body faded, the knots in her muscles eased. The particles clung to her, begging her to play with the darkness, an invisible current tugging at her hair and clothes, but she resisted the pull.

"Holy shit." Eddie's whisper drew her back from the edge.

Reminded her of her purpose.

She cupped her hands, carefully gathering the dust-like particles, and turned to face Eddie. Before she could doubt the wisdom of her plan, she blew the particles directly in his face, engulfing him in a cloud that left him no choice but inhale the darkness.

He immediately began to wheeze and hack. Ignoring them both, she stomped into the house, taking little satisfaction in slamming the door behind her.

Calling upon the particles wasn't as hard as trying to control them. Her head throbbed as the beginning of a headache built behind her eyes and exhaustion crept over her, as if giving him the particles instead of reabsorbing them had taken something out of her.

As soon as she entered, Mason spun from the stove and scanned her from head to toe, taking in all the details. Only when he was satisfied that she was whole and without a scratch did he grunt a welcome.

He lifted the plate next to him and carefully pulled off the lid to reveal mounds of breakfast food. Ever since she was taken from the woods under his care, he'd been hovering and feeding her every chance he got.

She was trying to be understanding and gentle, but she missed the old way of things.

I want my friends back, dammit.

She pushed aside her annoyance, tolerating his need to coddle her. She'd give him one more day, then she was going to kick his ass. She forced herself to smile and accepted the plate...then nearly grunted. The damned thing had to weigh at least five pounds. "Thank you."

When she would've turned away and scurried to her room, he cleared his throat. "I'll be walking you to class this morning."

He sounded nervous, like it was a date or something, and her annoyance with him faded, her smile turning more natural. "I'd like that. Give me a few minutes to get ready."

But as she placed her foot on the bottom step, yelling erupted from the basement. She hesitated for a second, the impulse to walk away so strong she actually took another step, then she sighed and retraced her footsteps until she was facing the basement door.

Sweat broke out between her shoulder blades, her heart began to pound so hard against her ribs she was having trouble catching her breath. Even though she knew nothing in the basement would hurt her—that she could leave any time she wanted—it took a concentrated effort for her to function past the paralyzing fear that wanted to take root.

Logan was trapped underground somewhere because of her. She couldn't afford the weakness of being afraid. Her fear of her uncle had gradually faded to rage over the past week, and her anxiety turned into determination.

It didn't matter where her uncle went to ground. She would rip the earth apart until she found the rat bastard and make him pay.

For every wound her uncle inflicted on Logan, she would bring him back from the dead just so she could kill him again.

More yelling erupted, interrupting her murderous musings and annoying the ever-loving crap out of her. Her anger surged forward, a familiar friend that never went away anymore, and tiny particles swirled around her as she yanked open the door and stomped down the stairs, her plate of food balanced precariously in her hand. That she was losing control, summoning the afterworld unconsciously couldn't be a good thing, but at the moment she didn't give a shit.

Ever since Terrance and his brother appeared on her stoop a week ago, they hadn't stopped squabbling. She wanted to give them time to work out their differences, but their constant bickering was going to make her lose her ever-loving mind.

Terrance stood beside the bed, his hands on his hips, glaring down at his sickly brother. But she could see the exhaustion and helplessness underneath his fierce facade.

"Enough!" When Terrance turned toward her, she shoved her plate of food at him. "Go get ready for class. School starts in an hour."

He automatically accepted the plate and turned to go, so dejected and beaten down he didn't even protest, and she swallowed the rest of her sharp words. It hurt to see him so broken after everything he'd sacrificed.

She and Kevin remained silent until Terrance trudged up the stairs, the door softly snicking shut behind him.

"You can keep your pity to yourself. Whatever you're going to say isn't going to change anything." The sullen kid lying on the bed crossed his arms and turned his head away from her.

The kid was right. Nothing she said would reach the stubborn fool, so she didn't try.

"You blame your brother for saving you." Annora turned away

from the sulking boy and curled her nose up at the stink permeating the basement. It was almost worse than when her uncle turned off the toilet in her cell when she refused to obey him. "And you won't get any pity from me. You did this to yourself. You have no one to blame but yourself."

That caught his attention—if the way he stiffened was any indication. "He should've left me to die."

Annora snorted at the absurdity. "You should know your brother better than that. I've only met him a few times, and even I know he would never abandon you."

At least the kid had enough shame to hunch his shoulders, then muttered under his breath, "He'd be better off without me."

"Oh, you won't get an argument from me. You're weak, wasting away, allowing your self-pity to destroy what little remains. After everything he sacrificed for you...*he* deserves better." She crossed her arms and glared at him, pleased when his dull brown eyes turned spiteful. "But what happens to lone wolves?"

The kid looked at her silently, refusing to speak.

"I mean, everyone knows his involvement in procuring the drugs. They're not going to welcome him with open arms. Even if they do accept him into a pack, he'll never be happy, never be complete. He'll never rise above being a virtual slave, a punching bag for the rest of them."

Using her foot, she nudged the clothes and rotten food scattered on the floor, disgusted by the mess. "Even I kept my cell better than this," she muttered in distaste.

She thought she would have flashbacks being underground again, but the comfortable room was big and spacious, taking up the whole span of the house. The bedroom barely took up a quarter of the area, the rest of the basement cluttered with training equipment and sparring mats. Windows lined the top edges of the room, admitting streaks of sunlight across the floors and walls.

"Your cell?" he asked tentatively.

She shook off her stray thoughts, the tightness in her chest easing until her breath no longer caught every few seconds. "Yup, my uncle decided I could be of use to him, so he trapped me in an underground prison for ten years." She shrugged at the horror darkening the kid's face. "I survived, but I don't think your brother will without you."

His face shut down again, and she stifled the urge to smack him silly. "You know what happens to lone wolves. Without a pack, they eventually go completely wolf. Is that what you want for him? To have him be hunted down and slaughtered? Are you honestly that selfish?" She leaned forward, yanking the blanket off the bed, completely fed up with him, the wave of sweaty warm air nearly making her eyes water. "Get your head out of your ass and stop feeling sorry for yourself. You did this to yourself. Pretend to give a fuck. If not for yourself, at least for him."

Kevin sat up in bed, his face turning a mottled red, his body so emaciated, she shuddered at seeing him move like a freaking skeleton wearing skin.

"You don't think I know what he sacrificed for me?" he snarled. "I'm a liability to him. I always have been. I thought with the drug…" Kevin laughed bitterly. "Without my wolf, I'm nothing."

Her anger deflated.

She could understand doing anything to help the guys, even sacrificing herself to save them. "You—"

"Just tell me if I'll ever get my wolf back." He stared up at her in defiance, a shard of hope lurking in his eyes.

But she couldn't give him what he wanted.

"You might not have your wolf, but you're not human. You may eventually gain your extra senses and strength back. You can live a full life, which is more than what you had the day before."

His eyes dropped in defeat, the hope burned to ash, and the last bit of life drained out of him. "I'd be useless, prey to every other supernatural."

"Not useless. You can—"

"Sit behind some desk?" he asked in revulsion, grabbing the blanket to cover himself again.

She lifted her brows at him, fed up with his poor-me attitude. "Grow up. You're not a kid anymore. You forfeited the rest of your childhood when you took the drugs that destroyed your beast. You have no one to blame but yourself."

"Don't you think I don't know that?!" His hoarse shout was

anguished.

A strange idea began to form. If he didn't want to live to help himself or his brother, she would give him what worked for her— vengeance. "What I'm saying is that you can still be part of the team. You're not useless...or at least you don't have to be. You know a lot about Director Erickson, his weaknesses and strengths. We need to go after him, which means we'll need someone to guide us in the outside world, do research...someone behind a desk who can lead us to the fucking bastard. Wolves are supposed to be cunning. Use that cunning to help your brother survive."

He stared at her mutely, as if too scared to speak...or hope.

"Erickson needs to be stopped."

"He needs to pay." Kevin nodded slowly. "And you'd trust me to have your back?"

"I trust that you want him to pay. I trust that you'd do whatever it takes to protect your brother." She sat at the edge of his bed, then leaned forward to rest her arms across her knees, suddenly tired. "Erickson has murdered hundreds of shifters during his reign of terror. He's insane, believing any sacrifice is worth it in his quest for power. His drug destroyed your life, and he'll keep doing it to others."

"He never forced any of us to take the drug." Kevin's brown eyes lowered in shame. "I did that on my own."

"And you're paying the price." She placed her hand on his blanket-covered ankle. "Who's going to make *him* pay?"

A heartbeat, then two, passed, until she shrugged and stood. "Think about it. Maybe if you decide to live, your beast might be able to heal. You might not ever be able to shift again, but maybe you'll be able to keep your extra senses, keep the extra strength. You could make it be enough."

As she turned to go, Kevin spoke, "You're going to get yourself and your pack killed going after him."

She halted, her mouth snapping shut against the urge to protest, everything inside her shutting down as she turned to face him.

"You're too nice." Kevin stared her down without flinching. "You help people who are weak, stick your nose in where it doesn't belong. People will notice, and they'll see your kindness as weakness.

It's a vulnerability they'll exploit."

She couldn't say he was wrong. Her uncle used that vulnerability against her often enough in the past, but she didn't want to be like her uncle or Erickson. She didn't want to harden her heart, because she was terrified she'd become an even bigger monster than the rest of them put together. Thankfully, the guys grounded her. They'd never let her go off the deep end. "That might be true, but you forgot to take something into account."

She strode toward the door, more than ready to leave, pausing at the bottom of the stairs to glance over her shoulder at him. "I'm more than willing to do whatever it takes to protect my pack. If I have to tear down the world to do it—I won't hesitate. I'm not afraid to get my hands dirty, even if I have to stick them into someone's chest and rip out their heart to do it. Get out of bed, eat, train, and for god's sake take a shower. We can talk to Director Greenwood when you're in better shape."

His face turned beet red. He dipped his head and smelled himself, then winced and jerked back.

She took it as a good sign. As she headed up the stairs, she forced herself not to charge up them like a lunatic, refusing to let her fears control her.

And she couldn't stop her thoughts from jumping to Logan again.

Ten days.

He's been gone ten fucking days.

Only the gods knew what tortures Logan was enduring at her uncle's hands. Every time she closed her eyes, she'd swear she could hear his screams. When she lay in bed at night, hovering between awareness and sleep, she could feel every lash of the whip against Logan's flesh, every cut of the knife.

As soon as Logan noticed her, he'd shove her out and sever the connection.

She wasn't sure how much longer she could remain sane before she broke and slipped into the afterworld to track down her uncle. She knew she'd be able to find him if she pushed the tenuous link joining them, if she gave herself over to the darkness.

The only thing stopping her was the fear that she might end up taking the rest of the guys down with her.

Chapter Three

When Annora headed down the stairs after her shower, her backpack over her shoulder, she heard the guys arguing in the living room. Their voices were harsh whispers as they tried to keep quiet, but they couldn't quite manage to mask the worry and anger.

Her first impulse was to slip away, not sure she was emotionally equipped to deal with another drama.

Her hand was on the knob when she heard her name, and curiosity got the best of her.

"I don't like her heading off to class for hours without one of us there to guard her." She winced at Camden's overprotectiveness. She'd swear that if she let him, he would whisk her away where no one would ever be able to find them.

The only thing stopping him was knowing it wouldn't solve any of their problems.

As she crept closer, she heard Xander grunt in disagreement, the sound so close she knew he must be leaning against the wall just inches from her, but she couldn't make herself move away. "Class is the only thing preventing her from training twenty-four hours a day. While I want to protect her, coddling her will just push her further away."

He wasn't wrong.

Mason's voice was gruff when he spoke, the floor creaking as he shifted his feet. "She's not sleeping, and when she does, she's having nightmares. She's hardly eating. She won't be able to keep going much longer without cracking."

She swallowed hard, surprised the guys had noticed so much. She couldn't help but feel like she was letting them down. She stepped under the archway between the rooms, her eyes immediately dropping to Eddie's unconscious form passed out on the couch. "What the hell happened?"

She strode forward and leaned over the back of the couch to examine him, expecting to find they'd beaten the shit out of him, but he didn't have a mark on him. She brushed his hair away from his forehead, and he leaned into her touch, but quickly fell back into unconsciousness of sleep.

"Whatever you hit him with outside knocked him out cold." Xander pushed away from the wall, gazing down at Eddie impassively. "I hauled his ass inside and dumped him in here, figuring you didn't want to leave him outside."

So touching.

She sighed when his last comment sounded more like a question than a statement. "Thank you."

Worried she might have harmed Eddie flashed through her, but she quickly dismissed it. He lived in the afterworld for years, so an influx of the energy wouldn't harm him now. She refused to admit she could've given him an overdose while he was stuck in his human form…or that he was weaker than he said.

After watching the steady rise and fall of his chest, Annora straightened and gripped the strap of her backpack. She smiled at Mason, completely ignoring the others and the conversation. "You ready?"

Mason grinned, his upper and lower fangs sticking out slightly, marking him as not completely human. His forehead was a little too broad, his features a bit exaggerated, not to mention the bright pink hair and the ring of horns adorning his head.

That he couldn't completely pass for human was what she liked most about him. While he might resemble a monster, he was an angel to her. She'd met a number of humans who were more of a monster than actual shifters.

He quickly crossed the room and held out his hand in a silent demand for her bag. His pink hair was slicked back, but strands sprang forward as if reaching for her, the strands of hair giving away his emotions more readily than his face. His lavender eyes were bright as he gazed down at her, waiting patiently for her to comply, and she knew the big lug wouldn't budge an inch until she obeyed.

She huffed in exasperation as she handed it over, her lips quirking. "You know I can carry my own things."

She followed him to the door, and he smiled at her over his shoulder as he turned and held it open for her. "But why, when I can do it for you?"

"Charmer." She reached up and patted his chest as she passed him on her way out the door, doing her best to pretend everything was normal…even if only for a few minutes.

Mason escorted Annora to her class, her presence calming his troll, who wanted to rage against the world that hurt her. He surveyed the students around them, seeing everyone as a threat. Since the rescue, her role in the whole mess has gotten out. While some people blamed her for taking away their drugs, the majority of the packs were grateful to her for saving them—despite a few who vehemently disliked being in her debt.

One thing was clear…everyone now knew who she was.

Annora ignored everyone around her, but that didn't mean she wasn't aware of everything. If anyone came too close and stepped into her personal bubble of ten feet around her, looked at her too long, or even whispered her name, she would tense. It wasn't even a conscious thing on her part, more like an extra sense.

It would only take a snarl from Mason to send them scattering, but he knew it wouldn't last for long.

They would get braver.

She was powerful, and they were drawn to her because of it.

"We could leave here, go into hiding." Mason would do anything to keep her safe. He wanted to take her away but knew she would never allow it. That didn't mean he wasn't going to try. "We could train you without being watched, your every move reported."

"And where would we go?" Amusement sparkled in her dark eyes, lighting up her whole face.

"My family." He cleared his throat, running a distracted hand down his shirt. "We could live with them for as long as you need. They vowed to protect you."

She cocked her head, her pace slowing as she studied him with narrowed eyes, like she was hearing everything he wasn't saying. "At what price?"

An ache burned in his chest where his heart stopped beating for a second. "My return. I would never be able to leave again."

"No." Her face shut down, and she stormed away, her short legs working so hard he actually had to skip a step to catch up to her. Wisps of black smoke rose from her skin, snapping around her like snakes in her agitation. "Not acceptable."

"The hell it isn't!" he growled, and he wanted to shake her for refusing to understand how important she was to him. "Your safety is worth more than my freedom."

"You'd be nothing more than a slave." She whirled and faced him so quickly he almost trampled over her. Instead of being intimidated, she popped her hands on her hips and glared up at him. "You'd give up being my mate?"

Her voice didn't wobble, but the vulnerability in her eyes slayed him, and he ruthlessly squashed his feelings. "In a heartbeat, if it meant that you would live."

His heart turned over in his chest, determination hardening inside him. "You will always be my mate, but I couldn't go on living if anything happened to you."

Her brows rose, her anger faded, and she placed a hand on his chest. "You can better protect me by remaining at my side."

As if she hadn't just taken him out at the knees, she calmly turned and walked away.

When they approached her building, her stride automatically

slowed, like she wanted to prolong their time together. Though he might not have known her long, he missed her when she wasn't near. If she wasn't in school, she was training. Without Logan, it was like a part of her was missing.

He very much feared things were going to get much worse before they got better. The only thing he could do for her was be there when she needed him and catch her when she stumbled. He quickened his steps, reaching over her shoulder to open the door for her, already aching at the coming separation.

Annora ignored the open door and paused in front of Mason, her insides melting when a smile spread across his face. His lavender eyes brightened, his pink hair swaying toward her, giving away his pleasure at just being near her.

Her breath caught at having anyone look at her that way—like she was the only thing that mattered.

Though it might be selfish, she couldn't give him up.

It would break something in her.

"I ran from my uncle last time instead of dealing with my problems, and it cost me Logan. I won't lose you or anyone else. I need to stay and fight."

When he looked ready to protest, she backed toward the door, wishing she had more time, but students were now hurrying past them to get to class. "If I remain in the public eye, they can't take any action outright. While people might report my activities and whereabouts, he can't attack without repercussions. But if I leave and go into hiding…if I disappear…no one would ever know what happened to me."

Instead of letting her go, Mason followed her step for step, a menacing expression on his already forbidding face. Then he crushed her to his chest, the frantic pounding of his heart thudding under her ear. "I would know. I won't let anything bad happen to you."

She wrapped her arms around him as far as possible, doing her best to calm him. When the halls began to clear, she reluctantly pulled away and grabbed her bag. "I have to go or I'm going to be late for class."

His grip tightened, squeezing the breath out of her, before he reluctantly released her. He sighed so heavily his shoulders heaved. "Go while you can." He gave her a sharp look as he began to pace the hallway. "One of us will be here to take you to your next class."

He didn't give her time to respond before he marched up to the door, grabbed the handle, and flung it open, the metal frame creaking and swaying as he stormed outside. She watched for a moment longer, not surprised when he took up residence under a tree to stare broodingly at her building.

Annora reluctantly turned away and hurried into her classroom. Theoretical magic—how it worked, and how to tell when magic was being used in close proximity. The class was mandatory for everyone, the group kept small to allow more one-on-one training. Thankfully, when she slipped into her chair, dropping her backpack at her feet, she had thirty seconds to spare.

The teacher shot a pointed look at the clock, annoyance shining in her eyes. The woman was a witch, resentment putting starch in her spine at being forced to teach other paranormals anything magical. She was youngish, maybe late twenties, and not very powerful, which probably explained how she got stuck with this job.

Her brown hair was spun up in a fancy twist, a glower permanently etched on her face, aging her prematurely. She wore a jacket over a silk shirt, jeans, and high heels, so pretentious Annora was surprised the woman could even bring herself to breathe the same air as the students she was supposed to teach.

Every day she would select a different student, then proceed to make the next hour of their life hell. Annora had a sinking feeling that she just landed at the top of today's shit list.

Slouching lower in her chair, hoping the teacher would forget about her, Annora opened the textbook and did her best to pay attention, but it was hard to concentrate with all the magic saturating the room. As each student entered the classroom, their magic was revealed for all to see...and feel. The force of it made her head pound, and it was all she could do not to sneeze and choke on the polluted air.

A slight tug on her pant leg had her stiffening, and she leaned over, spotting a small ferret at her feet. Shock washed over her. "Edgar?"

He promptly sat upright, pawing the air, as if begging for forgiveness.

The pleasure at seeing an old friend again faded, her smile melting away when she realized he was still Eddie. She faced the front of the class, her heart aching. "I can't just forgive and forget."

It didn't matter that he was an animal with no way to communicate with her.

He should have found a way to tell her the truth.

Even if in doing so he risked that she would no longer trust him, and he wouldn't have been able to protect her when she needed it most.

Knowing she was being unreasonable, she released a weary sigh and rubbed the tips of her fingers over his head, unable to resist petting him.

I miss my friend.

And the bastard knew it.

He'd somehow took a piece of himself and gave the critter back to her. She suspected he didn't do it as an act of forgiveness, but because only he understood how much the little guy had come to mean to her over the years.

As if he sensed her resolve weakening, he tugged on the zipper of her backpack and slipped inside, rummaging around until he found the snacks at the bottom of her bag that she didn't have the heart to clean out. For the next couple of minutes all she could hear were small rustlings, wrappers being torn open and crunching as he chomped down on his chips.

The teacher was going over the different ways to sense magic, and Annora tuned out her pretentious, snobby voice. She slipped out her phone and opened it to try and decipher the pictures she took of the spell book she'd pilfered from Director Erickson.

Most of the book contained handwritten passages, many from different eras, the scrawling notes crossed out and overwritten many times. To her frustration, a good portion of the writing contained more images than words. Going on a hunch, she allowed the particles from the afterworld to fill her eyes. While she still couldn't read anything, if she concentrated hard enough, the purpose of the spell began to slowly form in her mind.

Though she wasn't a witch, she suspected if she pushed enough particles into the spell, it would be strong enough to trigger it.

"Are you listening, Miss Greenwood?" The teacher stomped toward her desk, her voice sharp, the clickety-clack of her shoes giving away her annoyance. "Don't think because you're Director Greenwood's pet that you're exempt from participating in my class."

Ms. Hopper's eyes widened almost comically when she got a look at the screen, her mouth gaped open in surprise, greed written over her face a second before she lunged forward. Annora quickly blinked away the afterworld and snapped her phone off.

"Where did you get that?" The harsh demand echoed in the now-silent classroom, and she snatched Annora's phone away and clutched it to her chest. But no matter how often she mashed her fingers against the button, the screen remained dead. When she lifted her head, it was like a cat poised to pounce onto its prey. Her green eyes darkened to almost black, magic crackling around them as she tried to force the truth from Annora.

Static slithered along Annora's skin, leaving behind a cold trail of slime that made her want to scrub herself raw. It was invasive and aggressive, not at all like the subtle magic she was used to sensing.

Particles rose from under her skin in retaliation, pushing the magic away to give her a little bubble of breathing space, and Annora thrust out her hand. "Give it back."

Ms. Hopper scowled, taking a step back, as if she expected to be tackled. "This doesn't belong to you."

Anger ignited inside her like a tiny flame, and Annora rose to her feet, unwilling to let anyone else push her around. "You're mistaken. That's my phone. Give. It. Back."

Logan gave it to her, and no way was she going to let this hag take it.

Instead of retreating, Hopper stuck her nose up in the air, her lips pursed like she'd sucked on a lemon, and threateningly shook the phone clutched tightly in her fist. "There is a page of ancient text on this phone that belongs in the private section of the university library. One I've never seen. Where did you get it?"

Annora bit back her reply, instantly on alert. She was warned to keep the book hidden, and she'd fucked up. She'd been staring at the damned thing for hours, every waking second she had when she wasn't working out her frustrations with the guys.

And found abso-fucking-nothing about how to defeat her uncle or Director Erickson.

But she was learning about phantoms, their strengths and weaknesses…and their magic. No way could she let that information fall into the witches' unscrupulous hands. "The knowledge has nothing to do with you or the university. It's a family heirloom."

The class watched them like an old video game of pong, a few of them almost gleeful, subconsciously trying to stay out of range, as if waiting for a bomb to explode.

And Annora wasn't sure if they were more afraid of her or Hopper.

"Lies. Those were spells. They belong to *us*." The witch gave her a nasty look, then glanced down at the still-blank phone. Magic rose in the air, quickly followed by the burnt smell of melted plastic.

The phone gave a warbled chirp, a small wisp of black smoke rose from the device, and part of her soul shriveled as another connection to Logan was taken from her.

With a snarl, Hopper pulled out her phone, angrily jabbing numbers so hard her finger threatened to punch through the glass. As soon as the clock ticked down to the end of the class, the students shot to their feet.

Before Annora could take a step, Hopper whirled and pointed a finger at her. "We're not through. Stay here. Don't make me hunt you down."

Then she went back to chatting on her phone, no doubt talking to her coven leader.

One of the students paused next to her, bending down to whisper in her ear, his eyes locked on the witch across the room. "Be careful. You need to watch your back around them."

"Giles?" She blinked up at him in shock, hardly recognizing the change in the man since Erickson tried to harvest the magic from him. She'd used her magic to keep him alive when he hovered near death. In turn, he helped those held captive escape. How was it possible for him to have grown taller? And he had to have gained at least fifty pounds.

His eyes shimmered a bright yellow as his wolf prowled forward, then he blinked it away, and gave her a smile and a small salute before he looked over her head at the witch. His eyes widened just before he allowed himself to be swept away in the flow of students. "I'll just wait outside until your men show up."

In case she needed him.

It wouldn't surprise her to learn he'd been keeping an eye on her ever since their return.

As the students poured out of the class, she saw Camden, Xander, Mason, and even Edgar force their way into the room. Based on their long-combined histories of wars and battles among the shifter clans, witches, and vampires, she suspected they weren't there to walk her to her paranormal history class. Annora glanced at them for a moment, then looked down and glared at the ferret in exasperation when she realized what had happened. "You told."

He lifted his cheese-stained paws in the air, then tucked them together as if begging for forgiveness.

She rolled her eyes at him, heaving a sigh. She could never stay mad at the little guy. When she stooped to pick up her bag, he scrambled inside with a happy chatter.

The guys, however, were in warrior mode, all of them so handsome and lethal a thrill shot through her at knowing they were hers.

As they surrounded her, Hopper charged forward like a yappy Pomeranian and blocked their way. She held out the phone clutched in her fist like a sword ready to cut Annora down. "You're not going anywhere."

"Greenwood is expecting us." Xander stormed between them, his dark hair more prominent when the white tips bristled. Inhaling his fresh sea breeze scent eased her rage, and Annora watched Camden stride within touching distance, ready to drop the witch with just one brush of his poisonous fingertips. He spoke on the phone with Greenwood, the director's voice easily heard from the device demanding their presence immediately.

Mason stood guard near the door, his bulk blocking the entry so no one could slip past and steal her away. She couldn't see anything past his massive shoulders, and all she wanted to do was go over and lean against him and not think for just two seconds, desperate for just a whiff of his fresh pine and copper scent. His fangs peeked out of his mouth. It shouldn't be sexy, but she craved a taste of him, needing it to soothe her ragged nerves.

Xander blocked the witch's every attempt to go around him, her voice rising to a screech, while Edgar plucked Annora's bag out of her hand and tried to herd her toward the door. There was a self-awareness to him that made him stand out from other men, even the supernaturals. He had a strong jaw, giving him a stubborn look, though everything about him softened when his gaze landed on her. The pure joy and possessiveness shining from him was still present right now but dimmed.

Because of her.

He carefully kept his distance, a distance she insisted they maintain, and a pang of guilt made her stomach churn.

No matter how much shit she dumped on him, he always showed up when she needed him the most.

Despite the lies and deception, there was one thing she could always trust him with—her life.

Chapter Four

As the team crossed the quad, Annora could practically feel the witch breathing down her neck. The woman was so close, she could imagine her own shadow reaching out, ready to drag the twit into the afterworld and make her constant yammering on the phone disappear for good.

Fingers slipped between hers, clamping down hard, startling her out of her thoughts, and she was surprised to see her shadow shrinking back to normal. She'd been completely unaware that her thoughts were being put into action.

The past merged with the present—weeks of training vanished—and she flinched. She yanked on her hand, waiting to be punished for using her gifts without permission, waiting for pain to take away her ability to breathe or even think.

When the hand refused to release her, her heartbeat gradually stopped thundering in her ears.

It took a few seconds for the man's face to come into focus.

Edgar—not her uncle. He looked down at her with concern, the rest of the guys crowding closer, sensing her turmoil.

They were her friends.

Her family.

They wouldn't harm her.

But doubt shadowed her mind. Logan hurt her by vanishing. She wasn't sure if she'd survive the pain if something happened to the others. Physical pain was easy. It was the emotional pain that came with allowing people into her heart that was going to be the death of her.

After a minute, she stopped struggling.

"You're still leaking," Edgar leaned down, murmuring so softly the breeze threatened to dance away with his words.

Annora mentally scanned her body, checking for injury, until she realized he didn't mean blood. Her insides stilled, the air around her stalled, allowing the coldness of the afterworld to creep into the world as she focused on the darkness rising inside her.

Edgar was right. Particles of the afterworld were leaking out of her. Her shadow stretched across the groomed lawn once more, determined to finish its mission, resembling small puffs of dirt kicking up, reaching for the witch so stealthy Annora hadn't noticed, silently doing as she bid and eliminate the threat.

Instead of being appalled, Annora hesitated to make it stop.

Only when Edgar tightened his grip on her hand in warning did she reluctantly pull it back. The particles fought her for a few seconds, not wanting to obey, the darkness stinging along her skin as it wrapped back around her.

Only after the dark particles were firmly tucked away did common sense return.

Too bad she wasn't horrified by her actions.

The only reason she stopped was Hopper's disappearance would make things worse. Annora rubbed the tension between her eyes. Unfortunately, it did little to take away the building headache. She pursed her lips, glancing up at Edgar, and acknowledged the truth she didn't want to admit to, even silently.

"I didn't do it consciously." The confession burst from her in a rush. "Ever since I started visiting the afterworld, it has a mind of its own. Every thought, every urge…" She shrugged. "…it wants to please me. It takes more effort to hold back the darkness than it does to use it."

A muscle jumped along his jaw. "You can't lose control like that.

You *must* resist using it. The more you give in to it, the easier it will be for your father to find you." His grip tightened on her hand, his hard blue eyes troubled. "If he finds you…I'm afraid I won't be able to protect you."

He snorted, his bitter laughter twisting something inside her. "Hell, I wasn't even able to save myself when he came for me, and I was at full strength back then." When he tugged her closer, she didn't fight him, needing the comfort of his nearness just as much. "I'll do everything in my power to keep you safe, but you need to keep training. You need to get stronger if you want to survive. If not for yourself, do it for your men."

Survival.

Her life seemed to always come down to survival.

What was so wrong with her that she had to fight every damn day to simply stay alive?

That's when she realized she did want to live…for them.

Which meant she had to find a way to keep the witches on her side to prevent them from hunting her down like she was a helpless little mouse with no powers of her own.

Annora inhaled deeply, then gave him a nod. "I'll do my best."

The guys released a collective breath, none of them even bothering to pretend they hadn't been listening to every single word. Mason lengthened his stride, opening the door for her, and she nodded to him gratefully.

As they bypassed the elevator, Annora smiled when the witch sputtered in protest, taking malicious pleasure by forcing her to suffer while trudging up the stairs, if for only a few minutes. The click-clack of the witch's heels could be heard throughout the stairwell, everyone else making the climb soundlessly.

As they reached the top floor, the guys spread out in formation around her. Just as they reached Director Greenwood's office, the door opened and Kevin walked out. Shock held her immobile. Despite their conversation that morning, she'd never expected him to actually listen. Their eyes met for a fraction of a second, his widened, and he ducked away before she could gather her wits to demand what he was doing there.

As they piled into the office, the witch entered last, breathing heavily. She scowled at the way the guys hovered so protectively around Annora, and she planted herself in front of the desk. "The guards have seen her to your door. You can send them away now."

Greenwood eased himself into his chair, not in the least bit rushed. He leaned back, threading his fingers together, resting them on his chest. "The guards? You mean her mates? If you're bringing an accusation against Annora, then they have every right to attend this meeting."

If anything, his comments made her scowl deepen until she resembled a shriveled prune, which was surprising for one so young. It had to take years of practice to get that bitter. Just as she opened her mouth to protest, a sharp knock interrupted her. A smug smile lit Hopper's face, and she turned sharply on her heels to answer the door. "That will be the coven."

Annora didn't take her eyes off Rufus, but his expression was inscrutable...until he winked.

She blinked at him, trying not to gawk, not sure she could trust her eyes.

Then the wink became moot. The door opened and two women entered the room. They seemed to suck the oxygen out of the air, their magic beating greedily against her, demanding entrance to her mind.

Instead of giving in to the urge to annihilate them, Annora locked the darkness swirling inside her down tight against their combined assault. Edgar placed a warning hand on her shoulder, and she shrugged him off. The last thing she wanted was for the witches to focus their attention on him.

As far as they knew he was just her mate.

Nothing special.

She was determined to keep it that way. She would not permit anyone to take him away from her to experiment on him the way her uncle did on her.

"Enough." Director Greenwood's gruff tone brooked no argument, the snap of command in the one word rippling through the room.

The witches stopped immediately, turning their attention to him. "Our apologies, Director."

To her surprise, the witches weren't old and wizened. They were sisters, no more than thirty years old. One had longer hair tugged back into a messy knot, her glasses making her appear innocent, but there was a cunning in her eyes. The other was slightly older, her hair cropped short, her face sharper, more no-nonsense.

Magic bounced between them like a feedback loop, building and growing with every exchange. While she sensed they used spells to keep up their appearance, it was more for little things like keeping their hair its original color and their clothes wrinkle free.

"Thank you for coming on such a short notice, Hetty and Suesette. I'm sorry we had to interrupt your day, but your young novice insisted." Greenwood leaned forward and waved an arm to the chairs in front of his desk. "If you would, please have a seat."

"It's no problem," the youngest murmured, taking her seat. "It's our duty to come when summoned. Thankfully, we were in the area."

Despite sounding accommodating, there was an underlying hardness to her expression, as if annoyed about being called like a dog to heel.

Annora studied them more closely, saw the way they tilted their heads the same way, and suspected they were able to read each other's thoughts.

The older sister took her seat, her smile more natural. "Excuse us for getting right to the point, but there was mention of an ancient grimoire being discovered." She leaned forward in her seat. "May we see it?"

Though she was more polite, she was no less ruthless. She might care for propriety, but she was fanatical in her belief in magic, a true believer, which made her even more dangerous.

Rufus cast Annora a glance, but Ms. Hopper scuttled forward with her pilfered phone. "The pictures were on here."

Striking more quickly than any snake, the younger of the two sisters snatched the phone away, a moue of distaste curling her lips a second later. "You tried to use magic on technology. You destroyed it."

Hopper opened and closed her mouth, then almost seemed to cave into herself. She bowed low in apology, scuttling backwards as if to get out of range. "My apologies, Mistress Suesette."

The older sister, Hetty, dismissed the phone as unimportant. "If she's correct about what she saw, the ancient book belongs in the secured section of the library."

And once the book went into the library, Annora knew no one would ever see it again.

No one but witches.

"Actually, the book belongs to my family. Nothing in the book talks about the four devotions of witchcraft…unless you've been lying to the university, not to mention the supernatural community at large, and there are more."

Camden inched closer to her, going into protective mode, as if he suspected the witches would try to kidnap her right then and there.

Greenwood's attention sharpened at her accusation, but the witches didn't react, as if she hadn't just accused them of fraud.

The silence was deafening…and telling.

"The book is from my ancestors. It's dangerous, and not for those who weren't born to it." Annora refused to back down. "I'll destroy the book before handing it over to people who have no idea how to handle it. A single spell in the wrong hands once nearly enslaved an entire race and killed dozens."

All three witches gasped at her in horror, Hetty rising to her feet in protest, her face beseeching. "You can't do that."

Annora wasn't surprised to note they were more upset over the destruction of the book than the loss of life.

"The book will be safer with us." Suesette rose as well, her tone superior and more commanding than her older sister's. "We have centuries of experience dealing with dangerous magic. Proof of what happened with Director Erickson is just an example. Only we can keep it safe."

"And the instant you try to use the book, my family will come and tear through you to get to it. You're not able to access the spells, not without them shredding you from the inside out." Annora refused to give up the book without a fight. They could pry it from her cold, dead hands.

"Prove it." Suesette pushed up her glasses, her chin lifting with challenge. "Prove you're the rightful heir, and we won't object."

Smugness oozed from her.

The witches believed she was lying—that she would fail.

Greenwood gave her a warning look, while Edgar subtly shook his head. Even the ferret peeked its head out of the bag, patting her shoulder to remind her she couldn't cross over into the afterworld.

Annora stifled her frustrated growl and tried one more time to reason with them. "Using the spells would be inviting death. Every time you wield the book, it steals more of your life. It's addictive and twists you into something inhuman."

"Prove. It," Suesette said again, and crossed her arms, her tone imperial. A splash of magic saturated the air, trying to force Annora to obey. "Or hand over the book."

There was no choice.

Xander wedged himself between her and the witches, his broad shoulders blocking the rest of the room, ending the standoff. His teal eyes were stormy when he locked them on her. "You don't have to do this. They can't force you to do anything."

Despite his gruffness, she wasn't reassured.

"Actually, we can." The younger witch lifted her chin in the air. "We can bring you to the council and put it to a vote to have you suspended from the university until you comply."

When the guys didn't protest, Annora knew the witch spoke the truth.

The darkness inside her stilled like a predator ready to pounce, just waiting for her signal.

They wanted to take her men from her, take away everything that mattered to her, and her rage slipped the mental leash she'd been using to try and hold it back. "You want proof? Just remember you asked for it."

Edgar reached out just as she released her hold on the darkness crouched at her core. It exploded out of her and slammed into him with enough force that he grunted under the impact. His eyes flashed pure black as he tried to absorb everything, but it was too much.

Dark particles escaped his control and swirled around the room like dust. It absorbed all light, leaving a dim blue hue behind, the air murky like they were submerged in water.

The temperature dropped drastically, but the cold never touched her, the darkness cocooning her in warmth and comfort. Everything was calmer, and the aches from the morning workout vanished. Bruises shrank, the flames licking at her eyeballs turned cool, the headache threatening evaporated.

While the afterworld usually soothed her, this time, instead of blunting her rage, it fed it.

Her ragged nerves grew claws.

She felt better, stronger in this world…more powerful.

Strong enough to eliminate any threat to her or her men.

The walls began to crumble, the ceiling sagged dangerously, plaster and mice-infested insulation raining down. Black mold swept across the floor, and the witches retreated hastily. The desk tipped and crashed to the floor, tossing the director's papers into the air. As soon as they hit the ground, the sheets disintegrated and scattered like ash. The chairs melted down into a pile of sludge.

Black butterflies uncurled around them, their wings flapping slowly as they scented their prey.

"You want the book?" Annora glared at them, her smile turning vicious. "Fine. All you have to do is walk out the door of this office and survive."

Chapter Five

The witches automatically glanced at the door, Hopper and Suesette taking a step back when it resembled a doorway straight to hell. The wood was rotted, black mold nearly an inch thick caked the surface, while maggots appeared to be swimming under the surface, a few of them worming out to plop on the floor. They wiggled madly, inching their way toward Hopper.

She turned an alarming shade of green, swallowed hard, but stood her ground.

No one made a move toward the door.

Annora let her anger burn out. She shrugged off Edgar's hold and marched toward the door, the floor bowing and creaking under her feet. Ignoring the way the metal knob felt spongy under her grip, she flung open the door. The hallway outside the room looked mundane, almost surreal, compared to the sinister world surrounding them.

A few motes of black dust landed in the hallway, and the rot spread like water across the floor, black mold sprouting up and eating away at the normal world.

"Stop," Hetty snapped, her frown thunderous. "You've made your point."

While there was anger in her eyes, it didn't hide the greed.

Whatever power Annora had over the darkness, they wanted to control it and wouldn't let anyone stop them.

Annora had made a stupid mistake and allowed her anger to control her.

Not only did the witches want the book, they now knew she could use it.

If they couldn't get the book, they would settle for her. Or worse…if they got the book, Annora worried something in it would allow them to control her. She refused to have her life dictated by anyone else ever again, and the need to eradicate the threat burrowed into her mind like a compulsion.

Ribbons of smoke slithered across the floor, the darkness determined to do anything to keep her safe…starting with killing everyone in the room who knew the truth.

"Annora." Rufus didn't hesitate to step out from behind his desk. The ribbons of smoke plumed in the air under his footsteps, retreating from him as he stopped in front of her. "I won't let them touch you. But if you kill them, I'm not sure I'll be able to protect you."

She wasn't sure if her power recognized itself on him when she used her gift to save his life, or if it didn't sense a threat from him. Maybe it realized that she needed him to survive.

"If you attack them, you're just giving them an excuse to hunt you down." Without an ounce of fear, he placed his hands on her shoulders and gave a comforting squeeze. "If you run, your men will follow. You don't want them to get caught in the crossfire."

The small particles floating in the air like an invisible current stilled, coming to attention at the threat. Then, like the fog rolling in, the particles kicked up off the different surfaces, peeling back from the real world to wrap around her and seep into her skin. Rufus retreated, watching her and the witches both, as if he wasn't sure which was the biggest threat.

She couldn't blame him for his suspicions—hell, she wasn't even sure she trusted herself—but it still stung.

The darkness caressed her skin, a promise to protect her, before her body absorbed every last speck of the afterworld.

Lights flared in the room, the brightness burning her eyes. When everything came back into focus, the room looked dingier, as if being touched by the afterworld had tainted it somehow. The desk remained crooked, the floors covered with grime, the door warped, the chairs lopsided, having aged a hundred years in seconds.

It was the first time since she'd called on the afterworld that the outer world remained affected after the power vanished.

Like it was getting stronger.

Feeding from the human world.

Hetty recovered first, tugging at the hem of her shirt and clearing her throat, speaking toward Annora as if the rest of the room didn't exist. "You were right. We only teach the four devotions because the rest have been lost to us over the centuries. Magic becomes stronger or weaker depending on the individual students. Two witches who master control over air are almost guaranteed to breed a strong air witch. They may have minor talents in the other devotions, but it's rare."

"So you run a breeding program to make stronger witches." The knowledge made Annora's skin crawl. To be forced to breed against one's will reminded her too much of her uncle forcing her to perform on cue for the highest bidder.

Suesette clicked her tongue in annoyance and rolled her eyes. "No different than a wolf breeding a wolf. Like-minded devotions gravitate toward each other. The first child of any witch is always the strongest. We ask that each female give us one child in her chosen devotion to be raised by the coven. After that, they are free to choose whomever they want as a mate."

Even though no one else appeared the least bit surprised, Annora couldn't keep the repugnance off her face.

"Oh, don't look so shocked. Ask your friends what will become of them when they leave this school. If they don't find their pack grá, they must abide by the rulings of their alpha. They would have their future mates chosen for them, perhaps even be shipped off to another pack, separating them from their family and friends." Suesette's face twisted in disgust, like she'd smelled something bad. "At least we aren't so barbaric."

Almost afraid of what she would see, Annora glanced at the guys.

And was floored when they all nodded. Camden's vivid green eyes didn't waver as he met her gaze. "The rarer the species, the stricter the laws. It's to ensure the races don't die out. Too many have gone extinct. While some have mandatory mating, most only require you produce the allotted number of children before being allowed to seek your pack grá."

His skin rippled, a pattern swirling across it for a second, before he gained control and his skin smoothed out. The scruff along his jaw made him look dangerous and wild as he ran his fingers through his black hair, the strands shimmering a deep iridescent blue and silver as he sighed.

When he reached for her, she flinched away from his touch. The exotic smell of flowers she associated with him swamped her as his agitation increased.

Camden curled his fingers into fists but didn't back down. "Most packs don't follow the archaic rules."

"But yours do." She looked at each of the guys, a sick feeling invading her stomach when none of them denied it. "And when your alpha demands you do your duty? What then?"

She felt betrayed, her one tie to this world snatched away in a moment, her whole existence shifting.

"You are our pack grá." Xander grabbed the back of her neck, his grip just short of brutal, and she used the pain of it to ground herself. She peered up into his teal eyes, heart in her throat, silently demanding that he not leave her. She wasn't sure she was strong enough to let them go to another woman and not lose her shit and destroy everyone who dared touch them.

"We are yours and only ever yours," he growled. "Nothing anyone else can say or do would ever change that."

He drew her closer until she was pressed against his chest, his sea breeze scent wrapping around her. The white tips of his hair bristled, and she'd swear she could hear his gryphon's wings rustle around her protectively, staking his claim as well.

Mason's upper and lower fangs peeked out of his mouth as he hesitantly rested a hand on her back. "You are our alpha now. Only you have the ability to command us."

Annora tore herself away from the men, hating to have her weakness exposed. The witches wouldn't hesitate to use them against her if the speculative look in their eyes was any indication.

Instead of commenting, Hetty pretended like nothing happened.

"Each coven trains one or two main devotions. Selection is much like the university. The stronger your devotions, the more other covens seek you out."

Which Annora took to mean if you had no power, you were nothing more than a pawn or a slave. If a witch failed to give birth to a powerful witch, they were the black sheep of the family and shuffled out of the spotlight.

As if reading her outrage, Mason leaned closer, until his fresh pine and earthy copper scent soothed her ravaged emotions.

He brushed his fingertips lightly down her back…and projected his thoughts directly into her head using the mating connection. *Don't waste your pity. The weaker the witch usually means the more vicious and bloodthirsty they are clawing their way to the top in hopes of proving their worth.*

He said no more as the witch spoke.

"Each coven actively collects grimoires to store their unique spells." Hetty studied her closely, as if she could discern her ancestry with just a look. "The older the book, the more magic has been absorbed into it over the centuries. Ancient books have one keeper per generation, almost always a female. The grimoire only appears when that witch is born. While some might be able to open and even read the spells, only the chosen's blood is able to grant the spells their full power."

Annora blinked at the witch, not sure she understood. "Explain."

Suesette huffed in annoyance, but Hetty answered her question patiently. "A human would see the book and would likely not even be able to open it or read the spells. A shifter might be able to feel the magic in the book, read the spell, but it's doubtful they would feel anything but a snap of static. While I could read the same spell and make a light drizzle, if you read the spell, you could create a monsoon that lasted for weeks."

"Magic is stored in the blood," Suesette muttered, clearly annoyed to be explaining something so basic to an outsider. "Stronger ancestry usually equals stronger magic."

Hetty cast a reproving look at her sister, then glanced back at Annora. "Witches have certain markers in their blood that indicate what devotion will be the strongest for them. Most of the time it's accurate."

"But other times the person might hold the right markers, but they're duds," Suesette snarked, clearly believing Annora belonged in the last column.

Hetty's lips tightened, the only evidence of annoyance she permitted herself. "The marker for the dark matter devotion has been missing for decades. The elders tried to breed more witches with the talent when they tested for powers, but—"

"Let me guess, they disappear?" Annora tangled her fingers together to keep from reaching for the door and marching out.

Hetty's blue eyes sharpened, and magic rose in the air. "Explain."

The compulsion to do just that surged through her, and Annora snorted, crossing her arms. "Try your magic on me again and I'll take it as an invitation to retaliate in kind. Then we can see who'll still be standing in the end." Annora cocked her head and stared at them. "That's really what you want to know, isn't it? Who's stronger?"

Hetty bowed her head. "My apologies. No insult was intended. We use magic like your shifters use their extra senses. It's instinctive and automatic."

Annora didn't believe it for a second. What she would believe was that the sisters were so used to using magic to get their way it was second nature to both of them. Instead of ignoring the demand, she gave them the truth, hoping they would understand the foolishness of trying to resurrect this dark matter devotion nonsense.

Edgar glared at her, silently willing her to keep silent. And he was right. The more people who knew the truth about phantoms, the more dangerous it would be for them…and her.

But screw them!

If her father was coming for her anyway, it might be best to have an army on her side when the time came.

"While a few witches might have access to this dark matter, you're not the only people. My guess is you can only access a fraction of it…like a single raindrop compared to the ocean. Actual dark matter is a completely different realm of existence, one the residents don't like sharing. If they notice someone accessing it, they will investigate and remove any and every threat to their existence."

"Who?" Hetty leaned forward, and even Suesette seemed to be holding her breath.

Before she could answer, Edgar latched onto her wrist. The gathering darkness whirling inside her exploded outward like a small tornado, her form dissolving into smoke. Even as she wrenched away from him, it was already too late.

He'd ghosted them.

Feeling Annora pull away from him, panic seized Edgar, triggered by terror that he would lose her in the banished lands. He hastily dropped them into the empty stairwell and frantically ran his hands over her, searching for any injuries. When she tried to push him away, something inside him snapped, and he cupped her face, forcing her to look at him.

"Don't ever do that! You can never tell anyone." He shook her for good measure, his heart thudding so hard his ribs hurt. Blood whooshed in his ears. Fear rotted away his calm like a corrosive acid. He'd never felt it so strongly and didn't know how to stop the way his hands trembled. Her nearness helped, and he pressed his forehead to hers. "The consequences—they hunt down any rumors about them. When they find you, they will send you to the banished lands."

Her brown eyes were black pools when she peered up at him, her face softening, and he knew she didn't understand. She slipped in and out of the shadows too easily and didn't understand what it felt like to be trapped and hunted in the darkness. And he was determined to make sure she never did.

"Tell them?" She pursed her lips and blinked up at him. "Thanks to my demonstration and you whisking us away, I don't have to say a word."

He closed his eyes, cursing himself for an idiot, and prayed for patience. "Annora—"

"They're going to come for me either way, and you know it." A grimace made her nose scrunch adorably, and she pulled away, leaving his arms to feel empty without her. Her stubborn little chin rose in the air, and she planted her hands on her hips. "Would it be so wrong to have an army behind me?"

His teeth snapped shut with an audible click when he saw the cagey look in her eyes. His anger deflated, allowing him to breathe freely for the first time since taking human form. "You planned it."

He thought over the many ways her plan could backfire, the ways she could get hurt, and couldn't help but smile down at her. It went against all their laws, all their beliefs, but he had long ago given up on obeying the rules from his past. If it took a war for her to live fully and safely, he would lead the charge.

Annora shrugged, a small smile playing around her lips. "You said we can't win against them alone. The only way to change that is if we do something about it." She glared up at him, as if wanting to thump him on the back of his head. "But you should never have used your powers. I was trying to keep you safe for once. They didn't know about you. If the witches or phantoms come for you—"

"They will find I'm not easy prey." The doors above them slammed open, and he didn't need to look to know the rest of her men were descending on them. Edgar frowned down at the girl before him, so delicate and strong at the same time.

He'd been fascinated when she burst into his life so many years ago, like a beacon in the darkness. He would never have guessed the hell she had to live through just to survive, and he vowed to do whatever was in his power to keep her safe. But he'd never expected that she would save him in turn. "Whatever happens, we're in this together."

"Eddie..." Annora murmured distractedly, a smile breaking across her face when she glanced up as her men descended on them, and the love shining in her eyes shredded his heart a little because it wasn't directed at him. "...you'd better stand behind me. I don't think the guys are happy with you."

He snorted at the absurdity, crossing his arms and leaning against the wall to wait for them. While her men were a power to be reckoned with, they had one thing in common—her safety was paramount.

They would not fault him for protecting her.

"Edgar," he mumbled under his breath, barely biting back the snarl at the mention of the other name, and the distance she was putting between them. Darkness stirred inside him, awakened by his agitation, and he gritted his teeth and swallowed it down.

One way or another, he would earn back her trust.

Chapter Six

Annora jogged up a couple steps to head off the guys, watching Xander practically sail down the stairs as he leapt from one floor to another, the coattails of his duster flapping behind him like wings of a large bird of prey. Mason moved like a predator, swift and silently, while Camden took up the rear, guarding their backs.

Xander landed before her without a sound, his sea breeze scent curling around her. He scanned her from head to toe, then grunted, glancing at Edgar over her head. She expected him to lunge at the other man, and she braced herself to stand between them, but Xander only nodded.

Then Camden and Mason were there, and the testosterone went off the scale.

Instead of stopping, the guys took formation around her and swept her up, practically frog-marching her out the door. "Camden—"

"Greenwood has forbidden them to go after you, but I don't think it will stop them." They burst out of the building into bright daylight. Camden surveyed the quad, viewing everyone as a suspect, his usual status quo. The scruff along his hard jaw made him look intimidating as hell. Sunlight hit his black hair, highlighting the iridescent colors that only showed when he was feeling strong emotions.

And based on the way the muscle in his jaw kept ticking as he clenched his teeth, he was more than pissed.

Unfortunately, she had a feeling it was directed at her.

"I'm sorry. I—"

Camden whirled so fast she had no time to stop and ran smack into him. Before she could fall on her ass, he grabbed her close, making sure not to brush his toxic touch against her skin, the muted contact all he allowed himself. She wasn't sure if he wanted to strangle her or if this was his version of a hug. "What were you thinking?! Goading the witches to war will have consequences. They will never let you go now. They—"

Annora reached up, brushing her palms along his face, the scruff along his jaw prickling her fingertips. "You and I both know they were going to come after me either way. I'm willing to pay their price if it means I get to stay with you. I'll pay any price to keep you and the rest of the guys safe."

With a muffled curse, he tightened his grip around her hard enough to leave bruises. The bite of pain licked along her nerve endings, calming the rising panic at what she just set in motion.

"Foolish girl." He dipped down and brushed his lips across hers. Without giving her time to even taste him, he was gone, marching her back to the house.

The rest of the guys appeared to be just as resigned to her actions.

It was why she didn't warn them.

She knew they would've tried to stop her.

"They were after the book." Mason's voice was a low rumble. "They're going to keep coming for it. We need to stash it somewhere they can't find it."

Mason was built like a giant, his body still bulked up even though he'd calmed slightly, while still poised and ready to protect her if anyone got within five feet of her. She patted his arm and smiled up at him. "We don't need to worry about the book. It's someplace safe."

Edgar whirled to gawk at her in horror, and he wiped a hand down his face. "Tell me you didn't."

Annora pursed her lips and avoided meeting his eyes, not wanting to see the recriminations. He was doing everything in his power to protect her, but she couldn't seem to stay away from the afterworld. Each touch was like coming home. It called to something in her on a deeper level, an addiction that she couldn't—wouldn't—give up, despite his warning.

Edgar marched toward her, murder on his face. "It's too dangerous to go into the afterworld without—"

"I didn't set a foot across. I swear." She shrugged. It was the best she could give him. "I just opened it up a little and put the book in a safe place. Somewhere no one would look for it."

He opened his mouth, then closed it, his expression pained. The other guys gave him commiserating looks, and she resisted rolling her eyes at their antics, as if she was being unreasonable.

As they approached their house, her skin prickled almost painfully. Instantly on alert, Annora scanned the campus. The people had thinned out considerably, just a few dozen students using the paths on their way to their classes or dorms.

At first, her attention slid over the woman who looked like she was camped out under a tree, gazing intently at her phone, a fierce scowl on her face. Annora had to force her eyes back to her, like there was something around the woman that was telling her to look away—*nothing to see here.*

The woman was young, her prickly nature settled around her like a cloak. Her hair was black as pitch, long and straight. Bangs covered her forehead, her face so pale it gave her a classic beauty that people envied. She was slim and fit, her clothes expensive.

Though shifters were abnormally good-looking, this woman resembled a foreign princess.

She didn't belong.

Going on a hunch, Annora narrowed her eyes and allowed the dark particles to fill them…and nearly fell on her ass.

Another phantom!

Dark particles floated around Annora like a typhoon, ready to rip into the world when unleashed at any sign of danger. Now that she was using her power, if only slightly, she could feel the other woman like a cold chill against her skin, a light touch of death.

She immediately blinked away the dark particles, but it was too late.

The girl's head snapped up and their eyes locked.

The ferret poked his head out of her bag and perched on her shoulders, then hissed, tugging at her collar, urging her to run.

But it was much too late.

The whites of the other woman's eyes were swallowed by pure darkness while she scanned her surroundings, dismissing Annora as unimportant, her eyes locking on Edgar instead.

Every protective instinct surged to life.

"Edgar…"

He turned and gazed down at her, a smile playing about his lips, his eyes softening. "You used my name."

But he quickly lost his good cheer when her eyes flicked toward the stranger. Now, instead of sitting, the woman was on her feet, making her way toward them.

Edgar's face hardened, and he grabbed Annora's face, his grip just short of pain as he tipped her head back. "No matter what, you must *not* use your powers." Without giving her a chance to protest, he shoved her toward Camden. "Get her inside, and don't let her leave."

"What?!" She ignored the way the guys surrounded her and hauled her away. "Wait!"

But no one paid her any attention as they hustled her up the stairs.

The last view she had of Edgar was him striding toward the other girl with a massive scowl on his face. When he opened his mouth to talk to her, the girl gave him a brilliant smile and threw her arms around him.

Then the door shut between them with a snap.

Everything inside her burned white-hot.

"Hey, let me out of here." When she reached for the handle, Mason wedged himself between her and the door, then crossed his arms, refusing to move his massive bulk.

There was no way she would be able to budge his ass.

For a few seconds, the delicious urge to ghost them rippled through her.

That woman was touching Edgar.

Her Edgar.

Xander stepped up behind her, slipping his arms around her waist and pulling her tightly to his chest. Her ribs creaked, the pain grounding her, then twisted to pleasure as the sensors in her brain mixed up the wires. He knew just the right amount of pressure needed—stopping just short of breaking her bones—to pull her back from the edge of panic.

His touch was both a threat and a promise.

If she went, he was determined to go with her, and she refused to allow anything to happen to her men.

Only when she deflated against him did he reluctantly release her, trailing his fingers down her spine until she shivered.

Her lungs expanded, the air sweet as her body automatically inhaled. She turned away from them, chewing absently on her bottom lip, trying to resist peeking out the window like a jealous girlfriend.

Camden stepped into her path, reaching up to run the pad of his thumb along her bottom lip, easing the sting. The wild, exotic smell of flowers wrapped around her, soothing her ragged nerves. His vivid green eyes, the color of a venomous green tree frog, examined her face carefully, no doubt studying her for signs that she was affected by his touch.

She reached up and linked her fingers with his. He stiffened, his expression uncertain and she tightened her grip. "It's not the venom that's calming me—it's you."

He didn't look convinced, but neither did he pull away.

Footsteps stomped up the stairs from the basement, and Camden twisted them around until he was standing in front of her. Mason's form bulked up, while Xander calmly reached over and grabbed two knives from a wooden cutlery block on the counter.

Terrance entered the kitchen, flipping his sandy-blond hair out of his face. The friendly, boy-next-door persona was gone. He'd lost weight in the past week, concern for his brother weighing heavily on him.

His brown eyes were no longer laughing as his gaze locked on her. "He's gone."

Annora blinked at him in confusion. "Who?"

"Kevin." Terrance leaned against the wall as if he didn't have enough strength to hold himself up anymore. He glanced down at a piece of paper in his hands that she only just noticed. "He cleaned out his things and left."

The guys relaxed some, even going so far as to stand aside and set down their weapons. While they tolerated the kids in the house, they weren't part of the team.

No one was trusted with her protection but them.

"What?" Annora plopped down on the chair by the counter, guilt churning in her stomach. "That's not what we discussed at all."

Terrance's head snapped up, his face whitening. "You didn't kick him out?"

"Of course not!" Annora surged to her feet and began pacing. Then she remembered spotting Kevin walking out of Greenwood's office just as they arrived and blanched. "He went to talk to Greenwood without me."

"Greenwood? What does he have to do with anything?" Terrance pushed away from the wall, suddenly alert, life surging back into his eyes. "What did you say to Kevin?"

"I told him to stop acting like a victim, that other people had it worse. I told him to get off his ass and share whatever information he had on Erickson with Greenwood. I never meant for him to go off on his own!" Instead of retreating, she stood her ground when he approached.

She deserved his recriminations and much worse for meddling in their lives. Worry that he would seek out the drugs again to make him whole made bile rise to the back of her throat, but she quickly dismissed her fears. Kevin wouldn't risk dragging his brother down with him again.

The brothers were too dependent on each other. They fed off each other. If they wanted a healthy relationship, they needed to start living separate lives. She just never expected the kid to jump into the deep end. "I'm so sorry. I—"

Then another horrible thought occurred to her, cutting off her breath. "Logan. He's going to infiltrate Erickson's pack and go after Logan."

She turned toward the door, ready to charge after the stupid fool, when Terrance stepped into her path. "You didn't send him, then?"

"Of course not!" Annora reared back, dread tearing up her insides. "Fuck, he's just a kid. I can find Logan without your brother risking his life to do it."

Terrance gave her a small smile, a tendril of hope lightening his expression. "You got him out of bed. You gave him back the fire he's been missing, something I couldn't do. He was dying down in that basement." He glanced down at the paper clutched in his fist, then shoved it into his pocket and straightened his shoulders. "While he might be in danger, it's the first time he's acted like his old self since before he started taking those damned drugs."

Terrance glanced around the kitchen as if noticing the tension in the room for the first time. He went on alert, his face hardening. "What happened?"

Though he wasn't much taller than she was, there was an understated power to him, a kind of competence that made people think he could solve whatever problem arose. Too bad her problems were most likely to get them all killed.

"Or maybe the more important question is—what do you mean you can find Logan?" Edgar spoke from the kitchen doorway. Annora whirled to find him watching her closely, his face hard with suspicion. He'd entered so silently she hadn't even been aware that he'd joined them.

"I just meant that I won't put other people in danger." Annora backpedaled, but, judging by their forbidding expressions, none of the guys believed her.

"What did you do?" Camden's sharp question had bite, his accusation making her take a step back.

Instead of cowering, she lifted her chin mutinously. "The same thing I would do if anything happened to any of you. I'm searching for Logan."

Xander's brows slammed down, and he edged in front of her. "How, exactly?"

That was the crux of the problem, and likely to land her in hot water. She crossed her arms, suddenly feeling awkward with him so close, the chill of his anger not inviting her to touch. She swallowed past her dry mouth, pressing her lips tightly together to keep from spilling her secrets.

She might as well not have even bothered, since her silence gave her away. When the guys began to swear, Edgar wove between the others, coming to a stop in front of her. "What have you been doing?"

Annora refused to be intimidated and narrowed her eyes at him. "Don't you be changing the subject...who was that girl out there?"

She peered around the other Edgar to speak to the guys. "That girl is a phantom."

Xander and Camden surged into action, covering the windows and doors. Even Terrance swiped up the deadly knives from the counter and took up point in the living room, while Mason boldly stepped into her space and place a giant hand on her shoulder, as if to dare anyone to take her from him.

"She's like you?" The troll looked down at her with his lavender eyes, fear making them appear darker.

"No." Annora wasn't sure how to answer the question. "She's like Edgar."

The guys paused at her comment, and Camden turned to look at her over his shoulder. "What do you mean?"

Edgar was the one who spoke when she was at a loss for words. "Sadie is a pureblood, sent to check out a disturbance in the area. So far, she doesn't have a clue about you, and we need to keep it that way."

The steam left her suddenly, and Annora gouged her fingernails against the fleshy part of her thumb, using the pain in an attempt to stave off her anxiety. "She will report me to my father."

It wasn't a question.

Edgar gazed down at her, his blue eyes darkening with worry. "In a heartbeat."

Chapter
Seven

When Annora opened her mouth to demand more answers—like why the fuck the girl would be hanging off him like a monkey? Or, more important, why he didn't push her away—Edgar tucked a finger under her chin and tipped her face up to his, silently demanding the truth.

"What do you mean you can find Logan?"

The rest of the guys came stalking back into the room, maybe realizing that if a phantom was after her, there was no real way that they could stop them from claiming her when they could simply transport into a room and get out before any of them could blink.

Camden crossed his arms, Xander leaned his hip against the counter, and Mason squeezed her shoulder, their silent censure making her flinch. Even Terrance looked concerned, tucking the knives in his belt in case he might need them.

Smart man.

Blowing out a harsh breath, she admitted the truth. "I've been doing some digging."

They stilled, the silence in the room so sharp, the edges clawed at her conscience. She glared at them, daring them to take her to task. "I couldn't just sit around and do nothing!"

No one spoke, their condemning gazes nearly suffocating her.

Camden broke first. "Show me."

He looked more resigned than angry, like he should've expected her to do something and was kicking himself for not catching on and stopping her sooner.

Glad to escape a tongue-lashing, Annora nodded. "I have a map."

Without waiting for a prompt from them and needing space to gather her wits, she whirled and dashed up the stairs. It didn't take more than two seconds to find the map she taped under her mattress.

But when she turned to go down the stairs, she couldn't do it.

They were waiting for her, their disappointment making it hard for her to catch her breath.

With her uncle, she took the beating and could move past it, but her rebellion broke the trust between her and the guys, and she wasn't sure how to get it back.

She shouldn't care.

She was doing what they would do if they could to find Logan.

So why did she feel so horrible about it?

With a heavy sigh, she trudged down the stairs, each step weighing heavier on her. When she entered the kitchen, she found all five guys seated and waiting for her in silence. She swallowed hard, her feet frozen to the floor, her heart cracking a little at seeing them so united against her.

Only when Mason stood and pulled out her chair was she able to function again.

She hesitantly stepped toward them, not sure what to expect. She was raised with fists and pain, which was so much easier than this uncertainty. Unable to look at them and see their disappointment, she ducked her head while she unfolded the map and spread it out on the table.

Two dozen black marks were slashed across the surface.

Without speaking, the guys stood and leaned over the map. The five minutes of silence while they studied the map almost broke her. A beating, broken bones, or starvation she could handle, but being left out was breaking something deep inside her, and she shuffled her feet awkwardly, no longer feeling like one of them.

As if her movement caught his attention, Camden lifted his dark head and pinned her to the spot, his expression completely pissed. "You were going to leave us behind to rescue him."

It wasn't a question.

She wanted to protest and defend herself, but he wasn't wrong.

If she had a chance to get Logan back, she would take it in a heartbeat.

Mason wasn't just furious, he was hurt, and her heart actually cracked at his devastated expression. Xander didn't say anything. Though he might understand her reasoning, the tic in his jaw called her on her bullshit. He leaned over the map, his hands on the table as he surveyed her work. "How are you narrowing down your locations?"

She swallowed hard against a lump in her throat, not sure how to answer them.

Because she wasn't sure how she knew.

Edgar swore and straightened. "Tell me you didn't—"

"Of course not," Annora huffed in annoyance. "I said I wouldn't slip into the afterworld, and I kept my word. My dreams. I've been dreaming about Logan. It's so real that I could swear I'm actually standing next to him."

Tears pricked her eyes at what was happening to him in those dreams, her mind flooded with every devastating detail of what Logan was being forced to endure because of her, and she waited as the guys fell silent at the implications.

"Fuck." Xander's voice was hoarse, easily reading her tortured expression. "You're connected to Logan, picking up things from him when you sleep, living through whatever's happening to him."

She tried to convince herself the nightmares weren't real, but they were too similar to her childhood memories to dismiss. "And they're getting worse. Logan won't be able to take much more before he breaks."

Mason swallowed hard and grabbed her to his chest then dropped into a chair, his hold unbreakable as he pulled her onto his lap. She leaned against him, the reassuring beat of his heart helping her to breathe past the pain.

"I can withstand any torture my uncle inflicts on me, but I can't deal with Logan's pain. It's breaking me. How can I fight it?" Her voice wobbled pathetically. She glanced at the guys pleadingly, her lungs practically on fire as she waited for them to answer.

"By staying strong for him." Camden didn't hesitate to speak. "He needs you to stay strong. If you falter, he'll be the one to break. Can you do that for him?"

Annora swallowed hard and answered truthfully. "I'm not sure."

She pulled away from Mason, shivering when it felt like all the warmth left her, and faced Xander. "Why is it so much easier to take a beating than to watch him being tortured?"

Xander's face softened, and he stepped toward her, pressing his forehead against hers. "Because caring for others is a bitch. It means your uncle didn't break you. It means you survived. That you beat him. Don't let him win now."

Camden curled his fingers into her hair, pulling her toward him. "You're Logan's alpha. You've claimed him. You can give him the strength he needs to survive."

"Camden!" Xander snapped, his expression murderous. "Logan would want her to have a choice. He wouldn't want her to be tricked into claiming him."

The look that passed between the guys had her backing away, a dark suspicion worming its way into her gut. "Tell me."

Xander blocked her exit, leaving her trapped between the two men, each of them glaring at the other in a silent battle of wills.

Edgar broke the stalemate. "What they don't want to tell you is that your claim on them isn't complete yet. You have the choice to walk away from them if you want."

Camden looked ready to deck Edgar. His gaze dropped to her and his expression softened. "Logan is reaching out for you because he acknowledges you as his alpha. You anchor him. If you accept him as your mate, you should be able to reach out to him. The connection should help shelter him from the worst of the pain, allowing him to heal from his injuries faster."

She blinked at him in astonishment, wanting to smack every fucking one of them for not telling her sooner. There was no way in hell that she would leave him to suffer in that hell alone if she could help it. "How?"

"You can take control of his dreams and make him forget by

taking him to a place that makes him happy."

Her mind went completely blank. Logan was basically born a slave, his entire life dedicated to serving a woman who took pleasure in making him as miserable as possible. His life was as shitty as hers, just in a different way. She combed her fingers through her hair, completely frustrated. "Where?"

Camden's smile was crooked and devastating as he gazed down at her. "It's the same place for all of us...wherever you are."

Heat burned her cheeks, and she tangled her fingers together to keep from reaching out to Logan right now. She glanced over her shoulder to the stairs leading to her room, determined to reach him tonight.

Only to have Edgar step directly in front of her. "If you do this, there will be no going back. Not even death will break this bond. If something happens to you, chances are none of them would survive long without you."

How could she let Logan die lost and alone because something might happen to her later?

She couldn't.

She glanced around at the men and crossed her arms. "Then we better find a way to keep me alive."

Because no way in hell was she leaving Logan to his fate.

She refused to allow him to sacrifice himself to protect her.

"Logan wouldn't want this for you." Xander grabbed her shoulders, his conflicted expression torn between his deep yearning to belong against his fear that they were forcing her hand.

"It's my choice. None of you get to decide that for me. You're family. My family."

She looked at Edgar, finally understanding what he'd done for her. He'd been her lifeline for years, helping her survive her uncle. He saved her...and bound himself to her in the process.

How could she be mad at him when she was about to do the same thing? "I understand what's at stake. They're worth the risk."

He swallowed hard and gave a small bow of his head, accepting her silent apology for everything he'd sacrificed for her.

A little uncomfortable at the pure possessiveness shining in Edgar's fathomless blue eyes, she turned toward Camden. "Show me what I need to do."

Camden trailed Annora up the stairs, growing more and more anxious at the thought of being alone with her, knowing he'd be touching her bare skin soon. His nerves increased with every step, and he watched the sway of her hips, the way her hair swung back and forth across her back almost hypnotically.

Unable to restrain himself, he reached out and brushed his fingertips along the silken strands. The need to bury his face into the heavy mass, almost a compulsion, made him jerk back and ball his hands into fists.

It was harder to ignore the tremor that went through him at the thought of being allowed to hold her while she slept. He would have to touch Annora, feel the warmth of her skin, feel her body wrapped up in his arms as he held her to keep her from waking.

The rest of the guys cleared out of the house to give them privacy and investigate what the witches were planning, and it scared the ever-loving crap out of him to be alone with her.

What if something went wrong?

What if he hurt her?

Or worse, what if she never woke up again?

He blew out a heavy breath, a spiky bundle of temptation and fear churning inside him like cactus needles.

He'd dreamed about physical contact with her since he first met her, and his cock hardened just at the thought, but it was a dark temptation he didn't allow himself with anyone—ever.

His touch was toxic.

He couldn't forget.

He could never forget.

But she was different. A visceral yearning grabbed him every time she was near. The memory of her, the feel of her silken flesh the couple times he allowed himself to give in to temptation for just a few seconds, was imprinted on his mind forever.

And, like an addict, he craved more.

Could he really touch her without harming her?

What was the limit?

And, maybe even more important, could he dare allow himself to hope? If anything happened to her because of him...he would never forgive himself.

As they entered her bedroom, the bed loomed large in his mind. His chest felt tight, his breathing becoming short puffs, and his feet froze to the floor. Annora didn't show any such hesitation, marching directly toward the mattress and dropping down on the surface. She stretched out stiffly, like she was preparing for the guillotine, then looked at him and quirked a brow.

"C'mere." She sighed deeply and patted the bed next to her. "I want to get this over with."

Her anxiety allowed him to push away his own. This wasn't about him—this was about her and Logan. Camden perched on the edge of the bed, careful to keep his distance as he pulled off his shoes, not allowing himself the smallest brush against her until it was time. "Are you more afraid this won't work...or that it will?"

"Both." Her broken smile nearly crushed his resolve, and it was all he could do not to gather her up in his arms. Her face grew solemn. "If I'm right and we reach him...that means everything that's been happening..."

Her voice cracked, and she glanced away from him.

"It means that what you saw was real."

She nodded meekly, barely a movement, and his plan to just hold her hand vanished, her pain ripping open his heart. Camden slowly stretched out next to her, gingerly gathering her in his arms. "It also means we have a chance to get him back. We have a way to reach him."

She twisted until she rested on her side and pressed her face against his shoulder, the whisper of her breath against his neck nearly making him groan his torment out loud, his arousal hitting so hard, he couldn't even form a coherent thought. He shook his head to rid himself of his fantasies, and it took all his concentration to remember his purpose in her bed.

No sex.

He slipped his palm along her neck, cupping the back of it, and leaned forward to press his lips against her forehead. He didn't move, didn't breathe, as he waited for her to go limp.

Instead, she snuggled against him, and he found himself unconsciously brushing his fingertips along her skin, the tangy smell of lemon and warm jasmine drawing him closer to get another whiff of her intoxicating scent.

He hummed in the back of his throat, and she tipped her head back, their lips only separated by a fraction of an inch. Her dark eyes drew him closer, like he was the one under a spell.

Annora felt the pull of sleep but resisted for a moment longer, Camden's fear and need reaching out to her. She leaned up, brushing her lips lightly against his, his tortured groan cut short when she pulled away.

"We'll practice touching and kissing and pushing our limits later. I promise. Right now we need to stay focused on Logan." She swallowed hard, terrified what she might find when she closed her eyes, and fought against the need to sleep. "He—"

"You're right." Camden shook his head, a shutter falling over his face. He stared down at her, once more completely analytical, and she hated the distance between them.

She reached up, running her palm lightly along his jaw. He flinched at the contact, watching her for a second before leaning into her touch.

"I'm not hurting you." The awe in his voice nearly broke her heart. To go through life and never be able to touch or be touched by anyone was a different kind of torture than fists and words, but just as effective at destroying a person.

"Of course not." She rolled her eyes at the absurdity. "You would never hurt me." She settled against him once again, resting her face against his chest, feeling her body relax for the first time in a week. "I haven't been sleeping much. After watching them torture Logan, every time I close my eyes…" She took a shuddering breath. "I can't force myself to get back into bed. But now I know it was real…"

Rage burned through her like an inferno. She tightened her fingers into a fist, feeling her nails dig into her skin deep enough to draw blood, but the pain did nothing to dull her fury.

She'd lived with her uncle for years, even had a chance to kill him, but ran like a coward.

And now Logan was paying the price.

If she had a chance to do it all over again, she'd kill that man in a heartbeat. It didn't matter that she would've likely died in the process, she would take the chance if it meant the guys would be safe.

Camden gingerly settled his hand on her hip, pulling her mind away from the nightmare of her thoughts. He slid his palm upward until his fingers rested against bare flesh at her waist, effectively distracting her. His breath stalled in his chest, his body stiff beneath her, as if he was waiting for a rejection.

She placed her hand on his chest and slid it up until her fingertips rested against the pulse in his neck. The furious beating relaxed her, and she mentally counted each thump. "Don't let me drown in the nightmares."

She lasted no more than thirty seconds before sleep claimed her.

"Never." He kissed her brow, his murmured words the last thing she heard.

Annora wasn't sure what to expect, but finding Logan huddled on the cement floor was a relief. He wasn't strapped to a table, his chest ripped open for her to watch his organs move and struggle to survive. Her uncle wasn't hovering over him with a maniacal grin and sharp blades.

But her relief was short-lived. He curled into a tighter ball, keeping his back to her, as if sensing her presence. "You shouldn't have come. I told you not to come again."

His voice was hoarse and broken from too much screaming.

She knew the signs well enough.

Annora snorted at his comment and dropped to her knees at his side. "You should know by now that I rarely do as I'm told."

His huffed laugh was quickly cut off when he seemed to fold into himself. She touched his arm gently, almost afraid of what she would see. Her lungs stalled when she caught her first sight of him. His face was almost unrecognizable under all the blood. Hundreds of cuts and bruises and massive swelling distorted his features, and her heart slowly shredded, threatening to choke her.

Thick chains were cuffed around his arms, shackling him to the floor. The wounds around his wrists were so raw, bone gleamed through the meaty mess of what was left of his flesh, as if he was seconds away from gnawing off his own hands to be free. Blood continued to drip on the floor in an ever-widening puddle.

Acid curdled her stomach.

He'd given up hope.

His black hair was limp, the bright red tips dulled. While he was normally slim, now his bones poked against his skin, his body all angles and sharp edges. His clothes were stained and matted, sticking to his skin, and she knew he must be severely injured if he was still bleeding. The floor was more of a stained concrete…easier to disguise the blood when they had visitors.

Surprisingly, when people came to purchase your services, they didn't like to see signs of torture. They liked things nice and tidy. Knowing was one thing, but seeing the results was too much for their delicate sensibilities.

Not that any of the clients would have tried to help and rescue her—but because her value decreased if the client was distressed by all the blood and injuries.

She clucked her tongue and shook her head. "You think my uncle could be a little more original in his torture. How many cuts did he make before he gave up? I reached over three hundred before he got frustrated and slit my throat."

"Jesus." They both turned at the sound of Camden's voice.

"What the hell?!" Annora blinked at him in surprise. "You were able to follow me."

Instead of replying, he knelt next to Logan and carefully touched his hand to the back of the kitsune's neck.

Logan blinked, as if in shock, then reached out and locked his hand around Camden's wrist. "You're real?" His eyes quickly latched onto hers and tears flooded his eyes. "The dreams are real? You're not just in my head?"

"I've told you that a million times." Annora heaved a frustrated sigh but was more relieved than annoyed that he finally believed her. "Now tell me everything you know about this place so we can come and rescue you."

Camden's touch, or maybe just knowing he was no longer alone, seemed to finally reach Logan. He relaxed against Camden, allowing the other guy to lay him flat. As he described the fortress where her uncle planned to store her once he recaptured her, Annora rested her hand on the ragged edges of the massive wounds gouged into his torso.

She shut out their voices until they were just a murmur, focusing on doing what Camden suggested…healing Logan. Dark particles gathered under her skin and swirled into existence at her call. Without a clue what she was doing, she demanded that they stitch Logan together.

The darkness rose at her plea, swarming around her in a violent, churning mass, then slammed out of her so hard and fast that it stole her breath and left her a hollow husk. When she opened her eyes, it was to find Logan encased in a black swarm.

Camden rested back on his haunches but quickly caught her hand when she went to reach out and touch the mass. "Wait. Watch. Give his kitsune time to accept the intrusion."

Black dust floated through the air and settled over Logan's flesh. The darkness sparked bright for a few seconds, then rolled off his skin like dandelion fluff. The entire process took no more than a few minutes. When done, she was more than a little disappointed to notice that he seemed unchanged.

Until he sighed in relief and blinked open his electric blue eyes.

They were clear of pain for the first time in days.

The faint scent of fresh snow and heat rippled in the room, and her breath caught, the pain lodging so tight she couldn't make her lungs work.

Logan gathered her close, his arms feeling so real a sob escaped her.

"I'm fine." His arms tightened around her, belying his words, and she'd swear she could hear the silent swoosh of falling snow. At her watery laugh, he amended his statement. "While I might look like shit, whatever you did healed the worst of the injuries. I'll stay strong for you. I'll wait for you to find me. I'll stay alive."

She tipped her head back, clinging to him. "We're close. You have to fight."

He smiled at her ridiculous command, a hint of his old carefree charm restored enough to make her heart ache. He tipped his head toward her, as if he had any say in the matter. "I'll do my best."

But the humor never reached his eyes.

As soon as they woke up, his hellish existence would return.

"You need to go. Be careful. Trust no one but the guys. They have spies watching you. Stay safe. For me. It would break me if anything happened to you." He pressed his lips against her forehead, and it felt like her heart was being ripped out of her chest. Then he pushed her away, his face hardening, taking with it any signs of the Logan she knew. "They're coming. I can hear their footsteps."

Even as he spoke, the room around them became hazy, the touch of his arms less firm.

Reminding her that this was just a dream.

And breaking her heart all over again.

Annora resisted the pull, demanding the darkness inside her to take him with them, but it was no use. Like every other time she tried, everything around her slowly devolved into a smoky haze. Camden carefully gathered her to him, and she struggled against him. "No, please, just a few more minutes."

But it was too late.

Though she couldn't see the prison room any longer, she heard the creak of the jail door opening, heard the murmuring glee in her uncle's voice and the snap of a whip. Her back arched, as if it landed against her flesh instead of Logan's.

When Logan gave her one last mental shove, the dream dissolved, no matter how hard she tried to grab on to it. She bolted upright and gasped for air.

As she scrambled to get out of bed, Camden gathered her in his arms so tightly her ribs creaked in protest. It was the only thing that kept her from spinning out and losing her freaking mind. She used the pain to ground her, allowed it to push away the need to lie back down and drag Logan back with her one way or another.

But she knew from experience that no matter how hard she tried, Logan wouldn't allow it.

He wanted to spare her the pain, and she almost choked on her bitterness.

It was only then that she became aware of Camden whispering to her, repeating the same phrase over and over.

"We'll find him in time. I promise. We'll find him."

Chapter Eight

Logan didn't feel the lash of the whip as it flayed open his back, barely flinched from the pain, so focused on Annora that it was manageable for now. But he knew he would pay for it later. Her uncle would keep going until his arm was too sore to lift the whip or he got his screams.

Though Logan hated to admit it, he was close to breaking.

Every day, reality drifted further and further away.

Annora's daily visits had become his salvation.

He both lived and dreaded the nightly dreams. He almost gave in to the temptation to never wake, the only thing stopping him was knowing Annora needed him.

He had to fight for the chance to spend more time with her.

A single lifetime wasn't nearly enough, and he'd be damned if he gave up one second sooner.

He thought the dreams were another sign that he was losing his mind—until Camden showed up too. No way in hell would he use his last minutes on earth to dream of that asshole.

Everything became more real when Annora used her witchy powers to heal him.

He felt better, stronger than he had since before he left, and it took everything in him not to beg her not to leave him.

Until he heard the guards coming.

She had to leave before they discovered her.

As she faded from his arms, she left a gaping hole in his chest.

At his center—where his kitsune hid—rested a dark well of power so deep and vast nothing could consume it.

But instead of fear, his heart warmed.

It was Annora.

She was an unstoppable force that wouldn't rest until she came for him.

Fear and hope warred inside him.

For the first time, he allowed himself to believe in the possibility that he'd see her again.

A particularly nasty blow split his flesh open, ripping a groan from deep within him. The haze of the dream world beckoned to him, but he gritted his teeth and bore the pain.

Now that he knew the real Annora was waiting for him, his dreams of her would no longer satisfy him.

He gripped the chains pinning him to the floor, wrapping them around his hands, and continued to work on loosening the bolts holding him in place.

He'd be damned if he'd let this blowhard win.

He'd conserve his strength. Wait for the perfect time to strike. Because if it was the last thing that he ever did, he would make sure her uncle never laid a hand on her again.

Annora followed Camden down the stairs. Though they'd both showered, the cold dampness from the prison still clung to her, the smell of stale blood and the bitter taste of despair hovering around her like a toxic cloud.

The rest of the guys were seated around the table, waiting for them, and she knew Camden must have called them back. From their grim faces, he also must have told them what transpired.

Camden took his seat, but she was too nervous to make herself sit, like she was on trial or something. She leaned her hip against the counter, crossing her arms, not ready for the comfort they were willing to offer, not until she was sure she wouldn't shatter.

"The nightmares are getting worse." She spoke bluntly, staring blankly at the middle of the table instead of facing them, or she wouldn't be able to get the words out. "I swear I can hear him screaming even while I'm awake. Sometimes he calls for me, while others he begs me to stay away."

It felt like she was going fucking insane.

The guys were silent while she lost her calm, and she swallowed hard against the need to run out the door and allow herself to be taken just so she could be near Logan.

"They won't kill him." Xander reminded her, his voice a comforting rumble. "Not until they get what they want."

Me.

Annora gave a bitter laugh. "You don't understand. I'm not afraid they'll kill him. I can save him from death. What I can't do is put him back together if my uncle breaks him."

"Logan isn't as weak as you think." Camden stood and came to a stop in front of her. "His life hasn't been easy. He knows how to fight, especially now he knows you're waiting for him."

She refused to blink, refused to let her tears fall. She desperately wanted to believe him, but she knew the lengths her uncle would go to in order to achieve his ends. He would break Logan, try to turn him, make him into one of his minions if he could.

And it would destroy her.

"You have no idea what my uncle is capable of." She shook her head in despair, refusing to look at them lest they see her shattered expression.

"I do." Edgar watched her without a hint of emotion, always pushing her in a way the other guys were afraid to do. "And I know if I had you waiting for me, I would endure anything, survive anything to get back to you. Your kitsune will fight for you. Trust in him. Trust in us. We'll do everything in our power to get him back."

It sounded like a vow, and the guys nodded in complete agreement.

"What we need to do is practice, find a way that you can use your powers without alerting the other phantoms to your presence." Xander ignored the glare Edgar tossed at him. "She needs to practice taking us with her. If she finds Logan, no way in hell do I want her to go anywhere near her uncle without backup."

Edgar pursed his lips, unable to refute Xander's logic.

Hope surged through her at the possibility of actually being able to do something instead of sitting on her ass.

Edgar gave her a speculative look. "You have a rare gift, usually gained with age or a powerful lineage, one that before I met you I would've said takes a lifetime to master. But if we can ward the house strongly enough, we could practice ghosting distances without touching the afterworld."

"Like teleportation?" Mason appeared intrigued instead of disbelieving.

"I know a few witches who owe us favors." Camden pulled out his phone, already scrolling through the contacts.

Annora reached out, touching his arm. He jumped, startled at the contact, his head snapping up before he seemed to settle himself.

"And the kerfuffle of this morning?" she asked. "You don't think they're going to demand more?"

"We need this." Instead of being concerned, he just shrugged, like any price was worth paying. "They're going to be gunning for us either way."

When none of the guys objected, she let the matter drop. While she might not like the idea of inviting strangers into her life, if it meant she could protect the guys *and* rescue Logan, it was a price that she was willing to pay.

As the guys went into motion, Edgar pulled her off to the side. "Are you sure you're up to this?"

"I have to be." Annora answered honestly. "I don't have a choice."

His lips tightened as he scowled down at her. "The afterworld is a dangerous place. As much as it feels like home to you, there are creatures there that would be more than happy to rip you apart or keep you trapped to feed off of you. You have no idea—"

"I can do this." She gave him a smile to hide her own doubts.

She'd never been afraid of the afterworld the way he was. Maybe it was because she was never taught to fear it, or maybe he was right and she was just being naïve, but she needed to try.

No, she had to do more than try.

She had to make this work, whatever it took.

As if the witches had been waiting for their call, it didn't take more than an hour for them to show up at the house. She watched no less than five witches gather outside, casting wards strong enough that she could feel them brush against her like static.

When the witches were done, the guys headed out to the backyard. The witches carefully kept their distance, trying to remain quiet so they wouldn't be kicked out. Having them stay to observe must have been part of the deal to get them to ward the area. The witches gathered at the fire pit, lighting the fire with a simple flick of their wrist, the flame an odd blue color, as if they were using it more to spy than for heat.

The guys waited patiently by the tree line behind the house, pretending the witches didn't exist…all except Edgar.

He stood facing her in the middle of the clearing, legs spread, arms crossed, an imposing expression on his face. "You know how to ghost people by slipping into the afterworld, but I want you to practice ghosting without setting foot in the other realm before you try to bring anyone with you. The last thing we need is for anyone to get stuck or lost on the other side of the barrier."

She swallowed hard, not concerned about herself, but what would happen if she lost someone in the afterworld and wasn't able to pull them out. She gave herself a few seconds to wallow in her doubts, then resolutely pushed them away.

She could do this.

She felt each of the guys in the back of her mind like a warm glow.

If they got lost in the abyss, she would damn well go and get them back.

She thrust her shoulders back and nodded to Edgar. "I'm ready."

A muscle ticked in his jaw as he swallowed back any other protests. He knew she was right. This needed to be done. The only way she could protect herself from the other phantoms was if she was stronger, faster, and smarter.

"Travel to the guys and back without entering the afterworld." That was all he said before he retreated to stand next to Xander.

The first dozen times she tried—she failed spectacularly.

She felt herself slip into the afterworld every jump, no matter how hard she tried to resist.

The next two jumps, she did something different, using the darkness inside her instead of the afterworld, and didn't even manage to ghost at all. She growled in frustration, glaring daggers at Edgar, but he only shook his head.

"Again. I can still feel you pulling on the afterworld." He leaned against a tree and crossed his leg at the ankles, as if completely bored. "Try again."

She glared at him, the urge to skip over to him, smack him, and slip away again nipping along her nerves. Dark particles rose, as if to do her bidding, and an idea sparked.

Grabbing the darkness, she flung the particles out in front of her. Then, with her breath held, she stepped right through them.

They sucked her forward, twisting her inside out, before spitting her back out in front of Edgar.

His mouth dropped open in shock. When she staggered, struggling to regain her equilibrium, he caught her close against his surprisingly firm chest.

"You did it!" He blinked down at her, eyes wide in shock. "How did you do that?"

"It worked?" She smiled, then gave a whoop of victory. "It worked!"

Dizziness assailed her, like she had low blood pressure or something, and Mason steadied her when she would've stumbled into him. "Whoa, easy there, little-stuff."

His concerned gaze moved past her to land on Edgar. "So she can do it, but at what cost?"

The guys gathered around her, and Xander tipped her chin back, studying her eyes, unobtrusively measuring her pulse. After a moment, he retreated. "Physically she's fine." Then he glanced at Edgar. "But can you look deeper? See if keeping her from touching the other realm is harming her? While her afterworld might harm you, it might also be her lifeline."

"I'm fine." She tried to push away from them, but none of the guys stepped back, their bodies a solid wall. She rolled her eyes at their antics, then sighed and gave in to their silent demand, knowing they wouldn't stop unless they could confirm for themselves that she was unharmed.

She glanced at Edgar, then pointed to the barrier surrounding them. "Before you do anything, are you sure the wards will hold?"

The last thing she wanted was for the phantoms to come and claim him. Something about seeing Edgar with that girl this morning still rubbed her the wrong way.

Edgar was hers, and she wasn't letting some skank take him away from her.

Not without a fight.

"They'll hold." He grimaced, obviously not relishing calling on the darkness, and she hated that they asked it of him.

"You don't have to do this." She rested her hand on his chest, wanting to comfort him. "I feel fine. Honest."

But he was already shaking his head. "I won't have you risk yourself foolishly. Let me check you out first."

"Then I can go with you." But even before she had a chance to finish her objection, he exploded outward in a cloud of dark smoke, his form indistinguishable, the shape of him only a vague outline. Dark particles shimmered and flared brightly as they caught the sunlight.

Residue from the afterworld radiated from him, a cool breeze wrapping around her, urging her to come and visit, like he was a doorway to the world beyond. She reached out toward him, then gasped at the contact, her whole body tingling like she'd touched an electric current.

His form became solid under her touch, as if she'd called him back, and she pulled away, rubbing the tips of her fingers together. "What was that?"

Edgar's shoulders were heaving, as if he was struggling to catch his breath. The afterworld faded from his eyes, leaving behind a blue so dark they were almost black, pure joy and possessiveness shone from them as he gazed down at her. "It's said when a perfect match is found, that phantoms can join their powers together, making them stronger and faster. Making them unstoppable."

But something about his awe made the hair on the back of her neck stand on end. "But?"

"It's rare." He took a step toward her, as if lured closer by the power, but then forced himself to stop. "Most don't even try it. If they're not a close enough match, one phantom can easily consume the other…or worse, they shatter against each other, rendering them both barely a step above a null. Most never recover from the loss of their powers."

Annora swallowed hard, not sure she wanted to know the answer, not if it meant she had to send him away to protect him. But she couldn't bury her head in the sand. She would not be responsible for destroying what he held most dear. "And when we touched?"

Even before he spoke, she saw the hesitation in his eyes and knew the truth.

Her touch would consume him.

When he went to reach for her, she flinched, quickly ducking behind Mason. "Don't! I won't be responsible for hurting you. I won't—I can't—"

Her breathing went ragged.

She stumbled away, unable to find enough oxygen to fill her lungs.

"You misunderstand." Edgar didn't flinch or retreat from knowing she could literally destroy him with a touch. "Merging is giving and taking. There has to be a balance. With practice, we would be able to control the push and pull and use it."

But she was already shaking her head.

"It's about trust," he continued, his eyes sparkling with pure happiness. "I know you would never harm me—your magic doesn't see me as a threat. Plus, I know it's not possible for me to harm you. Even if I took all the power you have to offer, it would only weaken you at the very worst. The only threat to me is too much power burning me out."

He grinned, like it was miraculous news, but none of it eased the tightness in her chest at the thought of giving him up.

Because that's what would happen.

She had to send him away. She couldn't live with herself if she ever harmed him, even unintentionally.

The eagerness on Edgar's face faded when she remained mute.

Xander grabbed her arm and twisted her around to face him. He lifted up his scarred hands, staring down at them. "I've killed people with my bare hands, torn them apart without an ounce of remorse, and I will do it again."

He dropped his hands and glanced at her. "Are you afraid of me now?"

She blinked up at him, confused at the abrupt change in conversation. "No, of course not. You would never harm me."

She knew it down in her bones. He would rather kill himself than harm a hair on her head.

It was the same for all of the guys.

"Then you have a choice. Edgar has spent most of your life trying to keep you safe. You must trust him on some level. If all you have to do is practice in order to keep him in your life, don't you think he deserves that chance?"

Damn them for being so reasonable.

She rolled her eyes, wishing it was so easy. If she fucked up…if anything went wrong…she glanced at Edgar out of the corner of her eyes and felt her resolve softening. He had risked everything for her, saved her repeatedly. If the phantoms were really coming, they were going to be coming for the both of them.

He risked everything to escape them once.

He deserved more than her tossing him away to face his fate alone.

Why the fuck were people so damned difficult?

Living on her own was so much easier.

And so much lonelier.

She pulled away from the guys to glare at Edgar. "You'll tell me if *anything* is wrong? No matter what? You'll warn me before I hurt you?" She narrowed her eyes at him when he nodded after each question. "You have to promise you won't allow me to harm you."

His eyes darkened, the fathomless blue seeming to almost churn. He covered his heart, then bowed at the waist. "You have my word. Upon my honor, I will keep you safe."

It sounded like a vow, and she pursed her lips at the phrasing, feeling like she was missing something important.

But the guys seemed satisfied and continued the conversation, Camden getting straight to business. "Can she jump safely now?"

Edgar studied her for a heartbeat longer, then turned toward the guys. "The jump fatigues her, since she is passing over the afterworld without refreshing her well of power, but otherwise leaves her unharmed. The effect she's feeling is what most phantoms feel when they ghost. It's like a muscle. The more she practices, the better and stronger she will become."

Annora pressed her nails into the pads of her fingers, the sharp, quick jab of pain helping her focus as she processed the information.

She was so distracted, in fact, that she didn't realize the guys had stopped talking until Edgar came to stand next to her. "We're going to practice jumping with a passenger. Since I'm the least likely to get lost and could possibly find my own way back or hold off from being killed until you find me, I'm your first volunteer."

She blanched at the blunt way he phrased the way things could go horribly wrong, but she also appreciated his honesty. He held out his hand to her without hesitation, completely trusting, while he waited for her decision. Knowing that she needed to master this skill, she blew out a breath and squared her shoulders.

Without pausing, she gathered the particles that seemed so much a part of her, doubled the amount from last time, and cast the cloudy mixture in front of her. She wasn't sure what others saw, but the dark particles paused midair, a cosmic doorway opening up in front of her, the tiny specks sparkling like stars in the inky blackness.

Concentrating on a location just a few feet away, she reached out, grabbed Edgar's hand, and pulled him through the barrier. She met a slight resistance as the particles clung to her like dust. Pulling Edgar after her took more effort, like she physically had to haul his body though a tub of syrup.

Time stretched and pulled, twisting and bending around her. It was harder to find her footing, and harder to leave, when it felt like traveling through wet cement. When the darkness finally released her, she was thrown into the human world, smacking against the ground hard, landing on her hands and knees and dragging Edgar down with her.

He didn't seem to be in much better shape, struggling to keep himself from face-planting on the prickly lawn. Familiar arms curled around her waist from behind, hauling her to her feet. Her legs were too unsteady to stand on their own, so she leaned against Mason, not the least bit surprised that he reached her first. The warmth from his massive body made her shiver, and she realized the passageway felt like a freaking walk-through freezer set on freeze-your-nuts-off.

Only when she was sure she could stand on her own without falling over did she stumble back over toward Edgar, glad to see that he'd pushed himself up and was now sitting on his ass. He still looked ready to keel over, but he was upright instead of passed out.

"What the hell happened?" She staggered to a stop in front of him, setting her feet wider to keep from collapsing next to him. "Why did it feel like it was fighting me?"

Laughter burst out of him, and she narrowed her eyes when it felt like he was laughing at her. If she thought she could kick him without falling over, she would've tried. Instead she settled for crossing her arms and glaring. "Explain."

Edgar leaned back until he was sprawled on the ground, shaking his head at her as if completely baffled. "I don't think you understand how much of a struggle it is for a normal phantom to even ghost. Most can't access the afterworld the way you do, much less take to it like a fish to water. Most phantoms are drained after visiting your afterworld once, much like you're feeling now. It's unnatural for them."

He grimaced up at her, his humor vanishing. "*No one* can jump like you, especially not the way you just did. It should be impossible." He very slowly pushed himself to his feet like an old man trying to rise, as if his muscles refused to cooperate. "You have an affinity for the afterworld like I've never encountered in the past. My fear is that your father will no longer try to kill you, but instead do everything in his power to crush your spirit and mold you into is very own flunky to do his bidding. His ruthlessness is much like your uncle's, but with one exception..."

The worry on his face made panic tighten her insides until they felt liquid.

"…where your uncle failed, he will succeed."

Annora lifted her chin, refusing to be cowed. "I won't allow that to happen."

Pity darkened his eyes, the afterworld eating away all color and light. "You already gave him the key to owning your soul. All he has to do is kill your mates or threaten them, and you will be his willing servant."

Annora shook her head, denying the truth of his words, but Edgar followed her relentlessly, and grabbed her arms so she couldn't leave. "I know of only one person who might be strong enough to save your mates."

Everything inside her calmed, relief making her insides wobble. "Tell me."

"You—you just have to want it bad enough."

Chapter Nine

All Annora could do was open and close her mouth as Edgar strode away, completely at a loss how to respond. The guys were silent, watching her with concern.

But she hoped Edgar was right.

No one was more motivated to save the guys than her. If there was a way, she would find it.

She turned toward the guys and saw the same conviction on their faces.

Without hesitation, they believed she was strong enough to stand up to her father.

Swallowing hard, she focused on Xander. "If I'm going to have any hope of winning, you need to train me harder. You can't go easy on me—you can't let me lose."

Xander gave her a speculative look, then nodded. "Be prepared to move in thirty minutes."

Without another word, he turned and walked away.

The witches must have heard they were planning to move. They were on their feet, their phones out as they left. Annora doubted they had any intention of letting her out of their sight for one second, so they were calling in reinforcements. Even as the last one stepped off the porch, the fire in the pit stuttered, then died down to ash.

It took an effort on her part to shrug off knowing that her time was no longer her own.

She wasn't used to the attention and hated it. She didn't know how celebrities stood it, much less those who sought it out. She shivered at having all those eyes following her every move.

It gave her the heebie-jeebies.

It didn't take long for the guys to meet her at the front of the house, silently taking formation around her and escorting her to the arena. Edgar joined the others, falling in like he'd been a part of the group his entire life.

She easily spotted several groups of witches doing a piss-poor job of pretending they weren't watching her, but to her surprise, there were also a number of shifters who, while they watched her, seemed to be watching the witches with even more interest.

It was almost like they were protecting her from the witches. Then she realized they were the other teams who patrolled the campus. Either her guys called in reinforcements or Greenwood did.

She relaxed slightly at knowing someone out there would have the guys' backs if anything went wrong.

Not surprisingly, no matter how hard she searched, she couldn't spot the phantom girl, Sadie.

Annora wasn't sure if that worried her more or not.

When they reached the arena, instead of going topside, they went down through a series of passageways.

Three levels down, the entire floor was pitch black. One lone, naked bulb illuminated the tiny locker room. Xander and Edgar stayed near her, while the others disappeared off into the darkness. With her advanced hearing, she could tell they didn't go far, but she couldn't see anyone in the shadows, her eyes slow to adjust to the dimness.

"This is the training pit." Xander turned toward her, slipping a vest over his head, systematically dressing in the full training gear that waited for them in lockers. The rest of the guys followed suit, their movements practiced.

They did this often.

"Yeah, I can tell where you got the name." She smirked at him, shoving her hair back into a messy ponytail, then accepted the vest Mason slipped over her head. It was thin and versatile, allowing her arms and torso easy movement. "Very original."

But accurate. Even with her extra abilities, she couldn't see more than a few feet in any direction. It was almost like walking into a sensory deprivation chamber.

He cracked a small smile at her snark, but it wasn't enough to throw him off his speech. "There are no lights down at this level. You'll find more than thirty rooms of various shapes and sizes. Some of them are empty of furniture and others are packed full. We use this place to practice before we breach unknown locations. Witches come down here often, so the place is fully warded."

Thank the gods!

It meant she was free to use her full powers.

Without them, she was very much aware they wouldn't stand a chance.

Xander turned and walked away, then picked up a dark, lethal-looking paintball gun hanging by pegs on the wall. "Here's the scenario: your men are imprisoned down here. You must rescue them and escape. You'll have to work and move as a team if you want to survive. More than four hits and you're dead."

Without saying anything else, he turned on his heel and strode away, the rest of the guys disappearing in the darkness.

She sputtered for a few seconds, then grinned. She turned toward Edgar, feeling hopeful about their chances of getting Logan back. "I guess we're the rescue team. Ready?"

Edgar lifted an imperious brow at her, a small smirk playing on his lips. "How about we show them what it'll be like to go up against phantoms?"

Annora nodded, enjoying the idea that they would be training the guys just as much as they were being trained. The team took the impending attack from the phantoms in stride, not even fazed at the idea of fighting an opponent they couldn't see or track, and she was pretty sure they were underestimating their enemy.

They'd gone only a few feet when they came upon three different paths. Edgar let her take the lead, and she allowed instinct to guide her to the right—only to find a second divide in another twenty feet.

She took three more paths, passing no doorways, when another split opened up in front of them. She halted, hands on her hips and cursed. "It's a fucking maze."

They'd been underground no more than ten minutes and she was already hopelessly lost, her senses unbalanced by the lack of sounds and sight.

"I could always tell when you were in the abandoned world. It was like the air warmed in welcome. I could follow that connection like a tug right here." He tapped his chest, his expression intense as he gazed down at her. "You can do the same with your men, even if we're in the earthly realm."

He sounded almost afraid to mention their connection, as if she would try to cut him out, but reminding her at the same time that he mattered, that he was one of her men—in case she forgot. Feeling more and more horrible for making him doubt himself and his place, she nodded to him. "We're family."

He didn't move as he stared at her, his eyes flaring with hope. "Family."

He tucked a stray strand of hair that had escaped from her ponytail behind her ear. "In the true spirit of practice, you should avoid the afterworld as much as possible. Only use it in case of emergencies."

Annora couldn't help but wonder what part of avoiding the afterworld was practice and what part of it was actually his fear of the banished lands he'd been trapped in for so many years.

He was elegant in no way a human could duplicate, with a self-awareness she envied. Though his skin was smooth and pale, there was a sharpness to his eyes and face that hinted at the hardships he'd suffered, and a stubborn look to his strong jaw that, heaven help her, she was coming to admire.

Despite her resolve to keep her distance, she was failing.

And she was beginning not to care.

When he cocked his head at her, she brushed off her distractions and began moving again.

Focusing on the ties binding her and the men together, she sensed Mason was the closest, waiting just a few yards ahead of them. As she neared his location, she pressed her hand to the walls, trying to find an entryway.

And found nothing.

Dammit.

She was so close she could almost taste victory.

Left with no choice, she stepped back and followed the passageway. She only went a few feet before halting, scowling when she discovered it led them farther away from Mason. She growled in frustration, then raised her brow at Edgar. "Ready to make this interesting?"

His answering smile was devilish. "I thought you'd never ask."

Annora retraced her steps, then placed her hand on the wall separating her from Mason. She collected the darkness inside her, watching it curl around her fingers. The more she used, the more her senses expanded and seeped into the human world.

The wall was just normal wood, drywall and studs a few inches thick. "Follow me."

Then she allowed the particles to burst outward in a swirling mass, her form dissolving into mist, and she slipped clean through the wall. She took form on the other side, only to see Edgar appear next to her as if he stepped out of thin air.

She scowled, wanting to call foul that he'd used the afterworld when he banned her from it. He smirked, as if waiting for her challenge, and she pursed her lips, refusing to give him the satisfaction. He pointed to his eye, then tipped his head to indicate the three guys in the room guarding the door. Mason was leaning against the wall, reading on his phone. As if he sensed her, he lifted his head, surprise widening his eyes when he saw her.

He glanced at the door, then back to her, before grinning.

The guards were so focused on the doorway, they never once looked behind them.

Edgar gave her the option of taking out the guards or going for Mason. While removing the threat was optimal, the alarms had yet to be sounded. The better plan would be to sneak in and out and rescue as many of the guys as possible before they were discovered.

She reached Mason first. She touched his arm, allowing the darkness of the afterworld to wrap around them. To her surprise, she was able to take Mason with her as she stepped through the wall. It wasn't that he dissolved, but more like he could follow in the disturbance of her wake.

They were spit out on the other side, dumping them into another room.

Only it wasn't empty.

Four wolves were playing cards, clearly bored. At their entrance, they froze, staring at them in complete shock. Mason was the first to react, taking advantage of their inaction by charging them. Though the man was massive, he moved like a wild animal on the hunt...all lethal and deadly grace. Annora was a step behind him, not nearly as fast as the troll, the trip through the wall disorienting her slightly and leaving her off-balance.

She hid behind Mason's bulk, sliding out from behind him at the last possible minute, diving low to take the nearest wolf out at the knees. Without a hint of hesitation or remorse, she brought up her elbow and rammed it right into his nose.

The kid kept his cool, not reaching for his nose as she expected, but going for his gun while she was distracted. As he took aim, she grabbed the barrel and yanked it aside just as the ping of the paintball launching breezed by her ear. She took control of the gun, ramming it backwards, smacking him between the eyes and knocking him out cold.

As she hauled herself off the prone body, she saw Edgar was no less deadly, his movements sure and practiced as he popped in and out of existence, avoiding the punches directed at him, dodging the paintballs that went off with a muted potch of compressed air.

It didn't take more than a minute to incapacitate the four wolves. Her men moved as a team that had worked together for years. After the raid, they checked each other for injuries. She and Edgar were clean, but Mason had a bright pink splash on his outer thigh.

Though she didn't like that he'd been *theoretically* injured, the shot was in a non-life-threatening area at least. He was used to taking abuse, and she had to trust that he knew what he was doing.

What she didn't expect was for him to collect the paintball guns and hit each of the downed wolves with the requisite four shots to show they were dead. "Mason?"

"We must eliminate the threat." He shrugged those broad

shoulders of his, completely unconcerned that he would've murdered four people in cold blood. "If they were really after us, if it came to choosing between you and them, I wouldn't take any chances."

She tucked away her squeamishness.

He was right.

The kind of people who took Logan didn't deserve her mercy.

"Where to next, boss?" Edgar asked, while Mason wrapped the straps of one of the guns around his forearm. He offered one to Edgar, who looked intrigued, but ultimately waved it away. When Mason raised a brow at her, lifting up a gun in offer, she too declined.

"I have no training with guns. It would be more of a distraction." Then she focused on Edgar's question. "Since no alarm has been sounded, I say we avoid the hallways, move from room to room in a straight line, and clear as many as we can before they catch on to what we're doing."

It was a gamble not to head directly for the rest of her men, but she needed more practice, and the team needed time to fall into a rhythm of working together. In under an hour, they'd cleared most of the basement and collected the rest of the team members.

She also discovered that only one person at a time could follow in her wake. If she wanted to take more than one person with her, she needed to travel with them into the afterworld. She could keep the portal open and reach back for them, but it was taxing.

They were nearing the exit of the pit, but their escape had been discovered. The rest of the people hunting them would be waiting, and now they were prepared for her tricks.

A single wall separated them from their freedom.

The guys had various bruises, a few of them had paint shots—herself included, when she was shot in the back by none other than Vicki, and another one to the shoulder when Loulou gave her a disarming smile and shot her point-blank.

That shit hurt!

She almost felt bad for grabbing the gun and shooting Loulou four times to take her out. No way in hell could she punch her best friend. Thankfully, Lionel wasn't in the same room, so she was still alive and not shredded about the room in itty-bitty pieces.

Nearly everyone who broke free from Erickson's lab volunteered today. Lionel and more than a few members of his pack joined as well. Overall, there were more than forty people who participated in the training session.

She was exhausted from avoiding the afterworld and dragging the guys with her, sweat plastering her shirt to her, her hair snarled and matted. She was reaching her breaking point, but kept her mouth shut. They were close to the end. They would win, and she'd finally prove to herself that she could keep her guys safe.

While the guys noticed her deterioration, taking the lead more and more, they didn't protest or call it quits. Their trust in her pulled her back from the brink, their nearness having a calming effect.

She'd take the exhaustion and bruises over the anger and despair that had been threatening to consume her, the aches keeping her from going off the deep end.

Pain meant she was alive.

Pain kept her focused on the task that needed to be done.

As the men discussed options, she studied the last wall separating her from freedom. "Edgar…can we manipulate inanimate objects?"

As if seeing the direction of her thoughts, he shook his head. "Not normally, not without calling on the afterworld."

So not only could she not see into the other room without being spotted, she couldn't pull the guys in with her. Edgar was adamant that she refrain from entering the afterworld, and it was taking its toll on her mind and body.

She could feel it reaching for her, brushing against her, tempting her to just take a little, like an addict, and she was practically shaking with need. It was like someone was pressing on her chest, cutting off her air supply, allowing her just enough to function with only half her senses.

Mason gave her a broad smile and nudged her aside, cracking his knuckles as he did, his arms bulging. "My turn, pretty one." He pressed his fingertips against the wall, the paneling bowing under his touch, and he smiled. "I got this one."

Camden rubbed his jaw, his head cocked. "They'll be expecting us to come through the walls." He walked toward the door and placed his hand on the knob. "I say we send Edgar and Annora to pop into the center of the room, and then the rest of us will just walk through the door."

"We're at the end...I could just open up the afterworld and transport us all to the stairs." When the guys looked at each other, she knew they were going to say no, and she barely resisted the urge to stomp her foot. "You're asking me to fight with my hands tied behind my back while you guys are able to use your full shifter abilities—why deny my abilities when it could help us win...and possibly save us later?"

She understood their fears, but she refused to allow it to control her.

Edgar edged in front of her. "Because this is practice. You're getting better and faster each time you use your abilities. What happens if you use your abilities and the phantoms find you? What will happen to Logan and your men then?"

"Fine." She pursed her lips, hating that he was right. It was just so damn frustrating. "What about you? Why are you allowed to use your normal abilities?"

Edgar blinked down at her, then shook his head. "Because I can't do what you do. While I might be powerful, I can't manipulate the afterworld the way you can."

Annora stared at him for a heartbeat longer, unsettled to realize he was telling her the truth. "That's the real reason why you think my father will allow me to live, isn't it? How many people can actually ghost the way I do?"

Only very reluctantly did he respond. "A handful of people, most of them elders who've accumulated their powers over centuries."

Which meant that she was screwed.

Even if she fought her way free of the phantoms, they would always come for her, wanting to control her...unless she found a way to make them regret coming after her in the first place.

Acid churned in her guts as the answer came to her—she was either going to have to go to war or find a way to kill her father.

Fuck!

Chapter Ten

Annora didn't say anything after they breached the last room. The fight was intense and brutal, and though they managed to escape, they'd taken serious damage in the process. The guys were sweaty and covered in an assortment of colors from the paintballs.

While none of them took enough to die from their injuries, it left them weak.

Open to another attack.

As the guys talked strategies, she headed off to the showers, since it was too late in the evening to run through the pit again.

"Hey, wait up!" Loulou bounced into view, her energy boundless, her smile bright and cheery. She was splatted everywhere with paint, but instead of looking defeated, she wore them like badges of honor. Her almost-white hair was piled on top of her hair in a messy knot, making her too-large blue eyes appear even bigger and brighter. "Where've you been the past week? I've been trying to get ahold of you. Don't tell me the guys are keeping you prisoner, not when I know you can slip away to say hello to your bestie."

Annora had to look away from her earnest expression, guilt piling up around her like thick sludge that made walking, even breathing, a chore. "I'm sorry. It's been a rough week."

Sympathy oozed from Loulou for all of two seconds, when her eyes narrowed to dangerous slits. "That better be the answer. If you're trying to push me away because of the danger, you can forget it. I'm not going anywhere."

The stubborn little rabbit crossed her arms defiantly, her pointy chin hiked up in the air, her hair practically quivering in outrage.

"The danger—"

"Fuck the danger." She skipped ahead, then turned around until she was walking backwards, forcing them to walk face-to-face. "Some things are worth the risks."

Annora studied her fierce little friend and realized she meant every word. Her throat tightened, and she had to swallow the surge of emotion threatening to drown her. When she said nothing, Loulou smiled, her grin spreading across her face while she did a bouncy victory dance.

"I knew you'd see things my way." She twisted around, not missing a beat and began walking next to her again. "Next time, you call me."

She bumped shoulders with her, the girl nothing more than a ball of fluff. Then what Loulou said registered, and Annora narrowed her eyes. "Someone called you."

Loulou suddenly found the concrete walls fascinating. "I have no idea what you mean."

"Mmm-hmmm." Annora didn't believe her for a second. Right before they passed through the doorway, she flung her arm across the path, blocking the exit. "Spill it."

Looking guilty for a second, Loulou blinked up at her with those big eyes of hers, lips quivering, and Annora snorted. "Don't work your wiles on me. I'm not falling for it."

But she did have to look away.

Loulou sighed and grumbled. "Figured you'd be the one who could withstand my special allure."

Annora smothered her laugh, not willing to admit how close she came to cracking. "Spill."

"Edgar showed up out of the blue." Loulou ducked under her arm and continued out the door. "And I mean literally. Poof!" She flung out her hands like an explosion, humor making her eyes honest-to-gods twinkle. "I thought Lionel and his men were going to have a heart attack."

Annora's mind went completely blank. "He did?"

"Uh-huh." Loulou nodded like a bobble head, her hair flopping as she practically skipped down the hall. "He was worried about you."

Annora bit her lip, not certain how to react. Most of the time Edgar was a possessive asshole who thought of her as his property to protect. But getting Loulou…this was more than just returning the ferret to her. He was trying to be considerate of her feelings.

As they entered the shower area, Annora cocked her head at her friend. "What did your Lionel say about you coming out today?"

She couldn't imagine that he was pleased about it.

"Pshhh." Loulou shrugged it away with a flap of her arm. "We're not mated yet, and if he thinks he can tell me what to do after, he has another think coming."

She was all attitude and sass, but Annora saw the way her face softened when she mentioned Lionel. Annora lifted a brow and thrust her thumb over her shoulder to indicate the door. "Is that why he followed us down the hall?"

Instead of refuting it, a broad smile crossed her face, pure joy lighting her up from the inside as she practically bounced on her feet. She clasped her hands together, bringing them up to her chest, and fluttered her lashes. "Isn't he just the best?!?"

Annora snorted as the girl whirled away, leaving her alone with her thoughts. Loulou was so happy it filled her whole soul. Annora wanted that for her and the guys. She just wished it was as easy.

Then she kicked herself for the thought. Loulou and Lionel had fought hard for their love, and they deserved all the happiness they could get. Their life wouldn't be an easy one, but their love for each other was strong enough to withstand anything.

As she stripped and stepped into the shower, Annora wasn't sure if she was ready to call what she felt for the guys love. She was devoted to them, would do anything for them, but her emotions were too fragile and new to examine more closely.

Not yet, not until they were all safe.

As she walked out of the shower, she wasn't surprised to find a subdued Loulou dressed and pacing restlessly, the bubbly personality that made up so much of her was gone.

"Loulou?"

"I know Logan is gone for now." She stopped pacing then whirled and advanced on her, the rabbit's expression fierce as she waved her finger in Annora's face. "You call me if you need a good cry." Then a wry smile came to her face. "Or if we need to go get coffee and plot a war party to retrieve your boy."

Annora blinked away the tears before they could fall and rubbed at the heaviness in her chest. Taking a step forward, she engulfed the petite woman in a hug, nearly sobbing when Loulou hugged her back just as fiercely. "I will."

Loulou sniffled, ducking her head and pulling away. "Well, you do that."

Then she was gone, out the door faster than lightning.

No matter how determined Annora was to keep her distance from everyone when she first arrived at the university, she was glad she'd failed in such an epic fashion. Even with all the trouble that followed her, she couldn't—didn't want to—imagine her life without Loulou and the guys.

As she opened the door to leave, she nearly slammed into Xander. Freshly washed, his black hair hung into his face, the white tips stark against his tanned skin. Big and rugged, he made her want to snuggle up against him and forget her cares for a while. His teal eyes were sharp as he studied her, and she gave him a small smile. "I'm okay."

"Liar." His low voice was gruff, not letting her get away with anything. He looped his arm around her neck and pulled her close.

Annora sighed against his shoulder, allowing herself to relax against him, the fresh sea breeze scent he carried loosening her tongue. "Yeah, but I'm dealing with it."

Xander stifled the rage that threatened to consume him, the

piercing caw of his gryphon echoing his sentiments exactly. They both wanted to fight, maim, and kill anyone who would dare harm her. It was a physical ache to hold himself back.

But him losing his shit wouldn't help her. If he thought he could sneak in and retrieve Logan for her, he would do it in a heartbeat.

Every one of the guys would.

Unfortunately, it wasn't that simple.

No matter how well-trained, how deadly they were in battle, they couldn't win against an army.

Annora frowned up at him, standing on her toes to try and see past him into the hallway. "Where are the others?"

Her question snapped him out of his funk, and he stepped back. As much as he might wish to keep her all to himself for the rest of the day, he had to content himself with a few stolen moments. "They're waiting for us topside."

"No doubt plotting our next step without me." Annora winced and cast him a commiserating look. "Leaving you stuck babysitting."

Xander didn't even try to cover his snort. "More like I won the bet."

Annora was so worried they'd be too late to save Logan that she was becoming desperate.

Taking unnecessary risks.

Pushing herself too far, too fast, and that worried him. He'd been like that before he met her, focused only on the job, and he didn't want that life for her. She deserved better.

He meandered down the tunnel next to her, not in any rush to return to the others. Wanting to distract her, take her mind off her worries, he captured her hand when it brushed past his and wove their fingers together.

When she faltered, glancing at him sideways, he couldn't resist the temptation to see how far he could push her. He tugged on her arm, spinning her around in a dramatic, tango-like dance move, and pressed her up against the cement stone wall.

She peered up at him with wide-eyed innocence, nervously tucking her hair behind her ear. "What are you doing?"

"I'm not letting you get caught in the same trap as me." He ducked his head until their noses brushed. "There is more to life than training and work. You taught me that."

When she tried to duck her head, he caught her hand and put it over his heart, determined to make her understand. He worried that if he couldn't find the right words, she would slip through his fingers and fall prey to the insanity of hatred and war, forgetting what mattered most.

He was used to fighting with his fists, teeth and talons. He wasn't any good at expressing himself.

But for her, he would try.

"We're here for you...if you'll allow us. You haven't lost us. Don't shut us out." He cleared his throat, struggling to speak. "I'm here, and I'm not going anywhere."

Annora stared up at the big, gruff man, able to taste his anxiety. Knowing she was the cause of his unhappiness made her stomach lurch. She stroked the scruff along his chin, then brushed her fingertips along the crinkles worrying had etched across his forehead. "I have no intention of going anywhere."

He leaned down, his voice a demand. "No more shutting us out."

Before she had a chance to say anything, his control snapped. His lips slammed against hers, and she found her back crushed against the wall behind her, like he couldn't get close enough.

Then the outside world was forgotten as he devoured her.

He nipped at her lips, demanding more, and she relished the sting. She slid her hands down his shoulders to rest against his chest, savoring the way his muscles flexed under her touch. Knowing he needed more, she trailed her fingers down to the waistband of his pants, then shoved her hands up under his shirt, shivering at the heat pouring off of him.

A growl rumbled in his chest, igniting every nerve ending in her body, leaving her craving more. He bent, grabbed the back of her legs, and lifted her clear off the floor. She quickly wrapped her legs around his waist, and a hum of approval resonated low in his throat.

A second later, the tunnel seemed to be flooded with people, the kids whistling and catcalling as they passed. Xander lifted his head and snarled viciously. Wind picked up in the tunnel, as if a great creature was flapping its wings, sending the students scurrying like rats trying to outrun a flood.

His pupils were fully dilated, his body rigid as he tucked her away from prying eyes, his beast in full control. He wasn't being possessive, but trying to protect her virtue, and warmth flooded her at his thoughtfulness. Not sure how to calm him, she cuddled him close, running her nails up and down the back of his neck until he finally relaxed against her.

He slowly lowered her to her feet, not looking at her. When he would've moved away, she clamped her hands around his wrists, halting him as if she'd used a spell to freeze him. She trailed her fingers down the inside of his wrist to the center of his palm and spread her fingers wide, linking them through his.

His grip immediately tightened around her, and he stared impassively at their joined hands for a full minute. When he realized that she wasn't trying to get away, he seemed to deflate, the tension going out of him. Tucking her close, he guided her aboveground to join the others.

The team surveyed her and Xander when they emerged from the tunnels, their attention lingering on their clasped hands for a few seconds before they went back into protection mode as they headed out. To her surprise, Xander didn't release her until they got back to Grady House.

The absolute darkness huddled around the house caused her steps to slow.

Something was waiting for them.

As the guys escorted her inside and began making supper, Annora wandered into the living room, gazing out of the wall of glass, searching for what triggered her unease. "I need a few moments to myself. Is the backyard still warded?"

The guys paused, glancing at each other, when Camden spoke. "Yes, it's still warded. Stay within the boundaries."

She could tell that it cost him not to send one of the guys out with her, and she had no doubt she'd only have a few minutes to herself before at least one of them came searching for her. She'd have to work fast if she didn't want to be discovered.

Annora hurried toward the sliding glass door that made up most of one wall. As soon as she slipped outside, the cool night air was like a slap to the face, the touch of frost in it reminding her of Logan. Pushing away the distracting thoughts, she quickly stepped down off the porch, and made her way toward the darkness lingering just beyond the wards.

She stopped at the edge and crossed her arms with a scowl. "What the hell do you want?"

The darkness thinned for a second, then began to move and thicken. The cloud of particles condensed, sucked inward as it began to settle into the shape of a person.

A familiar person.

"Sadie." Annora kept her voice flat, struggling to hold back the rage that urged her to close the distance between them and rip the woman's throat out.

"Ah, he told you about me." Her midnight black hair was pulled back, which only seemed to accentuate her otherworldly beauty. The glow of the afterworld was only a shimmer in her eyes before fading to pure malice. "Funny, you weren't important enough to even mention."

Annora snorted, rolling her eyes at the stupidity. "Of course not. Why the hell would he share anything with someone we can't trust?"

The smugness melted away, hatred twisting her face into a snarl. "So cute. You actually believe you mean something to him, a tiny human."

Done with the games, Annora dropped her arms and marched toward the barrier, stopping an inch away from it. "Tell me, since you were his friend, how long did you look for him in the banished lands before you gave up?"

Shock made Sadie blanch. She shook her head, opening her mouth to respond, but snapped it shut without speaking, her eyes dropping.

The horrible truth dawned, and Annora couldn't speak for a moment under the crushing weight in her chest. "Dear gods, you left him there to rot, didn't you? You didn't even have the decency to search for him."

"You don't know what you're talking about." Sadie strode closer to the barrier, pointing an accusing finger at her. "No one who walks the banished lands ever returns."

"Except he did. He found his way back after you abandoned him." Annora grew up around people like this woman, claiming to be friends, then abandoning her when she needed them most. "What do you really want? Why are you here?"

"You think you're someone special? That he'll stay with you? Forget it." Sadie stared down her nose at her, derision twisting her lips. "He's heir to the controlling seat on the council. Do you actually think he would give that up for you?"

Annora had already figured out that Edgar was someone important.

She would never have guessed that he was her father's right-hand man.

Though she was relieved the girl wasn't in love with Edgar, at least not in the traditional sense, Sadie wanted him to take his rightful place and wouldn't stop until she got him back. "Edgar gave all that up years ago when he left. He would never return to that world."

Laughter burst out of Sadie, genuine amusement dancing in her eyes. "Oh, that's great. You don't even know his real name, do you?" Her grin widened when she looked down at her. "Alcott will return with me eventually. We've been betrothed since birth. It's our destiny to rule the council together."

A giant fist grabbed her insides and twisted.

Betrothed.

Annora stared up at the woman's smug face and put every ounce of her conviction into her voice. "Edgar is my mate. If you think I'm going to just hand him over to you without a fight, you have another think coming."

She took vicious pleasure at seeing Sadie's shock at the word *mate*.

"You lie." But the woman's voice trembled, the sour scent of her fear tinging the air.

Annora instantly went on alert. "I don't lie."

But it was like Sadie didn't hear her. "Phantoms don't mate. We're not allowed to for good reason. He would never allowed himself to fall into that trap."

"Trap?" Though Annora was ridiculously relieved to know the two phantoms weren't married already, her fear of losing him now that they were just working out their differences was a living beast threatening to devour her. "What do you mean?"

Sadie gawked at her incredulously, then tipped her head back and cursed up a storm. "Fuck! I can't believe the asshole allowed himself to be mated. What the hell was he thinking?!"

Annora could only gape at the outburst.

Sadie whirled toward her and held up her hand beseechingly, then jerked back when the wards set off a shower of sparks against her fingertips. "You have to release him from your claim."

Annoyance and incredulity went through Annora. "You've got to be kidding me. He's not a damned fish to be tossed back. He'd been lost to the afterworld for years—*decades*—while you left him there to rot. Where was this concern and friendship then?"

"I thought he was dead!" The girl whirled away, gripping the back of her neck as she cursed under her breath, dark particles floating around Sadie in her agitation. "You're holding him here just as much as if you shackled him. If you don't think he would return at the first opportunity, you're a fool."

As much as Annora didn't want to admit it, Sadie was someone important to Edgar...and incredibly dangerous. Annora could fight against fists and weapons, but how did she fight the past?

For some reason, Annora never considered that Edgar might have a life before they met, and she was more than a little curious about what he was like then.

Well, of course he had a life before her. She rolled her eyes and wanted to smack herself. She just never expected it to come back to bite her on the ass.

"Look, I don't give a fuck about your problems. I've got enough of my own." Annora rubbed her brow, wishing she knew how she got herself into such a mess. She just wanted a simple life, but it seemed that wasn't in the works for her. "I have no intention of releasing Edgar. If he wants to leave, he's more than capable of. making that decision for himself."

Sadie gave a maniacal laugh. "You don't get it. People like Alcott and I don't get a choice. Phantoms are under tight control. We're never allow to leave our realm. They can't risk our powers falling under anyone else's control. That's why we keep to ourselves. While it might be dangerous for us if people find out about us, it's infinitely more dangerous to the ones who discover us."

Sadie came to a stop in front of her, all artifice gone. "Alcott is too powerful to be allowed to live away from the phantoms. The others will find him, and they will force you to comply or kill you. That's your choice. Would you really risk his life for something as stupid as love?"

The last time he'd been given the choice, Edgar chose death by walking into the banished land.

He was never meant to survive.

"It's fine if you want to kill yourself, but don't get Alcott killed for your delusions of love."

"You love him." Annora's heart sank at the realization. She could fight other phantoms for a chance at a future with him, but she wasn't sure the fragile love she felt for Edgar was enough to keep him by her side.

"May the gods save me from delusional humans." Sadie plunked her fists on her hips and rolled her eyes dramatically. "Phantoms don't marry for love. Our betrothal is a union between houses. He was raised to rule. I won't allow him to throw away all our careful planning over some stupid human who doesn't know better."

In a burst of particles and smoke, Sadie seemed to fold into herself, then vanish in a puff of dust that glittered as it floated to the ground.

Leaving Annora standing out in the cold, her insides feeling like ice after everything she just learned.

Edgar was betrothed.

If he had the option to return, would he take it? He turned down ruling the phantoms once, entering the banished lands to escape, and suffered for it.

Could she ask him to give up even more to stay with her?

Then a more troubling thought popped in her head—if he was the heir, her father would be coming for him as well. He would never let Edgar go, especially not a second time.

Would she and Edgar be strong enough to hold out against her father and his phantom army?

Chapter Eleven

When Annora entered the house, she registered that the guys were preparing supper. Edgar was setting out dishes, seeming almost bemused to find himself doing chores among the men, and she realized that he probably never had to set a table before.

Needing time to process what she learned before she took any action, she stepped into the kitchen. "What can I do to help?"

"Feeling better?" Camden studied her face, then pulled out a chair for her. "The food is almost done. Sit."

The ferret scurried past her, reaching her chair first. He jumped on the bottom rung, then pulled himself up onto her seat. Then he whirled and hauled himself up along the back, before jumping on the cupboard and making a mad dash for the food dispenser Mason had installed.

Instead of going for the button to release the food, the little shit leaned down and wiggled his arm up into the device to pull out his own helping, chittering happily at his bounty. It didn't take long for his cheeks to be full, and she smiled at his antics, foolishly glad to have the little beastie back.

As everyone sat down and ate supper, she studied each of them in turn. They asked her to fight for a future with them. Annora had no problem fighting. She'd been doing it her whole life, struggling to survive one day at a time.

But she never had to worry about others when she fought.

She'd already failed Logan.

What if she failed them as well?

But as she looked around the table at her men—if she was brave enough to claim them—she realized something important.

They were worth fighting for.

She didn't want to live in a world that didn't have them in it.

Even as her gaze landed on Edgar, lying asshole or not, she couldn't imagine him not standing at her side. He'd protected her when no one else would…how could she do any less for him?

As she helped clean up the dishes, she noticed the silent looks the guys were exchanging, the way they lingered in the kitchen, practically bumping into each other. She dumped the last of the dishes in the hot suds, then turned to face them. "Okay, spill it."

They each snapped to attention like boys caught in the middle of a prank.

Camden scratched the back of his head, then crossed his arms and leaned against the wall opposite her in a casual pose that was anything but casual. "While you were outside soul-searching, the guys and I decided it's too dangerous for you to sleep alone."

Annora was more bemused than angry about their decision. But even before she could open her mouth to reply, he rushed on. "We'll sleep in rotation. Every night a different one of us will remain with you. That way, if Logan reaches out to you, we can use the time to get a lock on his location."

None of the guys blinked or even looked like they were breathing as they waited for her answer.

Annora shrugged. "Okay."

"Okay?" Camden raised a brow at her, then cocked his head. "That's it?"

She smiled, deciding to take pity on him. "It's a solid plan. It's only ever been me. The more of us who can help pin down Logan's location, the sooner we can get him back."

The rest of the guys deflated, as if they'd been expecting a fight, and she quirked a brow at their reactions. "Did you think I would say no?"

"Well…" Mason scrubbed so furiously at a spot on the plate in his hand, she was surprised it didn't crack under the strain. "You're very protective of your privacy."

"And skittish about touching." Xander murmured as he reached up to put a piece of glassware into the cupboard, the back of his shirt lifting up to reveal a tanned strip of flesh that beckoned her to explore.

She shook her head, trying to clear her thoughts. "That was before."

"Before?" Edgar swiped at the table, scattering crumbs across the floor, unconcerned with the streaks he was leaving behind as he was watching her.

"Before I realized we belong together." She pushed away from the counter, not surprised to find all the guys watching her as she sauntered toward the stairs. As she turned, she smiled to see the water pouring out of the faucet, overflowing the cup in Mason's hand as he stared at her dumbly. "Who has the first shift?"

Mason lifted his arm holding the cup, nearly dumping the water down the front of his shirt in the process. He cursed and swiped at it with a towel to clean up the mess while the rest of the guys chuckled.

As she headed up the stairs, she pushed away her nervousness at the idea of being alone with the troll. He would never harm her. She wished she could say the same. They were mates, so her powers shouldn't harm him, but that didn't assuage her fears.

But Logan was counting on her, not to mention that the guys trusted her.

They were banking on her powers recognizing them as her mates.

How could she do any less?

If she didn't take this chance, her fears would likely destroy them more quickly and thoroughly than any outside threat.

Mason stood at the bottom of the small staircase that led up to

Annora's room but couldn't make himself move. What if he rolled over and crushed her? What if he sweated like a pig in the middle of the night? Or if he groped her in his sleep like some caveman? Or worse, what if his ever-present erection didn't go away?

He glanced down at his sweats, shaking his head before turning away to pull on a pair of jeans. It would be torture to be confined in the custom-made jeans for the whole night, but he rather be tortured than freak her out.

He was hovering in the doorway of his room like a nervous teenager when she called down the stairs.

"Mason?"

He swallowed hard, feeling like a tennis ball was stuck in his throat, real terror making a tremor go through him.

"Yes?" He leaned forward and popped his head out of his door, then cursed himself for his stupidity when he saw her looking at him from upside down as she leaned over the half wall, her long, luscious hair spilling down like a waterfall of silk, begging him to touch. His fingertips tingled, almost like he could already feel the sleek strands sliding past them.

"Are you coming upstairs?" Frown lines kinked between her eyes, and he realized she must have asked the question more than once.

Feeling a blush crawling up the back of his neck, he ducked his head. "I was just going to get a pillow."

"Okay." The troubled expression melted off her face, and she flashed him a small smile bright enough to set-off shockwaves in his chest...because it was meant just for him.

He blew out a heavy breath, only to turn and find Camden and Xander leaning against the wall just out of sight of Annora, both of them grinning like idiots. He scowled at them. "Laugh all you want, chuckleheads, but your nights will come soon enough. We'll see how easy it is to keep your hands to yourself then."

He stomped away, their laughter following him, and he let his frustrations melt away.

This was one of the few times they'd laughed since Logan was taken. While it might be at his expense, he could take it. Annora gave them hope when she burst into their lives, and he'd be damned if he'd let anything ruin that.

Even with all the danger—or maybe because of it—the guys were finally coming together as a team after years of working together, and it was thanks to her. As he gathered his pillow and blankets and left his room, he sighed, relieved to find his teammates gone and the hall empty.

He placed his foot on the bottom step, then closed his eyes for a second and prayed to the gods that he would be able to keep his vow not to take advantage of her. While Annora was outside, they decided she shouldn't be alone, especially at night...but only to sleep.

She was off limits.

Unless *she* seduced *them*.

His cock twitched to life, and he cursed the stray thought that slipped past his control. As he climbed the stairs to her room, he recited the flora and fauna of North America.

In alphabetical order.

In Latin.

And as much as he dreaded this night, he was the first to volunteer, eager to spend more time with her. Time he planned to use to convince her that she was madly in love with him, before he allowed himself to lay a hand on her.

He nearly groaned when he finally stepped into her room to see her wearing an itty-bitty tank top and shorts that made her legs go on forever. He dragged his eyes away from her, afraid he'd turn into a drooling idiot, only to have his eyes land on her tiny bed.

He swallowed hard, calling himself all types of a fool for believing he'd be able to keep from touching her in that postage-stamp size queen bed, and nearly strangled while swallowing his tortured groan.

Annora looked at Mason's dismayed face, then at the bed, and wanted to smack herself for not thinking of his comfort sooner. No way was his massive frame going to be able to fit. The ferret grabbed her pillow, then loped across the mattress, dragging his prize onto the floor. She rushed toward the bed, quickly following suit and ripping off the blankets. She dropped them haphazardly next to the pillow, trying to spread them out, feeling flustered for not thinking about it sooner. "I'm so sorry. I didn't think. We can sleep on the floor."

At Mason's strangled laugh, she glanced back, only to find him watching her with his mouth hanging open. She chuckled and sat back, realizing she must look like she was playing some demented game of Twister.

He clutched his pillow and blanket to his chest, and damned if the pillow wasn't taller than her. Shaking her head at her foolish thoughts, she grabbed her pillow from the ferret and tossed it at Mason, smacking him right in the face. "Get down here and help."

With a chuckle, he dropped down next to her, and they had the bed sorted in five minutes. As she flipped off the lights, she glimpsed the ferret curled up in the center of the bed, the sheets a little nest around him, completely content to have the place to himself.

As she walked toward her makeshift bed on the floor, she saw Mason's bright lavender eyes following her every move. They practically glowed in the dark while he watched her like a predator ready to pounce.

As she settled, pulled back the covers, and crawled underneath, he seemed to relax, and she shook her head at her foolish thoughts. She wiggled her feet, seeking to stick them out of the bottom of the blankets. Only she couldn't. She glanced down to see what was the problem, then huffed on silent laughter.

His blankets were massive.

While she drowned in them on her side, they barely reached his chin and covered his feet. Giving up her struggle, unable to sleep, she shifted, but couldn't stand the awkward silence a moment longer, and blurted out the first thought that popped into her head. "What size are these?"

"California King." He reached up and laced his fingers behind his head, placing his massive arms on display. His tattoos rippled as his muscles flexed, and she couldn't help her curiosity, too hyped up by his nearness to sleep.

She hesitantly reached out and traced one of the bold lines that swirled down from his shoulder and peeked out of his shirtsleeve. "What do your tattoos mean?"

"Why do you think they mean anything?" His deep voice was a low rumble, the playful amusement in them relaxing her.

She didn't know how to explain what she felt when she gazed at his tattoos. "I don't know. Something about them reminds me of you."

"You're right." To make her feel more at ease, he looked up through the skylight, allowing her to look her fill of him. "Trolls grow into their powers as they age. The darker the lines, the more tattoos, the stronger the troll."

"Really?" Annora squinted at the tattoos partially hidden by his shirt, trying to make them out in the dark room. "How do you get them? Are you born with them? Or are they spelled?"

The only magic she sensed was from him alone. His pink hair was shadowed in the darkness, but she could see it swaying hypnotically, as if content, dancing to a song only it could hear. His scent of fresh pine and copper reminded her of the outdoors. After spending years trapped underground, she found it soothing.

"They're unique to each tribe and each troll." His gaze flickered toward hers, then resumed observing the sky. "We're not born with them, nor are they spelled. It's something in our blood. Our tattoos form at puberty, revealing and dictating our placement and standing in the tribe."

Something about the total lack of inflection in his voice made her stomach lurch. "But?"

He glanced down at her in confusion, completely unaware that he'd given himself away. "What?"

She propped herself on her elbow. "But your tribe doesn't think your tattoos count, do they?"

When his gaze flickered away and he shrugged, she decided she very much wanted to meet his family, just so she could give them a piece of her mind…and maybe give them a little peek into what hell would look like if they didn't start treating him right.

She cupped his face, waiting for him to look at her. His forehead was large, his face broad, his features exaggerated, he had a ridge of horns around the top of his head, and when he was riled, his upper and lower fangs were massive, protruding slightly out of his mouth.

And she wouldn't change anything about him.

He was a fierce warrior and defender, but he was more.

He was her friend and protector.

As he gazed up at her with his lavender eyes, she knew she couldn't have picked a better man to watch over her while she slept. "Your tribe is full of idiots. While your tattoos are stunning, they only make up a small portion of what I like about you. I'm glad they tossed you away, or I might never have been lucky enough to meet you, and that would've been a shame."

Annora gave his cheek a light pat. "I must warn you, though—if I ever meet any of them, I might take their fangs and horns and wear them as jewelry."

He blinked at her blankly for a moment, then full-out grinned. "Oh, they're gonna love you."

She just grunted and, resting her head against his shoulder, snuggled down for the night with a contented sigh. Mason went rigid for only a second before he wrapped his arm around her and gave a hum of contentment.

Annora closed her eyes, then frowned, curiosity getting the best of her. "How did you guys decide who would be staying with me tonight? Rock, paper, scissors? Or did you have to resort to picking straws?"

There was a beat of silence before he spoke. "Actually, we picked by choosing who needed you most."

Her eyes snapped open, and she was completely awake now. She opened her mouth, then silently closed it, not sure how to respond. She didn't sense that he meant it in any physical way. No, it was more than that. She worried that by being near them, being chosen as their pack grá, she was failing them in some way, too ignorant of what the role meant to know what she should be doing.

His large hand came to rest across her back, nearly spanning her from shoulder to shoulder, pulling her out of her chaotic thoughts. "Hush and go to sleep. We'll talk in the morning."

Instead of feeling confined, she was reassured by his touch. She closed her eyes, sleep claiming her in minutes.

When her eyes fluttered open, she was still in her room, but they were no longer alone. Logan was resting behind her, his arms wrapped around her waist, his fingers brushing back and forth along her stomach, just above the waistband of her shorts.

It felt so real her heart hiccupped against her ribs, and she was afraid to close her eyes, afraid to blink and it would all vanish.

"I've missed this," Logan whispered, his breath ghosting along her neck, and she shivered. She blinked away the tears burning her eyes, swearing he was so real she could actually feel him.

"How are you here?" Then her gut pitched wildly, and she swallowed hard. "You're hurt bad, aren't you? You're—"

"Still alive." His arm tightened around her, and she felt him brush his lips along her shoulder. "But I'm not sure for how much longer."

"Just hold on for a little bit more." She turned in his arms, studying his face. He looked like the same old Logan, but his eyes were shadowed and haunted, and dread tightened her guts.

They were running out of time.

He looked away, as if seeing something that she couldn't, his form flickering. She reached for him, desperate to hold him to her, only to have her hand pass clear through him as if he were a figment of her imagination, and her heart broke a little.

"Logan—"

"Your uncle saw the way I healed the last time I…fell asleep." His attention dropped back down to her. "This time, he's making sure I don't stay under more than ten minutes at a time before he wakes me."

He sugar-coated everything, but she knew her uncle and his methods. He would strap her down and connect electrodes to her, shocking her every ten minutes, wanting to test how long she could go without sleep.

Wanting to see if that would make her more pliant.

It nearly drove her fucking insane.

Annora cupped his face, allowing the particles inside her to capture him and hold him to her, giving him all the strength she could. "We're coming. Watch for Kevin. Trust him."

Before she even finished speaking, he dissolved under her touch, like wisps of smoke. No matter how hard she tried to hold him, he slipped through her fingers.

"No!"

Mason's arms wrapped around her from behind, but the warmth

of him barely penetrated the ice that filled her soul. "We're running out of time."

Instead of comforting her, Mason tightened his hold, his head bowing under the weight of the truth. "I know."

His grim voice made her breath hiccup in her chest, but she was infinitely glad the guys were no longer denying it. Her mind whirled with plans for how she could locate him before it was too late, and only one thing came to mind.

She would have to go into the afterworld to find where they were keeping him—even if it meant bringing her father down on her head.

Chapter Twelve

Annora was awake before dawn, unable to go back to sleep after Logan vanished. She went through her plans, determined to do what was necessary to rescue him.

She just needed to find a way to get the guys on board without them flipping their lids.

She carefully lifted Mason's arm from around her waist, stifling her grunt when she discovered the damned thing nearly weighed as much as she did. When she didn't make much progress, she shoved a pillow at his chest, then wiggled and twisted until she was free.

Only to find the ferret sitting on his haunches, watching her with his head tipped in curiosity.

She would swear he was laughing at her, the little bastard, and she resisted the urge to flick his nose. "You could've helped."

Honest to god, the little fucker shrugged.

Panting like she just been in a wrestling match with a slab of cement, Annora smoothed her tangled hair back, but then froze when Mason shifted. He tightened his grip on her pillow, then pulled it close, burying his face in it as if trying to catch her scent. With a contented sigh, he relaxed and went back to sleep.

Instead of leaving, Annora remained crouched next to him. Lines of sleep were pressed into his face, his hair tousled, his body relaxed. He looked different…unguarded.

Vulnerable.

Not the indestructible force he was when awake.

Unable to help herself, she leaned over, brushing his hair away from his forehead. The strands swayed sleepily, curling around her before relaxing back into sleep. Mason sighed, a small smile playing about his face, and she carefully rose to her feet.

With one last reluctant look, she collected her clothes and headed for the shower, quickly shutting the door in the ferret's face, chuckling happily when he thumped into the wood.

Payback's a bitch.

By the time she was finished, Mason and his bedding were gone and her own bed was neatly made. A pang went through her at the sight of the empty floor.

She was already missing him, and she shook her head at her own foolishness.

He was just down the stairs.

He hadn't left her.

But then why did her room feel so empty without him?

The ferret was resting near the stairs, waiting for her. When he saw her looking, he gave her a beckoning wave, as if to urge her to go faster, then bolted for the kitchen.

Shoving her feet into her shoes, she tromped down the stairs after him, coming to a halt when she saw the guys were already assembled, Terrance included, the breakfast waiting. With Logan gone, meals weren't the same. He was the resident cook, and while she was sure it was only her imagination, the food just didn't taste the same without him.

A glance out the window showed the sun just breaking across the horizon.

Edgar was mysteriously absent, and she couldn't help but wonder if he was with Sadie. She didn't begrudge him his friendship with the girl—okay, maybe she did just a little—she just didn't trust the other phantom not to try and kidnap him.

When she didn't see him in the backyard where she met Sadie last night, she turned to survey the rest of the guys. It didn't take a genius to figure out they'd been on guard duty all night, rotating shifts. She scowled and grabbed a piece of toast off a plate, taking a vicious bite before pointing it at them accusingly. "You could have come and gotten me. I could've taken a shift."

"That would've defeated the purpose of keeping you safe." Xander spoke with a completely straight face, focused on dumping ingredients into a blender for one of his workout drinks that always looked like revolting green sludge.

She stopped chewing for a beat, swallowing her mouthful of food before she choked on it. She wanted to argue with the guys, protest that she was part of the team, but the look in their eyes brooked no argument.

No matter what she said, they wouldn't budge.

She sat at her place at the table, setting her half-eaten toast on her plate, the mound of food making her stomach churn. Glancing up, she saw the ferret was on the counter, manhandling his feeding dish again. As if sensing she was watching, he straightened and gave her a nod of encouragement.

She lifted her chin, determined not to be swayed from her course. "I have a plan to get Logan tonight."

She waited for an explosion of protests, but the guys only nodded and took their seats.

"Tell us." Camden glanced up at her as he took a bite of food, completely calm, as if he'd expected her announcement.

She squinted at Mason, wondering if he'd suspected and told the others, but he appeared just as curious as the others. "You're not surprised?"

All of them looked up from their food. It was Xander who answered. "Of course not. We're actually surprised you told us about it first."

She stifled her huff of annoyance, because she had to admit the thought had crossed her mind. The tension melted out of her spine, and she slumped in her seat. She didn't like putting them in danger, but if she wanted to get Logan back, she needed their help.

"The only way for us to locate him in time is to enter the afterworld." Annora waited for them to explode and tell her it was too risky.

"Your phantom isn't going to like it," Camden warned, completely unfazed by her announcement.

She narrowed her eyes, studying each one in turn. "How did you know what I was going to say?" She didn't wait for them to speak because the answer struck her immediately. "You came to the same conclusion."

She shoved away from the table, glowering at them. "Why the hell didn't you tell me sooner instead of letting me waste all this time?"

It was Mason who spoke, "It had to be your decision."

Their absolute calm irritated the snot out of her, and she turned to glare at Mason, feeling her hackles rise at his betrayal. "So this was the real reason you guys decided I need a babysitter at night…so I wouldn't sneak off on my own? Maybe the real reason why you were patrolling the house?"

Without missing a beat, Mason shook his head. "Actually, that factored very little into it. You're foolish, not stupid. The best way to get Logan back is if we work together. We knew you'd never put him in danger that way."

She pursed her lips and crossed her arms, not sure she was completely appeased by his answer, but didn't want to dig into it any further. "And when my father and his minions arrive? What then?"

"They're going to come either way. At least this way we'll know when to expect them." Camden leaned back in his chair, humor dancing in his vivid green eyes at seeing her riled.

She harrumphed in annoyance, and laughter drained from Camden. She was sad to see it disappear, and her anger evaporated.

"Do you have a plan for what to do once we locate Logan?" Xander tipped back his drink and chugged down the slime as it oozed out of the glass, and she swallowed hard, unable to look away, practically able to feel the sludge slide slowly down her own throat.

Only when he set down the glass was she able to blink and break her gaze. "Once we locate Logan, your job is to get him out."

"While you do what, exactly?" That Camden didn't outright say no floored her.

Annora crossed her arms, letting her nails bite into her skin. "I'm going to take my uncle somewhere he'll never be able to hurt anyone else."

The afterworld.

And she was going to leave him there to rot…if he survived that long.

She waited for the guys to explode, but they only stared back at her resolutely.

Which meant…fuck.

They were plotting something.

She narrowed her eyes, but no matter how hard she studied them, she couldn't pick up anything through their connection, and none of the assholes cracked under her glare. Worry churned in her gut, but she didn't have a choice. Her instincts warned her that if she waited any longer, the Logan who came back wouldn't be the same boy who left.

"I want to get some more practice in before we leave." She gave a pointed look at Camden and Xander. "Since you guys were up all night patrolling, you can stay back and either rest or work on whatever secret plans you want to make for tonight." She glanced at Terrance and Mason. "They can escort me."

A muscle ticked in Xander's jaw, while Camden rubbed a hand across his face. They both looked at each other before nodding. She wasn't sure how she felt about them not arguing with her. Her bullshit meter was pinging, but she refrained from calling them on it.

For now.

She'd wait until after they got Logan back.

And then she'd kick their asses for worrying her.

Without waiting, she grabbed the cold toast off her plate and headed for the door. The ferret scampered off the cupboards, slipping into her backpack seconds before she picked it up. Swearing erupted behind her when they realized that she was leaving now. Chairs scraped, and she smiled to herself as Terrance and Mason scrambled to catch up while she headed out the door.

Terrance reached her first, and she spoke before he could ask. "You'll be staying behind. Since I'm not connected to you, I don't know what would happen if you travel with us into the afterworld." She lifted her hand to stave off his protest. "But I want you to get your own team in place. As soon as we find the compound where they're being held, the guys will call with a location, and then you'll need to ride in with the cavalry. While someone else might be able to handle it, I think you have a better understanding of the urgency. Can you do that?"

She was asking him to wait to rescue his brother.

She wasn't sure she would be able to do the same if he asked her to wait to find Logan.

His shoulders slumped and he stared at the ground for a few paces before nodding. "While I want to be there to breach the compound, I understand. My brother—"

"We won't leave him behind." Then she glanced at him from the corner of her eyes. "Though when I find him, I might give him a talking-to for running off like that."

Terrance laughed as he flicked his sandy blond hair out of his face, then gave her a tired smile. "You and me both."

As they made their way toward the arena, Mason was a silent watchdog at their backs. She was very conscious of more eyes than usual watching her, and it made her skin crawl. She wanted to go back to being anonymous, but she very much feared that ship had sailed on her first day of school.

They walked out onto the field, and she took off her sweatshirt, leaving her in a tank top, then bounced on her feet to warm up her muscles and nodded toward Terrance. "Let's work off some of that frustration."

He gave her a dubious look, then shrugged and peeled off his shirt, leaving him standing in pants and a very form-fitting, ribbed tank top. Her brain did a mental pause at seeing him stripped down, and she shook off her thoughts as he sauntered toward her, his face losing all animation as he went into beat-the-crap-out-of-you mode.

While he wasn't built like Xander or Mason, his sleek lines showed enough muscles to promise his opponents that he knew what he was doing. She managed to evade his first punch, bending backward, but missed the wind-up fist that hit her ribs with enough force to knock the air out of her with an oomph.

Using the pain, she smiled at him and swung out her foot, catching him behind the knee. Instead of going down, he did a backflip, and she narrowly missed being kicked in the face with the heavy, metal-tipped shit stompers he wore.

After twenty minutes of exchanging blows, her body aching deliciously, she danced out of the range of his swing and smiled. "Are we done with the warmup?"

He blinked at her, then gave a bark of laughter. "Are you trying to get me killed?"

He glanced behind her, and she followed his gaze to see Mason was barely holding himself back from a complete shift, ready to stomp the smaller man into a puddle of goo. Annora rolled her eyes at Terrance. "We both know you've been taking it easy on me. If I'm going to learn how to fight my own battles, I can't have you holding back."

Terrance studied her with his calculating brown eyes. He wore the cute neighbor next door look well, but his open, friendly face was a mask that hid a devious mind. After a moment, he lifted his chin and gave her a come-get-it wave. "Then show me what you got."

With a mischievous smile, she let the darkness take hold of her.

One second she was in front of him, the next she appeared behind him, nearly knocking him on his ass with a blow to the kidneys. By the time he whirled, she already ghosted away, appearing a foot to the right, swinging her fist into the side of his neck.

He grunted at the impact and staggered, barely straightening before she appeared in a crouch in front of him, sweeping his feet out from under him. He landed with a meaty thump, grunting at the impact and stared up at her in consternation.

Then a grin split his face. "You're on."

While she was getting better at ghosting without jumping into the afterworld, it took more concentration. After an hour, she was slowing, and her coordination suffered. A crowd had grown. While some people cheered in the beginning, the stadium had grown quiet while they sparred.

Only when Mason stepped onto the field did she and Terrance break apart.

The wolf had speed and strength on his side, while she had surprise.

Both of them were beaten black and blue, and a few minor cuts nicked her knuckles and face. Her bones ached from the jarring impact of flesh meeting flesh, but it was a pleasant ache that she'd grown used to while living with her uncle.

Terrance surveyed her critically, his own body more battered than hers, but he was already healing even while she watched, his wounds knitting together. "You're a fast learner. You're getting better."

But not good enough to win in an all-out fight against a shifter.

At least not yet…but maybe in a few more weeks.

Mason stopped beside them, glaring threateningly at the wolf, and Annora had to smother her smile when Terrance lifted his hands in surrender. Taking pity on him, she slipped between them and grinned impishly up at the troll. "No eating wolves today."

He grunted, giving one last glare at Terrance over her head, before he finally dropped his gaze to her, immediately locating every scrape, every bruise, his glower deepening. "Heal."

Annora stopped teasing him, his gruff tone warning her that he was on the edge of losing his shit. With a nod, she lifted her hands and allowed the dark particles resting under her skin to rise. A black smog hovered over her hands, then slowly wound around her hands and arms, licking at her injuries. Bruises faded, scabs flaked away, while cuts slowly stitched themselves together, the sting of pain making her inhale sharply.

Instead of feeling weakened by the healing, the pain and touch of the afterworld invigorated her. The smoke twisted through her fingers playfully before finally sinking back into her skin. Smiling brightly up at Mason, she held her arms out from her sides. "See? All better. No need to pound the wolf into mulch."

Whispers spread around the arena like wildfire, and her smile faded when she saw dozens of unfamiliar faces gawking at her. Mason and Terrance seemed to realize it at the same moment and sandwiched her between them.

The ferret grabbed her bag from the sidelines and dragged it after him as he scurried toward her side. She slipped her sweater over her head and barely had time to scoop the ferret into the bag and pick it up before the guys frog-marched her off the field.

She brushed her fingers over the ferret's head, silently vowing to come up with another name for him. She couldn't just keep calling him ferret.

Once away from prying eyes, the men gave her a little more

breathing room. Terrance eyed her arms with awe, reaching out to touch her, but stopped just short when Mason gave a little snarl of displeasure from behind them.

"That...was not smart." Terrance gave her a grim look, then glanced over his shoulder, as if he half expected a horde of people with pitchforks to be following them, clamoring for her blood.

She scowled at him, hating the way gooseflesh pebbled her skin at his ominous pronouncement. "What do you mean? All shifters heal." She snorted at the absurd idea that she was somehow different. "I've even seen witches do spells to heal just as fast. What's the big deal?"

Terrance grimaced, while Mason rubbed his forehead as if to ease a threatening headache. He herded her down the tunnels, skipping the showers completely. The troll's large hand came to rest on the small of her back as he hurried her along, practically sweeping her off her feet as he rushed her into the twists and turns of the dark tunnels. "Strength is valued in the paranormal community, but it can also be a curse. Those people saw you take a beating for hours, saw you fight in a way that they cannot beat, then saw you heal without any ill effects."

"What he's trying to say—" Terrance interrupted, bringing up the rear, guarding their backs. "—is that they want what you have and will do everything in their power to take it from you."

"Good." Annora couldn't repress her savage smile.

Terrance gaped at her, while Mason stopped walking, his hand sliding off her back for a second before he grabbed a fistful of her shirt and hauled her to a stop. She turned to find herself confronted by a very angry troll.

"You orchestrated this whole fight, didn't you?" He glowered down at her, his agitation making his hair puff up with static and stand on end all around his head.

If she didn't know him so well, she'd be intimidated.

Okay, maybe she was a little intimidated.

She couldn't work up a smile in the face of his anger, but she refused to lie. "Yes."

A shutter fell over his face and his arms flexed when he clenched his fists, his hair wilting. "That's why you asked for me. I'm so stupid and gullible that you thought you could put one over on me."

The dejected look in his eyes, the way he was no doubt calling himself all sorts of an idiot, tore up her insides. Annora turned toward Terrance, struggling to control the anger brewing in her gut. Tiny particles swirled around her like Hell was reaching beyond the grave to pull her back. "Go and make sure we're not being followed. Then head out and tell Greenwood our plans for tonight. Ask him how we can get in touch with your brother to let him know we're coming."

The kid glanced between her and Mason, as if he thought he should stay to protect her, then closed his mouth and took off with a nod.

Without waiting for him to go, she grabbed Mason's arm, and dragged him toward the stairs. She released him, took a few steps up before turning, almost putting them on eye level, then she crossed her arms and glared down at him. "Is that the kind of woman you think I am? That I would single you out that way?"

She snorted at the absurdity. "You're one of the most intelligent men I know. I picked you for the reasons I stated this morning. I would've acted the exact same way if any of the other guys came with me instead, and I resent that you would judge me by others' standards."

She was so angry she was shaking with it.

That he thought she would treat him in that way…hurt threatened to crush her.

Mason studied her a moment longer, his eyes searching hers intently. He must have found what he wanted, because his shoulders slumped, and he ran a hand over his hair. The hot pink hair reached out for her, as if begging for forgiveness. "I'm sorry. I thought…I don't know what I thought."

He gave her a sheepish look, and it was all she could do to hold onto her hurt and anger.

Before she had a chance to react, a fierce scowl crossed his face, his hair twisting wildly. "What the hell was that whole act outside about, then? Why make yourself a target?"

A beat of silence followed before he answered the question himself. "It's the same with the witches. You're building your army in preparation for your father."

When he narrowed his eyes at her, still furious, she gave a shrug. "I'm betting that the shifters would rather I fight with them instead of being used as a weapon against them."

"Unless they decide to eliminate the threat of you completely." His voice was a low rumble, the muscles of his arms flexing, as if he was already mentally ripping apart anyone who would try to harm her.

Annora reached up and cupped his face. His anger vanished at her touch, his expression startled. "It's a risk I was willing to take. I'll do whatever I have to do, fight anyone I have to fight for a chance to stay with you and the rest of the guys."

His eyes darkened and he reached up, grabbing her wrist, holding her to him. Giving in to impulse, she leaned forward and brushed her lips against his.

His eyes widened, then his breath left him in a rush. A second later, he lunged forward, wrapping her up in his arms and sweeping her off her feet, taking control of the kiss like initiating contact had given him permission.

She wrapped her legs around his waist, her eyes widening in shock when his thick erection pushed against her, and she made a startled noise at the back of her throat. The fucker was massive. She knew he was a troll, that he would be proportionate to his size, but couldn't imagine how he thought all that would fit.

Very reluctantly, he lifted his head. He gazed down at her with heavy-lidded eyes, then the corners crinkled in amusement, as if he could read her thoughts and couldn't contain humor. "Don't worry, I know how to use it. You'll be more than ready for me when the time comes."

She nearly choked on her laughter, giving him a dubious look, but he looked so smug, so confident, she believed him. Heat pooled between her thighs, and she shivered in anticipation. "Really? Maybe you should show me."

His breath exploded out of him at the dare, a deep groan vibrating from his chest as he lowered his head toward hers. He demolished her lips, taking control of the kiss. She was startled by his fangs, then moaned when he nipped at her, the sting making her skin extra sensitive.

Unable to resist demanding more, she reached up and tangled her fingers in his hair. The strands pulled her closer, enjoying the attention. Then she ran her fingers lightly along the crown of horns buried in his hairline and felt more than heard his tortured grunt. He stumbled forward, shoving her back against the wall, using his weight to pin her, then ran his hands down her body.

His palms ghosted along her skin, so gentle she barely felt them until her body was tingling with pleasure. He shoved his hands under her sweater, his touch rough, as if his control was fraying, and she gave a hum of approval.

He boldly cupped her breast, capturing the tip between his fingers and squeezing deliciously, and she couldn't stop the way her legs tightened around him, which shoved his erection against the growing ache between her thighs. Unable to help herself, she did it again. When his hand came to rest on her hip, he surged against her, taking over.

With each thrust, her lust increased until there was only his hands and his mouth and his erection as she fell apart in his arms. He pulled away, completely content to watch as her awareness came flooding back, a pleased, possessive expression on his face.

Then he dropped a chaste kiss on her lips, tugged her shirt back into place, and carefully lowered her to the ground. She staggered, her legs needing a second to remember how to function. Before she had a chance to catch her breath, he wove their fingers together and led her topside.

"I'll show you more after we get Logan back."

It was a promise, and she shivered at his husky tone, heat spilling into her stomach, already craving more. Before she could voice her thoughts, they stepped out into the quad. She took a deep breath, but it did little to calm the way her body longed for more of his touch.

They'd only gone a few yards when a group of five young witches surrounded them. Four of them were wearing clothes that cost more than what she made in a week from the university. All but one of them were girls.

"Hey, you. We need to talk." The girl in front was all attitude, her black hair sleek and perfectly groomed. She was a stunner, not a single blemish on her skin. Everyone in her posse was the same, so cloaked with magic that it snapped angrily along Annora's skin. Four of them were smirking. Only one of them hung back, clearly not pleased to be there…or associated with the others.

Mason gave a muffled curse, untangling their fingers to stand in front of her, his frame bulking up even as she watched.

"We don't want trouble." He crossed his arms in a way that made his muscles appear even more intimidating. "Leave."

"Not you," the witch snipped, then pointed at Annora. "Her."

Mason refused to budge, his smile displaying his massive fangs.

Completely undaunted, the lead witch rolled her eyes, waved her hand and said something in Latin. Magic splashed in the air, hitting Mason in the chest even as Annora tried to shove him out of the way, but his bulk was impossible to move.

The spell soaked into his skin, and the very air around him turned frigid.

She circled him, looking up at his eyes…to find him completely frozen in place.

Anger flared to life within her so fast and so bright the air around them became murky as a dark fog from the afterworld rose up from the ground and seeped into the human world.

She whirled on the lead witch. "What the fuck did you do?"

Chapter
Thirteen

The smirks slid off their faces. Two of the witches panicked and backed away, while the lead female and the single male lifted their hands, spells sparking along their fingers. The only one who didn't react, besides the widening of her eyes, was the witch standing in the back.

Smoke curled around Mason, snaking up his legs to wrap around him. Sparks flared where the particles ate away the magic.

"Do you feel that, Brittney?" The male held out his hands as if he could feel the magic, a tiny bit of awe on his face, which was quickly replaced by greed.

Just when Brittney held out her hands, a wisp of smoke curled up, then lashed out at the guy, quickly coating the tips of his fingers black.

They both jerked back, the guy hissing as he tried to scrape off the black gunk, but it was like his fingers were stained. "What the fuck is that?"

He glared, taking a threatening step toward her, when the black fog rose threateningly between them.

"You're such a child, Brad. Suck it up." Brittney huffed in annoyance and flapped her hands at him. "It's your own fault for touching that shit." She eyed the dark particles avidly, then dragged her attention away. "Give me the book and we'll leave you alone."

Magic reverberated in the air, the words echoing loudly. The spell slammed into Annora, hitting her chest hard enough to knock the air out of her. The compulsion to obey crawled over her, seeking a way to infect her. The darkness from the afterworld lashed out, curling around the magic and crushing it, sending glitter fluttering to the ground as it sucked all the energy out of the spell.

"You fucking bitch." Annora could feel the dark particles play with her fingers, weaving in and out of them, eager to devour the witches and teach them a lesson. "Did you really think it would be so easy?"

The spell around Mason fractured, and the dread holding her hostage eased, reducing her need to kill them and leave their carcasses behind as a warning. "My guess is that you have about two minutes to leave before Mason breaks free and hunts you down like vermin."

Brittney scowled, while Brad hiked up his chin in defiance, as if he thought he could take a troll and survive.

"Give it up, Brit." The girl in the back crossed her arms. "She's not going to buy your bullshit, especially when you iced her friend and tried to spell her. You were told to befriend her, not make her our enemy. Hetty and Suesette are going to be so pissed." She laughed gleefully, clearly eager to witness the upcoming smackdown.

"Like you could do any better, freak." If looks could kill, the girl sticking up for her and Mason would drop dead.

The freak lifted her hands and shrugged like she didn't give a shit. Her blue hair was cut like a bob, only it was short in the back and longer in the front, the strands brushing her jaw. "I didn't want to be here in the first place, and I wouldn't be if I wasn't ordered. You fucked up. Any chance of you getting the book is gone."

Brittney looked homicidal, but when Mason tore free with a roar, she whirled back, her magic swirling in the air.

Annora pressed her small palm against Mason's chest. To her surprise, he stopped. With a wave of her arm, a plume of black particles soaring through the air like a swarm of bugs. "Try it again. Let's see if you survive."

Brittney narrowed her eyes, as if seriously contemplating the challenge, when Brad swore. "Fuck—I can't access my magic!"

Brittney and her goons glanced at him, then to the blackness that still stained his fingers.

"You did this to me." Brad took a threatening step toward Annora, then hastily retreated when the dark particles rose like a beast ready to strike. "Fix it."

Annora crossed her arms, able to feel Mason practically breathing down her neck with the need to pulverize the threat. If she concentrated, she could feel the afterworld feeding off his magic, slowly draining him with each pump of his heart.

"I really don't see why it's my problem." She didn't flinch under their glares. "I want your word, under magical oath, that you will keep your distance from me and my people."

Brittney crossed her arms and stuck her nose in the air. "Fuck you."

Before Annora could do anything, Brad grabbed Brittney by the throat with his infected hand. "Your word—or I'll snap your scrawny neck, you bitch."

Her blue eyes bulged, hatred burning in them, but she relented with a small nod. When his hand loosened from around her neck, Brittney coughed, glaring at Annora and Brad the whole time. It took only a few minutes for four of the witches to give their oath, their magic sparking in the air, binding them.

As soon as they finished speaking, the sludge painting Brad's fingers flaked and floated away like ash on the breeze. Then the witches were spun on their heels and forcefully marched away by their own magic.

All except for the girl they called freak, who lingered behind. "A word of warning…the witches won't give up. They want your magic too much to just let you go. And you might want to watch out for Brad. Male witches are rare, which makes him a spoiled brat. He won't take kindly to you beating and humiliating him today." An evil smile crept over the girl's face. "Although I have to say I enjoyed it immensely."

A wisp of fog reached for the girl, brushed against her boot, then seemed to disintegrate and fall back to the ground.

It didn't see her as a threat.

"Why warn me?" The fact that this one warned them didn't make her less dangerous.

"I'm more of a hedge witch, and prefer to work alone, but they don't really give you a choice about joining the cult. Once you're classified a witch, the rest of the school considers you persona non grata. Witches are a whole pack of bitches that no one wants to hang out with." She crossed her arms and looked away. "The rest of the witches make sure of it."

Then she gave a shrug and turned to walk away. "Good luck. You're going to need it."

"Wait." Annora took a step after her, and the witch paused, glancing at her over her shoulder. "Come with us."

The girl turned and scowled at them. "Why?"

"Because we both want the same thing—the witches off our backs." Annora dropped her hand from Mason and strode after the girl. "If I have you as my liaison, the witches will leave me alone."

The girl snorted. "And how exactly does that get me out from under them?"

"You'll have a position of power. They want what I have...which only you will have access to. Meet up with us later at the café, check us out, and decide. If you agree, we can discuss what to share with the other witches. Win-win." Annora held out her hand. "Deal?"

The first spark of interest lit the girl's green eyes, and she surveyed Annora up and down. "I might not have a lot of power, but if you're fucking with me, I'll find a way to make you regret it."

Before Annora had a chance to respond, the girl grabbed her hand and shook it.

"I hope you know what you're doing," Mason murmured.

So do I, but she didn't say that out loud.

"Fine, I'll meet you back at the café in three hours." The girl didn't wait for a response before turning away. That should give her enough time to convince the guys of the soundness of her plan and convince them to allow her to go to the meeting.

"Wait!" Annora took a step after her. "What's your name?"

The girl glanced over her shoulder, humor dancing in her eyes. "Willa."

Then she was gone.

Not wanting to linger, Mason put his hand on Annora's back and propelled her forward until she practically had to run to keep pace with him.

It didn't take long for them to reach the house, Mason only seeming to breathe again when the door shut firmly behind them. The guys were talking in the living room, and she followed the sound to find Camden and Xander with maps spread out over the coffee table.

But no Edgar, which worried her. She nudged Mason. "Go and tell them what happened."

He gave her a suspicious look, and she patted his arm. "I'm going to find Edgar. I won't leave the house. Promise."

He slipped his fingers into her hair, his palm resting heavily on her neck. Instead of the threat she expected, he leaned forward and pressed a kiss to her forehead. "Call if you need me."

Annora watched him walk away, her mouth gaping open like a halfwit, while memories of him pressing her against the wall and ravishing her flashed through her mind. And he knew it, too, if the way he strutted into the living room, all proud of himself, was any indication.

The guys glanced at her. From the heated looks in their eyes, they knew exactly what happened.

No fair!

No way could a girl be expected to resist that much temptation.

Fighting a blush, she whirled and dipped back into the kitchen, only able to catch her breath when they were out of sight. She blinked and stared blindly around the room, trying to remember what was so urgent.

Then it hit her—Edgar.

And she wanted to smack herself for forgetting for even a second.

She edged near the basement, grabbed the knob, then took a bracing breath before she opened the door. Flashes of being trapped in her uncle's basement slammed into her, and she broke out in a sweat. It took her a moment to get her heartbeat under control and another moment to realize that the basement was dark.

He wasn't downstairs training.

Instead of feeling better, worry dug its claws in her mind.

He would never have left her of his own free will, she was sure of it. For the first time since she and Edgar were connected, she reached out for him. The threads binding them together were more like filaments, tiny and glowing, but weak…because of her.

And she didn't have a doubt that Edgar knew about the tenuous link and how much it had withered with her neglect.

She felt like an ass.

She touched the cords, allowing the afterworld to feed along the fibers until they glowed bright. She sensed Edgar on the other end, his confusion, his worry…his concern was all for her.

He was waiting for her in her room.

Turning on her heel, she charged up the stairs two at a time. When she reached her room, she saw Edgar standing in the middle of it, his head tipped back, staring out the skylight, completely still. Her heart clenched to see him so alone and adrift.

It boggled her mind that he had a life before her—friends, family…lovers.

Though she pulled him out of the afterworld, she now worried that she hadn't actually saved him—or maybe even made things worse for him. His new life was nothing compared to what he'd lost, and she couldn't help but wonder if he missed his old life and regretted his choices.

The ferret slept peacefully along his forearm, arms and legs hanging down both sides, completely passed out, while Edgar ran a single finger along the little guy's head and back to the tip of his tail.

"We're going to have to figure out another name for the little beast." Annora stepped into the room, and Edgar looked up at her with a puzzled frown. "Unless you would prefer to go back Alcott."

He flinched as if she'd slapped him, his voice hoarse when he answered. "No, I put that life behind me."

Annora nodded, coming to stop in front of him, then ran her fingers lightly along the ferret's ear. "If we're going to call you Edgar, we need another name for this little guy to avoid confusion."

Edgar straightened at her comment, his whole being centered on her, like a child waiting for Christmas. Suddenly nervous, Annora hesitated. "Unless…he's a part of you…keeping him weakens you, doesn't it?"

Edgar gazed down at her, his blue eyes searching. "It's minor. I barely feel the drain. When he's with you, he runs more off your power than mine, absorbing the excess energy that you tend to leak."

When she would've pulled her hand away, the ferret reached out, grabbed her finger, and bumped his head against it, begging for more cuddles. She couldn't resist his plea.

Edgar gently placed the ferret in her hands. "He's much more yours than mine now. Keep him, so when I'm not near, I know someone is watching over you."

Annora hugged the sleeping ferret to her chest, blinking up at Edgar. "But I thought he was a part of you? How is he more mine?"

Edgar reached out, hesitated for a second when she didn't flinch away, then pushed a strand of her hair behind her ear. "You are just as much a part of me as him. You hold my heart as surely as you hold him. You need him more than I do. If you won't allow me to keep you safe, maybe you'll allow him."

Her mouth opened and closed like a damned fish, but no sound emerged.

His smile was heartbreaking when he gazed down at her. "You didn't know?"

She shook her head mutely, beyond speaking.

He smiled down at her sadly. "Call him Prem—it means beloved."

Annora swallowed hard, stroking her cheek against the ferret's soft fur. All she could do was nod. She cleared her throat and glanced up at him. "Prem...I like it." She didn't mind that Edgar would use him to spy on her. He had too much honor to use Prem for any reason other than her safety.

She carefully placed the ferret on her pillow, then turned back toward Edgar and crossed her arms. "Now why don't you tell me about Sadie?"

Rage burned through Edgar when he learned that Sadie went against his wishes and dared to approach Annora. He scanned Annora for injuries, struggling to hold his form when all he wanted to do was eliminate the threat.

Only when she appeared unharmed did he cross his arms and glare down at her. "She's no one."

Her eyebrows shot up in surprise. "So she's not your fiancée?"

Son of a bitch!

His stomach lurched at the thought of losing Annora. If she thought for even one second that Sadie had a prior claim on him, she would push him away, and he couldn't allow it. "That man died a long time ago. Besides, the promise was made between our families. The only person I've ever pledged myself to is you."

Annora tipped her head to study him, and he'd swear the whole world narrowed down to her. She stepped toward him, and he clenched his hands at his sides to keep from shaking some sense into her.

But instead of saying anything, she placed her hand on his chest, then leaned up on her tiptoes, and his whole world stopped when she touched his face with her other hand.

"That's good, because you're mine. If she tries to take you back, I'm afraid I might have to kill her." Then she gave him a bloodthirsty smile that made his cock harden so fast it was almost painful. When her gaze dropped to his mouth, every thought in his head but the need to taste her vanished, and he forgot how to breathe when she leaned closer. "Mine."

Then her lips brushed his and his control snapped.

He wrapped her in his arms, sweeping her off her feet lest she thought to pull away. He kept his kiss light, seducing her, afraid she would pull away if she knew how much he needed her...needed this.

She was his everything, heaven and hell all wrapped up in a gorgeous package he couldn't resist. She burned bright like a star, and he was determined that no one would douse her spark while he stood guard. And if he got burned in the process, he was starting to believe she would be there to make everything better.

With shaking hands, he lowered her slowly, afraid if he didn't stop now he'd take things too far. He'd wanted her for too long, and what little control he had left was nearly ready to shatter. He lifted his head, the taste of her making him yearn for more, especially when her eyes fluttered open and she gazed up at him with what he wanted to believe was love. "I'm yours. I've only ever been yours."

He was enchanted by the light blush that dusted along her cheeks, and he pulled away to resist temptation, very conscious of the bed looming behind her. It was much too soon for her—she needed to trust them more—all of them—and he refused to push her too fast, too far, and scare her away again.

He grabbed the threads of their previous conversation. "You need to stay away from Sadie. She's dangerous, and I won't tolerate her harming you."

"You don't think I can take care of myself?" Annora retreated, her eyes narrowed in challenge as she glared up at him, and his heart tripped in his chest.

"It's not about strength. The life Sadie and I had growing up was brutal. While yours wasn't any treat, we were raised in cruelty and war. Each of us is basically a nuclear bomb waiting to go off if we lose control, and I don't want you to get caught in the blast. There is a reason our people keep to ourselves—we're dangerous, not only to ourselves but everyone else as well if the afterworld escapes our control. Only with a lot of practice can we survive the touch of other phantoms without destroying each other."

Edgar cupped her face, allowing his fingers to brush against her skin, unable to stop himself from stealing the light caress. "After everything you've been through, it's a miracle you survived as long as you have without killing yourself or others. I suspect that using your powers has helped bleed off the worst of the power buildup."

"So...fuck. You're saying that my uncle's torture saved me." She let out a bitter laugh that hit him like a blow to the solar plexus, and he tightened his hold on her when she would've pulled away. While he was sure she'd much rather have detonated and taken the fucker with her, Edgar was infinitely grateful she survived.

Hatred welled up in him at the mention of her uncle, and he looked forward to the next time he saw the bastard, relishing the moment when he could finally make him pay for laying his hands on Annora. "I'm saying that if you're strong enough to survive your childhood on your own, you're strong enough to stand up to your father. Your power is contained, keeping you camouflaged in a way that's unique."

"Or maybe it's because we're mates? Maybe that's why phantoms are so volatile...they have no one to hold them steady." She gazed up at him with her brown eyes so dark he'd swear the afterworld stared back at him.

He suspected that, while part of what she said might be true, it wasn't the whole story.

She was special in ways she couldn't imagine, and he'd do whatever it took to protect her. "Possibly, but now that others know about you, more will follow."

"How much longer do we have before Sadie reports us?" Annora reached up and wrapped her hands around his wrists, the heat of her like a brand as she gripped him tight.

"She'll keep quiet for now, but it's only a matter of time before the truth comes out." He pressed his forehead against hers. "I'll do everything in my power to keep you safe."

Even if he had to sacrifice himself to do it.

All he needed was to get close enough to Daxion. He'd been storing up his power. Once the man got close enough, he would let it loose and hope it was enough to destroy the man who had enslaved an entire race.

Annora didn't like the way Edgar went silent, no doubt plotting something she wasn't going to like, and she pressed against him, suddenly afraid. "Promise me you won't do anything foolish. Give my plan time to work first."

She listened to the steady beat of his heart, only relaxing when his arms came to rest around her. "By starting a war between the races?"

She tipped her head back to glare up at him. "If that's what it takes to keep you."

He was hers.

She was determined to do whatever it took so he wouldn't have to go back to that life of hell.

She pulled away, then walked over to the closet. Before she opened the door, she allowed the afterworld to spill into the human realm. Darkness crept along the wooden frame like mold. Then she grabbed the knob and opened the door.

Inside was the pure blackness of the afterworld. Although there were shelves inside, she could see the other realm beyond, the shadows moving in the darkness. Edgar latched on to her arm, the grip bruising, ready to rip her away, and she quickly grabbed the book.

She'd barely pulled it free when Edgar slammed the door shut, the wood practically nipping at the tips of her fingers. Dust plumed up from the door, then drifted to the ground like the magic had been expelled, leaving them staring at an ordinary closet again.

"Annora—"

"Don't." She turned with the book clutched to her chest. "I understand your unease with the afterworld, but the things beyond that gate don't frighten me. The human world is much more dangerous for me."

She could see he wanted to argue…and the moment he gave up. He combed his fingers through his dark hair, leaving the strands standing up every which way, very different from the impeccable way he usually looked. She wasn't sure she found the rumpled look cute or if it disturbed her. He smelled like the afterworld—like home— and it was all she could do not to try and comfort him.

Instead of giving in to the impulse, she held up the book and gave him a bright smile. "You can't protect me from everything, but you can give me the tools so I can protect myself. How about you give me a few lessons?"

She waited, studying his inscrutable face, every inch of him the royal pureblood. Taking the trick from Loulou, she blinked up at him with the innocent look that always made guys cave to her every whim. "Something in here might be the only thing that can save me."

He sighed in defeat and held out his hand. She smothered her victorious grin when he grabbed the book, then glared at her over the top. "But we do this my way. When I say we're done, we stop."

"Yes, sir." Annora barely resisted the urge to do a happy dance as she followed him to the middle of the room and took a seat on the floor.

She dropped down next to him, then leaned forward and craned her neck to get a better view of the book. Some of her joy drained out of her when she saw his solemn expression.

"It's a family grimoire." He ran his hand over the cover, a frown crossing his face, then his head snapped up. "But it's been infused with dark matter magic. My guess is your mother knew what you would become and was trying to prepare you for your life."

Chapter
Fourteen

"**W**hat?" She jerked back in shock, plopping back on her ass in a clumsy sprawl. "So the witches...my mother." Annora reached out but curled her hands into fists before she could touch the book. "She was a witch. That would explain how she knew about phantoms, but how would she be able to write about their magic? I was told the ability to practice dark matter magic was lost to the witches centuries ago."

Edgar gave her a steady look that made her swallow hard, and she wanted to turn away from the truth in his eyes.

"Your father—she knew he would come for you eventually, so she created this book to help you learn about your past without having to rely on him for anything."

She ran the tips of her fingers reverently along the edges of the book, then snatched her hand back, her face hardening with understanding. "And my uncle knew—or he suspected. He found the book, but he couldn't access the pages. That's why he took my blood, but it still wasn't enough for him to cast spells. He's a dud."

"Best guess...he sold the book to Erickson." Edgar tapped his finger on the front of the cover.

"And why Erickson thinks I belong to him. My uncle sold me to him, too."

Edgar didn't react beyond clenching his fingers into fists. "Most likely. He needs you to make the book work. He was able to use your blood for small spells, but he wants more. He's developed a taste for the power."

Annora sank her fingernails into the meaty part of her palm, trying to calm herself as the darkness rose at her agitation. The last thing she needed was to rip open the afterworld and bring her father down on their heads before they got Logan back and put their plan in action.

Blood welled from the tiny cuts. Before she could wipe away the evidence, Edgar clamped his hands around her wrists. She tugged on her arm once, then gave up control under his steady look. Instead of demanding that she heal, he took her hand and placed it directly on the leather cover of the grimoire.

At first nothing happened, then it felt like she'd picked up a live coal. The air around the book snapped and heated, her skin sizzling like a frying pan full of hot grease. When she tried to jerk her hand back, Edgar tightened his grip. But it wasn't him that held her still…the book was sealed to her palm. She gritted her teeth until she was ready to swear they'd crack, refusing to release the scream building up in her throat.

She would not be weak.

The cover of the grimoire rippled, and power shimmered up her arm. Her skin tingled like a numbing balm. By the time she lifted her arm and cradled it to her chest, she was shaking, her heartbeat erratic.

Edgar looked at her in concern. "Are you okay?"

Annora shrugged, using the pain to focus instead of letting it consume her. "A little warning would've been appreciated."

His fathomless blue eyes darkened as the afterworld swirled into them, rising with his agitation. "I'm sorry—if I had known, I would never have allowed it to happen."

Sincerity rang in his apology, and she sighed. He'd spent most of his life protecting her from pain. No way in hell would he have inflicted harm on her if he could avoid it. "I know you wouldn't."

She opened and closed her hand to get the feeling back into it, then nudged the book with her foot. "So what did that accomplish?

It better be good."

Edgar raised a brow at her, a smirk playing on his lips. Then he spun the book and flipped open the cover to reveal her mother's handwriting scrawled across the pages. Annora reached out, touching them reverently, struggling to hold back the flood of emotions threatening to drown her.

"When my uncle gained custody of me and learned what I could do, he tried to control me by threatening to destroy my mother's things." She rolled her eyes and gave him a self-deprecating smile. "Needless to say, nothing survived. I was nothing if not stubborn."

A muscle jumped along his jaw, and she pursed her lips, looking away. He took her beatings more personally than she did, like he'd somehow failed her. He didn't seem to understand that nothing was going to stop her uncle.

Only death.

His death.

And she was determined the man wouldn't escape her this time.

He would never lay another hand on her or anyone else, not if she had anything to say about it.

Annora flipped through the book, allowing Edgar time to regain his calm. The beginning of the book was older, the writing more slanted, the language older, and one she only vaguely recognized.

There appeared to be close to four hundred pages, possibly five or six authors. Only one section looked masculine. When she reached the end, a folded page fluttered to the ground. Annora hesitantly picked it up and opened it.

Her mother's handwriting jumped out at her, and a tremor shook her hands.

It had only one short paragraph.

I'm sorry I didn't have time to watch you grow up into the beautiful woman I see when I look at you. Keep this book close. It's the only thing that will keep you safe. Love you, baby.

The page blurred and she quickly blinked away the tears.

"What does it say?" Edgar didn't try to read the note.

She glanced up at him, studying him a moment, then handed it over for him to read.

"I think she dug up every bit of phantom lore she could find and wrote it in the book to protect you." He nodded toward the grimoire, frowned, and flipped back a couple pages, then ran his fingertips along the ragged edges where sheets had been ripped out.

He glanced up at her. "Do you still have the page you found?"

Annora scrambled to her feet and collected the page from her discarded jeans, then handed it over to him. He unfolded the sheet and held it next to the ragged edges. Much to her surprise, magic sparked along the seams, sealing them together until it looked brand new.

"How did you know it would do that?" Annora demanded, dropping down to get a better look at the newly restored page.

Edgar frowned at her, his brows furrowed. "I didn't. It was more of a hunch. The book practically radiates magic. It wants to be whole. You don't feel it?"

Annora bit her lip, opening her senses, and saw the book swirl with a rainbow of light and dark colors. "The magic is not the same as it is in the afterworld."

It wasn't what she was expecting.

She wasn't sure if she'd even be able to use it.

He only nodded, seemingly not worried in the least. "It makes sense, since your mother was a witch and not a phantom."

"So this isn't the ancient grimoire the witches are so eager to get their hands on?" It was all she could do not to snatch the book away from him to read more of her mother's legacy to her.

"Possibly." He shrugged when she forced her eyes away from the book to give him a questioning look. "The grimoire goes back five or six generations. In each generation, only one person in the entire family can access it and keep it up to date. The spells are unique to that family. So, out of hundreds of people in this family line, only you have access to it."

"Me?" She wasn't sure how she felt about the possibility of having more family out there, not if it meant they knowingly left her to suffer at her uncle's hands. Her mother never mentioned them, which was telling, especially since the two of them moved around so much when Annora was younger.

Unaware of her rambling thoughts, Edgar nodded. "You. Instead of continuing to record spells for the next generation, she recorded phantom lore to help you."

"But if she was a witch, how can the magic be helpful against actual phantoms? She couldn't know what would work if she couldn't cast the magic herself." When she flipped to the back of the book that held the information about phantoms, Edgar closed it with a snap. "Hey!"

"You are now bound to the book, but I caution you against using the spells until you know what you're doing. One wrong move can have dire consequences." He scowled at her when she opened her mouth to protest. "The afterworld behaves a little differently with each phantom. Not many can access it the way you do…they're not bonded in the same way…but that doesn't mean people can't find you there and hurt you."

"I do have one question…why did my mother not tell me?" If she'd known, she could've protected herself better, and never let her uncle discover the truth.

She could've had a normal life.

Edgar didn't flinch away from the question. "My guess? She was protecting you the best way she knew how. She bound your gifts when you were younger, but when she fell sick, it was too late, and she was too weak to help you. She must have been a powerful witch to even be able to conceive you. Phantom births are hard, and severely drain the mother, which is one of the many reasons why mating is banned between witches and phantoms. Death of the mother is almost guaranteed."

Annora could only nod, seeing her life through the eyes of a mother trying to keep her daughter safe.

"It'd also explain why you're so exceptional." He didn't say it to flatter her, but that didn't stop the way a blush heated her cheeks as his eyes caressed her face. "She couldn't let any other witches know about you for fear they'd take you away and claim you as their own."

"But I'm only half phantom," Annora protested.

"That doesn't matter to those who are addicted to power. Even if you were weak, they'd want you for breeding purposes. It's one of the reasons we try to rescue anyone with the dark, elemental power."

"Rescue?" Annora lifted a brow at him, her snarkiness evaporating at his blank expression. "You don't know."

A frown appeared between his brows. "Know what?"

"They've been killing those who refuse to go with them."

Edgar immediately shook his head. "No, they bind those who refuse."

"Edgar…my uncle said if I ever tried to escape, anyone who saw my magic would kill me. He said it was forbidden magic, punishable by death. After talking to the witches today, I was able to piece it together. The witches are desperate for power. They wouldn't kill off their own kind. That only leaves one who would do such a thing."

"Phantoms." Denial darkened his eyes at the horror of what she was saying, a muscle jumping in his jaw.

"They would have no choice. Even if they bound those who refused to bend to them, that would still leave their children open to inheriting the gift. They've been eliminating everyone who refuses to bow to them. They can't risk leaving anyone alive who is powerful enough to endanger their reign."

"I…didn't know." He stared down blindly at the book. "I've been gone too long, no longer involved in enforcing the laws, but I wouldn't put it past your father."

She flinched when he called the mass murderer her father, but she couldn't deny the truth of it. Being an asshole ran in the male side of her family apparently. "So what can you teach me about how to stay alive and out of my father's clutches?"

His calm returned as the conversation veered away from his past. He opened the book, flipping back to where her mother started adding to the grimoire. "It looks like she came into possession of the book a few years before your birth. There is a pause between when she was recording regular spells to when she switched to phantom lore."

Annora leaned closer, spotting the date. "When she became pregnant with me."

"She more than likely recognized your father as a phantom. When she became pregnant, she sensed you were different, maybe could even feel your growing power. In fact, your presence might have given her the ability to access the powers she needed to find out about phantoms and their capabilities. Phantoms normally can't do spells or magic, not in the same way as witches. Only the strongest phantoms are able to manipulate dark matter enough to cast spells, and I'm guessing you're one of the few exceptions, especially thanks to your mother's heritage."

"Is there a location spell? Can we find the missing pages? My uncle wouldn't go anywhere without them in his possession. If we can find them, we can find him, and if we find him, we can find Logan." She couldn't stop the hope that swelled in her heart and watched avidly while Edgar slowly flipped through the pages. She wanted to rip it away from him and search herself, but she didn't have a clue what she was looking for.

As if reading her thoughts, particles rose up around them, the tiny spots of blackness suspended in the air like raindrops. Then it was like they were sucked toward the book and soaked into the pages.

The pages turned slowly of their own accord, like a single finger was pushing at the bottom corner of each sheet, then another one, and another, each one faster until it was flipping pages faster than she could track. Edgar lifted his hand off the book and looked up, watching her with narrowed eyes, as if he suspected she had something to do with it.

She could only shrug. "I didn't do it on purpose."

But she would take it.

The pages came to an abrupt stop near the end of the book, leaving a single spell staring up at her.

"Fine." He gave her a stern look. "We'll look at it, but I want to go over a few of the self-defense spells first. You will not use the other spells without my supervision."

Since she knew he'd snap the book shut and refuse to teach her anything unless she agreed, Annora nodded.

Well, the good news was she didn't blow up the house, but it wasn't for lack of trying. In two hours' time, all she managed to achieve was memorizing a few spells.

And only one of them worked.

She could now make light—like light-up-the-fucking-world-with-the-sun-bright light—but that was about it. And since she and the guys could see in the dark, it wasn't very helpful, either.

While Edgar could cast faster than she could, his spellwork usually fell apart before he could finish, the spells a combination of witchcraft and phantom magic that he didn't have the skill to perform. He tried to show her simpler spells he learned as a child, but those were even worse. Trying to levitate a small pencil made the whole house shake and groan like she was trying to rip the foundation out of the very earth.

Unfortunately, casting spells appeared to be a skill that needed to be learned. Apparently, phantoms never really had a problem with drawing too much power and suffering the consequences, so Edgar wasn't sure how to restrict the flow of the afterworld. She'd memorized the location spell, but it was like she couldn't reach far enough or her uncle was cloaked somehow.

She just had to pray she'd be able to make it work when it was needed.

While she put the book away and took a quick shower, Edgar went down to apprise the guys of her lack of progress. If she wanted to meet Willa at the café, she was going to have to haul ass. She grabbed the newel post just before she was about to head downstairs, then backtracked and snatched the blades out from under her pillow.

They were a gift from Logan.

She hadn't worn them since he'd been taken, but she didn't want to leave the house without them, especially now her father was actively hunting her. She strapped them on under her shirt, touching the placement of the knives to make sure she could get at them easily, then tucked her shirt in again before heading downstairs.

Wearing them made her feel closer to Logan.

As she headed into the kitchen, she found Terrance in deep discussion with the rest of the team. They broke apart when they saw her, and she crossed her arms and narrowed her eyes at them. "Just tell me. I'm going to find out eventually."

Terrance was the first to break. "I got ahold of my brother and warned him we were coming. I told him to be ready and do his best to locate Logan." He ran his hand over his hair, flipping it out of his face. "He says that while they want the book, they want you more. They're willing to trade the kitsune for you."

Even before she had a chance to open her mouth, the guys exploded.

"You're not fucking doing it." Xander looked ready to tie her to a chair.

Mason's hair was standing on end, fairly vibrating with his growl, his frame bulking up, ready to go to battle, as if he knew she would fight him on it. What worried her more was that Camden remained mute—which didn't mean he had any intention of letting her go. No doubt he was ready to drug her at the first opportunity.

When she glanced at Edgar, he raised a brow and shrugged. "I'm with them. It's too dangerous to try a trade. They'd never keep their word."

"So what do you expect me to do? Wait for them to eventually capture and kill every one of you? Because that's what they'll do. What happens to me when you're all dead?" Annora wanted to stomp her foot or just ghost them and finish the job herself, but the stubborn bastards would only follow her and get themselves killed.

"Did Edgar tell you I haven't been able to get the locator spell to work?" She gazed at each of them, her heart threatening to break. "This is our only way inside, and you know it. Don't ask me to give up on Logan. I don't think I'd survive it."

A muscle jumped in Camden's jaw, fire blazing in his green eyes until they appeared to glow. He marched toward her, his hands fisted at his sides, looking ready to throttle her. He then leaned down, his eyes narrowed in warning. "If we do this, then we do it my way. No sacrificing yourself. The only thing getting yourself captured will do is ensure that we'll kill ourselves trying to get you out. You will do exactly what I say. Do I make myself clear?"

Annora swallowed hard at the threat, her chest aching at the idea of a world without them to keep her sane, and nodded up at him.

If she fucked up the rescue, they would die, and she refused to allow that to happen. "Understood."

Chapter Fifteen

As Annora left the house to meet up with Willa at the café, she couldn't have been more surprised when Camden volunteered to be her escort. "You don't want to stay behind and plot our course for tonight?"

He just shrugged as he surveyed the campus for any threat. "We're as prepared as we're going to be. The rest of the guys are going to scout for reinforcements." He glanced down at her, his expression as serious as she'd ever seen it. "We want Logan back as much as you do, but sacrificing you isn't an option. Trust us to know what we're doing."

They were the best of the best, having spent most of their lives training for this kind of situation. Annora leaned into him, resting her head against his shoulder. "I do trust you. If I didn't, I would have already tried to get him myself."

Camden heaved an exasperated sigh that was part laugh. When she tipped her head back to smile up at him, he brushed his lips against her forehead so lightly she barely felt it, and she wanted to cheer at the small victory. A few weeks ago, he would've cringed away from even allowing her within touching distance.

As they entered the café, Loulou popped up from her seat like she'd been launched from springs, and practically skipped over to them with a bright smile, her nearly white hair streaming behind her.

Lionel, her wolf protector, was only a few paces behind, a menacing presence poised to beat the shit out of anyone who dared threaten his mate. Where there was one, the other was sure to follow. She had to marvel that the guy had the energy to keep up with the high-octane bunny who didn't seem to know the meaning of slow or calm.

Loulou threw her arms around her. "I'm so glad you came."

Before Annora even had a chance to return the hug, Loulou jumped back and dragged her over to their table. "How did you even know I would be here?"

The rabbit looked at her over her shoulder, her large blue eyes a little too big for her face, and she shook her head pityingly. "Girl, nothing that happens on campus is a secret."

When Annora glanced around the café, she decided Loulou was right. The place was packed with an equal variety of shifters and witches, until it was almost standing room only. A glance out the window showed even more people were scoping out the place.

"Great." She resisted the urge to sigh while she wove through the tables after Loulou, doing her best to avoid touching anyone, still unused to being around crowds. While she hated her lonely childhood, her skin practically crawled at having so many eyes on her.

Camden pressed closer, guarding her back, and her unease lessened a fraction. Most gave him wide berth. A few curious people wandered a little too close, and he deliberately brushed against them. It didn't take long for their curiosity to fade to confusion after being dosed by his toxic touch, and they wandered away.

As they took their seats in the corner booth, Annora glanced around the cafe. The magic in the room was almost a living thing, it was so potent. It swirled and eddied like ribbons weaving between people, as if on the hunt or possibly trying to pick up her magical trail.

Camden waited while she was seated, then veered away to order their drinks, leaving Lionel to stand guard. Annora turned toward Loulou. "What on earth are you doing here?"

Loulou raised her eyebrows, then scolded, "I'm providing backup.

I'm sure you *meant* to call me. I just must have missed it."

Annora suddenly found the tabletop fascinating, avoiding those earnest eyes. "Loulou—"

"Hush." She waved her hand, and flashed Annora a bright smile. "Everyone knows something is going down tonight, and they want to help. Haven't you noticed no one is in class? *Everyone* skipped. No one takes one of our own without paying for it."

Annora blinked hard at Loulou's fierce vow, touched and overwhelmed by such support.

Then Loulou winked. "Besides, most of them owe you for rescuing their pack members. This is one way to return the favor. Shifters hate owing other packs."

Annora breathed a little easier.

That made more sense.

Camden made it back with her drink—hot chocolate—then leaned down to whisper in her ear. "Your guest has arrived."

Annora turned toward the entrance. Sure enough, Willa was waiting by the door, scanning the crowd with a grimace. Their eyes met, and Annora lifted her hand in a small two-fingered wave, ignoring the way Willa's glower deepened as she wove through the tables.

Willa was barely seated before she touched the wall and mumbled something under her breath. A spell activated, magic crawled up the wall and the rest of the café fell silent.

Annora could see everyone was still talking, moving, but the world around them was muted. If she concentrated hard enough, she could make out what the others were saying, but it was a struggle. She glanced at Camden, and he tapped his ear, indicating he could hear everything.

"Did you invite the entire campus?" Willa plopped down in her seat, shoving her shoulder bag between her and Loulou, forcing the rabbit to move over or be crushed.

Loulou glared at the witch. "Like we would let her meet one of your kind without backup."

Annora raised her brows at the antagonism between them, then shrugged. "Apparently nothing remains secret for long on this campus. We can move this discussion back to Grady House if you want more privacy."

"No, this is fine. Let's just get this over with." Willa finally broke eye contact with Loulou and turned toward Annora with a frown. She placed both hands on the table, her green eyes direct. "What do you want?"

Annora felt the spell the instant she spoke. It hit her chest and the pressure to speak increased with every second—trying to yank the truth out of her. The darkness at her core rose lazily, sucking in the magic. Instead of crushing the spell to ash, as soon as the darkness touched it, it shimmered black and was absorbed.

"You could just try asking," Annora chided.

Willa just shrugged, completely unrepentant. "Most people wouldn't know the truth if it hit them in the face."

Annora very much feared Willa was correct and conceded defeat with a tired sigh. "I want to survive, and I'm afraid I'll need the witches' help to do that."

Willa gave a near-silent whistle and shook her head pityingly. "They're going to own your ass for the rest of your life and beyond."

Annora took a sip of her hot chocolate, then gave a shrug. "Maybe...unless I have something they want. Which is where you come in."

Everything about the girl stiffened. "What do you want?"

Annora decided to be blunt. She didn't have time to waste. "I don't trust the witches to keep their word, so I need someone I can trust. Is that you?"

Interest sharpened the witch's eyes. "That depends...what do you need?"

"You want out from under the witches and so do I. They want my magic and will do anything to take it. Unfortunately, they aren't the only ones. I need the witches to stand on my side if it comes to a fight." Annora played with her cup, conscious of how much was riding on this conversation.

Willa didn't answer right away. "The people coming...they're like you."

Annora hesitated, well aware that the witches could try to make a deal with her father for the magic and turn her over to them. But she decided to take a gamble and nodded. If anything, her father would kill everyone before he turned over any information to them about dark matter.

Willa glanced away, surveying the rest of the café. "Witches get their power from the elements. What do you hope to gain by asking witches to join your fight? They'd be slaughtered."

"Dark matter might be stronger, but very few people can actually access it, and fewer still can control it without going insane or outright dying. But what if I serve as a filter? My strength with your magic?"

That got the witch's attention, and she turned to study Annora, raising a single eyebrow skeptically. "Are you sure that would even work?"

Annora just shrugged. "We could try it. As it stands right now, the witches are anxious to get their hands on my grimoire…for magic they can't even use. I can only imagine what they plan to do with it."

"So you would give me access, but only with your supervision." Willa didn't sound happy about that part, but she didn't say no.

"Exactly." No way could Annora allow the witches unfettered access to dark matter. They would destroy the world. Just from sitting across from her, Annora could sense Willa didn't have the markers needed to use the magic without annihilating herself in the process, the darkness had no interest in her.

Willa chewed on her lip for a moment, then narrowed her eyes. "Let's do a test to see if it's even possible first."

She dug in her bag and pulled out a fat candle, setting it in the middle of the table between them. While the rest of the room wasn't able to hear anything, Annora saw at least half the room lean forward with bated breath.

At her look, Willa just shrugged. "I'm a fire witch. While I can do a few parlor tricks in the other elements, I'm strongest with fire."

Annora tightened her grip around her cup, her hands ice-cold despite the warmth of the hot chocolate. She took another sip for courage, watching over the rim as Willa took a deep breath.

Okay, they were doing this.

She glanced at Camden, and he gave her a grim nod, his stance widening, as if he was waiting for someone to attack. Lionel stood only a few paces away from him, the two of them looking like matching-freaking-warrior bookends.

Loulou looked just as suspicious, but kept her attention glued on Willa, seconds away from pouncing with all her hundred pounds of fluff if the witch so much as breathed wrong.

"Ready?" Willa cracked her knuckles, then twisted her head from side to side.

Annora blew out a breath, conscious of the hundreds of eyes on them, then held out her hand and allowed a small bubble of the dark particles to form in her palm. The smoke curled in upon itself like snakes.

Willa gaped at it for a few moments, her eyes wide, then she straightened and cleared her throat. She mumbled a few words in Latin, twisting her fingers into strange symbols before she closed her hand into a fist.

Annora felt the tug on the dark particles, watched them twist around the wick.

Fire whooshed up from the candle, the flame nearly four feet tall. She was flung backwards, her back hitting the booth, the fire sucking the oxygen out of her lungs. Loulou gave a little squeal and ducked.

Camden grabbed her arm and yanked her out of the booth, twisting to protect her from the dancing flame. The blaze licked at the ceiling until Willa snapped out of her trance and slashed her hand through the air while muttering a few Latin phrases.

The next second, the candle was extinguished.

Or what remained of the candle.

All that was left was a puddle of hot wax dripping off the end of the table.

Lionel leapt over the booth and pulled Loulou in his arms, his wolf glaring out through his eyes, his fangs and claws extended, ready to rip apart anyone who got too close. Willa remained seated, staring at her melted candle, dipping her fingers in the hot wax.

She slowly lifted her head and met Annora's gaze, her green eyes glittering with anticipation. "I'll agree to help on one condition—take me with you tonight."

"Ditto! Don't think you're leaving without me!" Loulou peeked out from behind Lionel's shoulder, then quickly sidestepped him when he moved to reach for her.

Annora understood why Loulou wanted to help, but not Willa, and couldn't keep the suspicion out of her voice. "Why?"

"Because then you will owe me and won't back out of teaching me." She rose to her feet and faced off with Annora. "I won't go back to being a slave to those bitches."

Annora couldn't protest, because she knew what it was like to be at the mercy of a sadistic bastard, and she wouldn't wish it on anyone. "Are you safe where you're staying?"

Willa paused while reaching for her bag, glancing at Annora warily as she straightened. Then, ignoring her completely, she glanced at Loulou. "Is she really as innocent as she appears?"

"Oh, yeah." Loulou nodded and smiled. "But cross her and she'll make you regret it. There will be nowhere you can run that she wouldn't find you."

Annora glanced back and forth between the two of them, then sighed. "If you need a place to stay—"

"She can stay with us." Loulou interrupted, batting those big blue eyes up at Lionel. When he sighed in defeat, she grinned triumphantly and turned back to Annora. "You have enough on your plate for now."

Willa hesitated for a moment, glancing around at the many faces staring up at them, then shrugged. "That might be for the best."

Loulou nodded proudly, herding the witch toward the door like she was her charge now. "You're going to love staying with us."

Willa cast a glance over her shoulder, her eyes wide, almost pleading, and Annora just smiled and gave a little wave with her fingers. The girl wouldn't know what hit her. Smothering her laughter, she turned toward Camden, only to see him frowning at the smattering of wax that had splattered the front of her outfit.

She brushed off some of the dried flakes, then grimaced at the mess. "Can we stop by the bathroom?"

Indecision flickered across his face, then he heaved the put-upon sigh that guys gave when they're stuck doing something for their girl just because they asked and moved aside for her to go first. He followed closely behind her, not leaving room for anyone else to slip between them.

Before she reached the door, he touched her arm, then opened it and peered inside to make sure it was empty. Only when he stepped back did he give her a nod to enter. Annora was baffled by all the precautions but didn't protest.

If it made him feel better, who was she to judge?

But before the bathroom door could close behind her, his large presence followed her inside the room, securing the small space.

"What on earth do you think you're doing?" She planted her hands on her hips, tightening her lips against saying more. She wasn't sure if she was more annoyed or amused.

He gave her a hard look, then waved a hand at the two stalls in the room. "We shouldn't linger."

Knowing he wasn't about to budge, she turned toward the sink and slipped her shirt off. She shook off as much of the stubborn wax that clung to the material as she could, but it did little good. She grabbed a few pieces of the cardboard towels that didn't absorb shit, put in the bathrooms by some genius, and used it to scrape off the wax that dotted along her jeans.

It didn't take long to get most of the crap scraped off. She slipped on her shirt, then turned toward Camden…only to see him frozen in place, devouring her with hungry eyes.

"Camden?" She took a hesitant step toward him and could swear he actually growled at her like a dog with a bone. Her feet froze to the floor, her hand halting halfway between them. She stilled at the fierce expression on his face, fascinated by the emotions he normally kept locked down tight.

Instead of backing away like she should, Annora stepped toward him until her palm came to rest against his chest. He inhaled deeply, then shook himself like he was coming out of a trance. The yearning and longing were still there but banked.

He leaned down and grabbed her jaw, lifting her face up to his. "You should never take your shirt off in front of anyone but us. Too many others would see it as an invitation."

Then his fingers brushed along her jaw, making her skin tingle, and she licked her lips, suddenly craving the taste of him. The smell of exotic flowers and wildness clung to him, and she wanted to bask in the freedom of being close to him. "What if it was an invitation?"

His mouth slammed shut and a muscle ticked along his jaw. His eyes became fierce, narrowing dangerously, but it was the way his grip tightened on her face, the way his fingers trembled slightly, that gave away his need. Without giving him time to retreat, she stood on tiptoe and kissed him.

He stood frozen for all of a second before his control snapped.

His mouth opened over hers, and he devoured her, his lips and teeth demanding everything. The rest of the world vanished while he bit and nibbled at her lips, like he couldn't seem to get enough.

His arms came up to wrap around her, pulling her closer, and he scooped her up off her feet. She wrapped her legs around his waist, and he gave a groan of approval, walking her backwards until her ass came to rest on the counter.

Then he leaned her back, his lips trailing down her jaw to nip along her neck. The scruff along his jaw scraped her skin, making her squirm as every nerve ending flared to life and begged for more. Annora couldn't stop the way she arched into him, his every touch seemingly connected to her core, each brush of his lips sending her need ratcheting higher.

His hands slid under her shirt, barely trailing his palms over her skin, his touch reverent. Needing more, she tugged his shirt out of his pants, then nearly groaned when her fingers and then her palms encountered warm flesh. He was all muscle and heat wrapped up in a delicious package.

She could feel slight ridges under his skin as his beast rose to the surface, his black hair becoming iridescent. The need to taste him was like a craving. She shoved up his shirt and pushed him back, then set her lips and teeth to his chest. He cupped the back of her head, groaning as she nibbled at the delicious expanse of flesh.

His hip surged against her core, and it was her turn to moan. Then he trailed one finger down her spine, leaving shivers in its wake.

Until he got to the waistband of her pants.

He hesitated and pulled back from their kiss to stare down at her. Then his eyes dropped, and he traced the backs of his fingers along the patch of skin between the gap of her shirt and pants.

"Tell me to stop." His tone was tortured, his eyes shooting up to hers, the longing and fear there nearly tearing her heart to pieces.

"Do you want to stop?" Because the gods knew she didn't.

He swallowed hard, his eyes betraying his longing when they dropped to the button of her pants. Knowing he needed this almost as much as she did, needed to feel connected to another person, she reached down and unsnapped the button that had riveted his attention.

He didn't seem to be breathing.

As she slowly lowered the zipper, he licked his lips, greedily watching her every move. A tremor went through him, his breaths coming in great gulps when her panties were revealed, his neon eyes blazing with so much lust and longing that it was hard for her to swallow.

When he didn't move, she grabbed his hand and brought it to her lips to nibble at the tips of his fingers. "You can touch me if you want…or not. You won't break me."

The need to give him what he needed, what no other woman could give him, made her more daring. She ran his hand down the front of her torso, between her breasts, down her stomach until they reached her pants.

When she would've pulled away, he wove their fingers together, then leaned his forehead against hers. "Stop me if it gets to be too much."

She nodded weakly. Instead of drawing back, he watched every nuance of her expression as he slowly slipped their joined hands down the front of her panties. She bit her lip at the heat of him, then he used his other hand to pull her hips closer to the edge of the counter, making her legs spread wider to fit him between them, and guided their joined hands to slide over her core.

A moan tore from her as pleasure shot along her limbs, and she struggled to keep her eyes open and trained on his as her desire soared even higher. Then he moved his hand and she couldn't help the way her head fell back and her hips arched against his seeking fingers in a greedy demand for more.

She pulled her hand away from his hold, needing to be closer, and arched into him again when he rubbed against her harder. A gasp escaped her as pleasure sizzled from her fingers to her toes. Ravenous to touch him in turn, she reached for his pants. The instant her fingers brushed along his bare stomach, he sucked in a sharp breath, and she took advantage and slipped her hands into the small gap in the front of his jeans.

His body stiffened, as if he'd been completely unaware of what she was doing until then. She peered up at him from under her lashes, loving the way he had his head tipped back, the strong cords of his neck standing out, thrilled that she could make him lose control.

She wrapped her hands around his staff, marveling at the size and silken texture. He gave a tortured groan, then his other hand came up to settle on top of hers over the pants and he tightened his grip, showing her what he wanted. His head dropped forward, and his lips came to rest against her ear.

"Harder." As if to emphasize the point, he bit her earlobe sharp enough to make her jump.

Which sent his fingers into her core and elicited a groan from both of them.

She tightened her hand around him as instructed, following his lead as he grabbed her wrist and showed her how to pleasure him. For each stroke, he mimicked her movements, until her eyes fell shut and she crested...then all she saw were stars.

When his cock swelled in her hand, her eyes fluttered open. She needed to watch him reach his pleasure.

Only for him to pull her hand away, his breathing ragged.

"Hey!" When she reached for him again, he pulled his hand away from her core, and she couldn't help shivering, her body on the verge of another orgasm. Instead of answering her, Camden turned away and tucked in his shirt, refusing to meet her gaze as he buttoned up his jeans.

Suddenly feeling cold, she fussed with her clothes until she was fully dressed once more. "What is it? Did I do something wrong?"

He gave a strangled laugh, looking pained as he turned toward her, brushing a chaste kiss along her lips. "Sweetheart, if it was any more perfect, I would have come in my pants."

Heat singed her cheeks, but something about the way he avoided her eyes made her push. "Why didn't you?"

"We should go." When he reached to help her down from the

counter, she quickly wrapped her legs around his waist, refusing to budge.

She ducked her head until he met her gaze. "Tell me."

A dusting of red colored his cheeks, and he coughed a little nervously before he shrugged. "I don't know what my seed would do to you. My touch is toxic, my kiss is even more potent." His gaze met hers, direct and frank. "This isn't the way to find out if my body fluids would be harmful to you. I would never leave you vulnerable in a public bathroom stall."

Annora pursed her lips, wanting to argue, but she couldn't refute his logic. Then she gave him her best sultry smile.

She must have done it wrong because he stiffened in her arms.

Unwilling to admit defeat, still able to feel his arousal pressed between them, she rested her hand flat on his chest, brushing her fingers along the shirt that now separated them. Skimming her fingers lower, she trailed them over the front of his pants, dragging her nails over the rough material hard enough that he arched into her with a strangled groan. "We can easily find out."

He gave a start, searching her eyes, and her cheeks heated at her boldness. She wanted to duck her head, suddenly shy, but refused. This was too important. She would not allow him to run from her.

Sweet gods above, she was going to kill him.

Camden had to lock his knees as the image of him touching himself in front of her popped into his head. Then the image of her falling to her knees before him nearly had him spilling himself in his jeans. He struggled to get his breathing back under control before he hyperventilated.

He rubbed his hand along his jaw, then closed his eyes as the smell of her arousal tantalized him, and he couldn't resist the urge to lick his fingers.

Bad decision.

A feral growl rumbled from him, and it was all he could do not to push her back, strip her and taste her directly. The only thing that held him back was he wasn't sure what effect his poison would have on her after prolonged contact. Until they knew for sure, he had to keep his hands to himself.

Case in point, when she looked up at him with those sultry brown eyes, he had to shove his hands into his pockets or he wouldn't be responsible for his actions.

Fuck!

He'd had sex before but never like this, never skin to skin. He'd always remained fully clothed, wore gloves for their protection, and always wore three of the thickest condoms he could find. No kissing permitted. No hugs or cuddling afterward.

After a while it left him cold, and he simply stopped trying, the company of his own hand enough for him.

Then Annora walked into his life and turned it upside down.

That he could touch her...he shoved his hands deeper into his pockets to resist temptation, nearly groaning when he bumped his cock. The fucking thing was so sensitive, it throbbed with the need to be inside her.

Control.

He needed control.

She was everything to him.

He couldn't risk going any further until he knew what long-term effects it would have on her.

When she continued to gaze at him, her lips bruised from his kisses, her eyes still dazed with lust, he had to force himself to back away from her. "Not here, and not now. I want more than a quickie in a public bathroom."

Annora narrowed her eyes, then jumped down off the counter, taking a step toward him, and he backed away like a virgin protecting his virtue. He wasn't sure if he was afraid she'd eat him alive or more afraid that she wouldn't.

The cold wall hit his back, knocking the breath out of him with an oomph.

Then she was right in front of him, lifting her stubborn chin up in challenge.

"Then we'll wait until we get Logan back. We don't have to have sex, we can go as slow as you need, but I will prove to you, once and for all, that you don't have to be afraid of touching me. I've never felt safer than when I am with you and the guys. Nothing will change that." She reached up on her toes and brushed her lips against his jaw, then pulled away. "We should head back before the rest of the team starts to worry."

When she reached for the door handle, he slumped against the wall, not sure if he was happy with the way things ended or if he should be kicking himself for foolishly turning her away. As she sauntered away, he cursed, then pushed off the wall to follow.

Knowing smirks and even a few hoots rang out as they re-entered the café, making it obvious that the bathroom was a known hot spot for couples. Unfortunately, the few minutes away from the watchful eyes of the university had relaxed him, and he had to scramble to get his head back into the game and protect her.

The café had erupted in chaos after the demonstration, most of the people still lingering to keep an eye on them. The other half had already left, eager to share the news with their packs and covens.

Fuck!

She might as well just have stood up and yelled *come and get it* to a pack of starving animals. While the shifters could be vicious, witches were worse.

Even if she survived her father, neither group would stop hunting her—unless they could prove that she was a bigger and badder threat than the rest of them combined.

Chapter Sixteen

As they left the café, the cold air hit her like a slap in the face, and Annora shivered, still not used to the freedom of being able to walk outside at will...or the way the weather could change from one minute to the next.

But when Camden followed her outside and stopped next to her, she no longer felt the cold. He scanned the street, noting the pedestrians, even the drivers of the cars that went past. He was back in protector mode, quickly guiding her across the street. The sun was about to set, shadows were already stealing across the world, which meant they would be leaving to rescue Logan soon.

Nerves churned in her stomach.

Nothing could go wrong tonight.

Too much rested on this mission.

They were halfway home, each lost in thought, walking through the quad, when the air around her began to darken and stir. Instinct took over. Annora leapt away, barely missed having her head removed by a freaking sword that swooshed through the air, close enough that a breeze fanned her face. Black flames trailed after the blade as if it was eating away the metal.

The sword was there one second and gone the next.

Camden yanked her behind him, going into combat mode, turning in a circle, searching for the threat.

Only they were completely alone.

The darkness began to churn again and Annora tackled Camden, then squealed when he grabbed her around the waist and spun them until she was protected underneath him.

That's when she got a good look at their attacker.

Sadie.

That bitch!

Determination gleamed in the girls' eyes as she raised the sword over her head.

Without hesitation, Annora wrapped her arms around Camden and rolled them, the sword hitting the ground so hard the metal twanged and reverberated just an inch from them and cleaved the earth at least a foot into the ground.

Determination hardened Camden's face, and he was on his feet in seconds.

But Sadie had already stepped into the afterworld and vanished once more.

Annora concentrated on the guys, focusing on Edgar, doing her best to send him her location, hoping against hope that he'd get to them in time.

Only to be interrupted when Sadie popped back into existence in a swirl of dust. Camden quickly stepped in front of her, blocking the sword blow by grabbing Sadie's wrist. Her face went slack, her eyes dulling with confusion as Camden's venom pumped through her blood.

As if sensing the threat, she jerked away and swung a smaller second blade, nearly gutting him.

Camden leapt sideways and lost his hold—and Sadie popped out of existence again.

"Fuck!" Camden turned and went back to back with her, scanning the darkness. "I don't think she can jump if I'm touching her. I just need a couple more seconds for my venom to hit her."

Annora scowled, not liking the idea of him anywhere near the bitch, and quickly grabbed two of the blades she had stashed.

The darkness stirred to their right, and she didn't hesitate, throwing the blade hard and fast, the way Logan taught her.

Only to have Sadie swat it aside like a pesky gnat.

Camden swung, but she had vanished...only to appear behind him. Annora stepped between them, blocking the sword with her much smaller blade. Metal scraped along metal, skidded off her smaller weapon and hit her side. The sword slid along the blades she had stashed at her waist, then bit into her hip, the pain sharp and instant.

Sadie bared her teeth in a victorious smile.

Camden grabbed Sadie around her waist with a roar and flung her away.

Before the girl landed, she vanished in a puff of smoke.

Camden hauled Annora closer, checking the injury through the gap in her clothes, his face a mask of concern and worry.

When the darkness swirled again, Annora tensed and smacked away his hands. "Incoming!"

Camden barely whirled in time to duck out of the way of the damned sword. Annora flung her second blade, nailing the bitch right in the thigh.

Sadie screamed, yanking out the blade, then scowled down at the bloody knife. Camden ran to tackle her, but she vanished out of existence...and reappeared behind him again.

When Sadie raised the sword to plunge it into his back, something inside Annora snapped. She ghosted the small distance between them just as Edgar appeared a few feet away.

His eyes widened in alarm, and he reached for her. "Don't."

Annora gritted her teeth against Edgar's plea.

Sadie's head snapped up, and Annora used her hesitation against her and clamped her hand over Sadie's arm.

She had no choice.

While Camden was a trained warrior, he couldn't win against someone he couldn't see.

She glanced at the guys, then allowed the darkness around her and Sadie to swallow them whole.

Camden shouted in denial, while Edgar lunged toward them.

She dragged Sadie into the afterworld, releasing the girl when she whirled and swung her blade. Annora allowed the darkness to take her form, leaving her a ghost. The blade sliced harmlessly through her, the metal tugging at her chest, trying to drag her back, but she gritted her teeth and resisted.

Only when the blade passed through her did Sadie stop moving and glance around them.

There wasn't really a transition period. One second they were in the human realm, then next the world around them had gone dark with decay. The pathway was crumbling cement. The trees were just giant skeletons poised to snatch up the unwary. She'd swear that she could see emaciated corpses tangled in the tall branches. Tiny specks floated in the air on a current that tugged at her clothes, asking her to come out and play.

Sadie stumbled away, bringing up her sword, staring at the world around them with fear and awe. "What did you do?"

Black fog whirled next to them as Edgar took shape out of the darkness. He arrived whole, like stepping through a doorway. He glanced at her with a scowl, his fathomless blue eyes whirling with the afterworld. "Get to Camden and go home."

Annora bit her lip, every part of her objecting at leaving him alone with Sadie, alone in the afterworld that held him prisoner for so many years. "No."

"Alcott, what the fuck is going on here?" Sadie stormed toward him.

Annora ghosted through the darkness and appeared next to Edgar, grabbed another of her blades, and stood between them.

Sadie halted, bringing up her weapon, glancing between the two of them, her eyes narrowing. "Alcott?"

Annora snorted, resisting the urge to roll her eyes. "What the hell do you think is happening? We're in the banished lands where you left Edgar to rot all those years ago."

"Impossible." Sadie blanched, her sword wavering and she shook her head. "No one escapes the banished lands once they claim you."

But she glanced around them nervously, as if expecting the boogeyman to appear at any second. She tried to jump, use her powers to escape, only to reappear a second later like she'd smacked into a brick wall. She staggered for balance, her eyes widening in terror. "You stupid girl. Do you have any idea what you've done?

We're trapped."

Annora released a sigh and lowered her weapons. "No, only you are trapped. Now you can't hurt anyone else."

Edgar rested his hand on her shoulder, then gave a squeeze. "Annora."

It wasn't a reprimand.

He was leaving it up to her to decide what to do with Sadie.

She glanced at him over her shoulder with a frown. "She really was your friend?"

Edgar ran a hand over his hair and gave a shrug, suddenly looking tired. "At one time."

Sadie flinched, defeat bowing her shoulders for a second before she straightened and lifted her chin. "I'm trying to save your life, you stupid ass. Don't you see that she's dangerous? She—"

"She rescued me from the banished land," Edgar snapped, a fierce scowl crossing his face. "She's my mate."

Sadie gave a bitter laugh. "She put some sort of spell on you. Called you forth and bound you to her. She—"

"Dammit, Sadie." Edgar marched forward and yanked the sword out her hand. "She's Daxion's daughter. I didn't bring you here. She did."

Sadie's skin took on a green tint, and she staggered back as if struck, glancing back and forth between them. "Impossible. He would never break the laws. He—"

"Annora." Edgar turned away from his former friend, walking toward Annora, his concerned gaze coming to rest on the wound at her hip. "How badly are you hurt?"

Annora touched her wound, her fingers coming away with blood, but the pain barely registered. "Minor."

"You need to heal." Edgar studied the injury, ignoring the way Sadie watched them with narrowed eyes.

"It's not a big deal—"

"There are things in the banished lands that hunger for a taste of someone like you."

Annora glanced around the afterworld, convinced he was shitting her. "I—

"Not to mention if you go back to the house injured, the guys will never let you leave again and your rescue mission will fail." He spoke bluntly, but his eyes were glued to the blood soaking into her pant leg, as if seeing her wounded hurt him in some way.

But he did have a point. If the guys saw she was hurt, they'd never let her leave.

Giving him a nod, she swirled her hand in the air and the dark particles spun at her feet. It twisted up her legs like a snake, weaving around her, before skating up to her hip and licked along the injury, gathering into the wound.

Flesh stitched together in a painful wave, and she sucked in a sharp breath, letting it out as adrenaline surged through her veins. Pleasure and pain twisted together as the wound sealed shut, then even the bruise gradually faded.

"That's not possible." Sadie looked like she'd seen a ghost, staring at Annora like she was a freak.

Edgar inspected the rip in her clothing where the sword cut through, running the tip of his finger gently along the newly healed flesh, the touch on her sensitive skin making her shiver.

Only when he was satisfied did he grunt and straighten. "We need to head back before your men call in the cavalry."

Annora nodded, crossing her arms and cocking her head to the side. "What do we do with her?"

The need to keep her men safe rode her hard and being in the afterworld affected her more than she wanted Edgar to know. It wasn't a threat to her like he seemed to believe…it made her the threat. Breathing in the dark particles made her more volatile and vengeful.

She wanted to leave the bitch there to wander the banished lands the same way she'd left Edgar to suffer alone for all eternity.

As if catching the gleam of her intent in her eyes, Sadie lifted her arm in surrender and carefully crouched and set her sword on the ground. "You can't leave me here."

Sadie glanced at her, then turned to Edgar. "I'm not as strong as you. I won't survive."

Annora studied Edgar, only to see him wince, refusing to meet Sadie's gaze.

The girl closed her eyes, then straightened and lifted her chin.

Despite her moxie, fear lingered around her like a stench that would quickly attract predators.

And Edgar...he would leave his old friend here to rot.

To keep Annora safe.

She didn't give a shit about herself, but she worried what it would do to him if he left Sadie to suffer. "Edgar—"

"No." His head snapped up, and he glared at her. "She tried to kill you. She knows you're my mate and went after you anyway. She doesn't deserve your mercy."

Shame tinged Sadie's expression for the first time, and she spoke, her voice hoarse, barely above a whisper. "I thought I was saving you from a spell she cast over you. I didn't know."

Then her lips thinned, her face hardened and she turned toward Annora. "You need to know being mated is illegal. If they find out, they'll do anything to destroy you both, heir to the dynasty or not."

"But he left that life behind. He—"

"No one leaves...at least not alive. Edgar was the most powerful of us—before you. Because he wants to protect you, he's betrayed his own kind, and they won't easily forgive him." Sadie gave her a bitter smile. "Or you, for being born a half-breed. Daxion might excuse your existence, but never a rogue mating."

"But you breed your people for more power." Annora glanced between the two of them. "I don't understand why this is different."

Sadie gave her a pitying look. "The elders approve each union—a way to ensure they remain in power. They would never approve someone like you...someone they can't control. That's why Alcott was such a threat, why they needed to break him before he could take over. He didn't believe in the old ways. He wanted change." Sadie glanced at Edgar, but he refused to acknowledge her. "Instead of bowing down to them, he walked away, preferring to die in the banished lands than obeying your father."

Guilt over what her father did to Edgar threatened to strangle her.

"Stop it, Sadie. Annora did nothing wrong. She saved me, pulling me out of the afterworld without even knowing what she was doing. She's even stronger than her father...and you know as well as I do that he won't allow her to live unless she's completely under his control."

At the ominous tone, Annora stared at them, waiting for them to elaborate.

Sadie was happy to oblige. "If your father got ahold of you, he could mold you into his image." She turned to Edgar. "He'll break her until she's nothing more than a puppet, ready to dance for him whenever he pleases. If he has her, he will have no need of you." She reached out Edgar pleadingly. When he made no move toward her, she curled her hand into a fist, her arm dropping to her side and a snarl curling her lips. "You know what will happen if he gets control of someone with powers like hers."

Edgar snorted and shook his head. "If you think I'm stubborn, you haven't seen anything yet. I'm a pushover compared to her."

Calculation entered the phantom's eyes. "You'll need to challenge Daxion for his rule. It's the only way if you want to keep each other alive."

"Stop it, Sadie." Edgar slashed his hand through the air. "Stop twisting things to get what you want. Neither one of us want to rule."

Sadie marched up to him and poked him in the chest. "It doesn't matter what you want. We have to do what's best for our people, and our people need you."

"That's not my life anymore. It hasn't been for years. You have to let it go." Edgar pushed her away in disgust.

"Then help me do it." Sadie trailed after him like a persistent pit bull. "You owe—"

"Stop." Annora shoved her way between them, forcing Sadie back a step when she tried to get into his face. "He doesn't owe any of you a damn thing. You tossed him away like trash and didn't even bother to look for him. When he needed you most, you abandoned him."

It was all she could do not to haul back her arm and slug the bitch.

Annora turned away, ready to leave her ass behind in the afterworld.

Sadie called out. "What if I help you get your man back?"

Annora stilled.

She didn't trust Sadie an inch, and certainly not with the safety of her men. If it served her, that bitch would feed them all to the wolves and smile doing it. "You—"

"If she gives her word, she's honor bound to keep it." Edgar interrupted, then reached out, snagging her hand and pulling her close. "Though I don't want her anywhere near you, she might be the key to getting your kitsune out alive."

"But at what cost?" Annora was torn. As much as she wanted Logan back, she would not sacrifice Edgar to do it. She rested her head against his chest, and he pressed his hand against the back of her neck, pulling her fully against him.

"I won't let her touch you," he murmured into her hair.

That was the least of her worries.

"Sadie—"

"You have my word." She answered promptly, a victorious smile breaking across her face.

"And your promise you'll do nothing to harm or bring danger to Annora." Edgar stepped away to glare down at his former friend, nothing but icy disdain in his expression.

Sadie scowled and crossed her arms, looking Annora up and down before giving a defeated sigh. "Agreed."

A silent *for now* echoed between them.

"I'll take you with us when we leave in exchange for your help tonight—"

"Agreed," Sadie snapped, clearly not happy.

"—but I won't help you get us killed." Annora marched toward the girl.

Sadie dropped her arms and tensed, clearly longing for her sword. But instead of backing down, she lifted her chin.

"If you harm Edgar, there is nowhere you can run or hide that I won't find you. Understand?"

Sadie studied Annora, as if testing her resolve, then peered over her head at Edgar, an unreadable expression on her face before she nodded. "Understood."

Annora retreated to stand near Edgar, slipping her hand around the crook of his elbow. "Ready?"

He gazed down at her, his face softening from the imperial lord expression he normally wore. He reached up, brushing a strand of her hair back behind her ear. "I'll follow you anywhere."

When Sadie came near, sword in hand, he looked up, and any bit of warmth vanished from his expression, a clear warning to the other phantom.

Sadie gave a nod, then held out her hand imperiously, as if they were doing her a favor by bringing her back to the human realm.

Annora rolled her eyes, grabbed the girl's sleeve and watched as the world around them shifted and the shadows retreated. Visibility became clearer as the dark particles slowly winked out of existence. The sun hovered on the horizon, light barely stretching across the land as it began to sink. The air felt heavier here, less charged, the world duller.

Just as she released Sadie, Camden came up behind the girl, pressing his bare hand on the back of her neck. The phantom tightened her grip on her sword, only for Camden to clamp his hand around her wrist. They struggled for dominance for a few seconds before Sadie's eyelids fluttered and she dropped to the ground with a heavy thump.

Which left Annora staring at a very pissed-off Camden.

His hair shimmered in the darkness, the iridescent colors always more dominant when he was upset, but it was the scaly diamond pattern imprinted on his skin that gave him away.

He'd come to do war.

He scanned her from head to foot, and she barely stopped herself from fidgeting under his intense gaze. She waited for him to shout or vent his anger, but instead he strode to her side and inspected the now-unblemished skin where she'd been cut.

When she reached for him, he retreated, and a pit opened up in her stomach. He bent, then scooped up Sadie, tossing the girl over his shoulder like she weighed nothing, and laid his hand on her skin, the toxin in his touch keeping the girl from waking.

Annora frowned when he took off toward the house without a word, and she scrambled to catch up with him, not exactly sure what she could do or say to take his rage away. His anger made her anxious, and she hated the bitterly cold distance he was putting between them.

Edgar followed her, giving her a commiserating glance. "Give him time. He doesn't like that you vanished and he was unable to follow.

Men like him don't understand a helplessness like that...they can't bear it."

Annora nodded, feeling dejected.

But Edgar was right. Being helpless destroyed something inside a person.

She gazed at Camden's back, nearly distracted by the delicious flex and pull of muscles as he slipped in and out of the shadows. She winced at the hurt she'd unintentionally inflicted, determined to find a way to make it up to him.

As they entered the house, the guys were already waiting, fully decked out in their battle gear, every one of them looking lethal and intimidating as hell.

And fucking pissed.

She ducked her head and mutely followed Camden into the living room, where he dumped—or more like tossed—Sadie's unconscious body on the couch. When he made to head toward the kitchen, still refusing to acknowledge her, she scowled and stepped into his path.

"What was I supposed to do—let her kill you?" She plopped her hands on her hips, not about to be cowed. "I won't apologize for trying to keep you safe."

To her shock, Camden grabbed her and crushed her to her chest, burying his face in her hair. After a minute, he spoke. "You're my grá. Mine to protect." His grip tightened possessively, and she did the only thing she could...hugged him back. "I know what you did and why, but that doesn't mean I have to like it."

He pulled back, staring down at her, his green eyes devastated at the lack of control he had over his own life since she'd crashed into it. She reached up and cupped his cheek, watching the battle patterns slowly fade away under her touch. "I've never cared enough about a person to worry about them getting their feelings hurt. While I can't always keep myself from harm, I can promise I'll always come back to you...if you promise the same."

Breath exploded from Camden, like Mason just punched him the gut, and he gave her a crooked, broken smile. "Deal. I can't say I'll ever like seeing you in danger, but I know you'll do everything possible to keep yourself safe for us."

Annora placed her hands on his shoulders, dragging them down his chest, then smiled up at him. "We did learn one thing of interest tonight."

He gave her a questioning look.

"Your touch works on phantoms." She lightly scratched her fingernails across his chest, then stood up on her tiptoes and brushed her lips against his. "Logan is right…I was created for you guys."

He let out a tortured groan, and she slipped out of his arms just as he grabbed for her, sauntering out of the room with a grin, loving that she had the ability to throw him a little out of whack. She was conscious of the way his heated eyes followed her and couldn't stop the way her stomach fluttered in anticipation.

Camden needed surprise and love in his life or he was going to suffocate, and she was determined to give it to him.

She entered the kitchen and gazed at Edgar, Mason, and Xander, her determination hardening. She'd come too far, fought too hard, to lose them now. She was made for them, which meant if she had to set the world on fire to keep them safe, she would bring marshmallows and fucking watch it burn.

Chapter Seventeen

As the sun finally set, more and more people showed up at the house, until a veritable army had assembled in the clearing out back. They were waiting for the official call with details about the exchange.

Greenwood was on his phone, his expression thunderous. He turned and faced campus, as if he could see the person on the other end of the call. One hand rested on his hip, fury radiating from every line of his body. He ended the call and slipped the phone into his pocket with a cold, controlled violence that made her shiver.

He paused a moment, then turned toward her. As soon as their eyes met, she knew something bad had happened. As he strode toward her, the guys and a number of the other team leaders followed until they all stood on the back porch.

"A series of attacks is happening around campus." Greenwood barely finished before a bunch of growls erupted from the men. "We have no choice but to investigate. We'll be spread thin, which is no doubt what Erickson intends."

He ran a hand across his jaw, a burning rage hardening his brown eyes, something deadly awakening in them. "I'll take one team with me, and deal with them. I need the rest of you to stay focused." He gave a little rumbling growl, clearly not pleased about being left behind.

The group nodded and began to disband. Annora felt the compulsion he'd hidden in his words, the need to obey tickling along the edges of her mind. She pushed the command away and frowned. "Why you? Why—"

"I can either send out everyone to stop the attacks, or I can go myself." He gave her a self-deprecating grin. "I'm an alpha, strong enough to order most of them to back down without a fight."

Annora didn't want to see him go. A thread of worry tightened around her throat at the thought of her and the guys taking on her uncle and Erickson on their own.

But Greenwood was right. They couldn't do anything when others were in trouble. "I understand. Go."

His troubled brown eyes scanned her face, fondness and worry mixed in his expression. "I promise I'll find you as soon as I'm able."

"Be safe." Annora smiled and watched him walk away, his stride swift and sure, but she very much feared that, despite his vow, he would arrive much too late.

Greenwood collected a few men to accompany him and had a brief exchange with her guys before vanishing into the darkness. From where she stood on the deck, Annora could only watch in awe as the guys took charge like generals, giving instructions to those who remained behind.

Loulou bounced back and forth among the different groups, passing out weapons and coffee in equal measure without batting an eye. The teams who normally patrolled the campus showed up in force, plus a few dozen wolves, a couple of other shifters, along with Willa and a handful of witches.

They each milled about in their own groups, occasionally glancing at each other suspiciously. Loulou tried to get them to mingle, but they only stood in awkward silence. "This is never going to work if they can't even stand next to each other without a fight threatening to break out."

Xander gave her an appraising glance. "Actually, you might be surprised. They might not be a cohesive group like the elite teams, but they each know the part they must play and what will happen if they fail. They've grown up working this way. Trying to force them into a team will only make things more complicated for them."

Annora pursed her lips, and Mason gently patted her shoulder. "They won't do anything to jeopardize your mission. They know what's at stake. All of them have lost someone to Erickson, and they are not a forgiving people."

The guys wandered off to organize the different teams, and Annora struggled not to pace, needing to work off her nervous energy. When Sadie came to stop next to her, she stiffened.

"He would give up everything for you." Sadie watched Edgar instruct the witches, her tone indicating that she thought he was a fool. "A word of advice…fuck what your father wants. He's powerful and ruthless, which doesn't lend to making many friends. He has allies, but the tides can easily change. If you can win over the council, they might allow you to live just so they can subvert your father. They respect power more than anything else."

Then Sadie turned toward her, her tone serious. "But be warned, if your father doesn't think he can control you, he'll see you as nothing but a threat to eliminate."

"And he sent you here to…what? Spy on us? Kill us?" Sadie's sword flashed into her mind, and she snorted at the girl. "You preach about rebellion, but you obey him just like the rest."

Sadie's jaw tightened, and she spoke through gritted teeth. "I do what I must to survive."

"And fuck anyone else who is trying to do the same? Me? Edgar?" Annora shook her head and looked over the sea of people willing to help her. "I don't work like you. I suspect you're the kind of person who believes in something greater than yourself…until it might cost you something. Your rebellion won't go anywhere until the people find someone they believe will sacrifice everything for them." Annora glanced at her, then shook her head. "That person is never going to be you."

Sadie watched Edgar with sad eyes, her shoulders drooping for the first time. "I know. That's why we needed Alcott. Without him, we're doomed. The Daxion line has the ability to control the afterworld to a certain extent, but I've never seen anyone merge with it the way you do.

"The dark matter is what gives us power. Without it, we're vulnerable. Mortal. You're a half-breed, so maybe you can live without it. No phantom would ever give it up willingly."

Without saying anything else, Sadie turned, then halted with her back to Annora. "I never reported back to the council about you or him, but it won't be long before they begin to wonder what's happening, and they'll send someone to investigate sooner rather than later. Your power will only continue to grow if left unchecked, so the longer you can hold out and hide from them, the better chance you'll have to survive."

Then she stalked away.

The knot in Annora's stomach loosened slightly. While she didn't think she could ever be friends with the girl who was supposed to marry Edgar, Sadie wasn't their enemy, not yet. She wanted to support the girl's quest for freedom, but she refused to give up Edgar to make it happen. He was more than a pawn to her, more than a tool to use and discard whenever it suited her, and she would be damned if she'd just stand back and allow them to take him away from her.

A phone rang in the distance, and her attention was immediately drawn toward Terrance. Silence fell across the crowd like a wave, their stillness eerie.

Terrance met her gaze, his brown eyes turbulent as he answered the phone and listened for a few minutes before he hung up. He didn't utter one word the whole time. When he walked toward her, the rest of her guys quickly cut through the crowd to follow. By the time he reached her on the deck, the guys were already at her side.

"They've agreed to the trade. You are to take the book and meet Barnes in Oregon in one hour." Terrance glanced up at her, his gaze troubled. "You're to meet your uncle alone. They want the guys to meet up with Erickson. If they don't show, or if even one of them is missing, Logan will be killed."

Trapping her two fucking states away.

The world around her dropped away as the sound of wind rushed through her ears. It was only when the rest of the people gathered around them began slipping away that Annora was able to shake off the paralysis threatening to drown her.

The air surrounding her was murky, mold creeping across the wood, leaving a rotting, broken corpse of the deck barely standing. Tiny particles danced around her, and she flickered in and out of existence. No matter how hard she concentrated, it was a struggle to remain solid.

Thunderclouds roared overhead and fear flickered across the faces of the gathering crowd. More than a few wolf eyes gleamed back at her. Annora clenched her hands into fists, the sting of her nails biting into her palms calming her just enough for the dust to slowly fall out of the air like rain.

Prem streaked outside, crawling up the wooden post to stand on top of the railing. He stood on his hind legs, reaching out to her, chittering away. She scooped him up in her arms and ran her fingers down his spine, the motion soothing both of them.

She turned toward her guys, noting their worried expressions. Though they wanted to protest her going off on her own, she was thankful that they kept silent.

Then her eyes fell on Edgar and her hand froze mid-stroke as a devious idea began to sparkle at the back of her mind. "Edgar...are you still able to see through Prem?"

Darkness began to gather in his fathomless blue eyes, and a crooked smile crossed his face. "Yes."

Annora turned toward her team, excitement building in her gut. "You guys go. I'll take Prem with me. They don't know what Edgar can do. I'll be monitored the whole time. When I get to the location, you guys can confirm the handoff. If anything goes wrong, Edgar can get to me."

None of the guys liked the plan, but neither could they come up with anything better. The crowd split up into teams and disbanded, the majority going with the guys as backup.

While she and the guys were hoping for a clean exchange, none of them trusted Erickson, so a few of the members would remain behind on campus to keep a watch.

The guys wanted to send a few of the wolves and witches with her as backup, but Annora wasn't sure what the afterworld would do to them. She could travel with the team unharmed because they were her mates, but she had no idea what prolonged exposure would do to anyone else.

She wouldn't risk more people.

The few she pulled into the afterworld previously began to rot almost immediately. She wasn't willing to risk it—not tonight, not when so many other things could go wrong.

The ferret jumped down and scurried under the bench to the edge of the deck. He reached between the railings, wiggled his body, then plucked up something from the ground and jammed it into his mouth, glancing around furtively. When Annora leaned closer to get a better view, she saw a little plate was resting on the ground with a mound of dry cat food waiting.

She glanced at Loulou and Mason, unable to decide which one of them was spoiling him.

Both were likely culprits.

Xander grabbed her arm and dragged her into the house, the rest of the guys following only a step behind. He stopped in the middle of the living room, then began pacing back and forth.

Edgar glanced at the guys, then at her, every inch of him the stubborn lord. "I'll get the book while you say your goodbyes."

Edgar no more than left the room when Xander came to a stop in front of her and crushed her to his chest, squeezing the air out her. "If you run into trouble, get out of there. We'll figure out some other way to get Logan back."

Annora wrapped her arms around him and held him just as fiercely, knowing he was lying to her.

There would be no second chances.

She leaned back enough to look into his teal eyes and noticed the white tips of his hair were standing on end. The air around them stirred, and the sound of huge wings fluttered in her head. Reaching up, she brushed her lips against his. "Come back to me safe."

Without giving him a chance to reply, Mason plucked her from Xander's arms and hauled her against his massive chest. She clung to him, her feet dangling two feet off the ground. The troll practically vibrated with energy, the need to destroy their enemies riding him hard. Annora reached up and brushed her fingers along the wild mass of pink hair. Static crackled under her touch as the strands of his hair swayed toward her, curling around her fingers and brushing gently across her palm in a caress. "Be careful out there, big guy. You're not indestructible. I want you back in one piece, you hear?"

The only reply was a rumble, his beast in too much control for him to speak beyond a word or two. He lowered her gently to the floor, then slipped a finger under her chin and tipped her head back, clearly asking the same from her, and she nodded. "I promise."

Seemingly satisfied, he turned and left...leaving her alone with Camden.

"I'll get him back for you." He stood with his legs spread, his eyes hard, every inch of him the imposing commander.

Knowing he wouldn't touch her of his own accord, she went into his arms and rested her head on his chest. "Please don't do anything foolish."

He laughed almost silently, then kissed the top of her head before pushing her away. "I could say the same thing to you."

Annora pursed her lips, unable to argue, then she thrust out her hand. "Let's make a pact...we both promise to do whatever it takes to make it home alive."

There was only a slight hesitation as he slipped his hands into hers, but instead of shaking her hand, he brought it up to his lips, kissing the back of it lightly, looking at her over the top. "Deal."

Footsteps sounded in the kitchen, and Camden pulled away, then glanced up as Edgar entered the room. Camden tugged on her hair, giving her a nod. "I'll leave you to say goodbye."

Then he was gone.

Edgar stood with the book in his hand, looking slightly startled as she approached. Nerves fluttered in her gut, and she dug her thumbnail into her fingertips to give her courage. Instead of saying anything, she grabbed his arm and led him into the living room. "Sit."

He did as instructed, leaning back on the couch, his posture rigid, like he didn't know how to relax. The book lay forgotten next to him. She stepped between his splayed knees and cupped his face. Thanks to her being so short, there were only a few inches separating them.

Even sitting there was an elegance to him, an effortless self-awareness she envied. She smoothed her palms along the sharp angles of his face, his pale skin cool and smooth to the touch as she learned the contours. While he appeared only a few years older than herself, his eyes showed he'd weathered hardship that would've destroyed lesser men, and his jaw had a stubborn angle to it.

Then her gaze settled on his lips. They were generous, if a bit hard, and she gently scraped her fingernail over them. With a hum of appreciation and lust, he studied her with pure joy and possessiveness shining from his eyes. The afterworld swirled in the dark blue depths until she could get lost in them.

"I'm going to kiss you now, but I want you to know why first." She stopped caressing him, surprised to find curbing the impulse was one of the hardest things she'd ever had to do. This was too important for him to be distracted. "This isn't because you're a phantom, or because you saved my life, and certainly not because you've claimed we're mates."

She felt him flinch at the last one and tightened her grip by sliding her palm to the back of his head and combing her fingers into his midnight hair. "I'm going to kiss you because you're a man who has always had my back. At times, you've been my best friend—other times, a giant pain in my ass."

She leaned forward, resting her forehead against his, not sure he was even breathing as he watched her. "I'm going to kiss you because I'm falling in love with you. You're mine, whether I'm ready to admit it to myself or not."

His breath left him in a whoosh, and she tightened her grip on him when he reached for her, needing to maintain the distance between them in order to get out what needed to be said. "What that means is you don't get to sacrifice yourself or foolishly put yourself in harm's way. You need to return to me, safe and whole, or you'll shatter something inside me that can never be fixed. I don't need you as a fighter or a protector anymore, I need you in order to be able to live. Do you understand me?" She dropped her hands to his shoulders and shook him for good measure.

He scanned her face, his expression both fierce and vulnerable. His hands came to rest on her hips, his grip almost brutal in his hunger. "Then prove it. Kiss me."

She leaned down, closing the distance between them. Her lips barely brushed against his when he wrapped his arms around her and scooped her off her feet. She gave a startled squeak when he twisted and deposited her on the couch under his delicious weight. He took control of the kiss like he'd been dying for the taste of her, nibbling and licking and destroying her every thought but him.

She ran her nails down his back, then groaned when he arched into her. He pulled away, going only so far as to leave a gap of a few inches between them so he could gaze down at her. "Mine."

It wasn't spoken possessively, but with such heart-wrenching wonder that her breath hiccupped in her chest. She reached up and ran her fingertips along his cheek, unable to smile up at him, too many emotions clogging her throat. "Yes. Yours. That's why you'll come back to me."

He gave her a captivating smile that lit up his whole face, making him look devastatingly handsome and incredibly young. "I will always come back to you."

When she opened her mouth to protest, he sighed, then leaned down and kissed the tip of her nose. "I promise to take the utmost care of myself...if for no other reason than the chance to kiss you again."

Annora gave him a sharp nod. "Excellent."

He snorted, then sat back, giving her a hand to pull her upright, the amused gleam in his eye indicating he knew she'd manipulated him, but he didn't give a fuck, not if it meant getting exactly what he wanted—her.

As she straightened her rumpled clothing, his humor melted away and he leaned down, picked up the book and handed it to her. When she went to grab it, he didn't release his grip.

"The book is bound to you." He released his hold, tapping the cover. "What that means is it will always find its way back to you. Your uncle won't be able to access the spells anymore, and neither will anyone else. The more you use it, the more the spells will adapt to you."

"So the book will be safe if I have to hand it over?" Annora hugged it to her chest, concerned what other people would try to do if they got their hands on the spells. She'd rather destroy it than allow it to fall into the wrong hands again.

Edgar glanced out the window and nodded. "If they take it, you should be able to simply walk into the afterworld and find it waiting."

Relief poured through her, and she tightened her grip on the book, ridiculously pleased to know she literally couldn't lose her last connection to her mother. Her mother had handpicked the spells for her, because she thought Annora would need them. Annora only wished she had more time to go through them, time to look for a solution where no one would get hurt.

She gave him a crooked smile and patted his chest. "Thank you."

He reached up and grabbed her wrist, pressed her hand to his chest over his heart, then glanced out the window, his face hardening. "I'll keep watch over you. If you call for me, I will come."

Then he was gone, striding out to join the others. Annora took a deep breath and followed.

They were going to do this.

They were going after her childhood boogeyman and finally find a way to destroy the fucker so he couldn't touch her or anyone else again.

As the groups began to get into their vehicles, Sadie approached her, her expression both unsure and annoyed. "Where do you want me?"

Annora hadn't been sure the girl would actually keep her word. "I believe the guys are walking into a trap. Will you watch their backs and protect them?"

Sadie glanced at her sharply. "Why not just go in and kill your enemy? Between you and Alcott—"

"Edgar," Annora snapped and glared at the girl.

Sadie sighed heavily and crossed her arms. "Between you and *Edgar*, you can be in and out in seconds."

"Not all paranormals are stupid—they'll have an army waiting for us." Annora was annoyed at the girl for being so heartless, not sure she wanted to know more about phantoms if they were all like her. "Besides, they're holding one of my men. I won't leave him behind."

"So you'd rather put the rest of your mates in danger instead?" Sadie gave her a disapproving look and shook her head, completely baffled.

Instead of being offended, Annora gave her a pitying look. "You never leave family behind."

"They can't be allowed access to the afterworld," Sadie warned, then strode away.

Annora watched her and didn't have to wonder what would happen if she was taken.

Sadie would find and kill rather than let her power fall into the wrong hands.

Terrance took the steps up the deck two at a time, holding his phone out for her, the front displaying a picture of trees. "He said you should be able to find this place."

"Is Kevin—"

"He's okay for now." But Terrance looked worried, frown lines leaving deep grooves between his eyes.

"We'll get him out," Annora promised, but felt helpless as she watched the vehicles start to pull out onto the road, her skin itching at the idea of them fighting without her to watch over them.

Terrance nodded absently at her bullshit reply, knowing she couldn't promise him anything of the sort.

Her team milled about their vehicle in deep discussion, then gathered the maps off the hood. As they opened the doors to the SUV, they paused and glanced at her. None of them looked happy to be leaving.

She didn't blame them one bit.

Camden gave her a nod, a silent promise that he wouldn't let her down. Mason and Xander both watched her, as if committing her to memory, and she found herself stepping toward them to beg them not to go.

But when she opened her mouth, nothing came out.

They seemed to understand and ducked inside the truck. Terrance and Sadie were the last to enter, both of them crawling in the back. In less than a minute, they were gone.

Loulou stopped with one foot on the bottom step to the deck and gazed up at her. "They know what they're doing. They'll be fine."

But Annora could see the concern in the rabbit's too-large blue eyes. "Lionel will be fine. He won't let anything happen to himself, not when he's just found you."

"I know." Loulou's laugh came out as a sob, and she gave Annora a broken smile, rubbing her chest as if to ease the ache. She released a long, slow breath, then her blue eyes hardened. "When do you leave?"

"Now." Prem tugged at her pant leg, and Annora scooped him up, then grabbed the bag resting on the bench and opened it for him. Once he was settled inside, she eased the book in next, careful not to squish Prem, and slipped it over her shoulder.

"You can do this." Loulou looked her up and down, nodding her approval, then gave her a savage smile. "Now go kick some ass."

Chapter Eighteen

Annora glanced back at the house, the home now just an empty shell with the guys gone. The chill of it nipped at her, and she turned away, unable to remain there a second longer without them.

Prem pulled himself out of the backpack and rubbed his head soothingly along her neck. She reached up and scratched him between the ears. "What say we finish this once and for all?"

He bobbed his little head, brushing his head along her jaw, then patted her with a tiny paw before he popped back into the bag. Tugging Terrance's phone out of her pocket, she slid her thumb across the surface to unlock it. A picture of a bunch of trees in the middle of fucking nowhere popped up on the screen.

She'd never tried to travel so far, nor to a place she'd never been.

She wasn't sure if it was even possible.

Thankfully, the guys didn't know or they never would've agreed to the plan.

Since neither Edgar nor Sadie objected, it was something she should be able to do.

She just had to figure out how.

No problem.

Annora hesitantly reached for the afterworld, knowing that

touching it again so soon could draw the attention of her father.

Then she hardened her resolve.

She would be damned if she would allow him to take her, at least not before she got Logan back.

Hopefully her ability to remain camouflaged would hold out just a while longer.

Dark particles began to swirl around her, the wind more of a caress as it swirled around her. She brought up the phone and concentrated on the image. But instead of her entering the afterworld, the ground beneath her feet vanished and she fell through darkness, her stomach surging up into her throat.

There was a bright flash of light a second before she smacked against the ground so hard she lost her breath. She lay there stunned, her face planted in the dirt, and she used the pain to push herself up on her hands and knees.

Only to take a blow to the ribs that sent her flying.

As she rolled, her bag was ripped away from her, and she got the image of giant trees and fresh air before she smacked so hard into a tree trunk, her spine cracked ominously. Gritting her teeth, she pushed herself upright and lifted her head to see her uncle standing over her. He swung a bat absently while he studied her, his expression smug.

"I told him you'd show." He sauntered closer, then slammed his boot into her face and her head slammed against the ground, hitting so hard it bounced.

Annora growled and glared up at him, but the fucker knew that she couldn't—wouldn't—retaliate, not until she knew Logan was safe.

Which meant she was at his mercy until the guys completed the deal.

Fucking hell.

Memories of the past tortures flashed through her mind. Instead of giving into the fear, she gritted her teeth and spit out a mouthful of blood before smiling up at him. "Hello, Uncle."

He narrowed his eyes down at her, hating when she reminded him they were related. He tightened his grip on the baseball bat, winding up, and she chuckled. "Are we really going to do this again?"

Ignoring the grinding of bones, she pushed herself to her feet, using the pain to give her strength. The world tipped as her vision blurred and doubled before it righted itself. She staggered sideways to catch her balance, fighting to keep nausea from dropping her back to her knees. At the bare minimum, she had a concussion, maybe a fractured skull, not to mention a few broken ribs that ground together every time she moved.

Unwilling to give away how much stronger she'd gotten since they last met, she fought back the darkness, only allowing it to lick at her wounds. Which didn't mean she was giving in to his shit. She had to buy the guys some time. She tipped her head from side to side, bones crunching as she stared her uncle down.

Pissed that he couldn't bend her to his will, he swung the bat.

Annora caught it quickly, literally feeling the bones in her hand shatter. The flash of pain streaked up her arm, but she refused to release her hold. Darkness spiraled around the bat, eager to take a bite out of the bastard.

When his eyes widened with alarm, she yanked down hard on the bat, nearly jerking her uncle off his feet. It startled him enough that he released his hold and stumbled back.

Her bones snapped back into place, scalding heat melding the ragged edges back together, and she grinned at him.

A flash of fear crossed his face, which of course pissed him off more, and he narrowed his eyes. "No more games." He turned toward the trees and yelled, "Take her."

Half a dozen wolves emerged from the shadows, their eyes hard and determined.

And Kevin was one of them.

She gave him a hard look but couldn't tell if he was on her side or not. When he gave a small shake of his head, relief rushed through her, and she forced herself to concentrate on the others so she wouldn't give Kevin away. The wolves were young, maybe her age, with a feral and hungry look to them. Knowing she was outnumbered and about to get her ass handed to her, she flipped the bat and caught the handle.

As the wolves crowded closer, her uncle's attention fell to her bag.

Or more precisely, the edge of the book sticking out of it.

When he took a step toward it, she countered, and the wolves leapt between them. Her uncle gave her a sly smile as he stooped and picked up the backpack. He slipped his hand inside...only to yank it out a second later with a curse. The bag dropped to the ground with a thump, and he shook out his hand, glaring at her as drops of blood splattered around him.

Prem leaped out of the bag, and charged toward her, dodging her uncle as he tried to stomp on the little critter. She could finally breathe after the ferret scampered out of range. "I'm going to roast that filthy animal alive and make you watch."

Menace gave his eyes an unholy gleam.

He would do it, too.

She wouldn't put it past her uncle to eat Prem in front of her either.

The wolves didn't react to the ferret, just watched him scurry past. Though she wanted to scoop him up and keep him safe, she needed her arms free to fight. As if understanding, Prem zoomed up a tree and stood on the branch above her head like her very own guardian angel, chittering and waving his little paws like mad...almost as if he was telling them to fuck off.

Annora couldn't stifle the smile that broke across her face.

But when she turned toward her uncle, the humor vanished when she saw him grinning. "I've missed you. The past few days almost felt like old times. Too bad your little kitsune didn't hold up as well as you under the beatings. Disappointing, really. I was just getting started with him." He shook his head, his grin turning menacing. "It's a pity you couldn't have joined us to see how quickly I was able to break him."

Everything inside her went icy with rage. Darkness swarmed her until she nearly choked on it. The forest around them thickened with shadows, blocking out the evening sun, cocooning them in their own world. The darkness slowly stretched toward her, slithering through the trees, seeking prey. The wolves shifted restlessly as they watched the change, the temperature around them dropping twenty degrees in seconds. A few looked nervous, some impervious, while one or two retreated a few paces.

She grunted when her flesh wounds knitted together much too fast, the pain like she'd swallowed fire, until even the tips of her hair ached. She swallowed the agony and locked her knees, refusing to show weakness in front of them.

Kevin edged slightly away from the others, angling himself closer to her. His presence reminded her why they were there…to rescue Logan.

She sent a mental demand to Edgar, telling him not to come, then allowed the darkness to cut them off from the outside world completely, before Edgar had a chance to protest.

She couldn't release her wrath, not yet, not until her uncle gave the signal to release Logan.

Annora swallowed down the rage that wanted to rampage and destroy, feeling it burn through her like acid. Little bits of black smog seeped out of her, weaving between her fingers like a pet eager to be let loose to hunt.

Dark particles kicked up around her feet, like she'd stepped into a pile of black flour. It gusted up in the air, tugging at her clothes, until it was a struggle to hold her form.

Her uncle was oblivious, running his hand over the cover of the grimoire like it was made of pure gold, his eyes gleaming with greed. Feeling his polluted touch like it was running down her spine, it was as all she could do not to go over there and rip it away from him, feeling his.

"If all you wanted was the book, why did you even bother with me?" She would much rather have been abandoned in a ditch somewhere than grow up under his poisonous ministrations.

He glared at her, pure, venomous hatred simmering under the surface. "The grimoire was supposed to be mine. I was born with the ambitions in the family. Unfortunately, my sister got all the magical talent. She squandered her abilities, creating stupid trinkets and charms when she could've been moving up through the ranks in the coven.

"She could've run the damned thing, but the stupid bitch spread her legs for your father and got pregnant." A sneer twisted his face. "A one-night stand ruined her life. She left the coven as soon as she learned about you, threw it all away for you, you little brat."

He began pacing, his gestures ragged and jerky. "When she disappeared, the coven threw me out." He stopped abruptly and gave her a nasty smile. "Imagine my surprise when I got a call from her a decade later asking for my help. The cancer had ravaged her body, sucking away nearly all her magic. If she'd been in her right mind, she would've seen through my ruse, but she was so desperate to keep you safe, she gave me custody."

His nasty laugh sent goosebumps racing over her skin, and Annora struggled not to run from his caustic rant, knowing she wasn't going to like what he said next.

"But she was taking too fucking long to die. Two weeks after I arrived, I waited for you to go to school and smothered her in bed." His face darkened as he glared at her, spittle flying as he spoke. "Only to have the damned grimoire vanish."

Vague memories rose in her mind of him ripping apart their meager apartment, destroying everything in his path. Annora shivered, her body becoming heavy as she remembered coming home from school…and the beating that greeted her.

"It took me close to a week to realize you had the damned thing the whole time. At the first spill of your blood, the coloring book you carried around changed." He clutched the book tighter to his chest. "Your blood was the key."

"But then like an idiot, you lost it again, didn't you?" Annora strode closer to him, only to have the wolves stiffen and growl.

Rage darkened his face. "How was I to know it would vanish?! I ripped out three pages, and the fucking thing disappeared like a wounded animal. All I had left were three spells and a useless brat."

Hatred oozed from his glare, and she shivered from memories of his fists and her childhood conviction that it was all her fault rose like a ghost out of its crypt. The beating was incidental, a way to work off his fury, blow after blow pulverized her small bones, splattering blood with every hit.

It was the first time she died and came back.

"Imagine my surprise when I discovered you can heal, that you're special, but you fought me every step of the way, like your bitch of a mother. It was only when Erickson showed an interest in you that I realized just how special and started selling your…services." He gave a delighted laugh. "You were a fucking gold mine...when you cooperated."

His brown eyes sparkled with glee as he smiled. "With the book, I can take what I want. You'll finally learn your place and do what I say. And I'll finally have the power I deserve—all I need is your blood."

The wolves inched closer, practically salivating with a predatory urge to rip her apart.

"Wait." Her uncle held up his hand, then dug his phone out of his pocket and gave her a nasty smile. "I want you to hear them slaughter your friends first."

Her breathing stalled in her chest when she heard the phone ring.

"Erickson." The phone was full of static, dropping in and out.

"I got it." Her uncle met her gaze and grinned maliciously. "Kill them."

She snapped.

It was time to even the odds.

She allowed the afterworld to swirl to life inside her, the darkness demanding retribution. She gave her uncle a sinister smile, allowing every bad thing he'd ever done to her to fuel her rage. "I learned a few tricks of my own while away."

She allowed the afterworld to swallow her whole and stepped through the doorway to stand next to her uncle, then swung the bat with all her might.

Her uncle stumbled back, barely ducking in time to avoid having his head removed, lifting up his arm to protect himself and the wooden bat struck his hand instead. The satisfying crack of bones reached her ear, and she grinned at his scream. The phone shattered, tiny pieces of metal, glass and plastic flying in all directions.

Her uncle cursed and cradled his broken hand to his chest, smearing more of his blood on the grimoire cover. Instead of fear, he glared at her in defiance. "You can't kill me, not if you want to survive."

"Ah, but I've learned a thing or two while away, my dear, sweet uncle." She smiled as the first spark of alarm tinged his face. She lifted the bat again and took a step toward him. "Shall I show you?"

He stumbled away, glaring at the wolves, his squeaky voice

trembling with rage. "Don't just stand there. Kill her."

The wolves leapt forward as one.

At the last second, Kevin twisted, taking down two of them…leaving her with three.

Then Prem dropped down on one of the wolves aiming for her, landing on his head like some demented fur trader hat of old come back to life to seek revenge. The wolf shook his head violently, but Prem hung firm to his hair, his little claws gouging the wolf's face and sinking them into the gooey whites of the guy's eyes, and the wolf bellowed in pain, groping for the ferret as he spun in a dizzying circle.

Then she had no more time to watch because the other two wolves were upon her.

She swung the bat, cracking the first wolf across his temple. Wood shattered, sending splinters flying in every direction. Little shards bit into her flesh, peppering her face and arms. Ignoring the pain, she watched the wolf drop like a hunk of meat and skid across the forest floor a few feet before coming to a complete stop.

He remained unmoving.

These wolves didn't seem to be able to heal as fast as they would normally.

Before she had time to think, claws raked down her spine, ripping into her flesh, and she hissed in pain. She whirled, the claws slicing deeper before they were torn free of her body. She gritted her teeth, feeling rivulets of blood trickling down her spine as she faced the older wolf.

He bared his teeth, fangs gleaming as he leapt to rip out her throat.

Annora lifted her arm, and his teeth clamped down over it, biting with enough force to snap her bones again. Instead of dropping to her knees from the overload of pain, she brought up what remained of the broken bat and rammed the ragged edges straight into his chest.

A garbled howl caught in his throat, his eyes widened in shock, then their light dimmed, and his jaw went slack. As he dropped to the ground, he dragged her with him. She struggled to disengage his fangs from her arm, ripping flesh in her haste, when the last wolf charged her. His face had been peeled away like a medical cadaver, leaving behind strings of mangled tendons and shredded muscles.

She fell backwards and rammed her foot directly into his throat.

Bones crunched under the impact.

Claws dragged down her leg, leaving deep grooves in her flesh before he staggered back, grabbing at his own shattered throat as he struggled to breathe. Annora dragged herself to her feet and saw Kevin barely holding his own against the other two wolves.

Without the drugs or his enhanced shifter strength, they were slowly whittling him down, chunks of flesh and blood flying with each blow. He wasn't going to make it if she didn't help.

From the corner of her eyes, she saw her uncle take off into the woods in the opposite direction...and Prem racing after him in his loping gait, his furry little body matted with blood.

She skidded to a halt, the need to go after them like a craving, and she hated herself for hesitating.

Then Kevin shouted. "Go. I got this."

The sour taste of his lie hung in the air.

She had no choice.

He would die if she left him.

She turned toward Kevin and yelled, "Run!"

He gave her a startled look, taking a fist to the face. Shaking off the effects, he hesitated a moment longer before darting off into the woods like a shot. The wolves started to go after him—until Annora whistled sharply. "You go after him, you lose me."

The wolves hesitated, instincts demanding they hunt down their wounded prey. They sniffed the air, then turned toward her as if scenting her delicious blood, their eyes gleaming yellow and glittering with hunger. Fangs hung out of their mouths, their jaws misshapen, like they had too many teeth crammed inside.

Razor-sharp claws tipped their fingers, their arms too long and hanging awkwardly from their shoulders. Their hair receded, their foreheads shrinking, the bones of their faces crunching, while their flesh bubbled up from their skulls, like they were shifting in slow motion.

Annora stood her ground while they charged. She lifted her hand, blood dripping down her arm, and gave them a happy wave and smile. When they hesitated, exchanging a confused look, she released her stranglehold over the afterworld, doing her best to keep it from chasing after Kevin.

It burst into life around her, quickly eating up the forest floor and spreading like a dark plague through the trees. The temperature plummeted until the werewolves' breath fogged the air. Dark particles swirled on an invisible current, tugging playfully at her in welcome.

The sun had vanished, a bluish tinge taking over the world until the woods appeared haunted. The clearing turned gloomy, the trees broken and decayed, the leaves drifting to the ground, only to disintegrate on impact.

Her injuries were slower to heal, like she'd used all her energy to merge the two worlds, and her blood slowly dripped to the forest floor. She ignored the pain, her body numb to it, and she used the adrenaline to keep moving.

The shadows crept ever closer, and the wolves backed away, as if sensing the wrongness to it. Dark strands of fog crept closer, and the wolf she hit with the bat roused slightly, as if detecting danger. The shadows curled around him, and he screamed in terror.

He crawled toward her, claws gouging into the earth, but it was too late.

The shadows grabbed his leg and yanked him into the blackness of the trees beyond. He clawed at the ground, leaving deep ruts in the dirt, and his primal shriek of fear echoed through the trees like a dinner bell as more shadows streaked after him.

Only for his voice to vanish in a gurgle of death.

What the fuck?!?

Something was in the trees with them.

Something from the afterworld.

She edged away, cursing herself for not listening to Edgar when he tried to warn her.

The two remaining wolves scattered, their fight or flight response clearly stuck on the 'screw this shit' category. Not wanting to wait around for whatever it was to come back, she grabbed her backpack and hurried after her uncle.

Prem chirped from a tree, then waved a paw in the direction her uncle took. She reached up, scooping him in her arms, a sound of distress catching in her throat when he whimpered and curled around her. She grabbed the darkness and pushed it toward him, only for it to splash uselessly against him and drift to the ground like dust. He grabbed her finger and brushed his tiny hand against it, as if to say it was okay, and her heart shattered.

He was dying.

And she knew this time, there was no coming back.

Not willing to give up on him, she wove together a tiny blanket of darkness until the particles trapped inside began to sparkle with power. Edgar said he ran more on her power than his. If that was true, what healed her should also fix him. She hoped. She wrapped it around him carefully before slipping the now-unconscious critter into the afterworld, praying that he would heal and come back to her.

The need to seek out her uncle and dance on the mangled flesh and bones of his dead body roared through her.

It didn't take long to catch him. The stupid asshole was still plunging blindly through the forest, making enough noise to attract the dead. She quickly followed his path, hearing him curse even before she saw him trying to untangle himself from a thicket.

"Hello, Uncle dear."

He startled so badly he nearly fell back into the thicket when he whirled. When he saw it was her, anger darkened his face. "What the fuck did you do?"

"What?" Annora crossed her arms and raised an eyebrow. "You don't want to see where you'll end up after you die?"

It was like she'd kicked him in the balls, his eyes practically bulging out of their sockets as he scanned the darkness surrounding them.

"Lies!" But he didn't sound too sure of himself. "If you try to kill me, you'll only die yourself."

She couldn't stop the chuckle that bubbled up. "But Uncle, thanks to your tender care, I welcome death. There is nothing here for me to fear." She glanced at the fog that swirled around them, then back at him. "Besides, I have no need to kill you. You'll do that yourself."

The stench of his terror polluted the air. Shadows began to churn behind him, a form slowly taking shape. Then another. And another. The phantoms here were different—like the life had been drained out of them, leaving behind only their ghostly forms.

Then understanding dawned.

They were the banished.

The weak.

Without anything to tether them to the human world, they became nothing but shadows.

This world was what had terrified Edgar.

She remembered how they dragged off the wolf, and she wasn't sure if Edgar had been more worried about becoming one of them or being consumed by them.

As if seeing her looking over his shoulder, her uncle spun, then clutched the book closer to his chest, backing away from the new threat.

One of the shadows spilled across the floor like tentacles, the fog seeking out its prey. It slowly grew taller and taller, until the vaporous form of a man appeared, his face whisking in and out of reality like a ghost.

One moment he looked like a normal man, then his face would flicker until she saw what looked like his skeleton beneath, before he ultimately turned transparent once more.

Like his body couldn't hold its form.

He glanced at the book, then turned toward her, his expression softened. "You are as beautiful as your mother."

She opened her mouth, then closed it, her throat too tight to speak. She wet her lips and tried again, taking a step toward him. "You knew my mother?"

He gave her a broken smile and shrugged. "She was trying to help my brother. It was how we met."

Her world tilted on its axis.

This was how her mother met her father. It wasn't some random accident.

When her uncle turned and scurried into the woods, she narrowed her eyes and moved to go after him.

"Leave him," the specter said. "You did your job by getting him here. We'll take care of the rest. He won't escape, or hurt you, ever again."

Annora froze at the ominous tone, and she carefully looked at the man who was her uncle, then lifted her chin mutinously. "Are you going to kill me, too?"

She had too much shit to do before she died.

She couldn't leave the guys to fight alone.

They would never forgive her.

The specter shook his head slowly and turned to glance toward where her uncle had disappeared. As if it was a signal, her uncle's piercing scream of terror rent the air. A pleased smile twisted his face when he turned back toward her. Then his eyes turned sad. He lifted a chain over his head, the gold coin dangling from the end spinning wildly, the glints of light reflecting off it making it appear to glow.

"This isn't a safe place for you. You've stayed too long already. The phantoms are going to be coming for you soon." He carefully held out the chain for her. "Take this. It will protect you."

She held out her hand. When he set the chain in her palm, she half expected it to fall straight through. Instead the metal was bitterly cold, searing into her skin, and she curled her fingers around it. The phantom smiled down at her, like she just passed some sort of test. When he turned to go, she reached toward him. "Wait."

He hesitated, then glanced back at her over his shoulder, a brow quirked in question.

She chewed on her lip for a moment, eyeing the only relative she had left who didn't seem to hate her. She had so many questions to ask. "What's your name?"

"You may call me Valen." Then he disintegrated before her eyes. The dark particles blasted toward her, and she lifted her arms and staggered backwards as the tiny grains of sand pelted her. A brilliant light blazed behind her closed eyelids, the heat chilling her cold flesh, much like the spell she'd cast back at the house.

When she lowered her arms, the light was gone, taking any hint of the other realm with it, as if it banished the magic used to merge the two worlds.

She blinked at the change, swaying as she struggled to stay upright, blood loss making her dizzy. Though her wounds had sealed shut, they hadn't healed completely. Inviting the shadows into the human world created more like a dead zone, sucking the energy out of her instead of invigorating her the way they did when she opened a doorway to the afterworld.

She noticed the chain dangling from her fist, and slowly uncurled her fingers to see a gold coin shimmering in the night air. She carefully lifted it over her head, then groaned when her body protested such a simple move.

Like a craving, she wanted to slip into the afterworld and heal, but she was afraid of what she would find.

More specters?

Did they inhabit the afterworld?

Why show themselves now?

Did that mean her camouflage was well and truly gone?

She couldn't access the afterworld and take the risk that she'd end up trapped or worse, hunted by her father.

A branch snapped behind her, and Annora whirled, bracing herself for an attack.

Only to have Kevin walk out of the woods, his face grim. He glanced around them, but everything appeared normal, the unnatural silence loud in her ears.

"They never had any intention of releasing you or the book." He hurried toward her side, more of a limping gait than a walk, scanning her for injuries and frowning. "You look like hell."

She snorted, then waved a hand to indicate his nearly-destroyed body. Without his healing abilities, she wasn't sure how he was still standing. "You're one to talk."

He grimaced, then triumphantly held up his hand, revealing a small stone the size of a quarter resting in the center of his palm. "I have the spell to get us back to the base…only I'm not sure taking you back in your current state would be wise. You would be more of a distraction than a help."

"I could say the same about you." Annora narrowed her eyes at Kevin, feeling defensive. "I'm going, with or without you. If we go together at least we can keep an eye on each other."

The guys needed her. She refused to let them fight without her, and her determination to not be left behind hardened into resolve.

One way or another, she would find her way back to her men.

The darkness inside her was almost depleted, whisking up weakly at her probe. It licked at her wounds, healing her slowly, just enough to stop the internal bleeding, but not enough to knit her fractured bones.

Kevin huffed under his breath, knowing that he was getting played. Neither of them was willing to stay behind, not when the only people who mattered to them were in danger. "Deal—but promise you'll find me a nice burial site when your guys learn that I allowed you to go into battle injured and kill me for it."

"I would, but they'll no doubt bury me next to you after they wring my neck." Annora grinned at him, bouncing on her feet, ignoring the way her body protested. "Let's do this. All of this will have been for nothing if something happens to them."

Kevin nodded, then held the stone aloft. "You better not get yourself killed."

He twisted his wrist, dropping the stone to the ground. He crushed his boot against it, the fragile material shattering under his heel. Glass cracked, blasting out a weird green powder in a two-foot circle, surrounding them like it had been held under pressure. The smell of black licorice filled her senses as the green substance soaked into the earth. The ground beneath them turned spongy, and the world dropped away as they were sucked down into what felt like a whirlpool of molasses.

Chapter Nineteen

Logan woke to complete darkness, struggling for air, groggy and disoriented. The last thing he remembered was eating some gruel that was more water than food. It tasted like ass.

Son of a bitch!

They put something in his food.

He should've been suspicious, since they only tossed him scraps when they felt like it, but his beast had been so starved, the food was down his throat before he even thought about it.

He tried to twist, only to discover his arms and legs were hog-tied.

His breathing turned ragged at the thought of being trapped, gasping like the air was getting thin.

It didn't matter that he knew it was all in his head, that there was plenty of oxygen, he just couldn't seem to suck in any of it.

The past week had fucked him up far beyond what was done to his damaged body. Even now blood leaked from various wounds, leaving him lying in a sticky, crusted pool.

As he fought against the ropes, his broken ribs ground together, and he hissed in pain. He struggled against the urge to remain still, allow the pain to fade, but one thought filled him with determination—they were coming for him.

She was coming for him.

He blinked away tears at the thought of seeing her again.

His Annora.

A twinge of worry niggled at the back of his brain—what would she see when she looked at him?

He wasn't the same man.

He was broken.

Damaged.

He'd survived hell with his pack, but this was so much worse.

He shuddered when he realized he'd barely lasted a week before going out of his ever-loving mind. He was at the point he'd do anything to make the pain go away.

He couldn't comprehend how she'd survived years.

Alone.

With no hope of rescue.

His heart broke at what she had endured just to survive.

If only he'd known, he would've come for her in a heartbeat.

He trembled, adrenaline shooting through him at the thought of her coming for him, and he was determined she wouldn't find him trussed up like a damned turkey ready to be served. He had to figure a way out and find her.

His arms actually ached at the thought of holding her close.

He shook his head—first he'd kiss her, then hold her, and never let her go.

He needed to let her know she meant everything to him.

Gritting his teeth against the pain, he twisted and rolled onto his numb hands, making them feel like he'd stuck them in a woodchipper. With each move, the scabs crusted along his back from his last whipping just hours before broke open, and fresh blood spilled. He wanted to rage and fight, but he couldn't help but tremble when he thought of the punishment they'd inflict if he managed to escape and they caught him.

Only one thing snapped him out of his paralysis.

Annora was waiting for him.

He would never go back to that cell. He couldn't. He wouldn't survive.

He was already becoming conditioned by the pain.

How to avoid it.

Ways to please his captors so he wouldn't be hurt again.

The fear was like being wrapped in barbed wire. He couldn't help wondering if he was already too damaged, worrying that she wouldn't want him back…that he would fail her when she needed him most. With each thought, his doubts sent the barbed wire burrowing deeper.

He fought against it.

Only one thing was more basic than fear—his need to see her again. She was like air. Without her, he would drown in the pain. Only the image of them together when this was over allowed him to hold onto hope.

He could do this…he could escape…just for the chance to see her again.

Blowing out a shaky breath, he pushed through the pain and explored the area where they'd dumped him.

Small.

Cramped.

His brain was struggling to understand the sensory information.

It was the scent of oil and gas that gave it away.

He was in the fucking trunk of a car.

As his senses returned to him in fits and starts, he heard yelling and the sounds of battle.

The guys had arrived.

They came for him.

He inhaled sharply as hope burned bright, a sob of laughter catching in his throat.

Time to leave.

He grabbed the last spark of energy he'd been saving and called his kitsune. The way he was bound would ensure he would be turned inside out if he tried to shift. If he would even be able to change…his beast was beyond tired.

He needed to get the ropes off.

As he called on his beast, the fox lifted his dark head sluggishly, then gave a small nod at his plea and closed his eyes.

A spark of fire snapped and crackled between his hands until the scent of charred rope reached him, then it sputtered and fizzled like a blowtorch that was running out of oxygen.

Then it was gone.

Hopefully those few seconds were enough.

The rest of it was up to him.

He pulled and strained, the last strands of frayed rope binding him stretched and finally fell away.

Freedom!

A sob caught in his chest.

Then pain shot through his arms and legs like railroad spikes were being slammed into them as the blood flow returned. Panting like he'd been running for a week straight, he groped for the cord to release the trunk, gripping the spindly metal cable like a lifeline, and yanked.

Only for it to come away in his hand.

He burst out laughing, more of a wheezing sound than anything else, dark humor burning like acid in his guts. "Give me a fucking break!"

He wanted to rage at the gods but couldn't spare the energy. The fighting was getting louder. He refused to lie here helpless, waiting to be rescued...or slaughtered before he could even get out of the trunk. He ran his hands along the confined space, but knew he was too weak to peel away the reinforced frame. It was only when he searched the floor beneath him that he smiled.

Rolling to his side, he punched clear through the floor, ripping away the carpeted cardboard to the tire beneath—or more precise— the tire iron. Grabbing the slim metal rod, he wedged it into the trunk latch.

It took four tries for it to finally give and the trunk lid popped open.

Fresh air rushed inside, and he gulped it greedily.

Freedom lay beyond, just a few inches away, but he was paralyzed by fear. If he left and they caught him, they would torture him again.

It was the thought of Annora waiting for him that finally got him moving.

She was in danger.

She needed him.

Gritting his teeth, he clutched the tire iron to his chest and eased open the lid, then dragged himself out, nearly falling on his face before catching himself on the lip of the trunk. He staggered upright, suppressing a groan as his ribs and spine protested.

Then he tightened his grip on the tire iron and staggered off toward the sounds of fighting. His body didn't seem to work right, lurching instead of running smoothly, leaving a trail of blood behind him. Darkness surrounded him, ready and waiting to swallow him if he failed. His eyes were nearly swollen shut from his recent beating, and he could barely see a dozen feet straight ahead.

Despite the pain, he pushed forward, putting one foot in front of the other for only one reason...Annora.

If it was the last thing he did, he would destroy anyone who thought to harm her, even if it took his last breath to do it.

Annora felt solid ground under her feet, but it didn't keep her legs from buckling and dumping her on her ass. Kevin landed more gracefully, like he was stepping through a doorway, while she seemed to trip over the invisible stoop.

She glared up at him. "You could've warned a girl."

"Sorry." He grimaced and offered her a hand. "The landing takes a bit of getting used to. Those with a bigger affinity for magic are more affected by the ride."

She accepted his hand, grunting noncommittally at his comment, not sure how much of her magic was from her mother and how much was just normal for phantoms. Either way, portalling sucked donkey balls.

The din of battle filled the clearing, and she whirled, charging through the trees, climbing up a small hill to reach the peak...and stopped dead. The entire battlefield was stretched out before her, the full moon illuminating everything in all its gory, devastating details. She quickly spotted the guys as they tore through the army with an ease that she envied. They were amazing to watch.

Mason smashed his way through his opponents, while Xander

seemed to glide from one fight to the next, landing only long enough to eliminate the threat and soaring on to his next target. What freaked her out was the way Camden walked through battle with no fucking weapons at all. He wore his full armor from his lizard form, using his touch to knock out any who got within reach, and the wicked sharp spikes at his elbows to slice through the more stubborn opponents.

Each of the guys was fast and efficient in his takedowns, shouting orders as they moved onto their next targets. They remained in a group, often working back-to-back to protect the unit.

No wonder Greenwood considered them the best.

She couldn't hold back the awe and love that swamped her, unaware she was broadcasting until the guys' emotions flooded her…relief at knowing she was alive, fear and worry for her. Then they redoubled their efforts with one shared goal—no one touched her.

Camden shouted orders to the surrounding teams, and the soldiers surged toward Erickson's location. To her surprise, Sadie was in the midst of the battle, her sword swinging, lopping off limbs of any who dared get too near the guys, but sticking especially close to Edgar as he waded fearlessly through the battle. They moved like they'd fought together many times, and Annora shrugged away the pang of jealousy, refusing to let it distract her.

The witches hung back, performing spells to keep the shifters from transforming into their animal counterparts. Anyone who dared get too close was doused in a spell that melted whatever it hit, the magic dirty, but very effective. The rest were on the outskirts, shielding the whole battlefield with a dome to keep the sounds of war contained and discourage the wrong sort of people from investigating.

Erickson's men fought hand-to-hand. They weren't as efficient as the trained teams, but what they lacked in skill they made up for in sheer numbers and determination. A few of the larger shifters hung back, protecting Erickson.

While the director remained in his human form, there was nothing human about him in the way he picked up one of the wolves fighting nearby and ripped him to shreds with just his not-quite human teeth and claws.

It only took seconds to end a life.

She searched the teeming masses for Logan, but she couldn't see him anywhere—there were just too many people, too much movement for her to be able to track everything. Anxiety tightened her throat at the possibility that she might be too late.

Near their perch, one of Greenwood's men went down under a pile of bodies. Annora glanced at Kevin, but he was watching his brother struggle to fight off two wolves at the same time. "Go."

Kevin hesitated another moment, indecision twisting his face, then gave a nod. "You better not die on me."

It was a demand and a plea.

He was off before she could reply.

Then there was no more time to think or watch.

Cursing herself for her lack of weapons, she grabbed a sharp rock and hefted it, testing the weight, before she charged into battle. She grabbed one shifter, still in human form, by his hair, wrenched his head back and brought down the rock sharp and fast, ignoring the threatening flash of his fangs. The meaty thunk sounded juicy. His eyes rolled back into his head and he dropped to the ground with a grunt.

Unfortunately, he would be back in action in a few minutes.

Knocking them out wouldn't keep shifters down for long.

The shifter that went down slashed and clawed at the remaining opponent until he slumped over, his bulk threatening to suffocate the smaller man. Annora leaned over, quickly grabbing the unconscious guy's shoulder and yanked, while the shifter beneath heaved. Together they were able to pull the nearly three-hundred-pound guy away.

Annora turned...only to find Vicki glaring up at her. "You."

"Me." Annora gave her a crooked smile, then offered her hand. Despite the she-wolf hating her since she'd showed her up the night of the party, Vicki hesitated only for a moment, then grabbed it.

Once on her feet, Vicki stepped back and shook out her hands and arms, scattering blood and tissue everywhere. Worry tightened Annora's gut as she watched the battle, wondering if they could even win. They were massively outnumbered. She hadn't realized how many wolves would come to Erickson's aid and fight.

She must have said it out loud, because Vicki snarled. "They don't have any choice. They must obey their alpha. If the wolf doesn't have a strong enough alpha to hold them, Erickson rips them away and forces them to fight for him."

Horror sliced through her while she looked across the battlefield again—so many innocent people were being killed.

And for what? More power?

She watched the battle with new eyes...and realized what must be done. "We need to get to Erickson."

"Be my guest." Vicki waved her arm, indicating the far side of the battle, a whole field of wolves and shifters between them.

Annora glanced up, then watched in sickening fascination as Erickson picked up a kid half his size, cracked him open by nearly snapping the kid's head off and drank his blood like the kid was a wine cask. Blood and gore spilled down his face and chest in a red wave, and she gritted her teeth against the need to vomit.

He grabbed another kid, then another, seemingly at random, uncaring what side of the battle they fought.

After her uncle sold her blood, she'd done a bit of research. A few people actually believed they could steal the strength of their opponent by drinking the blood of the defeated. She'd discovered that the magic in her blood usually broke down quickly, so she didn't think much about it.

Her blood must have driven Erickson insane.

While the guys said shifters normally couldn't get diseases, she wondered if ingesting too much had rotted his brain.

And her guys were heading straight for him.

Her insides turned to stone—none of them would stop until the other was dead.

Sorrow turned her heart heavy when she realized what needed to be done. The afterworld called to her, instinct warning her that time was running out.

She needed to act before it was too late.

The phantoms were coming.

She could feel someone searching the afterworld.

Determined to make the rest of her time matter, she gathered the few dark particles that were struggling to heal her, then turned toward Vicki with a trembling smile. "Tell the guys I love them."

Vicki's head snapped up, her eyes widening. "Wait—what?"

Without giving Vicki a chance to stop her, Annora allowed her body to dissolve and reform a few yards away from her target. As she landed, Vicki's cursing cut off abruptly. The afterworld clung to her, and her hands shook with the need to absorb the swirling mass.

Fuck it.

Her father was coming for her either way.

It was only a matter of time.

If accessing the afterworld was going to get her killed, she was going to make it worthwhile.

Annora tore down every wall she ever built to keep herself safe— and darkness welcomed her with open arms.

Her back arched as power slammed into her with the force of jumping out of a plane without a parachute and hitting the ground. The world around her vanished as her vision darkened. Her injuries stitched together in a vomit-inducing second, the pain lingering under her skin for just a moment before the adrenaline took over and sloshed in her veins.

Energy filled up her body like she was drowning. As she gasped for air, darkness spilled down her throat. Every nerve tingled painfully to life, her body going weightless until she could no longer feel the earth beneath her feet.

When she opened her eyes, the roars and snarls of battle came rushing back. Blood landed on her like mist, so thick she could taste it with each breath. The sharp scent of pain and fear clogged the air.

Her body became heavy—solid—and her feet slowly touched the earth. Only then did she become aware of Erickson watching avidly, licking his lips like he was trying to figure out how to take her apart and get to the gooey insides.

"I told your uncle he was a fool. He should've turned you over to me immediately, then all of this could've been avoided." He studied her clinically, seeing her only as a commodity to be owned. While her uncle loved torturing and enforcing his dominance, she suddenly wondered if his *loving care* might have saved her from something worse.

When she stared at Erickson, pure insanity looked back.

Whatever was left of his soul was fractured and twisted. His lust for death and blood was bottomless.

He thrived on it.

Nothing would ever convince him to surrender.

The only thing that would satisfy him was the complete and total decimation of anyone and everyone who thought to oppose him.

He honestly believed the lives of others were his for the taking…because he could.

She had only one choice—he needed to die.

"That's cute." Annora smiled at Erickson, allowing the afterworld to weave through her fingers. "You actually believed I would have obeyed."

Erickson's smile was all teeth, his eyes completely devoid of amusement…or any sign of life for that matter. "There are ways to make people submit."

He was more of a monster in human form than any animal could hope to be. No wonder her uncle got along with him so well. She knew the instant the guys spotted her. Mason let out a roar that shook the air and charged forward. With each step his form bulked up more, his big frame knocking down and scattering anyone unlucky enough to get in his way.

The guys must have been used to the tactic, because they quickly fell in line in the empty space he left behind and followed the path of destruction. They were determined to get to her, keep her safe, and were willing to pay for it with their lives. Erickson would use them against her, and she couldn't allow that.

She had five minutes tops before they reached her.

She hadn't even finished the thought when Edgar winked out of existence and appeared at her side. Black smoke clung to him, curling around him like a lover's caress. Before she had a chance to open her mouth, he attacked the wolves sneaking up behind her.

Only there were too many to hold off for long.

It was time to act.

A blood-splattered Sadie appeared in an explosion of black dust. Her eyes immediately latched on to Edgar. She turned and cheekily saluted Annora with her sword. "I got him. Go do your thing."

Without waiting for a response, Sadie charged into battle, hacking at everyone who dared get too close to Edgar. Annora hesitated, then took a leap of faith. Although she wasn't sure if she trusted the girl, she knew without a doubt that the phantom would protect Edgar within an inch of her life. It was good enough for Annora.

Pushing away her thoughts of battle, she focused on Erickson.

She would be no match to him in a fair fight.

Good thing she had no intention of fighting fair.

Grasping onto the darkness, she threw herself forward—and appeared behind him.

Before she could land a blow, he whirled and snarled at her. He lashed out, claws slicing through air, and she barely ducked in time to miss having her throat torn out. She tried twice more, but his reflexes were too sharp for him to be taken by surprise.

They were too evenly matched.

The vengeful side of her was perfectly fine with destroying him at the cost of her own life, but her heart twinged at the thought of losing her men.

It was much too soon.

She hadn't had enough time with them.

Then there was no more time to think because Erickson snarled and charged. For every blow she landed, he got in two. After a nasty slash that nearly gutted her, Annora realized this plan of attack wouldn't work. They were both healing too fast.

Conscious of the guys getting closer, she grabbed the first reckless plan that popped into her head—bait.

She would wait for Erickson to get close, then strike a killing blow and hope he didn't take her out as well. She was tempted to drag his ass into the afterworld, but she wasn't sure what awaited her.

She would save the nuclear option as a last resort.

As Erickson circled her, his blood-soaked shirt clung to his torso and glistened ominously in the dim light. She allowed him near enough to land a couple blows, then refused to let her body heal. It didn't take long for her to begin bleeding like a slaughtered pig.

"I don't need your obedience." Lust gleamed in his eyes at the sight of her blood. He lifted his hand, licking the dark crimson off his claws with a look of ecstasy. "I'll take it. Power thrums in your blood. Unlike the others, you're a never-ending fountain. I can drink you dry, and you'll come back to feed me over and over."

But Annora wasn't sure she would be back.

Had Edgar been the one who forced her back to the human realm, or was it the afterworld itself? If Erickson killed her, it could very well be permanent, and she refused to die unless she took him with her. "You're addicted to blood, and it's driven you insane."

Erickson threw back his head and laughed, the booming sound reverberating across the battlefield. "I've never been saner. I've been killing for years, and none of these fools even suspected. Shifter blood has allowed me to heal faster and made me stronger. Only it wears off."

He scowled, clearly pissed to have that rush of power denied him. "That's when I discovered your blood. Your uncle gave me a sample, and I created an elixir that lasts even longer." Practically slavering, he stared at her. "But imagine how strong I could be when I have your pure blood pumping through my system! I will be unstoppable. I will be immortal."

It took everything in her to remain still and ignore the way the darkness nipped and stung along her wounds, demanding that she heal.

A wickedly dangerous idea slammed into her.

He wanted her blood—what would happen if she gave it to him?

One little taste and he already craved it.

If she could somehow get more of her blood into his body, she wouldn't need to lay a hand on him to end this. While he might be strong, he wasn't built to withstand the powers of the afterworld. If called, the darkness would respond to the demands of her blood.

She was staking her life on it.

The only problem was she had no clue how much blood was needed. To be on the safe side, the more the better. She'd wait until the last moment to test her theory.

Putting her plan in action, she pressed her hand against the wicked cut along her thigh, forcing more blood to spill between her fingers and coat her hands. When he got close enough, she lashed out, smearing her blood on whatever skin she could reach, gasping when his claws raked down her side in a move that nearly gutted her.

She staggered away, dropping to one knee when she lost her

balance, then glanced up to see his smug face gloating down at her, and her soul shriveled at the malicious gleam in his eyes.

"Oh, don't worry, dear. I have no intention of killing you—yet." His smile vanished, leaving only cruelty behind. "Not until you suffer for what you've cost me. We need some time alone, time that won't be interrupted by your pets."

Heart slamming against her ribs, her gaze shot past him to scan the battleground. She spotted her guys instantly—they were cutting a wide swath through the troops, and she sucked in a sharp breath of relief at seeing them alive.

"Take down her mates." Erickson's command resounded across the battlefield, the order so full of power, the battle around her halted, and fighters from both sides turned toward her team.

Her men halted their charge, going back-to-back as they surveyed the threat. Their faces were hard masks of determination while they waited for the first wave of attack. There was no fear or worry, only pure determination to reach her. Something inside her shriveled when snarls rippled through the air, and the different packs all lunged at once.

Edgar, despite all his power, went down hard, the expression on his face resigned…like he'd never expected to come out of the battle alive. Only a few yards away, the rest of the men were buried under an avalanche of bodies.

She felt each blow, each slash of claws.

Felt bones crunch and splinter.

Beyond the pile, she saw Greenwood and a handful of men work their way toward the writhing mass, flinging people away right and left. His gaze met hers, and she saw the devastating truth in his eyes—he would never reach them in time.

He would try, but he would fail.

She gave him a nod of understanding, silently urging him to try anyway.

Greenwood bowed his head in acknowledgment, bringing his fist up to settle over his heart—a vow he would do everything in his power to save her boys.

It had to be enough.

He bent and picked up the pelt that lay at his feet and swung it around his shoulders. She watched in fascination as it wrapped around him, fur spilling down his chest and arms until he dropped down onto all fours in the shape of a raging, half-ton brown grizzly bear.

He lifted his head and let out a giant roar that vibrated in the air, his mouth opening wide enough to crush skulls. He was both majestic and beastly, a monster born to kill. Then he charged into battle, grabbing one unfortunate soul by the leg, snapping it in half and flinging the poor sod a good twenty feet to land in a heap.

She'd never seen a skinwalker in action, and she hoped she'd never have to come face-to-face with one in a fight. Knowing he'd do his best for her men, Annora turned toward Erickson, just in time for him to grab her by her throat, his claws digging into her flesh until blood trickled down her neck.

He lifted her off her feet, leaving her dangling off the ground like a fish on a hook. She grabbed his wrists, kicking her legs, but didn't try to escape.

Not yet.

It was too soon, especially if she only got one chance to bring him down.

She inhaled through the pain, letting it flood her system, feeling her senses heighten.

He inhaled deeply, his eyes dropping betrayingly to the fresh wounds, and he licked his lips. "By the time you wake up you'll be completely mine."

His very own fucking cornucopia. She'd never run dry, never die…at least not permanently.

He pulled her closer, tipping his head to lick at the blood along her neck, his tongue feeling like a slug crawling across her skin. She grimaced, everything inside her rebelling at the thought of being a snack. When his breath touched her skin, repulsion made her shudder, and she couldn't stop the way she squirmed to get away, shoving at his shoulders to put distance between them.

Then all thoughts of her plan scattered when she saw the wreck of what was once Logan as he staggered across the muddy battlefield.

It looked like he'd crawled out of hell.

And he was the most beautiful thing she'd ever seen.

But her joy was short-lived. Something was horribly wrong. As she studied his blank expression, she saw nothing of her Logan remaining in his faded blue eyes. He looked neither right nor left, as if the only thing he could see was Erickson.

The shifters on the battlefield fought like good little brainwashed monsters, none of them even bothering to attack Logan, and she realized Erickson hadn't rescinded his order for Logan to remain unharmed while under his care.

Thank fuck.

She'd needed a bit of good news.

Erickson lapped at her wounds, the feel of his wet tongue sliding along her skin making her gag. He dug his fingers into her flesh, squeezing hard to keep the blood flowing, so consumed with his hunger he was oblivious to everything else.

Fear turned her stomach sour.

There was no more time to stall.

If Logan got any closer, Erickson would kill him if for no reason other than to punish her. Annora lifted up her legs, planting her feet against his chest, doing her best to shove off him.

Only his grip remained unbreakable.

She was too weak, allowed him to take too much blood.

Black spots speckled her vision, and she blinked slowly, struggling to remember the plan.

Dark particles nipped along her skin, setting every nerve ending afire with the urge to kill. As agony pierced her, rational thought returned, along with her determination.

Eyes locked on Logan, she pulled on the afterworld. It licked hungrily at her flesh, slowly healing her. No matter how hard she tried to push it into Erickson, it refused her demand, determined to see to her wounds first.

Just as she was beginning to feel her heart sputter, Sadie appeared next to them with her sword raised. She brought the blade down on Erickson's arm hard enough to cut through his flesh. The edge became wedged securely into the bone, his enhanced body making him stronger than other shifters.

Annora landed on the ground, barely strong enough to keep herself from collapsing, the breath knocked out of her.

Erickson roared in pain, his huge fangs flashing, and he backhanded Sadie across the face. She sailed a few feet away and landed with a thud, too dazed to move, stuck at Erickson's mercy.

Annora could do nothing while she watched Erickson yank the blade out of his own arm with a grunt, then swing it toward Sadie.

The phantom scrambled backward in slow motion…much too slow to escape.

Only for the sword to falter when Erickson stumbled forward.

Instead of taking off her head, he'd sliced her clear across the throat.

Sadie grabbed her neck, tried to stem the bleeding, but it spilled through her fingers and down her chest. Eyes wide, she dropped to her knees, wheezing as blood gurgled out of her mouth. Their eyes met, her dark ones pleading with her to take care of Edgar after she was gone.

Then Edgar was there to catch Sadie, cradling her in his arms as he lowered her to the ground. Annora felt a devastating wrench that he went to Sadie and not her.

He was bleeding, his impeccable clothing rumpled, his hair wild and untamed, but it was the tortured look in his eyes that shattered her heart.

Feeling sick, Annora dragged herself to her feet.

When Erickson turned, she saw what appeared to be a crowbar sticking out of his back, clear through his spine. Bones gleamed as he dropped the sword and tried to reach behind him and wrench out the weapon.

Logan was breathing heavily, swaying on his feet, looking like a light breeze would knock him flat, clearly at the end of his endurance.

He'd used the last of his strength to get to her.

Then he grinned like a fool, his teeth coated with blood, his lips cracked, his face swollen and bloody, accepting his death, almost happy to leave the pain and suffering behind.

Annora recognized the sentiment, having felt it plenty of times herself.

She refused to let him go so easily.

"Erickson!" She screamed his name, scooping up the sword and slicing the edge across her palm. Blood immediately pooled from the wound, dripping between her fingers, and she waved the bloody hand at him, only backing away when his wolf caught her scent. "If you want to survive," she taunted, "you'll need my blood."

His eyes gleamed yellow as the predator in him rose to the surface.

He dismissed the others and began to stalk her.

Chapter Twenty

Erickson cocked his head at her, wolf cunning staring out at her from behind his eyes. Then he licked his lips, as if he could already taste her blood pouring down his throat. He reached back, ramming the crowbar through his torso, more blood spilling down his chest. Then he calmly reached down and wrenched the metal out of his ribcage.

"Annora, no." Logan scurried toward her, stumbling over his own feet, only to have Erickson kick him in the chest hard enough to send him flying backwards. Bones shattered under the blow. He landed with a crunch, then lay unmoving, and something inside her snapped.

The afterworld spilled out of her in a rush of vengeance, the darkness filling the space between them like angry storm clouds brewing. It hit Erickson full in the chest. His back arched, his arms were flung wide, and a jubilant chuckle as his wounds began to stitch shut. "I will be unstoppable."

Only when she was sure the dark particles had infected every cell in his body did she pull back with all her might. The golden strands of his life force were frayed and decayed, stolen from others and cobbled together like gossamer cobwebs.

Erickson staggered, his arms dropping heavily to his sides, and he blinked at her in confusion. He stumbled toward her like a drunk, tripping over his own feet, and he glared at her. "Stop it!"

Annora no longer felt any pain.

No worry.

No fear or anger.

Only one thought consumed her—vengeance.

Power thrummed through her as she gathered his life force. It fought her, not wanting to leave its host, but she ruthlessly, remorselessly yanked it away. It began to gather in her hand like a ball of frayed yarn, slowly growing bigger and brighter.

Though her body was healed, the sheer amount of power she used left her raw and empty. The blood covering her body felt tacky as it dried, the stench of his fear feeding her pleasure, and she smiled maliciously at him. "How does it feel to be fed upon like some fucking parasite the way you did to so many?"

A growl rumbled from his wolf, only to turn into a whimper, and still she didn't stop. The afterworld gathered above them, brewing like a tornado gathering force. Wind tugged at the world around them, debris pelting those who dared get too close, but none of it touched her. She'd almost swear she saw the spirits of all the dead Erickson had consumed waiting for him.

"Stop!" It wasn't a plea, but a demand—a weak compulsion. Erickson lunged for her, barely able to stay on his feet, the desire to crush her burning in his eyes.

Annora danced out of his reach, cocking her head to study him, no longer seeing him as anything other than prey. He ceased being human after his first kill, and she taunted him like he'd taunted so many of his victims. "How many times have you heard that over the years and laughed while you slaughtered your own people?"

The fighting around them had come to a complete halt. The guys were gathered around Logan. The rest of the people kept their distance, and she wasn't sure if that was because they believed he deserved death or because they feared her.

The thought of her guys no longer wanting anything to do with her nearly ripped her guts out, but the darkness crushed it. She gave herself over to the afterworld completely, using it like a shield nothing could penetrate. It welcomed her home, the cool air making their breath fog, but she embraced the numbness, the afterworld taking away all emotions but the need to maim and kill the creature before her.

The necklace she wore burned, nagging at her, refusing to let her surrender completely. It kept her grounded in this world when all she wanted to do was burn it down. It refused to let her forget her pain, refused to let her forget the men she loved so much.

It shackled her to the land of the living, and she reached up and grabbed the chain to rip it away. Only the instant her hand came into contact with the metal, she heard the guys yelling her name. Every wonderful, wretched emotion she felt for them came flooding back, the avalanche of feelings threating to overwhelm her, and her hand jerked away like she'd been scorched.

Not wanting to deal with her grief and loss for fear that she would be crushed under the weight, she did the one thing she'd promised to do from the start—save the men, no matter the cost.

As the last of his life force left Erickson, his flesh began to shrivel. Skin slowly sagged against his bones like he was a deflating pool toy, leaving him a ghost of himself. His wolf snarled at her, then the yellow gleam in his eyes flickered to brown like a light had been doused.

"No!" The roar ended in a scream as the shadow of a mangy, feral wolf slipped out of his human form, slinking low along the ground. It managed only a few feet before it staggered and dropped to its side and began to flake away and scatter like ash.

The pathetic thing that remained of Erickson was barely human.

Then the ball of light in her hand sputtered, and she watched the cord between her and Erickson finally snap. He dropped to his hands and knees, clawing his way toward her with a breathy wail of rage and denial.

The sphere of threads she'd gathered from Erickson pulsed like a heartbeat. The power felt like it was the opposite of hers—full of light and life instead of darkness and death. The longer she held it, the more it burned her skin. She could see the strands slowly wrapping around her hand, trying to graft themselves to her, and she shuddered at the thought of having anything that belonged to Erickson anywhere near her.

The pain in her hand began to feel like she'd stuck her arm in a shark's mouth, teeth ripping and sawing into her flesh. She had two choices...toss it into the afterworld to be consumed, or...give it back to those he took it from.

Annora pitched the glowing ball up into the swirling cloud mass raging overhead. Lightning cracked as it exploded across the sky, and she watched the golden sparks of light glitter in the darkness like a light show at Christmas. Then the glitter began to rain down like tiny fairy lights, healing everything they touched.

Once spent, the tiny sparks winked out of existence, leaving behind ash floating in the air like snow.

A clump of the golden liquid stitched together like a web over Logan. Power soaked into him, and her heart froze like a lump of ice until she saw his chest rise and fall. The tightness in her throat made swallowing impossible, and she bit her lip to hold back the sob caught in her throat.

In every direction, the darkness retreated, and her sanity returned...along with the magnitude of what she'd done.

She'd killed Erickson.

She didn't regret it, but she would undoubtedly be punished for daring to slay an alpha. However it turned out, though, she took fierce satisfaction in knowing Erickson's final act was to give back to those from whom he stole so much.

Annora slowly made her way over to where Sadie lay. The witches and shifters watched her in awe, their attention feeling like spiders were crawling all over her skin. Though Sadie was struggling to heal, the darkness trying to stitch her flesh together, it only dissolved before it could finish, her injuries too severe.

She was dying.

Annora didn't understand why the afterworld wasn't bringing her back.

Maybe she was too weak?

Or maybe the sword was built specially to kill their kind?

The devastated expression on Edgar's face was like a lance to her chest, hitting harder than any physical blow.

Annora glanced down at her hand, still able to see the tiny etches where the strands of light had tried to worm their way into her flesh, leaving her palm coated in the stuff. Chest hollow, knowing she was going to regret it, she knelt and carefully placed her palm over Sadie's chest.

The moment she touched the girl, her back arched off the ground, and she wheezed for air, the sound raspy and painful. Annora watched while tiny threads of gold forked their way under the girl's skin. With every pulse of her heart, the wound at her neck healed a bit more. Little nicks and bruises faded.

As the gold light faded, Sadie collapsed back to the ground, unconscious but alive.

The battlefield was so quiet it was eerie.

No one moved or even made a sound.

When Edgar reached for her, Annora flinched. As she pulled away, dizziness struck her so hard, it was like the earth was trying to swallow her. A babble of voices rushed to her ears, and she staggered to her feet.

She grabbed the sword, the tip leaving deep gouges in the ground as she dragged it behind her. When she reached Erickson, he lifted his arm out toward her, his bones creaking. His tongue was nothing more than dried jerky as he licked his lips. He grabbed her foot and tried to drag her closer so he could get to her blood.

Annora lifted the heavy sword, feeling it drag her backwards under its weight before she caught her balance. Then she brought it down, hacking off Erickson's head with one clean blow. Dark particles clung to the blade, and she could feel what remained of him being sucked into the afterworld. In her head, she could hear his scream of rage and denial...then his terror when he discovered he wasn't alone.

The sword dropped from her numb grasp. Just as her knees gave out, strong arms wrapped around her and swept her off her feet. The warmth almost burned her, and she shivered as the cold seemed to be anchored in her very bones.

"Easy there." Xander's voice was low and rough and soothing to her nerves. Glancing up, she saw his battered face come into a blurry focus. She tried to lift her hand to touch him but didn't have the strength.

He closed his eyes and pressed his cheek to the top of her head with a shuddering breath. The scent of the sea swept through her, easing the tight ache in her chest. A light breeze ruffled her hair, while the soft brush of feathers slid over her skin, no doubt checking her for injuries, and she found the sensation soothing.

Trusting Xander to keep her safe, she surrendered to the beckoning darkness.

"Annora."

Her eyes snapped open with a start at the sound of Logan's rough voice. Strong hands held her steady as she jolted, then she groaned while pain ricocheted throughout her body from head to toe, her bones feeling like they were tied in knots.

A quick glance showed they were in the truck. Mason drove without regard for speed, laying on the horn whenever another vehicle refused to get out of his way fast enough. He watched her in the rearview mirror more than the road, only seeming to relax when she gave him a small nod.

Edgar watched her from the front seat, an unconscious Sadie in his arms. Bile rose in her throat at the image of them so cozy together. When he saw she was awake, he leaned toward her, but she quickly turned away, fearing she'd be sick while her stomach felt like it was trying to eat itself.

Xander cradled her in his arms, while her legs were stretched over the bucket seats. Camden had his hand wrapped around her ankle, his fingers nervously tracing her skin over and over. That's when she saw he sat in such a way that he was reaching down to touch something.

When she moved her head to see what held his attention, a tortured groan escaped. She grabbed her head, feeling like it was about ready to fall off. Xander's arms tightened around her, and she'd swear she felt his lips brush her temple.

"Are you okay?" He slid his fingers under her chin and tipped her head back toward him, his teal eyes sharp with concern.

She opened her mouth, then licked her lips, her mouth so dry her voice was barely above a whisper. "Fine. Sore."

The vehicle swerved, the guys all looked at each other, and Annora winced. Since she never complained, they must be thinking she was at death's door. Maybe they didn't know it but dying was the easy part. Surviving and living were far worse.

Then she bolted upright, frantically searching the vehicle. "Where's Logan?"

At the sharp movement, a groan tore from her before she could stifle it, nausea making her mouth water unpleasantly, while her stomach churning threateningly.

Both Xander and Camden wrapped their arms around her so she couldn't move. Camden leaned close, pressing his hand to the side of her face, his touch calming the blast of panic. "Breathe. Logan is right here. He's resting."

He gently turned her head, and she saw Logan was lying stretched out between the seats. Annora reached for him, then curled her fingers into a fist and pressed it against her stomach to resist temptation. He was so bruised and battered, so damaged, she was afraid to touch him.

Her uncle did that to him.

Because of her.

Just the sight of her must be repulsive.

No doubt the thought of her touching him would make his skin crawl.

"Annora." Logan spoke her name again, mumbling it in his sleep. He shifted restlessly, grimacing, until Camden reached down and gently brushed his fingers along the side of Logan's neck. The kitsune settled down almost immediately.

"He wakes every few minutes, searching for you." Camden leaned back and tightened his hold around her ankle when she tried to pull away and curl into herself, as if bracing for a blow.

"Why hasn't he healed?" she whispered, so she wouldn't disturb Logan. She refused to look at him. Couldn't. What if when he looked at her and she only saw hatred staring back?

"He's exhausted." Xander cradled her close, as if he could feel her pulling away and wanted to stop it. "He can only heal so much, so fast, before his body shuts down."

"I'm fine." Logan's voice was a broken rasp.

His eyes met hers before he quickly dropped his gaze and her heart imploded with pain.

Physical pain was easy, she used it to fuel herself.

This?

This she didn't know how to handle.

She tried to swallow, tried to breathe, but couldn't seem to get enough air in her lungs to make them work. Logan dragged himself upright, leaning his back against the seat, chest heaving, the small motions exhausting him. He opened his arms, and Xander carefully deposited her sideways across his lap.

She sat on the floor of the van, between his splayed legs, afraid to move.

Afraid she would shatter.

Logan blew out a shaky breath, then gently placed his hand on her back, running his fingers lightly up and down her spine. After a moment, the tightness in her chest eased a fraction, and she became aware that he was speaking.

"You don't have to see me anymore. I'll leave. The last thing I want to do is hurt you. It's not like I'll be any good to the team anyway. I—"

"What the fuck are you talking about?" Annora turned and glared at him.

He swallowed hard, his throat bobbing painfully, and he quickly dropped his gaze when she looked at him. "I'm damaged. Broken. I can barely feel my kitsune. I don't know if I'll ever be able to shift again. I'm useless. I won't even be able to protect you. You need a mate you can rely on to keep you safe."

His voice broke on the last word, and the panicked buzz in her brain quieted. Hesitantly, she reached out and rested her hand on his shoulder. He sucked in a sharp breath, his head snapping up.

"I thought *you* hated *me*," she spoke in a broken whisper. "You have every right to hate me."

He scowled down at her, his split lip busting open again. "What the hell made you think such a thing?"

"My uncle—"

"Is an asshole." He shook his head as if she was a foolish child.

"What he did was not your fault."

"But if it wasn't for me, none of this would've happened." She gazed down at her lap, twisting her fingers together. "He never would've come into your life, never would've touched you."

A vicious growl rumbled between them, and he grabbed her arms, forcing her to look up at him, wincing at the harsh movement, but refusing back down. "I'm glad it was me and not you. I wouldn't trade even a second of the time we've had together. Every bit of pain was worth it, because it brought you into my life."

Annora searched his face for the truth.

His blue eyes never wavered, and the knot in her throat threatening to strangle her since he'd been taken finally relaxed. Tears blurred her eyes, and she quickly blinked them away. "You're not damaged in my eyes. You're perfect, and I wouldn't trade you for anyone."

His grip tightened on her arm, his voice fierce and ragged. "Tell me you mean it."

"Of course I mean it, you idiot." She leaned closer, resting her forehead against his. "I'm going to kiss you now."

He swallowed hard, his breathing ragged, and she'd swear he was nervous, which was ridiculous. He was a known womanizer. Her inexperienced fumbling should've made him take off running, not make him look at her like she was a goddess come to life.

Not wanting to hurt him, she closed the distance between them and gently pressed her lips against his. His mouth parted on a groan, and the darkness inside her rose. It mingled with her breath, leaving her and entering him.

She pulled away as he sucked in a startled gasp. His eyes went wide, then fluttered shut and he slumped sideways. Panic grabbed her by the throat, and she quickly caught him, gently laying him down.

"What the fuck did I do?" Her hands shook, and she quickly released him and scrambled back, pressing herself against the door, terrified she would hurt him even more.

Camden scooped her up onto his lap, while Xander leaned down and checked Logan over. "He's fine, just dropped into a healing sleep."

Her heart hiccupped against her ribs, and she glared at him. "You promise?"

Xander nodded, easing Logan into a more comfortable position. "His worry that you'd reject him kept him from surrendering fully to the sleep until he spoke with you." Xander leaned back into his seat and faced her. "If you don't believe me, you can check for yourself."

She didn't think he meant by checking Logan's pulse. Annora hesitated, not sure she trusted the afterworld the same way she used to, not after the way it nearly took her over.

Camden leaned forward, his face brushing lightly against hers. "Trust yourself. We won't let you fall."

Annora nodded, then braced herself and called upon the darkness until it filled her vision. She observed Logan and could easily see that his form was practically glowing.

He was healing.

Black welts and cruel marks were like shadows against the bright glow, and sorrow pierced her, knowing they were scars that would never heal. He hadn't been able to heal fast enough, some of the injuries were just too deep, and she wished she could take his pain.

She blinked away the darkness, both relieved and saddened. "He won't ever be the same."

"He'll be stronger." Mason glanced at her from over his shoulder, then went back to driving. "That's not a bad thing."

Annora glared at him. "No one deserves what he went through."

Mason shrugged, not bothering to look at her, avoiding her anger. "He's grown up since he met you." His grip tightened on the steering wheel as they drove through campus. They were almost home. "This was a hard lesson for him to learn, but he'll be stronger for it. He'll understand you better and in a way that only someone who went through the same thing could."

He drove the vehicle in the driveway, slipping it into park before turning to face her. "This will draw you closer together. He grew up very privileged. While he knew pain, he didn't know true suffering. This will make him more alert to the dangers you face."

Annora didn't like it. "I stole the last of his innocence."

Camden snorted, blocking her from reaching for the door and making her escape. "Logan was in no way innocent. He understood pain, grew up battling it every day of his life, but he's never known the fear of caring what happens to anyone else but himself. Never known true sacrifice. He didn't know what it meant to truly love someone else so completely that he would give his life for them. Until now."

As the guys opened the doors, Annora didn't move. "I never wanted that for him. Not because of me."

"Don't." Xander paused halfway out the door and turned toward her. "Don't diminish his sacrifice. Don't treat him as if he's broken. He did what he did out of love. Any of us, including you, would've traded spots with him in a heartbeat. Because of love. Don't pull away from him because of your fear. What he needs most right now is just you. When he looks at you, he won't see your uncle. He won't feel the pain. He'll see only you. The woman he loves. Unless you can't let it go. If you hang on to your guilt, you'll drown him with it."

Then he jumped out of the vehicle and stormed toward the house.

Annora watched him go in shocked silence. He was so stoic, so contained, she struggled to understand him at times. She wanted to deny what he said, but the pain in his eyes was a living beast that was consuming him, and she knew he spoke from experience.

Edgar was the next to exit. He gave her a worried look, only to have Sadie mumble something and cuddle closer to him in a way that triggered a pang of searing jealousy. She crushed it ruthlessly. She would not take his choice away from him. If he wanted Sadie, she wouldn't keep him from the woman he loved. His face shut down at whatever he saw when he looked at her, and he strode toward the house without speaking.

Mason shut his door, then came around back and gently lifted Logan out, as if the kitsune weighed no more than a kitten. She struggled with her guilt, not wanting to leave the comfort of Camden's arms while she sorted through her conflicting emotions.

And came to one conclusion…Xander was right.

She had to let go of her anger, her fear, and her guilt.

She'd been living with them for so long, she wasn't sure she knew how.

With a weary sigh, she made to stand, only to have Camden's arms tighten around her. He pressed his head against her shoulder, so she couldn't turn to face him. "Not yet. Please."

"Camden?" She gripped his arm at his softly spoken plea, worry dousing her like a bucket of ice. "What's wrong?"

Chapter
Twenty-one

"**Y**ou almost died!" Camden couldn't hold back the roar. By the gods, he wanted to shake sense into her, but he didn't think it would do any good. "We felt every blow, every cut, every bone crack and snap. We fucking felt your heart slow and nearly stop. Why the hell do you think Xander is so pissed?!"

He was breathing heavily at the end of his rant, but it did nothing to make him feel any better. He knew if it came down to the same choices, she'd do it again.

Because she loved them.

Fuck! How could that feel like both heaven and hell?

His hands shook, and he tightened his arms around her, pressing her closer, but it wasn't enough. He needed to confirm with his own eyes that she was okay. Damn if his heart wasn't thumping so hard it felt like it was trying to bash its way out of his chest.

Annora turned sideways on his lap, then held her arms out straight. "Go ahead. Look for yourself."

He swallowed hard, searched her face for any reservations at the thought of him touching her.

And found none.

Very gently, as if she was made of spun glass, he lifted up her sleeves to find smooth, unblemished skin. He lightly ran his fingers along her veins, the reassuring warmth of her skin calming him.

He turned over her arm, running his palm along her elbow. Then he methodically searched her other arm, inspecting every inch. When he was done, Annora grabbed the bottom of her battle-stained shirt and pulled it off over her head, leaving her wearing nothing but a minuscule tank top that barely covered her breasts.

He nearly swallowed his tongue when she tipped her head aside, silently urging him to finish his inspection. Blood flaked off her skin as he ran his hands over her exposed flesh. Though he found her sexy as hell, there was nothing sexual in his touch.

The longer he examined her, the more his control returned. She didn't protest when he slipped his hand beneath her shirt, checking her stomach, then her back, trailing his fingers up her spine. His hands ran along her shoulders, then slid along her neck.

Without prompting, she turned her head the other direction. He ran his finger from her ear down to her collarbone, settling his palm possessively over her throat, wishing he had the power to remove the image of Erickson's hand digging into her neck.

"Do it." Annora grabbed his wrist to keep him from pulling away. "It's the only way you'll feel better."

Camden swallowed hard, his breathing turning ragged at her husky demand. His cock hardened so fast it left his head spinning, and he stifled his groan. Unable to resist her, he leaned forward and placed his lips against her neck, every kiss, every caress marking her as his mate.

When she squirmed in his lap, he growled, the urge to bite her like a craving, and he jerked back. While she might be immune to his touch, he wouldn't risk infecting her with his venom, not until he was positive it wouldn't harm her.

Very reluctantly, he pulled back...only to find her smiling up at him, batting her pretty lashes. "My turn."

Every drop of blood in his body headed south, and he struggled to think coherently. Despite knowing it was a horrible idea, he couldn't resist her plea or the chance to know what it felt like to be touched, skin on skin.

Gooseflesh spread across his arms and torso at the thought, and he shifted restlessly, clearing his throat as he waited for her to make her move.

Her grin widened, and she reached out, pinching his shirt between her fingertips and tugging. "It would work better with this off."

Camden opened, then closed his mouth, swallowing hard, and obeyed. He grabbed the back of his shirt and wrenched it over his head. The reality of what they were doing made his stomach lurch alarmingly and he held his shirt in front of him like a simpering, spinsterish maiden, suddenly nervous.

What if she didn't like what she saw?

Then he wanted to kick himself for acting like a hormonal teenager. They wouldn't be in this situation if she didn't want him. But a little niggle of doubt remained like a worm, eating away at his courage and he couldn't make himself drop his shirt, not when his entire future literally rested in his lap.

Annora watched the flicker of emotions cross his face and hated that her presence made him doubt himself. She knew what it was like to yearn for a kind touch and be denied. She refused to let him feel the same way ever again.

She carefully picked up his hand, noticing blood still caked his nails, bruises darkened his knuckles. She turned his hand over, tracing her fingertips lightly down his fingers and across his palm, carefully trailing them up his arms like he had done with her, peeking up at him from under her lashes. He watched her avidly, his harlequin green eyes swirling with emotions. She wasn't sure he even breathed. Pleased to have his full attention, she skimmed her fingers along the crook of his elbow, enjoying the way he shivered as she explored him.

She didn't have to turn his arm…he did it for her, guiding her touch. She raked her nails lightly along the tender underside of his upper arms, then dragged them around the outside and up to his shoulders, loving the way he shuddered.

Unnoticed, his shirt sagged to the floor, leaving him bare for her to touch wherever she wished. Though she felt drugged by him, it wasn't the way he thought.

She didn't feel tired or scared.

She craved more.

She loved knowing she could affect him as much as he affected her. He didn't try to hide it, didn't shy away. As she ran her palms down his chest, his breathing became erratic. Muscles jumped when she reached his stomach.

As she traced the edges of his waistband, he snarled, then quickly captured her wrists and pulled her hands away, dragging her close until their breaths mingled.

She swayed forward, lured by the need to taste his lips, but he jerked back and shook his head. "No."

Her haze of lust evaporated, and she pulled back, only to be halted by his grip on her. She scanned his face, wondering if she'd read him wrong. He gazed at her so tenderly her heart quivered. "Why? You want me."

She wiggled her fingers and raised a brow at him. "I've more than proved that I'm not afraid. You would never hurt me."

"What if I'm afraid?" He gave her a lopsided smile.

His expression was so earnest and vulnerable, her stomach dropped and her body went ice cold. Of all the things she'd considered, she never thought he'd be afraid of her. She'd always assumed he felt the same way she did—and she quickly shook her head, too embarrassed to meet his eyes.

Her throat tight, she tried to pull away, desperate to lick her wounds in private. She didn't want him to know how much his fear hurt.

Only he tightened his grip and slipped his arms around her until she was plastered against his chest. "Annora...you misunderstood. I want to go slowly and treasure each moment with you, every touch and kiss. I want to take you out on a date, eat dinner with you, and make you laugh. I want to walk you home and hold your hand. I want to leave you at your door and kiss you goodnight. I want to do everything we missed together. You are my one and only. You deserve to be treasured. I want...I need to show you what you mean to me."

He pursed his lips then dropped his arms from around her and wiped his hands on his jeans as if he was nervous. Then he licked his lips and stared right into her eyes. "Would you do me the honor of going on a date with me?"

Tears immediately flooded her eyes, overcome by the enormity of her emotions. When his expression turned panicked, she gave a watery laugh and nodded. "Yes. Yes to everything."

She threw herself against his chest, wrapping her arms around his neck. His arms came around her, nearly crushing the air out of her, but she didn't care. She rubbed her face against his jaw, then reluctantly pulled away.

Before she could crawl off his lap, he lifted her and deposited her on the other seat. He picked up his shirt, tugged it over his head, and she couldn't help but gawk at the flex of muscles. When he pulled the shirt down, she must have hummed in protest, because when she looked up, it was to catch him smirking at her.

Her cheeks burned, and she ducked her head. She grabbed her own shirt and grimaced. No way was she going to wear the blood-encrusted rag again.

He jumped out of the vehicle, then offered his hand.

Pleasure bloomed in her chest, and she paused to memorize the tender expression on his face. It wouldn't last. She'd drive him crazy soon enough and wanted to savor the moment. When their hands touched, her skin tingled.

He wove their fingers together, and they walked back to the house, neither of them in a rush. When they reached the door, he leaned down to give her a gentle kiss, more of a quick brush of lips.

Then he was gone much too quickly.

When she opened her eyes, he was at the bottom of the steps, his hands in his pockets, rocking back and forth on his feet. "Go. The others need you."

She frowned, taking a step after him. "Where are you going?"

He looked off into the darkness, then back to her. "I'm going to check in with the patrols and help with the others when they return. There will be injured to help and prisoners to question."

Annora took another step after him, not wanting him to go off alone. "I can help."

Since the whole thing felt like her fault, it was the least she could do.

But Camden was already shaking his head. "Logan needs you more right now."

Annora stopped instantly, as if her feet had grown roots, then nodded, worry for Logan suddenly at the forefront of her mind. She turned, taking the last two stairs up to the house before she paused with her hand on the doorknob. A glance over her shoulder showed Camden was waiting until she was safely inside.

"Be safe," she said, then entered, closing the door behind her.

A quick look showed the ground floor was empty, and she charged toward the stairs, convinced something dreadful had happened.

She made it to the second floor, but it was empty as well. Her heart pounded so loudly in her ears she could hear nothing else but the erratic beat. Hand on the railing, she called upon the darkness, feeling it snap around her, hungry and searching for the threat.

She placed one foot on the stairs to her room when an arm wrapped around her waist from behind and lifted her off her feet. She was so focused on getting up the steps, her feet were still running. She threw back her elbow, slamming it into her attacker's stomach. Air whooshed out of him with a grunt, and she recognized the warm sea breeze scent only a second later, just as the darkness began to lick at his boots.

"Xander?" Her voice shook as she hauled back on the dark particles. They resisted, slithering up his legs to twine around him like a lover's caress, seeming to have recognized him before she did. When she realized that the darkness wouldn't harm him, she twisted and smacked at his arm. "Why the fuck did you scare me like that? I thought something awful happened."

He lowered her to the ground, gently turning her until she was facing him, and she burrowed against his chest, a shudder going down her spine at the thought of everything she nearly lost. He wrapped his arms around her very hesitantly, patting her awkwardly, as if he'd never given a hug before.

Well, she hadn't received many, so he could just get used to it.

Apparently she was beginning to like them.

"I was outside burning Logan's clothes. Mason is upstairs helping him get ready for bed." When she turned to go back up the stairs, he caught her arm. "Logan would like you to wait."

She glanced back, saw his pale face, and her gut tightened in dread. If Logan's injuries were enough to shake Xander, they were worse than she expected. "I can help. I can—"

"He's taking a shower. He just needs to get clean first. Wash away the blood and pain. He doesn't want to bring it into the house, doesn't want you to see him until it's gone." Xander gently tugged on her arm, leading her to his room.

It hurt to be excluded, as useless as a hovering bug that would only get in the way, but she pushed the whiny feelings away. If that's what it took for Logan to feel normal, she would respect his decision.

The hurt was her problem, not his.

A tiny chittering sound drew her attention to the top of the steps and she whirled to see Prem looking down at her with a ferret grin. Her throat closed and tears blurred her vision.

He's alive.

She didn't understand how or why, but she was infinitely grateful.

She gave the ferret a watery smile and wiped her hand across her mouth when her chin wobbled. He limped carefully down two of the steps, then put his paws in the air, shooing her away, silently urging her to go, that he would look after Logan until her return.

She reached out, careful not to hurt him, and bumped her finger against the side of his face. He rubbed against her, then pulled away and drudged back up the stairs to stand guard at the top.

With a sigh, she reluctantly turned away and followed Xander into his room, absently taking note of the starkness of his bedroom—it was devoid of anything that might mark it as his. The place was neat as a pin. A dresser, bed, and nightstand were the only furniture, and a single peg had been installed in the wall where his large leather duster hung within easy reach.

The bedspread was a dark, speckled blue that reminded her of the sea. The whole place smelled of him, and the tension in her shoulders eased a little more with each breath. She didn't get to see much more as he pulled her toward a door across from his bed.

The bathroom was massive, constructed in three sections. A huge tub took up most of the first room, the whole space screaming luxury, a place where a person could forget the world and simply soak. Without being told, she knew this was his private domain, his true home. Small bits of his personality were scattered around the room, carefully preserved—a broken shell, a tiny bird's nest, a neatly stacked selection of books.

She craned her neck to see more as he hauled her along, gasping when she saw the next room. The vanity was huge, spread along the whole side of the room, a different sink for each guy. She could tell which sink was whose just by looking at the clutter.

Logan's was an absolute mess, his shit scattered everywhere, even on the floor, like it'd multiplied while he was gone. Camden's section had his bottles lined up neat as a pin, everything in its place. Xander had the bare minimum, nothing on display but his toothbrush. Mason's was more of an ordered chaos, each of his few items was carefully maintained, as if he treasured even something as simple as a brush. Given that he was a troll, one on the bottom of the food chain in his family, maybe each item was a special gift.

There were two toilet stalls, but she didn't get to see more as she was dragged into the last section. A giant shower stood waiting for them. Besides a door to the hallway, the room only had a counter full of soaps and shampoos and an open closet full of huge towels.

She only became aware that they had stopped when Xander released her. He studied her carefully. When he seemed sure she wasn't going to run, he opened the shower and turned the water on full blast. Steam instantly billowed out from the multiple showerheads and filled the room.

Just imagining the feel of them pounding on her sore muscles made her groan.

Beyond worrying that he was still in the room with her, she stripped off her camisole. She wasn't ashamed of her nudity. Having grown up in what was virtually a glass box, observed every second of her life, she had quickly been stripped of any shyness. While she normally wouldn't take off her clothes in front of any of the guys, her need to get out of her stiff, bloody clothes was like a compulsion.

She could practically feel death clinging to them.

Her pants proved to be more difficult, the fabric sealed to her skin with dried blood.

Frantic to get them off, she wiggled and pulled. The sound of Xander clearing his throat made her freeze, and she glanced up at him.

His face was devoid of emotions, but the white tips of his black hair were standing on end. His teal eyes were sharp…and focused over her shoulder, allowing her privacy. The man was big and rugged, his facial hair giving him a roguish look…except he acted like the perfect gentleman.

"If I may?" He held up his hand, and she saw his fingers were tipped with sharp talons.

Annora crossed her arms over her chest to cover herself, more for his sake than her own, then walked over and presented him with her back. "Please."

He dropped to his knees behind her, and all the breath whooshed out of her at the suggestive pose. Her body came alive as she watched him carefully lift a single talon and slide it between the pants and her flesh.

He dragged the talon down the back of her thigh, the fabric separating easily, like under a sharp blade, and she shivered as his touch lightly caressed her skin. When he inhaled deeply and swayed closer, she knew he could smell her arousal.

But instead of acting on it, he carefully repeated the same performance with the other leg. Once done, he gently peeled her pants off, leaving her standing naked with him still kneeling at her feet.

Chapter
Twenty-two

Xander couldn't move. Annora looked down at him from over her shoulder, her gaze smoldering, and his muscles locked tight against the need to touch her and follow through on the promise in her eyes.

They were both covered with blood and smelled of death, but he'd never seen anything so fucking beautiful in his life, and he clutched his knees in a brutal grip to keep from reaching for her. Underneath the scent of battle was her own unique, intoxicating smell, and he couldn't stop himself from licking his lips at the thought of tasting her again.

His cock pressed demandingly against his fly, imprinting the zipper on it, but fuck if the bite of pain didn't make him want her more.

When he realized most of the blood covering her was her own, he struggled against letting his mind drag him back to the horror of battle, the image of blood pouring down her body and soaking into her clothes seared into his brain, and his hands shook at the stark knowledge of how easily he could've lost everything.

He wasn't strong enough to survive starting over again...not without her.

"I'm here. I'm alive." Annora slowly lowered one hand to touch his face. He closed his eyes on a rough exhale and shuddered, then bowed his head, leaning heavily into her.

She turned to face him fully, leaning against him, and he wrapped his arms around her hips.

He wasn't sure if she lowered herself or if he pulled her down to straddle him, he only knew her naked body was the only thing grounding him in reality. He clutched her close, knowing he was leaving bruises on her, but he couldn't stop himself.

She'd been so close to slipping away from him.

He must have spoken aloud, because she said, "I'm here, and I'm not going anywhere."

When she scraped her fingernails along his scalp, he pressed his face into the crook of her neck until he felt surrounded by her. After a minute, the tightness in his chest loosened enough for him to breathe properly again, her touch giving him life.

He cleared his throat, his voice gruff when he spoke. "I should leave you alone to shower."

He leaned back, respectfully dropping his gaze to the floor—only Annora didn't untangle herself and leave. If anything, she leaned closer and tightened her hold.

"What if I don't want to be alone anymore?" Her whisper fluttered along his skin, his cock throbbing painfully at the husky sound of her voice. "What if I want you to stay?"

His head snapped up, and his beast gave a fierce cry of triumph. It was all he could do not to growl and stake his claim. His searched her face for the truth, struggling to crush the impulse to take her hard and fast.

His frayed control screamed at him not to be a fucking idiot by turning her away, and he gritted his teeth against the urge to take her up on her offer, determined not to fuck this up. "Battle has a way of charging one's emotions. People make rash decisions they later regret. In the morning, you—"

"I've died more times than I can count, and never once have I run out to fuck the nearest man." Annora gave him a crooked smile, her eyes dancing with humor, then darkening suddenly as she scanned his face. "But I never had to watch people I care about fight and almost die for me. Never had anyone risk their life to keep me safe."

She cupped his face, leaning in close until her breath caressed his lips. "I've never felt such terror as I did when I knew I could've lost you without letting you know how much I love you."

Something inside him snapped at her simple, straightforward confession, and he launched himself forward. Annora squealed as she flew backwards, but he caught her close, inches from the ground and crushed her to his chest, her scream cut off as he covered her lips with his. Eager for the taste of her, he thrust his tongue in her mouth…then nearly came in his pants when she sucked on it lightly. He could practically feel each pull directly on his cock.

He slowly pulled away from temptation.

Not like this.

Not on the floor like the heathen he'd been accused of being so often when he was younger.

Feeling like he was tearing off his own skin, he pulled away and stood, although seeing her sprawled naked on the floor nearly made him drop back to his knees.

Instead, he reached down and offered her his hand, pulling her to her feet. At her questioning look, he kissed the tip of her nose and pushed her toward the shower. "I won't take you while your blood still stains your skin. I won't take advantage of you."

Annora gave him a soft smile. He wasn't the type of man to give her flowers or poetry. His gruff comment was his version of romance. She mattered to him, enough that he was trying to look out for her.

If she was just another one of his girls, he would've fucked her without a second thought.

Instead he wanted it to be special for her.

Wanted to treat her like she mattered.

When he tried to back away and give her space, she quickly grabbed his shirt. "But what if I want to take advantage of you? You have blood on you, too. We could share…the shower."

The last thing she wanted was to be alone with her thoughts. It wasn't because she was having doubts, it was because he was part of her soul. Touching him made her feel whole and loved. Like all the loss and pain had been worth it.

His teal eyes darkened with lust and he stepped into the shower with her fully clothed.

Hot water pelted them, soaking his clothes and painting the shower stall red with their blood.

She slipped her hands between his back and his soaking wet shirt, running her palms up the powerful muscles, checking for any injuries…but the instant she touched his skin, she was distracted. A hum of pleasure caught in her throat when he pushed her against the cool tile and kissed her like he couldn't get enough.

He didn't let up, didn't let her catch her breath. His hand was pressed against the wall near her head, while the other rested at her waist, his fingers tracing lightly against her skin, the complete opposite of his demanding mouth.

Annora pushed at his chest, and he backed away, searching her face, as if checking to make sure he hadn't pushed her too far, too fast. Without giving him a chance to ask questions, she grabbed the hem of his shirt and pulled up on it, then scowled when she couldn't reach high enough to remove it completely.

Being short fucking sucked. "Off."

He smirked at her demand, but obeyed, tugging it over his head before tossing it aside without bothering to look where it landed with a splotch.

Narrowing her eyes at him, mostly to stop herself from licking the water off his chest, she lifted her chin and crossed her arms. "Pants, too."

There was no smile this time when he glanced at her from under his brows, just straight lust. Without hesitation, he reached for his pants, freeing himself.

Dear gods above—the man didn't wear underwear.

Steam curled around them, playing peek-a-boo with the goods. As if knowing he had her completely captivated, he quickly stripped and straightened, making no move to touch her while she looked her fill.

The man was built, not an inch of fat on him. She noted the silver marks of old scars but barely noticed them at all, too distracted by the delicious muscles on display. His thighs were huge, matching the expanse of his chest and strong arms. A light dusting of hair covered his chest, and it was all she could do not to close the distance between them and nuzzle against him.

When he moved, he didn't touch her. Instead, he reached down and cupped himself, running his hand over his erection. Heat swamped her cheeks, spreading down her neck, but she couldn't pull her eyes away from watching him stroke himself.

Memories of the last time she watched him in the shower nearly made her groan. "No fair."

The way his eyes darkened said he was remembering, too.

She licked her lips, aching to touch him.

Then he stopped, and her head snapped up. Before she could open her mouth to protest, he bowed his head to her. "I'm yours to command."

Giving her complete and total control over him.

Lust weakened her knees, and she leaned back against the cold wall when her legs wobbled.

He did that once before when he was worried about rushing her, when he thought she was afraid, trying to give her time to adjust to touching him.

There was something wicked about knowing she could do whatever she wanted to him. Giving in to temptation, she leaned closer and licked his chest.

And was startled when he groaned and trembled.

Gently resting her hand on his chest, she marveled at being able to touch his hot, naked skin, the hairs tickling deliciously against her palms. His tortured expression was both heaven and hell, and every drop of water was a caress, leaving her wanting more. "Next time we can play your game. Right now, I need you."

She nipped his chest when he only stared down at her.

Then she was lifted clear off her feet when he exploded into action. She wrapped her legs around his waist, moaning when she felt his erection press against her. His grip was rough, his lips bruising when he smashed his mouth against hers.

The kiss was demanding and consuming. He nipped and sucked, granting her no quarter.

He made her feel alive and cherished, his hands rough as he dragged his callused palms over her body. The heat of him burned, and she rubbed against him, reveling in his nearness.

He slammed her against the cool tiles, the roughness startling a groan out of her. He ripped his mouth away from hers, then leaned down and nipped at the tip of her breast. She shuddered, the pain twisting to pleasure until she burned right along with him.

It was almost too much, her senses on the verge of overload. Feeling his teeth and claws caress her skin made her shiver, and it wasn't long before she was marked from head to toe. When she tried to touch him in return, he resisted, like he was on a mission to drive her insane.

Determined not to let him get away with taking charge, she reached between them and grabbed his cock, setting her nails against the warm skin, and he instantly stilled.

She finally had his attention.

He pressed one of his hands against the tile near her head, the other still supporting her...once again giving her complete control over him.

Smiling in satisfaction, she tightened her hold and stroked him, leaving him panting in under a minute, thrusting his cock into her hand. He gave a tortured groan, the muscles in his neck straining as he tipped his head back and struggled not come in her hand.

The tile under his hand cracked.

Realizing that he needed the closeness between them as much as she did, Annora leaned in to him and bit his shoulder.

Something inside him broke. He lifted her, then slammed into her hard and fast. The pleasure-pain was addicting. Neither of them lasted more than a minute as he pounded relentlessly into her. Her orgasm blasted through her first, taking all the worry and pain away until there was only the two of them. As she tightened around him, he flexed his hips in a way that robbed her of breath, sending her shooting even higher.

He gave a tortured groan, and she felt him pulse inside her as he found his own release.

She felt boneless, both of them panting as they struggled not to collapse and drown.

The sex was rough and beautiful, just like him.

He reached up, smoothing her hair away from her face, searching her eyes, his expression pensive. She smiled up at him lazily, using her fingertips to trace his lips. "Wow."

Only then did his serious expression melt away.

His shoulders relaxed, his half smile a little smug as he turned and began to wash her clean. Once done, he then gave himself a perfunctory swipe. As he stood under the spray, she moved closer to him, slipping her arms around him from behind, setting her hands over the taut muscles of his stomach and pressing her face between his shoulder blades.

Xander stilled, bowing his head, then rested his hand over hers, holding her close. Peace settled over them. Though she knew it wouldn't last, she savored the feeling.

Much too soon, he turned the water off, then swept her off her feet before setting her down gently on a fluffy rug. Walking naked to the open closet, he selected the biggest, fluffiest towel and wrapped her up in it, covering her from shoulders to ankles.

She smiled, suspecting it was one of Mason's.

Xander patted her down, making sure every inch of her was dry before he was satisfied, then grabbed his own towel, wrapping it around his waist, leaving it hanging deliciously low. When he grabbed her hand and began dragging her back to his room, she stumbled after him, completely distracted by the view and water droplets trailing down his back.

Shaking her head to clear it, she reached behind her, quickly snagging another towel and began to pat her hair dry, anything to get her mind out of the gutter.

He left her standing in the middle of his room as he went to his dresser and rummaged through the top drawer. He returned with one of his shirts. Without asking permission, he tugged her towel off, letting it drop to the floor, and pulled his shirt over her head.

He stood back, his head tipped to the side as he studied her, then grunted and nodded, seemingly pleased to see her wearing his shirt. Once satisfied, he cuddled her into his arms, leaning down to sniff at her neck and hair with a rumble of pleasure, seeming content to have her covered in his scent.

When he pulled away, he went back to his dresser and dropped his towel. She made a strangled sound to see he was fully erect again. He glanced at her over his shoulder, brow raised, then shrugged when he saw the direction of her gaze and lazily pulled on a pair of sweatpants, completely ignoring his erection.

"Ready?" He came to a stop next to her, hesitantly holding his hand out, not quite looking at her.

As if he expected her to pull away and pretend what they shared never happened.

Pursing her lips at the idiot girls in his past, she slipped her hand into his, enjoying the slide of his callused fingers against her palms, and tightened her grip until he looked up at her. "Any time."

His expression brightened, his teal eyes sparkled at the promise, and he tugged her out the door. As they headed toward the stairs, she stopped at the bottom, her chest constricting at the thought of seeing Logan again.

"Annora? May I speak to you?"

She whirled to see Edgar waiting at the bottom of the stairs, partially hidden in the shadows of the kitchen. Grateful for the reprieve, she nodded. "Fine."

She lifted Xander's hand and kissed the back of it. "I'll be right back."

He leaned closer and kissed her forehead, then disappeared up the stairs. Blowing out a breath, she headed toward the kitchen with a heavy heart, bracing herself for the pain of having Edgar leave her for another woman.

Edgar was pacing back and forth, his head down, looking completely lost, and it hurt her to see him so defeated.

"Do you love her?"

Edgar jerked as if she'd shot him. As she waited for him to answer, it was like all the oxygen had been sucked out of the room.

Chapter
Twenty-three

Edgar whirled and scowled at her. "Of course not."

Her relief was instantaneous, the churning in her stomach settled, while the world around her finally came into focus again, and she glared at him. "Then why did you go to her?"

She bit her lip, cursing herself for even asking.

It was selfish, but she couldn't help feeling like he abandoned her.

Edgar grabbed her hands as if he could stop her from slipping away. "She was *dying*. Dying for a phantom is beyond frightening. We don't just die—we're sent to the afterworld to be hunted down. I couldn't let her face that alone."

His voice cracked, and she felt like an ass. He had been alone for so long in the abyss, and no one went after him. Of course he couldn't let her die alone. She dropped her forehead against his shoulder, feeling like an idiot for not figuring it out sooner.

"Why didn't she heal?" She pressed her hand over his heart, only relaxing when his arms wrapped around her.

Edgar rubbed the back of her neck, the touch soothing both of them. "She doesn't have an affinity for the afterworld like you do. The sword that cut her was created with dark matter, making the wounds burn deeper, the injuries more severe. The combination was catastrophic for her."

He ran his hand down her back, cuddling her closer, almost as if she was the one he nearly lost. "What you did was absolutely amazing…but it's going to attract the attention of your father. He's going to come for you now."

She shivered at his certainty, then brushed it off. "He was going to come after me either way."

His arms wrapped around her, crushing her to his chest. "You risk getting captured if you go help her."

"Not for her, you idiot…for you." Annora pulled back to look up at him, needing to know how he really felt. "But are you sure this is what you want? You could have your old life back, everything you lost. I—"

"I'm sure." He buried his face against the crook of her neck. "I can't lose you, not after I just found you. I can't go back to that empty life—I won't. We're in this together."

Her heart seized at his conviction. While his vow should've thrilled her, she was terrified instead. She didn't want sole responsibility for his happiness. She was toxic to those she loved. People would keep coming for her, targeting them to get to her.

But she was too selfish to let them go.

She pressed against Edgar, vowing to do everything in her power, even break the veil separating them from the afterworld, if that's what it took.

Edgar straightened and kissed the top of her head. "Your men are waiting for you."

Upstairs.

In her bed.

She should be nervous about the prospect of sleeping next to them—touching them—but it felt odd not to have them close. She craved their touch after so many years of being isolated. Pulling away from him, she turned toward the stairs, then reached back and held out her hand when he didn't follow. "You coming?"

He straightened, his shoulders going back, his eyes suddenly blazing with emotions, and he grabbed her hand. His grip was tight, a silent promise that he would never let her go again, and the cage holding her emotions in check creaked open a little. As they reached the second floor, she paused at the bottom of the steps, suddenly worried about her welcome.

Edgar squeezed her hand, standing quietly at her side to give her time to shore up her ragged emotions. When she released a heavy sigh, he brushed his thumb along the back of her hand. Touching was still new for both of them, and she glanced at him to see his dark blue eyes staring at their joint hands in wonder.

As if sensing her attention, he glanced up and gave her a gentle smile. "You have nothing to fear. Your battered heart is safe with them."

"How do you know?" she asked, her voice hoarse. She could survive a beating and swallow pain with a laugh, but just the thought of her men turning away from her was enough to destroy her.

Edgar lifted her hand to cover his heart. "Because if they feel even a tenth of what I do, the thought of blaming you never entered their minds."

She searched his face for the truth and saw what she had been too afraid to look for earlier—and her breath caught in the back of her throat. "You love me."

"Always." He gave her a crooked smile. "With everything that I am."

Wonder and joy bubbled through her, and she reached up to cup his face. He leaned into her touch, his eyes closing, as if he'd finally come home.

"How do phantoms pledge themselves to each other?" Her heart skipped a beat at the very idea of someone taking him from her now she finally found him.

His eyes snapped open, and he gazed down at her with the pure afterworld blazing in his eyes. He searched her face, then released a shuddering breath. "You're sure?"

"Absolutely." Annora placed her hand directly over his heart. "We almost lost each other once. I want to be your anchor, so you'll never be lost or alone again."

He wet his lips, his hand trembling under hers. "If you have any doubts, we can wait. Once done, it can't be undone. You'll never escape me."

"I'm sure. One hundred percent." Annora tipped her head to the side and pursed her lips. "But the same goes for you. If you're doing this out of a sense of obligation, or because of my father—"

"Your father never crossed my mind." Edgar gave her a savage grin, the afterworld fading from his eyes and the fathomless blue she adored swirled in the depths as he pulled her closer. "I'm selfish and greedy and want you for my own. I want the family you're building here, not the one that tossed me away, and I will defend you and this new future with my life." He quickly searched her eyes. "If you'll have me."

Her skin tingled at his vow, her heart ready to burst. She tightened her hands on his shoulders, possessiveness and yearning sweeping through her. Everything he described sounded like a fairytale come true. "Yes—yes to everything."

Edgar drew away from her, pulling out a knife from somewhere on his person. He held out his hand, silently asking for her trust. Without hesitation, she placed her hand in his, palm up. Gazing into her eyes, he ran the blade across her flesh. Blood beaded up from the small, shallow cut to pool in her hand, and she gave a hum of pleasure at the bite of pain.

She watched him make the same cut across his own palm, then reach for her, his bloody hand closing around the inside of her wrist. She followed his example, clamping his arm in her hand, and she peeked up at him.

Raw hunger and possessiveness blazed in his black eyes. She felt the tug of the afterworld as dark particles began to swirl and twine around their clamped arms. The darkness solidified until they were bound together by a curl of smoke. It licked at her flesh, and pain prickled along her wrist where his blood touched, searing into her skin like a brand.

She sucked in a harsh breath, her grip tightening on his arm as her fingers spasmed. Edgar grunted as if she'd kicked him in the balls. Then the smoke seemed to absorb into their skin, leaving her whole arm tingling.

He unclasped his hand from around her wrist. Instead of releasing her, he cradled her hand in his, and she looked to see that all evidence of the injury was gone. He slowly pulled her arm closer until the underside of her wrist came into view, and she gasped.

A tiny tree was etched into her skin, spanning her wrist from side to side, almost completely circular as the branches reached down and the roots curled up. The afterworld swirled in the black lines like it was alive.

She grabbed his hand, twisting his arm to find the same symbol stamped into his flesh.

"For eternity," he murmured, running his fingers over the symbol.

The leaves seemed to sway until she'd swear she could see his name in the twisted branches. Emotions poured through at his touch—possessiveness, love, devotion, and an all-consuming need to protect.

His emotions.

He released her, running his thumb over his own wrist, as if to make sure it didn't disappear. "Lore indicates that most couples start with a small symbol. Each phantom couple is imprinted with their own image specific to them. As they grow together, so does the mark. It's tied to our health and emotions. As we grow stronger, the roots and branches can wrap around our entire arm...or wither and die."

Annora covered her wrist protectively.

Edgar smiled, then bowed gallantly before her and offered her his arm. "Come...you need your rest. Tomorrow will be here soon, and we'll need to plan and train for your father's arrival."

She accepted his courtly gesture, no longer nervous about facing the others, not with Edgar's love wrapped around her. As she walked into her room, she paused when she saw the guys had spread the sheets and covers across the floor to create a makeshift bed.

The whole team was waiting for her. Logan was in the middle, already fast asleep, a little furrow between his brows. An open space was waiting for her next to him. Camden was at the end, while Xander was at the other end, both clearly keeping watch. Mason scooted over, making enough room for the two of them.

A little self-conscious about wearing just a shirt, she hurried under the blankets. Edgar hesitated a moment, but when no one protested, he took his place next to her. Being near the guys was like a contact high, their touch calming her. Logan sighed in his sleep and wrapped himself around her, and all her worries and anxieties over the day melted away.

Logan jolted awake, terror gripping him as he searched the room, his heartbeat only calming when he recognized his surroundings.

He was home.

His breath whooshed out of him, and he cradled his head in his hands, his insides shaking so hard he was afraid he would vomit. For a second he thought being rescued had been a cruel dream, and he'd wake up in that hellhole again.

But he knew this room, could feel the wood floor beneath him, see the familiar objects. Although he was ridiculously pleased to see the guys were gone, giving him some privacy.

He inhaled deeply, humming when he caught Annora's delicious scent. It was hard to explain the smell…the closest he could come up with was a combination of warmth and flowers just after the rain.

He leaned over her sleeping form, joy bursting through him simply because he could actually look at her whenever he wanted. He gently brushed a strand of hair away from her face, marveling at her silken skin.

She blinked up at him sleepily, nestling into his touch, a bright smile curling her lips and something inside him unfurled at the unguarded moment. He leaned down and brushed his lips against hers.

Annora jolted under him, then pulled back to cup his face, her eyes wide awake. Then her brows knitted, and she began to poke and prod him, shoving up his shirt to run her hands along his chest.

"If you want to get me naked, you only have to ask." He smirked down at her when she froze, her eyes widening almost comically when she realized what she was doing. When a blush swept along her cheeks, his heart warmed.

The worry that she'd look at him differently, might be repulsed by him, evaporated, and he fell to his side next to her and cuddled her close. She buried her face against his chest and he hugged her tighter, running his hand up and down her back.

When his stomach growled, he could feel Annora smile against his shoulder. She pushed away from him, shoving her hair away from her face, and kissed his chin. "You're hungry. Let's get some breakfast."

Logan rolled onto his back and watched Annora kick away the blankets, her night shirt hiking up dangerously, and he sucked in a sharp breath when his cock sprang to attention in response. After being tortured, nearly every inch of his skin cut and burned, part of him had been afraid that he'd never be able to function completely again.

As Annora fluttered around the room, picking out her clothes, he cupped himself through the sweats, then sucked in a startled breath, quickly dropping his hand away from the almost too-sensitive contact. A second later, a joyous smile spread across his face, ridiculously relieved to know that he was fully functional.

When she slipped into the bathroom, he gingerly hauled himself to his feet, his bones creaking like an old man. It took a good five minutes for his muscles to respond and warm up. By the time he could straighten completely, he was shaking from the exertion.

"It'll take time for your body to feel like it's your own again."

He whirled to find Annora leaning against the doorway of the bathroom, concern darkening her eyes as she tenderly assessed his scars. She didn't look disgusted, more like sad she couldn't have prevented them.

He unconsciously ran his hand over the jagged markings. While his body felt familiar, it was different, not so completely under his control anymore, and it disturbed him.

He could live with the marks, but it was harder to deal with the knowledge that she'd survived under that sadistic fuck's care for nearly ten years. How—he wasn't sure. He barely survived a week. Bile rose in his throat at the thought of all the pain and horror she endured without hope of rescue.

"How long did it take for you to feel normal?" Logan picked up a discarded shirt and pulled it over his head, feeling suddenly shy about her seeing his body.

She gave him a crooked smile, then leaned down and began

straightening their scattered bed. "I never knew what it was like to be normal, not until I met you and the rest of the guys."

Fuck if his heart didn't crack right then.

Determination burned in his chest—if it was the last thing he ever did, he would do devote the rest of his life to making her happy.

When she straightened, her arms full of blankets, her eyes sparkling with mischief, he felt the first flash of familiar fire in his chest. He was afraid to move, afraid he might lose the feeling and fall back into the black hole that was his life for the past week.

Needing a distraction, he cocked his head. "What are you thinking?"

"I have a way for us to reclaim your body as your own." She dropped the blankets at her feet, nearly stumbling over them when she headed toward the stairs. She stopped at the top, then turned back toward him and held out her hand. "Trust me?"

His damned cock jumped at the mention of her claiming his body, and he gave her a crooked smile, knowing she didn't have a clue what she did to him with her innocent comment. He slipped his hand into hers, a weight lifting off his chest when she didn't flinch away, and the part of him had been petrified that the bastard had ruined him faded.

He tightened his hold, her touch making him believe that he could be normal and whole again. "With my life."

Annora told Mason what she needed—that's how they ended up in the tiny hole-in-the wall place in the middle of nowhere. The building was rickety, the paint chipped, the sign out front so faded it was hard to read.

Rick's Tattoos and Piercings.

The guys took formation around her, Logan at her side, as they studied the building.

"We should be back at the house training," Sadie snipped, pacing while she scowled at them. "The sheer mass of magic you used is going to attract an invading army, and none of you are remotely ready to fight."

"Enough." Camden didn't have to yell for Sadie to shut the fuck up. His voice carried enough command that her mouth snapped shut with an audible click. But it didn't stop the glares and muttering as they began to walk toward the building.

The guys had agreed to give her a few hours alone as a family without training or worrying about their future.

Time for them to heal.

Terrance and Kevin had returned home that morning bruised, battered, splattered with blood and gore, but they were laughing and talking. They promised to guard the house while the rest of them were gone and call if there was any trouble.

Lionel and Giles were working together to help organize the stray wolves who lost their alpha, so things everywhere across campus were in an uproar. Some of the wolves and shifters fought willingly in order to keep up their drug supply, but most of them had been forced to fight by an alpha who was too strong for them to disobey.

Loulou took charge of the magic users who had begun calling to demand an audience.

It was a fucking mess. Call her a coward, but Annora wanted no part of sorting it out.

As they piled into the building, she was relieved to see the place was neat as a pin, a fire flickering in the entryway to keep them warm. There were a couple of other shifters in the place, watching them warily, and Annora pushed her way to the front.

"I'm here to see Rick." She brushed her hands along the counter, only to have Logan link their fingers together to stop her nervous gesture.

A man came out of the back. His beard shadowing most of his face, while his eyes were a deep brown that matched his long, shaggy hair. What startled her the most was he practically oozed magic.

The man stopped a good foot away from the counter, crossed his arms as he surveyed them, then grunted. "I'm Rick."

Annora chewed her lip and glanced up at Logan. "This was a dumb idea. You don't have to do this."

"Hush." Logan leaned down, brushing a kiss across her lips,

effectively shutting her up. Then he straightened and gave the man a nod. "I'd like to get a piercing."

Annora could feel her eyes widen, and she spun to gape at Logan. For some reason, that was the last thing she expected.

Rick tipped his head to the side to study them with narrowed eyes. Magic splashed into the room, licking at them. With a sigh, he dropped his arm and lifted part of the counter, then stepped back. "Follow me."

When Annora went to obey, Mason grabbed her from behind, easily picking her up off her feet and carting her away. Logan gave her a wink and disappeared into the back with Rick.

The guys seated themselves at various spots around the room, but Annora couldn't sit still and began pacing. The other people in the place watched them for a few minutes, then seemed to decide they were harmless and continued to page through the books, talking quietly among themselves.

It was over in only a few minutes but it seemed to take forever for Logan to appear again. As he emerged from the back room, she scanned his face, then frowned.

She couldn't see any piercings.

Then understanding dawned and her eyes widened. Her glance dropped to survey his body, and her cheeks heated while her mind hummed with possibilities.

Mason came to her side and snorted, waving his hand in front of her face until she blinked. "I think you broke her."

The guys snickered and snorted at her expense, while Logan just gave her a smile. He stopped right in front of her, his spine straight, his shoulders back. "It...helped. I just need one more thing."

"What?" she asked, her voice barely above a whisper. She'd do whatever was in her power to make him feel like himself again instead of a prisoner.

"This." Logan picked up her hand, then turned her arm up and ran his thumb over the small tree that was branded into her skin. "I want you to mark me."

The rest of the guys gathered closer and nodded.

Sadie stood in the back, her mouth hanging open as she looked back and forth between Annora and Edgar and the mark. Instead of looking pissed for once, she sighed and glanced at Edgar. "You could've done a lot worse."

Something inside Annora eased at the acceptance on the young phantom's face.

"Don't get me wrong, I still think you're an idiot." She shrugged, nudging her friend with her shoulder, giving him a smirk. "But at least you're a happy idiot."

Edgar snorted but didn't protest, pure happiness blazing from his eyes.

Annora studied him, wondering if it would bother him to have the other guys wear the symbol he'd shared with her. He nodded at her silent question and gave her a slight smile in understanding.

She went through the same process that Edgar had shown her, slicing her palm and then theirs, wincing when she cut them despite their encouragement. When they tried to do it themselves, she shook her head.

It was her mark, her responsibility.

The afterworld rose at her call, marking each of them with the same tree. The guys either grimaced at the pain or grinned, but none of them protested as a tree was branded on their wrist, each a different color. She wasn't sure what the colors meant, but she liked seeing them bear her mark. With each new tattoo, a leaf on her tree changed colors to match theirs.

If she looked closely enough, she could see their names etched into her skin…and she could feel their joy and possessiveness at being claimed, the warm glow of their love filling her heart.

They were finally hers, and she was determined to keep it that way.

It was time to go home and prepare for war.

Chapter Twenty-four

Fuck!

Annora scanned the yard as they pulled up, her heart sinking when she saw the house was packed to the rafters with people. She wanted to tell the guys to keep driving, craving more time alone with them, but it wasn't an option.

She needed to train for the real possibility of meeting her father.

She should be excited or nervous at the possibility of seeing him for the first time, but since he was probably coming to kill her, it kinda squashed any curiosity.

Had he known she was alive?

Had he left her in hell to suffer at the hands of her uncle on purpose, hoping to be rid of her?

Had he loved her mother, or had she just been a convenience?

As the van pulled into the yard, she tucked away her childish thoughts. No, if her father had ever thought of her, it wasn't with kindness.

Camden parked the vehicle but didn't turn it off. None of the other guys got out either, as if fighting the same impulse to just leave.

Unfortunately, no matter where they went, her father would find them.

Camden must have come to the same conclusion—he turned off the engine with a sigh.

As the doors opened, Sadie boldly strode out of the house, having used her abilities to beat them home. A harried Loulou scrambled outside a second later, practically bouncing on her feet, babbling a million miles an hour.

A cluster of witches were gathered near the door, glaring as if angry she and the guys dared to be away from home when they came to visit. Willa looked annoyed by the proceedings, standing off to the side, leaning against a tree with her arms crossed, her blue hair making her stand out from the rest. She looked exhausted, the dark circles under her green eyes making the color appear even more vivid.

Their gazes met for a fraction, and Annora could have sworn the witch rolled her eyes.

The shifters were different, prowling around the perimeter of the property, each alert and waiting for attack. They snapped to attention when the vehicle pulled into the yard, every one of them anxious to be noticed. Lionel and his men were maintaining order, glaring at anyone who got too rowdy or belligerent...which looked to be a full-time job.

Neither group was happy to be in the same vicinity as to the other.

"What do they want?" Annora slumped back against her seat, reluctant to leave the privacy of the vehicle.

"The witches will either demand the book be returned to them or insist you start their training immediately," Mason murmured, then glanced at her with a half-smile. "Most likely both."

"The shifters no doubt have petitions they want you to review." Camden glared at the intruders, grumbling under his breath. "I'll deal with them, and let you know if there's anything of interest."

Annora knew she should protest, that it was her job to decide those types of things, but she didn't feel she had enough experience to judge issues in the shifter world. She'd rather leave it to someone who knew what they were doing. "I'd appreciate it."

Yet no one made a move to leave the vehicle.

Logan broke first and reached for the door. "I'll work on making lunch."

"I'd like to join you when you train the witches." Edgar crowded closer to her. "I don't trust them not to try and trap you in some way."

The rest of the guys grunted their agreement.

As the doors opened, no one even pretended they weren't staring and waiting for them. The guys circled her, falling into protective formation around her as the shifters and witches surged forward. Only when she started up the steps did she feel unfettered magic snapping around her and the guys.

"We came here for our training." Brad and Brittney smirked up at her, pretending like they hadn't tried to force her hand with a weak, witchy potshot at her and Mason.

"Actually, I don't remember you helping or even showing up for the battle." Annora stopped and turned to face the spoiled twins, then looked beyond them. "Willa? I trust you to select the appropriate candidates—if you trust any other witches, that is—and we'll start training in half an hour."

Ignoring the shouts of protest, Annora grabbed the door handle and addressed the shifters. "Give us five minutes to get settled, then Camden will come out to hear your…petitions."

Giving into the need to run, she wrenched open the door and shot inside.

Only when the door snapped shut behind her and the guys was she able to finally catch her breath. Sadie immediately pulled Edgar aside, and Annora had to work on biting back the sting of jealousy at seeing their two heads so close together.

She brushed the pad of her thumb over the slightly raised tattoo on her wrists. Warmth instantly flooded her, leaving her skin tingling. Edgar lifted his fathomless blue eyes toward her as if sensing her attention, his gaze warming from its usual biting chill, and he smiled at her.

Logan distracted her by giving her a kiss on her forehead, then disappeared into the kitchen to prepare dinner. Mason gathered her close, giving her a quick hug, rubbing his large hands soothingly up and down her back before he kissed the top of her head and went to help Logan.

Xander cupped the back of her neck and pulled her close. "I'll get things set up for our training session."

"Umph." Annora leaned into him, her head dropping forward to rest against his chest, her body already aching at the thought of his training.

It was pointless to ask him to go easy on her.

He gave her hair one last tug, then pulled away. As he headed for the basement, she noticed Kevin and Terrance were waiting off to the side. Xander gave them a sharp look, noting their battered appearance, then sighed and opened the door. "If you're going to live here, you're going to have to train harder. You're no way in shape enough to train with the elite teams."

He disappeared down the stairs. The brothers looked at each other, grinned like fools, and followed him down into the darkness.

Camden ran a single finger along her jaw, then bumped his knuckle under her chin before he dropped his hand. "I'll just be outside if you need me."

Edgar turned from Sadie, bowing slightly toward Annora. "I'll go collect Willa and be back shortly."

It was both a warning and a promise.

He didn't wait for her response, simply disappeared outside by way of the door.

Annora headed up the stairs, stopping when she noticed something was slightly off about her room. The air smelled different. Odd. Slightly dark and earthly, and she cursed.

Witches.

The fuckers searched her room, no doubt looking for the book.

Her eyes darted across the room to the closet. Even though she knew the book wouldn't be there, she was drawn anyway. As she reached for the door, the afterworld curled around the edges without even being called.

The doorknob was cold against her palm, then warmed as if recognizing her touch, welcoming her home.

She was floored when she opened the door and saw the book was waiting for her.

"Annora?" Sadie was standing at the top of the stairs, scowling as she surveyed the room. Then her gaze locked on the closet door, her eyes widened almost comically. "What—"

Annora slammed the door shut, dispelling the afterworld, tiny grains of sand drifting down like rain, only to vanish in a puff of smoke as they hit the floor. She lifted her chin and looked at the cool, beautiful princess. "Are you here to kill me?"

Sadie's attention snapped toward hers, then she shook her head and chuckled. "I think even if I tried, it wouldn't be possible, would it?"

Annora wasn't sure any longer and answered honestly. "I don't know. You might have better luck than most if you use your sword. Nothing lives forever."

Sadie heaved a sigh, the tension draining out of her. "To answer your question, no. I have no intention of harming you." She ran her fingers through her hair, looking conflicted and confused. "I no longer know the right path anymore. Nothing is as I've been told."

She straightened, as if she'd come to a hard decision. "But I do know that your Edgar is no longer my Alcott. He's changed. For the better."

She looked down and played with her fingers, her shoulders slumping. "I used to think he was the answer to all our problems. Now I know I was right—because it led me to you. After what you did last night, the sheer power you were able to gather…I only know one other person who could do such a thing."

Annora's stomach tilted wildly.

She already knew the answer. "My father."

Sadie nodded, her face grim. "And he won't be pleased. He's stronger and faster thanks to years of practice, but you rival him for sheer power. Given time, I think you'll surpass him, and he won't be happy. If he can't control you—"

"He'll kill me."

But Sadie was shaking her head. "He'll try to break you first. He'll go after you where you're the most vulnerable."

The guys.

Fury rose in her hard and fast, dark particles seeping from her skin at the threat.

"The bindings—the tattoo connecting you to the others—might be the only thing that saves you and them. You can draw power from them but also send power to them. If their lives are threatened, you can keep them alive."

"By draining myself."

"Yes." Sadie cocked her head, studying her. "But I suspect you already know that, or you wouldn't have agreed to it." The phantom touched her own wrist, a slight movement that Annora almost missed.

"You're envious. Why?" It wasn't jealousy or anything so simple, but maybe Annora was wrong. She still wasn't very good at reading people.

Sadie grimaced, quickly dropping her hands, but she didn't deny it. "Phantoms used to mate for life. It was said to be one of the greatest honors to be chosen. The markings don't show up unless you find your perfect match, someone who will love you beyond life and into death. That was taken from us when it was decided we'd be stronger devoting ourselves to our race and not one person."

Annora slumped, not needing to guess who ordered such a thing. "My father again."

"Actually, no." Sadie shrugged when she caught Annora staring at her. "But he upholds the laws made by the council ruthlessly and without mercy."

"Do you think they're wrong?" Annora shifted on her feet, not sure why the answer was so important to her.

"Before today, I would've said no. I didn't know any different until now." Sadie looked out the window, as if she couldn't bear to look at the future that had been denied her. "But after meeting you and seeing your men...I don't know anymore."

Footsteps pounded up the stairs. Sadie quickly sidestepped, going into warrior mode, seeming to snatch her sword out of thin air, the afterworld still clinging to it.

Only to have Edgar and Willa barge into the room.

Annora glanced beyond them, then raised a brow and smiled. "Don't trust the others?"

"Not even an inch." Willa snorted, her green eyes bright, and she lifted her chin, the humor vanishing. "In case you're not aware, I'm only a half witch. Most witches are fanatically loyal to their covens, while we mixed bloods are assigned to them like heifers at an auction.

My coven isn't happy about my little rebellion. They've demanded loyalty and threatened to banish me if I didn't take them with me today. I'm sure they'll think of something unpleasant to do to me as punishment, but I refuse to bend to them, not when I finally have a choice and the power to enforce it."

"We're more alike than I thought. I'm not very good at taking orders either." Edgar and Sadie both snorted, and Annora glanced at the two phantoms who stood off to the side. Neither of them protested her training Willa in the forbidden dark matter magic— something so dangerous it would mean an immediate death sentence if other phantoms discovered the truth.

She studied them a moment longer but couldn't detect any reluctance about her training an outsider. Annora took that as a giant step in the right direction. She lifted her hand, then called up a ball of churning smoke and held it out toward Willa. "You won't be able to conjure the dark matter, but let's check to see if you have an affinity to using it."

She tossed the ball up in the air, letting it hover between them. A true smile crossed Willa's face, determination to master this new ability sharpening her stare.

It was an hour before lunch was called, but it was enough to leave Willa swearing and sweaty. While the witch could use dark matter, it was taxing. She couldn't cast using the dark particles directly, but she could use them to boost her own spells. The destructive force was awe-inspiring, the proof leaving Annora's room covered with feathers and splinters of wood when the spells went awry.

As they headed down the stairs, Annora nudged Willa. "Want to join us for dinner?"

Though she looked tempted, Willa ultimately shook her head. "I'd better not. The longer I'm gone, the more restless the coven will get. If I don't show up soon, they're going to storm the house."

Annora grimaced at the thought.

The witches gathered like sharks scenting blood.

"You're welcome to sneak out the back," Annora offered. When they reached the bottom of the stairs, the kitchen was empty except for Mason and Loulou. The troll was leaning casually against the wall, patiently waiting for her, while Loulou was partially hanging out of the fridge, her backside wiggling and bobbing around while she dug around for something.

Willa hesitated at the offer, then sighed in defeat. "No, it's better to face them on my own terms. They'll only track me down later and make me pay for it."

She headed toward the door, then hesitated. "You're not what I expected."

Annora lifted her brows, not sure whether that was good or bad.

"I don't like many people, but I find myself liking you." Willa sounded grumpy and resigned as she turned and exited through the front door.

Annora stared at the door, a bit bemused and flustered by the backhanded compliment when Loulou popped up next to her. She had her hands full of so many drinks that they threatened to spill out of her arms. Then Annora noticed Loulou had a carrot tucked in one of her hands, and she had to suppress her chuckle.

Loulou squinted at the door, still and silent for once, then heaved a sigh. "I hate to admit it, but she's not bad. For a witch."

After her grudging approval, Loulou bumped Annora's hip with hers, then scooted out the kitchen toward the back door, practically skipping to a tune only she could hear, not missing a beat as she juggled the drinks while chewing her carrot stick.

Mason grabbed Annora's hand and dragged her toward the living room after the rabbit. "The guys decided to have a barbeque."

Annora stopped in the middle of the room when she saw the deck and backyard were packed. She wasn't used to being surrounded by so many people, and barely managed not to back away and bolt back to her room. Some of the shifters were the ones who'd been waiting for them out front when they returned from battle, the ones Camden must have approved, but she recognized more than a few of the others as pack leaders by the power radiating from them.

Alphas.

There was nothing remotely human about the group. They were pure predators in human form, ready to kill anyone who threatened them.

She wasn't foolish enough to think they were her friends.

If she became a threat, they wouldn't hesitate to eliminate her.

It was the way of their world.

But at the moment she was the lesser of two evils, the only thing standing between them and the phantoms who could destroy them on a whim if they so chose.

But not all the people on the deck were strangers.

A few people she would consider friends mingled in the crowd, allies who would fight alongside her through anything. They were standing with her men, watching the rest of the group for any sign of trouble.

Mason didn't like the stillness around Annora, the way she retreated into her shell where he couldn't reach her. He gently nudged her toward the couch. "Sit."

She obeyed without protest, blinking up at him until awareness flooded back into her eyes.

He took a seat next to her, then reached over and picked her up, placing her on his lap so her back was to him. She let out an adorable, startled squeak, and he had to suppress his smile. That she didn't get up and leave or ask him what he was doing warmed his heart.

She trusted him.

He gathered the long, silky strands of her dark brown hair into his hands and began to comb through it with his fingers, enjoying the way the wispy strands clung to him. He could almost pretend she was like him, and her hair revealed her emotions.

She melted with a sigh, her head falling forward, giving him free access.

After a moment, he broke the silence. "Want to tell me what's wrong?"

She gave an elegant shrug with one shoulder and waved her hand at the window without looking. "I thought I was getting better at being around people, but the moment I saw the crowd on the deck, the need to run and hide came flooding back. My uncle is dead. So why am I still so afraid?"

"You're not afraid." She sounded so disgruntled, he slipped his hand around her neck, sliding it up to cup her face and turned it gently toward him. "You were never afraid of us, not really."

Annora rolled her eyes and tsked. "You guys are different."

His cock throbbed at her husky tone, and he stifled a groan. It seemed that any time she even breathed in his direction his body reacted the same way. He brushed the backs of his fingers against her cheek, unable to keep himself from stealing the touch. "Damn right we are. You knew from the beginning that we'd never hurt you. Being cautious around others is normal. It's called self-preservation. But we would never let anything happen to you."

She sighed, turned sideways and snuggled against him, her slight weight delicious against his chest. "I know you wouldn't. I just thought that after a time I would be…" She shrugged, looking down and fiddled with the hem of her shirt.

"Normal?" He easily guessed what she wanted to say.

Her one shoulder lifted in a shrug, but she didn't look up.

"If you were normal, we would never have met." Her eyes snapped up, an adorable scowl on her face. "If you were normal, you would've run from me and the rest of the guys the first chance you got." Unable to resist, he leaned down and kissed the tip of her nose when she opened her mouth to protest. "We're broken in a way that only you can make whole, because you know what it's like to be so wrecked it's a struggle to survive. You know how to find the pieces of us and put them together again."

Like a cat, Annora squirmed until she was wrapped around him, her little claws kneading and petting his chest to soothe him. Unsurprisingly, his troll calmed at her touch, giving a little rumble of approval. His hair settled around him, almost subdued.

When her stomach grumbled, he chuckled, then scooped her up and stood.

Instead of jumping at his touch, she leaned into him. It took all his control to deposit her back on the couch when what he really wanted to do was take her back to his room and show her how much she meant to him.

He leaned forward to brush his lips across her forehead. She took advantage of the situation and tipped her head back, her lips meeting his, a silent demand to be kissed. He squashed his smile, his heart light at knowing his plan to make her fall madly in love with them was working. Every day she was becoming closer and closer to the guys.

When she tried to deepen the kiss, his dick throbbed painfully. He nipped at her with his fangs, then pulled back at her throaty moan, refusing to give the people on the deck a show. He had no problem sharing her with the team or watching them pleasure her. Making her happy was a job they shared equally.

But no one else had the right to see her that way.

That privilege was reserved only for them.

He straightened, stifling a groan when his cock stood at attention, nearly level with her heated gaze. She looked up at him from under her lashes and licked her lips, and he'd swear all his brain cells shut down.

"You're hungry." He stumbled away from her, struggling to remember why he released her in the first place.

Annora folded her hands demurely in her lap, her eyes trailing up his body, the heat of them leaving flames licking along his skin, and it was all he could do not to lunge for her. He reached down, unconsciously cupping himself, watching as her eyes dilated with lust.

The sound of laughter broke the spell, and he swiped the sweat off his forehead, backing away from her. "For food. I'll get you food."

Fresh air swirled through the room as Mason made his escape. He headed straight for the food, clearly on a mission, and she chuckled when he began to stack food on a plate. When he was only halfway through the line, he scowled at the plate, then went back for another one, hesitated as if debating with himself, and gathered two more before he headed back to the line, obviously determined to make her try everything.

Her heart softened at having the big man fuss over her.

The others seemed to know she'd only allow that from him.

While Annora knew Mason wasn't sexually inexperienced, his reaction to her made it feel special—like she was the only woman who mattered.

Everything was new and fresh.

She wasn't some weeping virgin. She felt no shyness or shame when she was around the men, not anymore. The knowledge that they were hers made her feel bold. She'd never felt desire before them, never yearned for a kiss or wanted to be touched.

With them, it was different.

Each touch, each kiss made her feel more alive than ever before.

Like they were awaking her from a horrible dream.

They were the real world.

They were her life and future.

With that thought, needing to be close to them, she got to her feet and made her way toward the sliding doors. She was no longer afraid to face the others on the deck, not with her men at her side. It was where she belonged.

As she reached for the door, the room behind her cooled dramatically. A shiver snaked down her spine, but it had nothing to do with the temperature.

"Good afternoon, Daughter dearest. I thought it was best that we finally meet, don't you agree?"

Chapter
Twenty-five

The voice was deep and cultured, every word modulated in a way that was guaranteed to annoy the piss out of her. Annora's gaze flew to the guys, but even as she watched, the glass separating them began to fog.

It only took seconds to black it out completely.

Darkness stirred around her fingertips. Though she could easily dispel it, she decided to wait. The last thing she wanted was to put her men at risk.

Very slowly, Annora turned and faced her father.

He…wasn't what she was expecting.

He wasn't a big man, more medium height and slim build, and reserved, like he'd emerged from a different era. Since phantoms could live for centuries or even longer, she shouldn't have been surprised.

He didn't look like the power-hungry megalomaniac she was expecting.

Until she got to his eyes.

Pure ruthlessness stared back from those black pools. No hint of color was revealed in their dark depths, like he'd swallowed the afterworld. She tore her eyes away, checking the room, but he was alone. She wasn't sure that was much better than if he'd brought an army.

He could easily kill her without any other phantoms being the wiser.

"Hello, Daxion. I would say this was a pleasure, but I detest lying." She didn't bother smiling at the man who was her father. Though her mother was the complete opposite of him in personality, she could easily imagine her slight, petite mother, who never had a hair out of place, standing next to him.

That's where the comparisons ended.

Her mother loved and laughed and lived to help others. This man, the way he looked down his nose at her, would be content to cut her throat without blinking if she dared get in his way.

"What do you want?" It chilled her to see him study her with curiosity. She'd take his disdain, or no emotion at all, over that.

"You're causing quite a stir." He sauntered toward her, unbuttoned his tailored coat and sat, resting his arm along the back of the couch…revealing two small blades tucked into his jacket. "I decided to investigate."

He was so calm and collected, not a hint of emotion marred his expression. She didn't make the mistake of thinking him cold and unfeeling. She'd met enough men in her life to know that psychopaths came in all flavors and could strike at any time.

Instead of provoking him, she took a seat opposite. "What do you want to know?"

He pursed his lips, clearly not liking her taking control of the conversation. "You seem completely unaware of the phantom realm and your place in it. You're upsetting the balance."

Annora widened her eyes, going for the innocent look. "Whatever do you mean?"

He cocked his head like a curious bird, the afterworld clinging him, ready to yank him out of danger if he came under attack. Annora kept her hands on her knees, making no sudden moves, very conscious of those shiny blades easily within his reach.

"Phantoms have a very precarious place in the world. We don't share our magic with others. Imagine if the world discovered eternal youth. What if no one ever died or had to face the consequences for their actions?"

Annora grimaced, recognizing the truth of what he was saying.

The world would descend into chaos.

"So you go about killing anyone who challenges...your way of life?" Annora frowned and leaned forward. "But what if phantoms don't deserve that type of power either?"

His smile was sharp and lethal when he leaned forward to match her pose. "We have checks and balances to make sure that doesn't happen."

"Explain." Annora should be thrilled to finally meet her father and talk with him. Unfortunately, the creep vibes coming off him erased any pretense of fatherly love or devotion. She didn't need to be told that she shouldn't get too close to him for fear he would turn on her and ordered her tossed in a dungeon just as graciously as he smiled.

"Most phantoms live in a delicate balance. Too much of the darkness will poison us and not enough will slowly starve us to death. Imagine if everyone had access to it. The well of power would shrink, putting our way of life and our people in jeopardy." He shrugged, not the least bit perturbed. "No one has complete control over the darkness. Only the very strongest can spend any time there without losing themselves to it."

His eyes dropped to her neck, and the first hint of true emotions entered his eyes—awe mixed with wonder, not to mention a huge dose of greed and anger. "Where did you get that?"

Annora didn't dare take her eyes off him. She reached up, her fingers tangling in the chain around her neck, and she curled her hand around the coin that dangled and spun in the air. "A friend gave it to me. He thought I would need protection."

She refused to acknowledge that it was his brother.

Only after she tucked the coin back into her shirt did Daxion seem to shake himself out of his stupor.

"Hand it over." He shot to his feet, and thrust out his hand, glowering down at her. Blackness seeped from him and crept across the floor toward her, the inkiness almost sinister in the way it moved, like it was prepared to take the necklace from her. "Now! Or I'll make you regret it."

Before she had a chance to respond, Edgar appeared behind him, Sadie's sword in his hand, the tip pointed at her father's neck. "Step away from her. Now."

Death gleamed in Edgar's eyes, his gaze narrowed on his former mentor as if barely resisting the urge to swing the sword and sever his head from his body. Daxion stiffened and backed off, glaring daggers at them both.

Annora kicked out at the hovering fog, watching it curl up in the air before dissipating harmlessly back into the afterworld.

"Alcott...you managed to survive, I see. Pity." Daxion lifted his hands in surrender, clearly knowing the other phantom was more than capable of following through on his threat.

"No thanks to you." Edgar moved to stand in front of her. "And not on my own."

Daxion lifted his brows at her, his curiosity sharpening as he looked back and forth between them. "Ah, I see."

"Annora—touch the seal on the room. Your men are locked out, but your touch should be able to key them into the house." Edgar didn't lower his sword or take his attention away from Daxion for even a millisecond.

Although Annora wasn't sure she wanted more volatile emotions in the mix, she trusted her men. If her father thought to harm them, she would destroy him. She walked over to the glass wall and placed her hand against the cool surface.

The dark particles whisked up to lick at her hands in welcome, obeying her without hesitation.

She felt the instant the guys entered. They were silent, each of them entering at different points to clear the house.

They reached the living room in under a minute.

Daxion didn't say anything, studying each of the guys with shrewd eyes, before turning toward her. Without speaking, he lifted his arm, unbuttoned his sleeve, and rolled it up. Imprinted on his wrist was a raven in midflight. The black lines were faded, the wings a little molten.

"I used to be mated like you." He brushed his fingers along the symbol and shook his head at the folly. "More than five centuries ago arranged alliances were the norm. It allowed families to merge power during the wars. When humans began to persecute shifters and witches, we fought alongside them, only we ended up taking the brunt of the damage in battle.

"We lost many. After the wars, we withdrew from the outside world. To keep ourselves safe, we allowed everyone to believe we'd perished. It was only after the wars that we became aware of how dangerous it was to bind two phantoms together."

He turned his back toward the room and stared out the darkened window at something only he could see, his hands on his hips. Camden and Xander crept deeper into the room, while Logan and Mason moved into position on either side of her.

When Daxion started speaking again, everyone froze. "I lost my mate in the war, only she didn't die when she went into the banished lands. Our connection bound her to me, giving her enough power to survive in the dead zone. Since then we've banned the barbaric practice so we won't make the same mistake twice. That coin you wear is the only way for a phantom to enter and leave the dead zone unscathed. The only way I can get my wife back."

He turned toward her, his gaze beseeching. "Your mother was helping me find an alternative way into the deadly realm. We managed to create the coin as a type of portal, but something went horribly wrong. We lost the coin, and your mother vanished."

"Annora, you can't believe a thing he says." Edgar took a step back to stand at her side. He rested a hand on her shoulder and squeezed hard enough to hurt. "He manipulates the truth to get what he wants. If he hasn't already tried to take the coin, it's because it has to be given freely or the magic won't transfer. You—"

"I'm not stupid." Annora reached up and patted his hand. Edgar searched her face, relaxing when he saw she believed him.

Oh, she had no doubt what Daxion said was true, but the facts were twisted to suit him. Her mother hadn't trusted him for a reason and gave up everything to go into hiding. It was a lesson she wouldn't soon forget. "What is this dead zone?"

Daxion's eyes flashed toward Edgar in surprise before addressing her. "When phantoms die, we don't just rot like humans. Our spirits are sent to the banished realm. Reapers often roam there from the dead zone, consuming the souls of the weak. The strong fight back and often turned into reapers themselves. No one survives long unscathed."

Annora was appalled at the choice—either die or turn into a reaper. Horror clawed down her spine when she saw the truth of what he really wanted. "When your mate died in the war, it was because you killed her. She chose to become a reaper to get her revenge. You don't want to save her, you need to kill her to sever the connection between you so you can finally be free. She's draining you faster than you can replenish your powers."

Everything began to fall into place. "You tricked my mother into helping you—possibly made her believe you loved her. It's the only way you could have gotten her to willingly participate in your scheme." She turned toward Daxion in time to see his face harden, all artifice gone, leaving behind the cold man who first entered the room.

"My mother wasn't a fool. She was a very powerful witch in her own right. She discovered the truth, the real reason you wanted the coin, and used her magic to keep it out of your hands before she gave it to Valen." She saw a muscle jump in Daxion's jaw and knew she was right. "In order to keep the coin away from you, he vanished into your dead zone."

"Valen followed me on one of my trips to visit your mother, the impetuous boy," he huffed in exasperation. "The fool fell in love with her, ruining months of careful planning. He couldn't mind his own damned business. When he learned the coin could open a portal to the other realms, he took it for himself. He always craved my power. Unfortunately, he wasn't strong enough to control it."

Annora cocked her head, recalling the image of Valen…his kind eyes, his genuine worry and concern about her safety.

He offered her the coin he gave his life to acquire in order to protect her from his brother.

It wouldn't surprise her one bit to learn he was the one who helped her mother make the grimoire for her, infusing it with his own magic, another layer of protection to keep her hidden.

"I think it was the other way around." Annora cocked her head as she studied Daxion. "You were the one who was jealous."

Daxion scowled and began to pace, his face so forbidding she could practically feel the air in the room cringe away from him. "He didn't understand what we could've achieved. With the coin, we can raise an army of undead and taken our rightful place at the head of the supernatural world."

He stopped and put his hands on the hilts of his weapons, as if he could go back in time and kill them both. "Instead, Valen took the coin and entered the dead zone to keep your mother safe. I lost track of him there. When I returned to confront your mother and get her to create another coin, she was already gone. Imagine my surprise when I learned she created a half-spawn like you, one who could pass between realms and thrive."

He gave her a nasty smile. "In the end, she did exactly what I wanted her to do. I have no need of the coin, not if I have you."

Annora rose to her feet, her chin lifted in defiance, not the least bit frightened. She'd gone through worse and survived. She wasn't about to allow herself to become that frightened girl again. "And you think I'd help you?"

"Maybe not willingly." Daxion laughed, a cackle that sent chills down her spine. "But as a half-breed, your kind has no legal standing in my world. The only way you'll survive is if I publicly claim you."

He stalked toward her, ignoring the sword pointed at him and grabbed her chin in a cruel grip. "If I don't vouch for you, phantom soldiers will hunt you and your men down and kill you one by one. The only way for you to survive is to become my pet, a slave to do my bidding."

Annora burst out laughing, startling him so much he dropped his hand and backed up with a glower. Any fear burned away under the rage that he would dare threaten her. Darkness licked under her skin, craving violence. Black wisps of smoke curled around her, the afterworld seeping into the human realm. "Send your soldiers. I'm not so easily killed. Harm my men, and I'll make it my life's mission to make sure you never get the coin or me."

Darkness wove between her fingers, eager for the taste of vengeance. Daxion studied the way the darkness obeyed her, narrowing his eyes when more fog seeped into the room, swirling protectively around the guys like a pack of eager hounds ready to rip apart anyone who ventured too close.

The guys were hers to protect, and no one was allowed to touch them.

Instead of fear, Daxion turned calculating eyes toward her. His smug attitude pissed her off, as if she was already under his control, her submission a forgone conclusion, and her control snapped. "You want to control the living and the dead? You want your reapers? Why don't we call them now and let them drag each and every one of your soldiers into the dead zone you so fear. You won't even see them coming."

The coin burned cold against her chest, keeping her from falling completely into the darkness of the afterworld. She stalked toward Daxion, ignoring the way Edgar followed hard on her heels. She glared up at the man who was supposed to be her father. "Checkmate, Father dearest."

Edgar wanted to snatch Annora away from Daxion, hating that she stood so close to the vile man who saw her as nothing but an obstacle to getting what he wanted. She couldn't know how very dangerous and underhanded he really was—the lengths he would go to achieve his goals.

He saw the other men exchange glances, silently communicating with each other, preparing to move at the first hint of danger. Though they didn't know Daxion well, shifters could sense his evil.

By prior agreement, they were to remain silent and vigilant and wait for his signal before taking action. They protested until he reminded them that if they put themselves in harm's way, Annora would throw herself into danger to protect them.

If anything happened, they would keep Annora safe.

He made them promise before he agreed to bring them inside.

If anything were to go wrong, he would use his power to lock Daxion inside the shields, giving the guys a few precious minutes to kill him before reinforcements could arrive.

If they didn't all die first.

When he glanced at Annora, he couldn't see an ounce of fear in her. She would battle the world to keep them safe, but Edgar was very much afraid it would get her killed.

Losing her would destroy him.

He couldn't allow that to happen.

"A compromise." Edgar lowered his sword and turned toward Daxion. "I'll hunt down your wife if you vow to leave Annora alone."

Daxion's smile slowly curled his lips, a malicious gleam making his dark eyes shimmer.

"Wait a fucking minute." Annora slammed her palm against Edgar's chest, managing to shove him back with the power of the afterworld still clinging to her. "No deal. The instant you step into the dead zone, they'll rip you apart. I won't send you there."

Edgar gently ran the back of his fingers down her cheek, not allowing himself to indulge himself the way he wanted. "No need. I can enter the dead zone through the afterworld without your help."

Annora flinched as if he'd struck her, confusion flavoring her words. "But...only the dead can get into the dead zone."

She blinked up at him, her mind rejecting the truth for a heartbeat longer, when anger suddenly darkened her face, and she slammed her palms against his chest and shoved. "Fuck you! If you think I'm just going to let you go without a fight, you're more of an idiot than I thought. Do you honestly believe sacrificing yourself will keep me safe? As soon as you complete your end of the bargain, he'll send his soldiers after us. He won't even have to lift a finger himself. He'll always find a loophole and weasel out of any bargain you make."

Edgar gritted his teeth, biting back the urge to curse.

Because she was fucking right.

He studied her beautiful face and his determination to protect her hardened. "But I'm not wrong. We need a compromise, something to keep him from coming after you."

Some of the fire in her eyes banked, the sharp edges of her fear easing, and she nodded up at him. "He'll honor his promise?"

Edgar glanced over her head and faced the man who had practically raised him. For so long he'd believed the man was a god. He'd been a fool. He pulled Annora close, his racing heartbeat only slowing when she was tucked safely against his chest. "Yes, he'll honor his vow or he'll risk losing his standing in the phantom realm. He cares about that more than anything else."

He was gratified to see Daxion glare at him in fury.

At least some things haven't changed.

"You will publicly claim Annora as your daughter."

It was Annora's turn to scowl, and Edgar quickly covered her mouth with his hand, silently urging her to trust him. Only when she gave a slight nod did the tightness in his chest ease. She grabbed his wrist, the gentle squeeze giving him a boost of courage to do the right thing.

The right thing for *her*.

"Agreed." Daxion gave them a smug smile that made his hackles rise. "In return, she'll eliminate the threat of my wife."

Annora piped up before Edgar could speak. "Agreed, but on my terms. I won't murder her. I'll look into a way of breaking the bindings linking the two of you together."

Daxion snorted, as if the idea was preposterous. "No phantom would willingly give up their power by dissolving the bindings. The only way to break a binding is by death."

Annora matched off with Daxion, going head to head in a way that made Edgar want to snatch her away and shove her behind him. "I'll track her down. If she doesn't agree to the terms, I'll find a way to break the bindings myself."

Interest sharpened Daxion's face, similar to a hawk studying his prey. "You think you have the skill and strength where so many others have tried and failed?"

He was dismissive, but a tiny thread of curiosity lingered. It was chilling. If Annora did manage it, Daxion would never allow her to leave his control. The men on her team must have come to the same conclusion, because displeasure hardened their faces, but none of them protested.

"Like you said, I'm a half-breed. My mother was a powerful woman in her own right." Annora shrugged like it wasn't a fucking big deal to admit she could do magic. "Who knows what I'm capable of?"

"Then I must insist that you be trained in our ways." Daxion gave her a crocodile smile that held no warmth. "We have far more research materials for you to review."

Everything inside Edgar rebelled at turning her over to be trained by the sadistic bastard.

That was if she even survived the training.

The smug fucker was trying to lure her in with knowledge of her past.

Knowledge that Edgar kept hidden from her for fear she would crave the life that he'd given up.

Daxion would try to destroy her, bend her to his will, trap her in a way that she would have no choice but obey him.

Edgar would not allow her to be broken.

Actually, he wasn't even sure she could survive it.

"Fine. Agreed." Edgar crossed his arms and narrowed his eyes at the man he despised. He couldn't believe he was going to agree to allow the man anywhere near Annora. "But her men will go with her. All her men."

"Unacceptable." Daxion sneered at the others. "Being a half-breed will already be a mark against her. My name might not be enough to protect her if she doesn't cut herself free of the shackles they placed on her. None of the others will accept her with them as baggage."

Edgar's gut sank like a stone, because as much as he wanted to deny it, he was right.

They were albatrosses around her neck.

If they wanted her to survive, she'd be better off without them.

The rest of the guys looked just as conflicted. They didn't want any harm to come to her because of them, but Edgar wasn't sure he—or any of them—were strong enough to let her go.

"I—"

Before he could agree, Annora turned and slammed her knee into his balls hard enough to drop him. He cupped himself, trying to breathe through the agony. He reached forward to clamp his hand around her ankle before she could do anything foolish.

"Don't." He pleaded with her with his eyes, and her expression softened slightly.

"I'm not shackled to these guys. I don't see it as a punishment, and I won't give them up. I don't give a fuck whether the phantoms accept me or not." Annora turned to face Daxion, her expression defiant. "I'll agree to your other terms as long as your protection extends to them. If any of them are harmed, the agreement is null and void, and I'll bring your whole empire down around your ears. Understand?"

Chapter
Twenty-six

Dark particles invaded her lungs while she waited for her father to accede to her demands. If he attacked, she had every intention of dragging his ass into his dreaded dead zone and leaving the fucker there, even if she had to stay and make him.

She was tempted to do it anyway. The only thing holding her back was it wouldn't stop the other phantoms from coming after them in retaliation.

As she waited for Daxion to respond, she kept the spell her mother left for her at her fingertips, ready to cast it, positive the bright light could banish him from the house or at the very least, cut off his power before he could attack her men.

"Very well. I agree to your terms." The seal on the room immediately lightened, the darkness evaporating to reveal more than three dozen shifters waiting on the deck, every one of them staring unblinking at the house. More than a few of them wore fangs and claws.

Daxion smiled, as if he found the lot of them quaint, and he lifted his hands up in surrender. "I concede. I doubt you want our petty family squabble to start a war that they'd have no hope of winning."

Was it so very wrong to want to punch your father in the face?

Everything about the man rubbed her the wrong way.

As if reading her mind, his smile spread, and he bowed to her. "Until we meet again."

Without giving her a chance to do anything more than scowl at him, he dissolved into nothingness, leaving behind a small wisp of smoke that evaporated a second later, seemingly sucked in on itself.

She reached out, almost able to feel the pull of the phantom realm, and couldn't help but wonder if she could follow the trail. Before she could test her theory, Camden grabbed her arm and spun her to face him. He cupped her face, checking her for injuries before he crushed her to his chest.

Fine tremors went through him, and she wrapped her arms around him, the enormity of what just happened slamming into her. His soothing touch seeped deeper into her, dissipating the worst of the reaction before it set in and she gave into the urge to puke.

Logan's hand landed on her back, and she found herself scooped up into his arms and deposited on his lap. Mason sat next to them, sweeping her feet up to rest them across his thighs, while Xander stood at attention on the other side, ever alert. He rubbed a strand of her hair between his fingers, then rested his hand on the back of her neck.

"Is he gone?" Camden stood next to Edgar, searching the shadows, looking ready to dismember anyone who got near them.

"He's gone—for now." Sadie slipped into the room from the kitchen, her face pale, her eyes hard. "But he'll be back. Count on it."

Annora sighed and leaned against Logan, his heartbeat thundering under her ear, his hold almost brutal.

He rested his chin on her shoulder with a heavy sigh. "I'm not going to let him take you. I won't let him hurt you."

Annora brushed her lips against his cheek. "He won't harm me, not in that way. I'm too valuable right now."

His lips turned down, clearly not happy with her observation.

"She's right." Mason slipped his hand around her ankle, then tugged off her shoes and began to rub her feet.

She nearly moaned…it felt so incredible she swore her eyes rolled up into her head. Then she caught his slight smile and realized she must not have been very successful in masking the sound. Her thoughts went back to Daxion, and she shuddered. "I can't believe that man is my father. Did I make the right choice? Should I have just killed him?"

She didn't have any doubt in her mind that it would eventually come down to that.

"He's a chameleon." Edgar knelt at her side, covering her hand with his. "He's very good at getting what he wants. You managed to outwit him and get away with it, which is more than most people can say. He won't like being forced to bend to your will, but you made the right choice."

He turned her hand up, rubbing his thumb over the tattoo on her wrist and murmured, "You scared the shit out of me."

"Is my whole family batshit crazy?" she lamented, dropping her gaze to their joined hands and played with his fingers.

"No." A smile flitted across his face, but the humor faded as he gazed up at her. "Those who crave power and chase after it—it breaks something fundamental in them. Valen, your mother, and you are proof that goodness exists." He threaded his fingers into her hair and pulled her closer, resting his forehead against hers. "You are proof that we can make our own future."

"Daxion is a threat. He won't stop coming after you," Sadie warned, retrieving the sword that Edgar had set on the floor next to him. "You can't trust him."

Annora ignored the way the guys stiffened and fell silent. "What do you suggest?"

"Send me back to be your spy." Sadie held up a hand before Annora could speak. "I know you have no reason to trust me, but I only ever wanted what was best for our people."

Annora believed Sadie…to a point.

As soon as the young phantom discovered someone or something that was better for her people, Annora would be persona non grata.

"If he catches you—"

"I'm dead." Sadie smirked as she bounced on her feet, expertly slashing her sword through the air. "But he would have to catch me first."

Without waiting, Sadie gave them a cocky salute and a sly smile before she fell backwards and vanished in a puff of smoke.

Annora stared broodingly at the now empty space. "I hope I didn't just send her to her own execution."

"You didn't send her anywhere. She would've gone with or without your approval." Edgar shrugged away her concern. "She's a survivor. If anyone can pull it off, it'll be Sadie."

Xander tightened his grip on her neck, and she glanced up at him. "We're going to need to practice fighting as a unit."

"You're also going to have to get more comfortable about us interacting with the afterworld." Camden watched as the shifters on the deck broke up in teams and began to patrol the grounds. "Think of it as an inoculation. The more comfortable we are in the afterworld, the better prepared we will be when we visit your phantom realm."

Fear was like acid in her gut, but she shut it down hard and fast…because Camden was right. Despite knowing reapers could come after them, the afterworld was a weakness they couldn't afford. All she could hope was the coin she wore would keep them safe until she learned to protect herself and them. "Agreed."

"You're going to also need to prepare yourself to meet other phantoms." Edgar grimaced, then pulled away from her and began to pace. "The central city is different from anything you've ever seen."

Annora crossed her arms at the thought of leaving her comfortable little home. "And if I refuse to go?"

The last thing she wanted was to bring more danger into their lives.

"Not an option." Edgar immediately shot her down. "Claiming another is very public—and mandatory. At the very least you must attend the ceremony. Since you're a half-breed, they'll see you as the runt of the litter, insignificant and weak, which will make you a target."

Instead of being offended, Annora snorted and grinned up at him. "Aren't they going to be surprised when they meet me, then?"

His troubled expression faded, the darkness in his blue eyes melting away, and he gave her a brilliant smile that made her breath catch. "Indeed!"

Annora pulled away from the guys and rose to her feet, feeling more like herself than she had in a long time. She wasn't out of danger, but her men were with her again, and they weren't going anywhere. Plus her uncle was finally dead and couldn't hurt her or anyone else ever again.

Overall it had been a good day.

She smiled at both of Mason and Logan. "I missed supper. What do you say we find something to eat?"

Both of the men grinned and got to their feet. Something about the mischief on their faces had her eyes widening, and she turned to run. She didn't make more than a few feet before Mason scooped her up in his arms, tossed her over his shoulder and headed toward the kitchen. At her squeal of laughter, the guys grinned and turned to follow.

Whatever the future held, they would face it together and come out on top.

She wouldn't accept it any other way.

THE END

~ Academy of Assassins ~

ONLY ONE THING STANDS BETWEEN HUMANS
AND THE DEADLY SUPERNATURAL WORLD…THE
ACADEMY OF ASSASSINS.

Abandoned as a child and unable to remember her past, Morgan was
raised as a hunter, one of an elite group of fighters sworn to protect
humans from the dangerous paranormal creatures who invade our
world…creatures such as herself. Her life changes the day she's
summoned to the Academy of Assassins, a school that trains witches
and hunters to eradicate paranormals who prey on humans. Her first
assignment—find and eliminate the killer who is using the Academy
as their own personal hunting ground.

As Morgan delves deeper into the investigation, she will need to
dodge assassination attempts, avoid the distraction of romantic
entanglements with the devilishly handsome security expert, Kincade,
and his maddeningly overprotective teammates, while keeping the
volatile magic in her blood concealed from those who would use it
for their own purposes. When the danger increases and the school is
threatened, Morgan must unearth her missing memories before
someone finishes the job they started so long ago—killing her and
unleashing a plague that will consume the world.

An Academy of Assassins Novel.

~ Coveted ~

Discover what happens when a woman stumbles across a Scottish werewolf imprisoned in a thousand-year old dungeon. Magic and mayhem, not to mention a lot of kick-ass action and some sexy hijinks, of course.

Pack alpha Aiden   vows to do whatever necessary to protect his people. When he discovers a plot to harvest blood from his wolves to create the ultimate drug, he's determined to stop them at any cost. And quickly finds himself taken captive. After months in prison, Aiden barely manages to hang onto his sanity. The last thing he expects is a shapely little human to come to his rescue and bring out all his protective instincts.

Shayla is being stalked because of her abilities as a seeker. When offered a job in Scotland, she leaps at the chance to escape. With danger pursuing her at every turn, she must decide if she could give up her magic in order to live a safe, ordinary life. Never in her wildest fantasies did she expect to find a feral-looking man imprisoned in a thousand-year-old dungeon...or be so wildly attracted to him. She didn't need more trouble, but when fate presents the means to help him escape, she doesn't hesitate.

Now they are both being hunted, and Aiden is determined to do everything in his power to protect Shayla...and seduce her into becoming his mate. As the danger intensifies, Aiden begins to suspect that Shayla might be the key to saving not only his people but also the future of his race...if he could keep her alive long enough.

~ BloodSworn ~

Ten years after they bound her powers and banished her, Trina Weyebridge had successfully carved out a new existence in the human world. She put her life as a witch behind her. But, her magic would not be denied, the bindings holding them in check are weakening. Vampires who crave a taste of the powers stored in her blood are hunting her with deadly force and have kidnapped her sister to lure her out. In a desperate bid to free her sister and gain her own freedom, Trina bargains with the all-too-tempting lion shifter who calls out the long forgotten wild side in her...she would be his concubine in return for pack protection. She'd be safe...until they found out the truth.

UNDENIABLE DESIRE. FORBIDDEN LOVE. INESCAPABLE DESTINY.

When Merrick spots a female intruder living on his property, he's intrigued by her daring. Curious to find out more, he follows her and comes to her aid when she falls prey to an attack. After weeks of unnatural silence, his beast awakens at her touch, and he suspects that she might be the only one able to save his race from a disease killing his kind. Not willing to take the chance of losing her, he binds her to him the only way he knows how...by claiming her as his own. All he has to do to save her is uncover the secrets of her past, stop a pack revolt, convince her that she's desperately in love with him in return, and prevent a war.

~ The Demon Within ~

As a punishment for failing his duty as an angel, Ruman finds himself encased in stone in the form of a guardian statue. Every few decades he is given a chance to repent. And fails. Until the totally unsuitable Caly Sawyer accidentally brings him back to life. Nothing is going to prevent him from gaining his freedom, especially some willfully stubborn human determined to kill him.

Caly doesn't trust the mysterious stranger who came out of nowhere and risked his life for hers. As a demon hunter, she knows there is something not quite human about the sexy bastard. Her ability to detect demons is infallible. She should know. She used to be one.

War is brewing between demons and humans. The demon infection that Caly had always considered a curse might just be the key to their survival…if Ruman can keep her alive long enough. Despite the volatile attraction between her and her sexy protector, Caly's determined to do whatever it takes to keep everyone alive. The more Ruman learns about his beautiful charge, the more he questions his duty and loyalty…and dreads the call to return home. If they can't learn to trust each other in time, one of them will die.

~ Electric Storm ~

A WOMAN WITH TOO MANY SECRETS DARES TO RISK EVERYTHING TO CLAIM THE PACK DESTINED TO BER HERS.

Everything changed when Raven, a natural born conduit, accidentally walks in on a slave auction. She only wants a night out with her friends before her next case as a paranormal liaison with the police. Instead, she ends up in possession of a shifter and his guardian. When your touch can kill, living with two touchy-feely shifters is a disaster waiting to happen.

POWER ALWAYS COMES WITH A PRICE…

To make matters worse, a vicious killer is on the loose. As mutilated bodies turn up, she can't help fear that her new acquisitions are keeping secrets from her. The strain of keeping everyone alive, not to mention catching the killer, pushes her tenuous control of her gift and her emotions to their limits. If they hope to survive, they must work together as a pack or risk becoming hunted themselves.

A Raven Investigations Novel : Book 1

~ Druid Surrender ~

A DARK, ENCHANTING TALE OF LOVE AND MAGIC IN
VICTORIAN ENGLAND.

Brighid Legend has been on the run for over a year, hunted by the
people who murdered her mother. Born a Druid with the power to
control the elements, Brighid knows her pursuers will never stop
until she is under their control. To escape detection, she struggles to
hide her powers and finds safety in a small, out-of-the-way village.
But after a series of mysterious accidents, she fears something sinister
has invaded her new home. While she searches for the source of the
trouble, suspicion falls on her, and Brighid flees, only steps ahead of
the villagers seeking vengeance.

Wyatt Graystone, Earl of Castelline, retires when the life-and-death
clandestine investigations he did for the Crown becomes more
tedious than adventurous. Something vital is missing from his life.
The last place he expects to find the missing spark is in a woman he
literally leaps through fire to rescue from being burned at the stake.
But the danger is far from over. To his frustration, the infernal
woman adamantly refuses his assistance, pushing him away at every
turn, when his only desire is to claim her for his own.

But someone has targeted Brighid for a reason. As the threats to her
life intensify, Wyatt is determined to uncover her secrets and do
whatever it takes to ensure she survives. When their pasts come back
to haunt them, they must overcome their worst fears or risk losing
everything. Saving her life is the biggest battle he's ever faced...and
the only one that has ever mattered.

WILL THEIR LOVE BE STRONGE ENOUGH TO SAVE
THEM . . .

A Druid Quest Novel: Book 1

ABOUT THE AUTHOR

Stacey Brutger lives in a small town in Minnesota with her husband and an assortment of animals. When she's not reading, she enjoys creating stories about exotic worlds and grand adventures…then shoving in her characters to see how they'd survive. She enjoys writing anything paranormal from contemporary to historical.

Other books by this author:
BloodSworn
Coveted

A Druid Quest Novel
Druid Surrender (Book 1)
Druid Temptation (Book 2)

An Academy of Assassins Novel
Academy of Assassins (Book 1)
Heart of the Assassins (Book 2)
Claimed by the Assassins (Book 3)
Queen of the Assassins (Book 4)

A Raven Investigations Novel
Electric Storm (Book 1)
Electric Moon (Book 2)
Electric Heat (Book 3)
Electric Legend (Book 4)
Electric Night (Book 5)
Electric Curse (Book 6)

A PeaceKeeper Novel
The Demon Within (Book 1)

A Phantom Touched Novel
Tethered to the World (Book 1)
Shackled to the World (Book 2)

Coming Soon:
Daemon Grudge – Clash of the Demigods (Book 1)
Ransomed to the World (Book 3)

Visit Stacey online to find out more at **www.StaceyBrutger.com**
And www.facebook.com/StaceyBrutgerAuthor

Made in the USA
Middletown, DE
05 March 2020